Lucky Stiff

Forge Books by Deborah Coonts

Wanna Get Lucky?
Lucky Stiff

DEBORAH COONTS

A Tom Doherty Associates Book
New York

LUCKY STIFF

A Forge Book
Published by Tom Doherty Associates, LLC
175 Fifth Avenue
New York, NY 10010

www.tor-forge.com

Forge® is a registered trademark of Tom Doherty Associates, LLC.

Library of Congress Cataloging-in-Publication Data

Coonts, Deborah.
    Lucky stiff / Deborah Coonts.—1st ed.
        p. cm.
    "A Tom Doherty Associates book"
    ISBN 978-0-7653-2544-0
    1. Resorts—Fiction.   2. Customer relations—Management—Fiction.
3. Las Vegas (Nev.)—Fiction.   I. Title.
PS3603.O5818L83 2011
813'.6—dc22

                                                           2010036256

First Edition: February 2011

Printed in the United States of America

0   9   8   7   6   5   4   3   2   1

For Michael

ACKNOWLEDGMENTS

Somewhere along the way during the Shameless Self-Promotion Tour for my first novel, *Wanna Get Lucky?*, a reporter, upon reading the acknowledgments, commented that apparently it took a village to write a book—at least, MY book, anyway. He acted surprised—and a bit disappointed that I apparently needed so much help. I don't know why he felt that way. Novels are huge projects. Writing one is akin to eating a cow—one bite at a time and eventually you've accomplished your goal. But not without help, support, hugs, kisses, laughter, the occasional butt-kicking, attitude enhancers, hand-holding, brainstorming, an occasional overindulgence or two, a serious stockpile of antacids and aspirin . . . and Pinot Noir.

So, at this juncture, I would like to thank those who provided the above. Tyler, my son. The loudest cheer at a triumph. The first to offer a hug when the clouds gather. A constant in an uncertain life. A truly remarkable human being.

Barb Nickless and Maria Faulconer, writers, readers, critiquers, cherished friends to walk through time with.

Polly List, kindred spirit, tireless champion, friend by chance, sister by choice.

Robin and Marshall Cloyd, family in the very best sense of the word.

Annis and Tom Buell, my parents, and my brother Tom, folks who have known me forever and who still will take my phone calls.

Susan Gleason, agent, staunch supporter, friend.

The folks at Forge Books: Bob Gleason, Tom Doherty, Linda Quinton, Patty Garcia, Phyllis Azar, Cassie Ammerman, and Ashley Cardiff, and all the other dream-makers. Thank you for turning writing dreams into reality.

The Tuesday Night Group—Linda, Reggie, Dulcinea, Robin, Sonja, Jane—laughter, stories, and more than I ever wanted to know about sex toys.

Dr. Kirby Stafford, state entomologist, the Connecticut Agricultural Experiment Station—my bee expert. Thank you for time, attention, and all things bee related. If there are errors in this story, they are my fault entirely and due either to my inability to understand insect esoterics or to use creative license (I like the last excuse the best). Thank you for sharing your expertise.

And my Michael, the man who holds my heart. Thank you for my wonderful life, for making dreams come true.

Lucky Stiff

Chapter

O N E

♡

Millions of enraged honeybees had done the impossible: Single-handedly they had brought the Las Vegas Strip to a standstill.

Alerted by our limo driver, who was stuck somewhere in the mess, I bolted out the front door of the Babylon, down the drive, and screeched to a halt at the Strip. Momentarily speechless, I joined several hundred Vegas revelers gathered in clumps. Gawking, they encircled a large tractor-trailer. The cab lay on its side—I could see the driver still trapped inside, staring out at us.

Momentum had wrapped the trailer around the cab. The thin aluminum skin had given way, exposing smashed and broken hives. A trickle of golden goo, which I assumed was honey, oozed from the trailer's open wound.

Clouds of bees launched themselves through the jagged tear

into the cool night air. They swarmed over and through the crowd like tiny avenging angels. The mass of hurtling bodies and flashing wings reflected the multicolored signs on the Strip in a free-form light show that put the Fremont Street Experience to shame.

Lifting half-full glasses in salute, the crowd *ooohed* and *ahhhhhed* as if this was another Las Vegas extravaganza provided for their benefit. The party atmosphere lasted but a minute or two—right up until the bees got angry. Swatting and twitching, the revelers did the bee dance. Then, realizing the bees meant business and outnumbered them by a large margin, they tossed their glasses and bolted. I never knew drunk people could run that fast.

Like a herd of wild horses in a mad panic, they stampeded past me, making a beeline for the relative safety of the hotel.

I was congratulating myself on my mixed metaphor when one of the little swarmers decided my neck was the perfect place to bury its stinger.

"Damn!" I slapped at the tiny creature, then plucked its squashed body from my skin and tossed it away. For such a small thing, it sure packed a punch. The pain galvanized me to action. I ran upstream through the crowd, heading for the truck.

Geoffrey David-Williston was right where I knew he'd be—in the thick of the action. Of course, I didn't have to be Einstein to figure that out—Geoffrey was the head of the World Association of Entomologists and their chief bee guy.

For months we'd been negotiating and planning the entomologists' conference at the Babylon, which would start the day after tomorrow. He had promised me we could populate an exhibit with millions of honeybees without incident. Fool that I am, I believed him—then.

Now I wanted a piece of his ass!

Reaching out, I grabbed his shirtsleeve, pulling him around to face me just as another little bugger planted a stinger in my left calf. Geoffrey's shirt still clutched in my fist, I bent down and swatted the bee away as I started in.

"You assured me no one would ever know you'd carted millions of bees through the streets of Las Vegas. Well, they damn well know now! In fact, you told me honeybees were docile and wouldn't harm anyone." I waved my free hand toward the bees. "They sure as hell don't look docile now, do they?" I ducked, hiding as much of myself as possible behind Geoffrey as the angry swarm buzzed past.

Several inches taller than my six feet, with hawkish features and deep-set eyes, Geoffrey was so thin he looked as if he hadn't seen a good meal in decades—making it hard for me to hide much of my bulk behind him. He didn't look at me. Instead he concentrated on the bees—his eyes following them as they raced through the night. When he spoke, I had to strain to hear. "Be calm. You're agitating the bees."

"Calm?" I brushed a little gold and black body from the sleeve of my sweater. "Agitating the . . ." I paused, closed my eyes, counted to ten, then opened them again. Nope, still seeing red; so I repeated the whole counting thing. This time, when I opened my eyes, I was only seeing a slight shade of pink. Better. "Geoffrey . . ." I started again, but he wasn't listening.

"Do you think you could get someone to turn off all these lights?" he said, as he watched the buzzing cloud whirling around. "The bees are disoriented. We're going to have a hard time getting them back into their hives."

"Turn off the lights? On the Strip? Sure, it'll only take me a minute." My voice was deadly. "Fortunately I've been entrusted with the secret code to the switch that will kill the power to the beating heart of Las Vegas."

Geoffrey looked at me, a quizzical look on his face. "You can't turn them off?"

What was it about sarcasm that eluded brilliant minds? *"Of course* I can't turn them off. You'll have to think of something else."

"Get me something to burn, then. Quickly." His eyes again followed the billowing mass of bees.

"A jackknifed tractor-trailer, a cloud of angry insects, a first-class traffic jam, and a panicked mob aren't enough for you? You need to start a fire?" My eyes were getting slitty—a bad sign.

"The bees are starting to sting. When they sting, they release an alarm pheromone that attracts other bees to help in the fight. Smoke can sometimes mask that pheromone." He turned and gave me the benefit of his full attention. "I think stopping the stinging first would be a good thing, don't you?"

I slapped at another bugger attacking my neck, then stomped my feet. Maybe I was imagining it, but I felt bugs crawling all over me. Real or imagined, the bugs propelled me to action. Geoffrey's plan being the only viable one at the moment, I grabbed my push-to-talk and barked orders to Security for barrels filled with something flammable.

"Once we get the smoke going, that should stop the bees from attacking. Then call the fire department," Geoffrey said when I was done, his words heavy with defeat. "The bees are simply too riled-up."

"And, pray tell, what will the fire department do?"

"They'll have to knock the flying bees down with foam." A baleful expression settled over Geoffrey's features. "That will kill them."

"Don't look so hang dog. You're not going to make me feel guilty about massacring millions of bees," I lied. "That solves the flying bee problem. What about the crawling ones?"

"I've called my team. They should be here any minute with the bee suits. We have to try to put the hives together and then, hopefully, the bees will return to them."

My hand began to cramp, so I let go of Geoffrey's shirt and swatted at a few bees crawling on my skirt. Since I knew nothing about taming bees (which sounded as improbable as teaching fleas to dance), and Geoffrey's plan was the only one we had, I decided to go with it. "Okay. Work your magic. I'll call the fire department." He started to speak, but I held up a finger to silence him. "And the police department needs to cordon off this area before these bees do a real number on someone."

"I'm sorry," Geoffrey whispered, his eyes again turned toward the sky.

"That's okay. I'm sure you didn't envision the truck dumping its load."

He turned and looked at me, his eyes struggling to focus. "I was apologizing to the bees, not to you."

"Of course you were." I felt the color rise in my cheeks as I wrestled for self-control. "Get these bees out of here and clean up this mess." I poked Geoffrey in the chest for emphasis. "But first, get the driver out of that truck before the bees eat him alive. Do it now!"

He gave me a look that told me, in no uncertain terms, I had exhausted my usefulness, then turned back to his charges. I paused to make sure he was moving toward the cab of the truck, before I turned to stalk off in a vain attempt to keep my dignity intact. I refused to slap at a bee that had punctured my elbow.

Stung, dismissed, and more than a little browned-off, I fought the urge to wring Geoffrey's scrawny neck, which was a bad idea anyway.

Then the bees would be *my* problem.

You see, problems are what I do. My name is Lucky O'Toole and I am the Head of Customer Relations for the Babylon, the most over-the-top resort/casino on the Las Vegas Strip. And as such, the hotel's entertainers, employees, and guests—oh yes, the guests; the weird, the wacko, the drunk and disorderly, the slightly naughty and the truly wicked—are all my responsibility.

I started in the business when I was fifteen. In the intervening years, I'd dealt with cockroaches, snakes, cats (both man-eating and domesticated), dogs, various reptiles (poisonous, venomous, and vile) and rodents (four-legged and two-legged), but tonight was my first experience with bees. And, frankly, I was at a bit of a loss.

Tired of offering my exposed skin to irate insects, I'd decided total retreat was the better part of valor when my phone rang. I flipped it open. "O'Toole."

"OhmyGod, ohmyGod, ohmyGod—"

"Paolo, calm down. What's wrong?" Paolo drove our limo on the late night shift.

"The bees! The bees! They are coming after me! How do they get into the car? OhmyGod! Mary, Mother of God, protect me." A staccato mix of English and Spanish, he fired the words at me. "Help me!"

"Where are you?"

"In the limo. Behind the fallen-over truck."

I squinted my eyes and stared beyond the light into the darkness. I caught the glimmer of silver and the reflection of light on black, like a black hole in the night. "I see you. I'll be right there."

I bolted toward the car, my arms crossed in front of my face, breathing through the loose weave of my sweater. I had no intention of discovering what it would be like to inhale an enraged bee.

Bees crawled all over the car. I could just make out the filmy aura of Paolo's face peering at me through the driver's window. He waved his arms frantically as if fighting off an invading horde. Using the sleeve of my sweater, I brushed the bees off the handle and wrenched the door open.

Paolo recoiled at the cloud of insects that swarmed through the opening. I reached in, grabbed his lapels, and lifted the small man clear of the car, setting him on his feet. We both ran like hell up the drive and through the front door, which we slammed behind us. Our backs pressed to the glass, we sagged against it, fighting for breath.

Color was returning to Paolo's face. Dotting his otherwise flawless Latin complexion, I noticed several red welts. I'm sure I sported a set of my own.

"I don't know about you, but I'm asking for hazardous duty pay," I said, when air again filled my lungs and I was no longer teetering on the brink of homicide.

"Hazardous duty pay? What is this?"

"Ask your boss when you insist on a raise."

Paolo crinkled his brows. "*You* are my boss."

"Oh, right." I straightened and smoothed my skirt. "Then forget what I said."

His eyes twinkled. "Paolo never forgets."

I raised one eyebrow as I looked at him. "Then you won't forget our limo which you abandoned in the middle of the Strip?"

"You want me to go back out there?"

I bit back a smile at his stricken look. "When it's safe, get the car."

THE dispatcher at the fire department didn't miss a beat when I explained the problem—she rallied the troops. Their sirens already sounded in the distance. My call to the Metropolitan Police Department didn't go quite as smoothly. In a snippy voice, the dispatcher assured me Metro had the incident "under control," which I thought highly unlikely. Metro had a disdain for directing traffic and regularly left motorists to their own devices when dealing with gridlock—an interesting approach in a state with a Concealed Carry law.

As a precaution, I keyed Security again and asked for reinforcements outside to help untangle the snarled traffic before somebody started shooting.

My footsteps echoed off the marble floor as I strode through the lobby. The revelers chased inside by the bees had filtered away, leaving the vast space virtually empty. I paused for a moment, drinking it all in. I rarely saw the place this quiet—two thirty in the morning wasn't my usual gig.

A work of art, the Babylon had been designed to incorporate all of the ancient wonders of the original Babylon—with a Vegas twist, of course. Large and grand, the lobby resembled an ancient temple with polished marble floors and walls inlaid with intricate, iridescent mosaics. Chihuly blown-glass hummingbirds and but-terflies of all shapes, sizes, and colors covered the ceiling. Long and low, the registration desk hid under the colorful tents of a bazaar that formed the pathway into the casino.

The Bazaar, a vast array of high-end shops, the entrance to which was on the far side of the lobby opposite the registration desk, beckoned weary revelers, and big winners. What the gambling gods gave at the tables, the retail gods could take away. We had all the best names—Chanel, Louis Vuitton, Tiffany, Cartier, Jimmy Choo, Dolce&Gabbana, Hermès, Escada, Ferarri—to name but a few.

An indoor ski slope, replete with manmade snow and moguls, lurked behind a wall of glass adjacent to Registration. Of course, I rather doubted the ancient Babylonians strapped on a pair of K-2s and threw themselves down a snow-covered run, but, after all, this *was* Vegas, and some latitude with reality was expected. At this time of night, all the skiers were doing the après ski thing; the mountain was closed.

Completing the picture, a winding waterway—the Euphrates—snaked through the public areas of the ground floor. Lined with flowering plants and spanned by numerous footbridges, the Eu-phrates was home to myriad fish and fowl.

Sitting on one footbridge, half-hidden from view, a man and a woman caught my eye. Anger infused their posture. Even with their backs to me, I could tell their conversation was not a pleas-ant one. At this time of the morning the combination of too much alcohol and too little sleep was often incendiary. As the problem solver on duty, it fell to me to put out the fires.

I edged closer for a better look. The guy's wavy brown hair looked familiar. So, too, the tailored tweed jacket. Damn! The Beautiful Jeremy Whitlock! What was he doing here? And what was he doing with that petite woman with long strawberry blond hair? Actually, as Las Vegas's ace private investigator, Jeremy was often nosing around, so seeing him wasn't that unusual. But seeing him with this woman certainly was, since Jeremy was involved in a hot-and-heavy with Miss Patterson, my senior assistant, who was neither petite nor a redhead.

The woman stood. Jeremy leapt up and grabbed her arm. When she turned to yank her arm from his grasp, I got a good look at her face. With a sinking heart, I realized that I also knew her. Numbers Neidermeyer—the scourge of every bookie in town. Our very own sportsbook manager swore the woman had no soul. I agreed with him—she'd sold it to the Devil a long time ago.

Numbers and I had history. When she was a blossoming odds maker and I was the Director of Operations for one of the Big Boss's lesser properties, she'd tried to put us over a barrel. I'd won that round, and, luckily, our paths hadn't crossed since. But, if the grapevine could be relied upon, she'd continued playing the same game, although with bigger stakes. To hear it told, she'd ruined several dozen careers not only in the gaming industry but in professional athletics as well. Because she was the best in the business—such was her reputation that one word from her would cause the big money to jump in before the casinos could change the odds, leaving the casinos with their pants down—she'd emerged from the various wreckages unscathed.

With a glance toward the front door, Numbers turned on her heels and headed in the opposite direction, leaving Jeremy alone. We both watched as she disappeared into the casino.

I wandered over to Jeremy's side. "Slumming tonight?"

He jumped at the sound of my voice then shook his head. "You have no idea." He ran a hand over his eyes. "That woman. She's a bloody cow."

"Can you speak American rather than Australian?" Actually, I'd sit and listen to the Beautiful Jeremy Whitlock speak Swahili if he wanted—those brown eyes flecked with gold, the wavy hair begging to be touched, the dimples, the perpetual tan, the great ass, the delicious accent. . . . If he and I weren't both already spoken for, I could definitely embarrass myself in his presence.

His dimples flashed then disappeared.

"Rubbed you the wrong way, did she?" I asked. "She has a habit of doing that. For all the years I've known her, I've been convinced she sees no reflection when she looks in the mirror." I took a good look at Jeremy. He looked whipped and more than a little peeved. "Is she involved in one of your investigations?"

"Up to her pretty little neck. I just can't prove it . . . yet. She's as cunning as a shithouse rat."

"My thoughts exactly." I glanced at my watch—almost three hours into the new day. "Is there anything I can do?"

"No, but thanks."

I didn't think he'd accept—client confidentiality and all of that—but he looked so miserable I had to offer. "You look beat. Are you going home?"

"No, I'm bunking with your right-hand man these days."

"I'm not sure I'd put it quite that way. Somebody might get the wrong impression."

Clearly too tired to smile, Jeremy gave me a peck on each cheek and an unenthusiastic little wave as he turned to go.

I watched him until he disappeared into the casino.

I spent the next hour wandering among the tables and slot machines as the gambling day wound down. A cloud of smoke hovered above the thinning crowd. Having abandoned the rows of empty slots, the cocktail waitresses lurked near the few tables still hosting some action. At the beginning of the evening, the waitresses wore broad smiles and little else. Now the smiles were nowhere to be found, and the women looked cold and miserable as they shifted from one foot to another. I marveled at their composure. A long night in the mandatory stilettos would have reduced me to tears.

A small crowd of Babylon employees clustered around a lone slot machine. Paxton Dane, a long, tall drink of Texas charm and the Gaming Control Board's expert on cheating—actually he was an expert on lying and cheating, but that's another story—was holding forth on all the latest ways to rig slot machines for a large payout. The required presentations to the staff were always held at four o'clock in the morning, when the fewest number of quarter-pushers were around. While the gambler might sleep, the hotel staff merely changed shifts. Which reminded me, my shift was almost over.

Just when I was actually beginning to believe I might escape on time, my push-to-talk called my name. I flipped it open, glanced at the number, then said, "Hey, Jer. Whatcha got?" Jerry was my counterpart in Security.

"What'd you do, draw the short straw or something? How come the boss is working the graveyard?"

"You know how I like to be in the thick of the action."

"Right," he snorted. "Your main squeeze working tonight?"

"Playing piano in Delilah's Bar."

"Thought as much. I got a call you need to take."

"Sure," I said, with a sinking heart. The possibility of some shut-eye before dawn was diminishing by the second.

"A guy in 12410 locked himself out of his room. The typical story—he was heading for the bathroom in the dark and went out the wrong door. Apparently he's buck naked and hiding in the laundry room."

"You checked his name against our registration records?" I asked, my brain switching to autopilot.

"Yeah, they jibe."

"How am I supposed to ask him for ID before I give him the key?" I really didn't want to go into a room alone with a naked guy who was most likely three sheets to the wind.

"His name is Lovato. I think you can put two and two together."

I whistled low. "Interesting. How'd he get hold of you?"

"Employee intercom."

"On my way."

AFTER a stop at the front desk to get a new key programmed for room 12410, I headed for the elevators. Standing in front of the main elevator bank and its shiny brass doors, I took stock of my reflection. A recent makeover had converted me from bottle-blonde to my natural light brown. Although I liked the transformation, I still wasn't used to the new old me.

I even wore a bit of makeup to accentuate my blue eyes and those darn cheekbones that had to be coaxed out of hiding. Still tall, I'd lost a few pounds—one of the effects of falling in love—that was recent, too. My mother told me I lost the weight because now I had something else to do with my hands. My mother, Mona, ran a bordello in Pahrump. Subtlety and gentility were not two of her stronger suits.

Once an elevator arrived, the ride was brief. I found the laundry room halfway down the hall on the right. I paused in front of the door. Should I knock? Feeling magnanimous, I decided I should.

Two taps and a voice called out, "You better goddamn well have my key. I'm freezing my butt off in here."

I paused, savoring the moment—I didn't get this sort of opportunity very often and I wasn't above making the most of it. This made staying up way past my bedtime almost worth it. I opened the door and froze in mid-stride.

Scrunched into the far corner of the small closet, swathed in white, with a scowl on his face, sat Las Vegas's own district attorney, Daniel Lovato. Most people called him Lovie—a nickname he well deserved—but Lovie Lovato the Lothario was too alliterative for me, so I stuck with Daniel.

"Daniel! Isn't this interesting?" My shit-eating grin would have been impossible to hide, so I didn't even try.

"Oh, Jesus, O'Toole. What are you doing here?" Lovie gathered the folds of sheet around him. "Shut the damn door."

"Does Glinda know you're here?" I shut the door behind me, then leaned against it, arms crossed across my chest. Glinda, in a fit of bad judgment I still didn't understand, married Daniel years ago. The fact that she hadn't killed him by now was a true testament to her self-control.

"I'm here with the bi—my wife." Daniel lowered his gaze and glared at me from under his bushy black eyebrows, which matched his thick black hair. Handsome, yes, but charming? To my knowledge, no one had ever accused him of that. "I beat on the door, but I couldn't wake her up. Now give me the damn key."

He extended his arm imperiously. With a sheet draped across his lap and over one shoulder, he looked just like a Roman Emperor— except the throne from which Lovie ruled was a pile of dirty laundry. Where was my camera when I needed it? Even my push-to-talk didn't have a camera feature. I resolved to do something about that.

I handed him the key. "We've got to stop meeting like this. People will start to talk, and I don't want to get on Glinda's bad side." Glinda was a bodybuilder and she scared me.

Daniel grabbed the key. Wrapping the folds of sheet around him, he levered himself to his feet, then brushed past me through the door.

"You're welcome," I said as I watched him stalk down the hall.

Here with his wife? *And I'm Mother Theresa.* When our great district attorney was out of earshot, I keyed security.

Jerry answered immediately. "You okay? Any problems with the naked guy?"

"Everything's fine, but do me a favor. Keep the last twenty-four hours of video from the hallway in front of 12410." I paused as I watched the district attorney let himself into his room. "And you'd better keep the next twenty-four hours as well. I don't know what games are going on up here, but I have a hunch we had better do some prophylactic CYA."

. . .

"MY day is officially over," I announced to no one as I rode the elevator to the lobby. Teddie would still be in Delilah's Bar tinkling the ivories, so I headed in that direction. Time to round him up and hit the trail.

Two months ago Teddie became the new man in my life. Actually, that's not really true. Two months ago he became the new man in my bed (not that there was an old one). Prior to that we'd been platonic best friends. Then, out of the blue, Teddie got a wild hair and kissed me right in the middle of Delilah's Bar. That kiss had changed everything.

Delilah's Bar—an oasis in a vast forest of machines and table games designed to relieve gamblers of their money—sat under a colorful tent on a raised platform in the center of the casino. Flowering bougainvillea streamed from latticework suspended between columns. Water gurgled from fountains and trickled down the wall behind the long bar. Thankfully, the televisions had been turned off. One lone patron, a cigarette dangling from his lips, played video poker at the far end of the counter.

Our head bartender, Sean, wiped down a glass with a bar rag. He nodded and smiled as I climbed the steps. "Your man's a real hit."

I took a seat on a stool and turned my full attention to Teddie, who was seated at the baby grand.

As Teddie played, he studiously ignored his audience of one, a lady seated close to him who had kicked off one shoe and was running her bare foot up his leg. In this day and age of rampant plastic surgery, I couldn't hazard a guess as to how old she was, but she was clearly trolling—and she had taken a shine to my man.

She had good taste—he *was* beautiful. Spiked blond hair, chiseled features, sparkling blue eyes surrounded by lashes females would kill for, broad shoulders, small waist, perfect ass. When near him, I found it next to impossible to keep my hands to myself.

Teddie's real name is Ted Kowalski, but when I brought his show to the Babylon, he was known as the Great Teddie Divine—Las

Vegas's foremost female impersonator. Everybody assumed he was gay, but they were wrong bigtime. He's not even bisexual, which makes it nice for me.

Now Teddie busies himself writing songs and hoping for a music career. Julliard-trained with a Harvard MBA, I had no doubt he'd get it. But in the meantime, he wrote music when the spirit moved him and played the piano in Delilah's on the nights I worked the graveyard. In addition, he still had his hand in the female impersonating thing—he now produced the show and was the headliner's understudy in case of an emergency.

I'd never tell Teddie this, but secretly I was glad when he hung up his dress. Having a lover who looked better in my clothes than I did was more pressure than I thought it would be. In addition, now I was the beneficiary of all his hand-me-downs—another plus.

His baby-blues closed as he sang an old Frank Sinatra ballad, Teddie wore his ubiquitous blue jeans. Tight, but not too, they always got my attention. In place of his favorite Harvard sweatshirt, he wore an open-collared shirt, the top several buttons undone. I could see the hint of chest hair, which I sorta liked. For a long time he waxed on a regular basis—chest hair and his Oscar de la Renta gown with the plunging neckline would not have been pretty.

Mid-ballad, Teddie stopped. "Mrs. Hitzelberger—"

"Norma," said the lady with her foot wedged up the leg of his blue jeans.

"Mrs. Hitzelberger," Teddie countered, this time a bit more forcefully.

Before he could continue, I slid onto the piano bench next to him. "Hey, handsome." With one hand, I turned his face fully toward me and gave him the very best kiss I could muster at almost four A.M.

Mrs. Hitzelberger grabbed my arm and tried to pull me away. "Honey, I was here first. This one's mine."

Like a flea trying to move an elephant, she had zero chance of pulling me away from Teddie—especially since he was kissing me back.

"Theodore," Mrs. Hitzelberger said imperiously, "Would a thousand dollars buy a few hours alone with you in my room?"

Words prevailed where force had failed—Teddie and I broke the kiss and turned to look at her, unsure whether we'd heard what we thought we'd heard.

"What?" Teddie asked.

"A cool grand for a few hours with you."

"What makes you think he's for sale?" I asked when I finally found my voice.

"Honey, everything in this place is for sale." Mrs. Hitzelberger waved her hand dismissively. "The only thing left to determine is the price."

I wasn't going to argue—she was closer to the truth than I cared to think about. "If that's the case, this one . . ." I shrugged toward Teddie, ". . . was bought and paid for long ago."

Mrs. Hitzelberger sized me up for a moment. Then she drained her drink and slid off her stool as she worked her foot back into its shoe. "Lucky you." She gave me a squeeze on the shoulder, then turned and headed for the bar.

"Truer words were never spoken," I said as I leaned into Teddie. "Play something for me."

He cocked his head at me. Then, a smile tugging at his mouth, he began to play. Frank Sinatra gave way to Bryan Adams.

I put my head on his shoulder as he sang a beautiful song about lovers who had started out as friends. Closing my eyes, I smiled—the guy had a song for every occasion.

AFTER I'd turned over the reins of power to my youngest assistant, Brandy, home beckoned. With Teddie's song in my heart and his hand firmly in mine, I pushed through the front door of the hotel and out into the cool night air. A few bees still buzzed against the glass. Thankfully, they ignored us.

At the end of the drive, we stopped to survey the damage. In full turnout gear with hastily rigged veils attached to their helmets and all openings bound with tape, the firefighters still manned the open hoses, washing dead bee bodies into the gutters. A commercial tow truck had righted the cab of the tractor-trailer. Men in white suits and veils worked on the shattered hives. Despite the conspicuous absence of the Metro police, traffic again crept down the Strip.

"What happened here?" Teddie asked.

I gave him a brief summary as I pulled him away from the lights of the Strip and into the velvety cloak of the darkest time of night.

"I was wondering about those red welts on your neck. I knew I hadn't put them there and you aren't the type to engage in extra-curricular necking." Teddie wrapped his arm around me, pulling me close.

The guy knew me pretty well. "Bees are going to be the least of my worries this weekend."

"How can I help?" He gave me a quick kiss on the temple for no apparent reason.

I liked it. "Keep me relaxed."

"They say sex is one of the great stress relievers."

"I like the way you think, Mr. Kowalski." I looped an arm around his waist. With my free hand, I grabbed his hand dangling over my shoulder.

The heat of the summer finally had broken, leaving the air as smooth and refreshing as a fine wine. We strolled the few remaining blocks in silence, savoring the quiet and the dark. Most of the stars had faded in anticipation of dawn, but one or two still twinkled valiantly. Except for a few bats winging in the darkness, the world was still.

Conveniently, home for both Teddie and me was a tower of glass and steel, called the Presidio, located behind the Babylon.

"Your place or mine?" Teddie inquired as he held open the front door for me.

"I like sleeping at your place—waking up in a man's bedroom makes me feel naughty."

"Naughty is good." Teddie shot me a grin as we stepped in the elevator. He inserted his card, and pressed the PH button, then folded me into his arms. "As long as you restrict yourself to this man's bedroom."

"Shouldn't be a problem. One man at a time is all I can handle," I murmured as his mouth closed over mine, setting my every nerve afire. How he did that remained an intoxicating mystery, but as they say, better not to look a gift horse in the mouth.

The ride to the top floor passed without notice. At the ding of the bell announcing our arrival, we unclenched and staggered out of the elevator into the middle of Teddie's great room.

I leaned one hip against the sofa and grabbed Teddie's shoulder. "Stand there a minute, will you?" I bent over and shucked off a shoe, then shifted feet and shucked the other. "Better."

"Let me help you." With a glint in his eye, Teddie boosted me so I was sitting on the back of his sofa, feet not touching the floor. He stepped between my legs and I wrapped them around his waist. He eased off my sweater then went to work on the buttons of my blouse.

I watched as he deftly worked through the lot of them. While the future with Teddie still looked a bit murky, the present was shaping up nicely.

"Woman, you have the most incredible underwear." He hooked a finger under the strap of my black lace bra and worked it down my arm. His breath caught when the sheer fabric fell away.

"My mother always told me fast cars and short skirts got a guy's attention, but the lingerie sealed the deal." His skin on mine shot sparks of warmth to my very core.

"She knew what she was talking about." Teddie looked at me,

his eyes the deepest shade of blue. He looped one arm around my waist.

"She should." Warming to the game, I snaked my arms around his neck. "But I don't want to think about my mother right now. I don't want to think about anything."

"Have it your way." My body anchored to his, his arm firmly around my waist, Teddie bent me back.

When his mouth found my exposed breast, rational thought evaporated.

Chapter

T W O

*D*on't you know somebody named Numbers Neider-meyer?" Teddie asked.

I folded aside the sports section of the after-noon paper to look at him. Half submerged on the opposite side of the hot tub, he hid behind what looked to be the front section.

Bright daylight streamed in the windows when we had gotten to sleep. Entwined, we had slept the day away and had almost slumbered through the cocktail hour, which would have been a crime against nature since I didn't have to work tonight. As the day faded toward night, we had decided champagne and fresh croissants—both to be savored in the hot tub on the deck—were in order. Teddie popped the cork on a bottle of Dom Pérignon, which we sipped from flutes of Steuben crystal while warm bubbles

burbled around us. Our larders bare, we'd called out for the croissants, which had yet to arrive.

The patio of Teddie's penthouse offered a panoramic view of the
Strip—the lights pale in the fading light of day. Behind the skyline,
in a ball of exploding oranges and pinks, the sun balanced on top
of the Spring Mountains. Bordering the terrace, the privacy hedge
of rose bushes, verdant and laden with blossoms, infused the air
with its perfume. A single hummingbird of shimmering green, a
splash of ruby red at its throat, hung in the still air.

"Numbers Neidermeyer? If you're trying to shatter this sublime
moment, you're doing a darn good job." Lowering myself until the
water touched my chin, I stretched my arms along the rim of the
tub. Savoring the delicious feel of the water as it caressed my body,
I closed my eyes and leaned my head back. The uglies of the real
world were not going to infect the rest of this day. My resolve lasted
but a moment or two—curiosity reared its ugly head. "Why do you
ask?"

"She's dead."

"What?" I opened one eye, but didn't move anything else.

Teddie extended the paper to me. "You might want to read this."

Reluctantly, I floated to a sitting position and took the paper. If,
in fact, Numbers Neidermeyer sported a toe tag, it wouldn't exactly ruin my day. The article was short. I scanned it quickly. Bile
rose in my throat as I reached the end.

Of all the ways I had imagined the demise of Ms. Neidermeyer,
being tossed into the shark tank at the Mandalay Bay Resort and
Casino as a predawn snack for the tiger shark was not one of
them.

"Heck of a way to go." I imagined her thrashing about as the
shark tore off parts—I'm very visual. Sometimes that can be fun.
This wasn't one of those times.

"Did you read the whole thing?" Teddie's voice was low, his expression serious.

I shook my head.

"Read it."

I did as he said—this time I read past the part about Numbers being a tasty tidbit. Apparently murder was sufficient to get Metro's attention. In their collective brilliance, the police were investigating the demise of Ms. Neidermeyer as a "suspicious death." No shit, Sherlock. Who would *voluntarily* hit the shark tank for a few laps? I read on. Already they had named a person of interest. The blood drained from my head.

The Beautiful Jeremy Whitlock was Suspect Number One.

I found my phone under the couch in Teddie's living room. For a moment I wondered how it had gotten there, then the warmth of the memory washed over me. Oh yeah.

Clad in jeans with a hole in the right knee, Teddie's Harvard sweatshirt, and an old pair of Merrells on my feet, I sat cross-legged on the floor. Flipping open the phone, I hit number three on the speed-dial.

Brandy answered on the first ring, "Customer Relations, Brandy Alexander speaking."

"Brandy? What are you doing there?" I rose to my feet. In a few strides I had crossed the room. I grabbed my second set of car keys off a hook by Teddie's door, and jumped into the elevator he was holding for me. He'd already pressed the button for the garage. I gave him a quick kiss good-bye before the doors closed. "Wasn't your shift over a couple of hours ago? Where's Miss Patterson?"

"She's at home—something about Jeremy. She said she'd call when she headed my way, but I haven't heard from her." The girl sounded exhausted.

"Why didn't you call me?" I tapped my foot as I descended. One could get a good buzz from 3.2 beer in the time it took our elevators to travel from the Penthouse to the garage.

"I was about to. I didn't want to get anybody in trouble."

The doors opened, and I ran for my car, a thirty-year-old Porsche 911. Like its owner, the car could be temperamental. I said a few quick prayers to the car gods as I folded myself into the tiny vehicle—someone my size didn't so much drive the thing as wear it. "We both told you, Brandy. We are a team. The only thing you can get in trouble for is lack of communication. I can't pick up the slack if I don't know whose rope it's in."

"I'm sorry." Now she sounded devastated.

I gave myself an internal tongue-lashing as I shifted the phone to my right ear. Holding it with my shoulder, I turned the ignition. The engine caught with its recognizable low growl. "No, I'm the one who's sorry. Two months on the job isn't a long time. You're doing great. Now, go home. Get some rest."

"But there's no one here."

"Call Miss Patterson, tell her to stay put. Then call Security. Speak to the supervisor on duty. Ask him to cover for you—he won't say no. Then forward the phones to his cell and hit the road." I piloted the car through the garage to the exit. "I'll be there as soon as I can. I'm leaving home now, but I have one stop to make."

Miss Patterson lived in east Vegas, just past the airport. Traffic willing, I'd be there in twenty minutes.

I'D been a bit optimistic. Cars, trucks, and the occasional RV packed the Strip, and Tropicana Avenue was backed up all the way to Maryland Parkway. Thirty minutes after I'd left, patience long exhausted, I finally pulled up to the gate of Miss Patterson's subdivision—an enclave of cute single-stories clustered around an elaborate pool, replete with waterfall and hot tub, and bordering a public golf course. Technically, in a vain attempt at gentrification, public courses were now known as daily-fee establishments, which is like calling a janitor a waste engineer. I punched in the code and waited for the gate to slowly open, then shot through the gap as soon as it was wide enough.

Miss Patterson's house occupied a premier lot. Three houses from the pool, it backed up to the first tee box, close enough to hear the golfers' expletives—which had been a bit disconcerting the first time she'd had a dinner party on the patio. Now, the invectives were part of the ambiance, or so Miss Patterson wanted everyone to believe.

A black Hummer hulked in the driveway. I assumed it was Jeremy's. I wondered if that was a sticking point for the Prius-driving Miss Patterson. However, the two vehicles combined probably had a neutral carbon footprint, but I didn't know. I had difficulty calculating my correct bra size—determining carbon footprints was well beyond my math skills.

Wrestling my thoughts back to the business at hand was harder than usual. An early morning of bedroom calisthenics and my brain had gone AWOL.

I parked along the red-painted curb in front of Miss Patterson's house, shrugged out of the Porsche, and hurried up the drive. Lights lined the path to the door, guiding guests as night closed its grasp. A single brass sconce illuminated the front porch. The door flew open as I approached.

Put together beautifully, Miss Patterson stood in the doorway. I still wasn't used to her recent transformation. Before Jeremy, who was fifteen years her junior, Miss P had been a frumpy almost fifty. Now, her short golden hair purposefully spiky, her makeup understated, competent yet stylish in her tailored pantsuit and heels, she personified fabulous, feisty fortysomething. A cascade of golden chains and flashes of gold at her earlobes added glitz. Altogether she presented the embodiment of a future Head of Customer Relations—if you ignored the scrunched skin between her eyes, the dark circles beneath them, and the taut line of her mouth.

"Lucky! Thank God!" Miss Patterson stepped aside, welcoming me inside. "I knew you'd come."

"Brandy got hold of you?" I walked down the small hallway to the great room at the back of the house.

Overstuffed couches dotted with throw pillows in bright colors filled one side of the great room. A glass-topped dining room set, each chair a different color, occupied the other side. A curved bar separated the kitchen from the other areas. Pastels and watercolors, each capturing a different mood of the desert, graced the walls. Plants softened the corners. Floor-to-ceiling windows, framed with plantation shutters, extended the length of the back of the house. Photographs of friends and family, lovingly displayed, nestled among the books in the bookcase and dotted the coffee table.

As I parked myself on a couch, I picked up the photo of the two of us taken at the Babylon's opening gala. Arms thrown around each other's shoulders, we grinned like fools and looked like we'd had far too much to drink, which we had. Unfit to drive home, Miss Patterson had spent the night at the hotel. Somehow I had staggered home—I still don't remember how. It had been a great night.

"She said you'd called, and I was to stay put. Knowing you, I figured you were on your way."

I set the frame back on the table. "Is Jeremy here?"

Miss Patterson paced in front of me, wringing her hands. She cast a furtive glance out the back windows. "He's sitting on the patio by himself. He refuses to come in."

"Has he been drinking?"

She shook her head. "No. He just sits. I was afraid to leave him like this. I can't tell if he's angry or scared."

"Both, I suspect." I pushed myself to my feet. "Let me handle your Aussie. Are you up for work? Brandy's catatonic after fourteen hours on the job, and I have a nine o'clock dinner with the Big Boss."

"Work sounds like the tonic I need." Miss Patterson straightened her shoulders. "I can handle the office if you can figure out how to get Jeremy out of this mess."

"You got it." My voice held more confidence than I felt. Clearing people in murder investigations was a bit outside my areas of expertise. Now, if he had a pesky little rash . . . "I'll give it my best shot," I said as I gave her shoulders a squeeze. While she was made of stalwart stock straight from America's heartland and could probably handle more than I could, a hug never hurt. "Now scoot. I'll check in on you before my dinner."

MY eyes needed a moment or two to adjust to the darkness before I located Jeremy sprawled on a chaise near the back fence.

"Mind if I pull up a chair?" I asked as I dragged one over to him. If he glanced up, I couldn't tell.

"Man, I really blew it giving that cow such a mouthful. Nothing like being a dickhead for the cameras." Jeremy's voice, while tired, still had a sharp edge.

"It doesn't mean you killed her." I paused for a beat. "You didn't, did you?"

"Don't be a dill."

"Not being fluent in Aussie slang, I'll take that as a no," I said as I leaned back on the chaise and stared up into the velvety darkness. Living under the canopy of light over the Strip, I'd forgotten how many stars hung in the night sky. "Want to tell me what happened? In American?"

"I don't know what happened. My client hired me to check out her hunch that somebody was playing fast and loose in the sports book at her casino. The house had lost money it shouldn't have."

"And that led you to Numbers Neidermeyer?"

"Not directly. I wasn't checking leads as much as following hunches. I hit a nerve when I cornered Ms. Neidermeyer. She lit into me. I didn't handle it well, but I didn't kill her."

"Is that what you told the police?"

"Yeah. Your buddy, Detective Romeo, banged on the door here around noon. He wanted to talk. I didn't see any harm in that, so I agreed and followed him to the station. I told him everything I know, but the bloody wanker kept me there for five hours." He rolled over on his side, facing me. "If I was going to kill anybody, right now he's at the top of the list."

I could see Jeremy's eyes, but the darkness shadowed his features, hiding any emotion lurking there. However, the line of his body betrayed his anger.

"Understandable." Secretly I was glad it was Romeo. The kid owed me, big time. "How do you think they tied you in so fast?"

"I've been wondering the same thing myself. Somebody must've ratted me out."

"Yeah, but who? The casino was practically deserted when I saw you two going at it."

"Were you the big mouth?" Jeremy asked, his voice tight.

"To quote a good friend of mine, don't be a dill." I shivered. The night air had turned cool. Even Teddie's sweatshirt wasn't quite enough. "Who's your client?"

"You know I can't tell you that. If it's any consolation, I didn't tell the police either."

"Last time I checked, this country had done away with thumbscrews and waterboards. You don't have to tell the police anything."

"I do if I want to keep my P.I. license. But my client isn't germane to the investigation. At the time, I hadn't given her a report so she didn't know anything."

"Except what she suspects," I reminded him. "You're splitting hairs with the police—not wise considering they have your neck under a boot. You'd better tell them and, if I'm going to help, you'd better tell me."

"Your young detective is in over his head," Jeremy said after a moment of staring into the darkness. "He let me run him around a bit, but I suspect he'll figure out he's been had and come sniffing around again. When he does, I'll tell him then."

"A wise man." I rose to go. "So, tell me. Where do I start turning over stones?"

Jeremy followed my lead, pushing himself to his feet. "The yellow brick road starts with your Aunt Matilda."

.   .   .

AUNT Matilda! Terrific. Lately, life had been going swimmingly—I should have known it wouldn't last.

After a good look at Jeremy in the light, I'd sent him to the shower, then to bed for a couple hours of shut-eye. Matilda wouldn't be receiving guests until at least eleven, and, in the meantime, I had a dinner with the Big Boss.

This time I drove more sedately as I piloted the Porsche toward the Babylon. Earlier, when I was coming the opposite direction, halfway to Miss Patterson's and weaving in and out of traffic like a maniac, I realized I'd left my purse and my driver's license with it at the office when my shift had ended early this morning. At four in the morning I was lucky to still have my sanity intact. Rounding up personal possessions was an impossibility. So, my prized Hermès Birkin bag, a gift from the Big Boss, was locked safely in my office—I hoped.

Traffic much lighter now, in the fifteen minutes it took me to get back to the Strip I barely had enough time to chase down the young Detective Romeo on his cell and invite him to breakfast. Since Miss Patterson always parked in my parking space, I spent another ten looking for an appropriate place to stash my baby. Not finding anything, I gave up and turned her over to the valet.

MISS Patterson manned her desk in the outer vestibule. She looked up when I entered. Worry clouded her eyes.

"How's Jeremy?"

I shrugged. "Shaken. Angry. I sent him to bed for a couple of hours."

"This is going to be okay, isn't it?"

"Sure. In time."

"But the police—"

"—Are doing their job," I said, finishing her thought for her. I headed toward my office with Miss P in trail, clipboard in hand. "Speaking of which, expect a call from Romeo. He'll want to verify when Jeremy came home."

Her eyes widened. "What should I tell him?"

"The truth." I stopped before rounding my desk and gave her hand a squeeze. "As corny as it sounds, the truth will win the day. We just have to find out what exactly the truth is. Trust me." I adopted an exaggerated stance with a hand in the middle of my chest, and, I hoped, a semblance of a grin on my face. "Really, have I ever let you down?"

She tried to smile, but didn't quite make it. Taking a deep breath, she gave herself a reassuring nod as if giving herself a talking to. Then, focusing on her clipboard, she switched gears and started in with the rundown. "Jerry called. He said he had the tapes of the twelfth floor you wanted. The police seized all the tapes from the lobby and casino cameras. There were too many for him to make copies in the time he had."

"The police showed up pretty quick." I checked my closet for my Birkin. Still there. "You wouldn't happen to have a copy of their search warrant, would you?"

Miss Patterson gave me a look over the top of her glasses.

"Of course you do. May I see it?"

She pulled a piece of paper from under the clip and handed it to me as I plopped myself in the chair behind my desk. Miss Patterson remained standing.

"Would you sit?" I said as I scanned the document. "You're lurking and it's making me nervous."

Miss Patterson perched on the edge of one of the chairs opposite the desk. She looked like a bird ready to take flight as she waited while I finished reading.

Our very own district attorney had signed the application and Detective Romeo had John Hancocked the probable cause affidavit. Interesting.

"Anything else?" I asked when I'd finished.

Miss Patterson scanned her list. "Not of any importance, for now."

"That will change."

The biggest fight of the year was scheduled for this Saturday night. A guarantee of $64 million had lured Tiny Tortilla Padilla out of retirement for one final fight. His opponent, the current titleholder, was some upstart from Germany who had fought to a 46-0 record. The promoters anticipated a record crowd. The first wave would hit tomorrow, but the real craziness would begin the day after—on Thursday.

We'd doubled the security staff to handle the incendiary mix of Hollywood celebrities, big money, and hookers, both professional and amateur, from all over the country. The good ones cleared thirty grand in the three days spent flat on their backs.

Sleep for me and my staff would be in short supply—we had the unenviable task of trying to keep a lid on this insanity. And now I had Jeremy's problem dropped in my lap. Good thing I didn't need much shut-eye.

"I think we're ready." Miss Patterson's eyes scanned down her list. "I can't imagine anything we've missed."

"There'll be something. There always is." Las Vegas had the same problem with fight weekend that the military had with war—what we prepared for was rarely what we got. "Have we heard anything out of L.A.?" Unbeknownst to Teddie, I'd sent a CD of his original tracks to an agent I knew in California. Impressed, she'd been schlepping the thing all around Hollywood and Vine or wherever the center of the West Coast music biz had migrated to.

Miss Patterson, my co-conspirator, shook her head. "Not yet."

I rose and rooted around in my closet. Dinner at the Big Boss's required more than tattered jeans and Teddie's sweatshirt. Several outfits covered in plastic hung in the very back—this wasn't the first time I'd found myself short on time and in need of an appropriate costume. "Heard anything out of Mr. Padilla's camp?"

"Not a word. For a big-time fighter he has the smallest entourage I've ever seen. And they don't ask for anything." Miss Patterson finally settled back in the chair. "The staff really likes him. He doesn't gamble, he doesn't drink, he's approachable and friendly, and he tips big. I heard the employees were thinking of adopting him."

"An interesting idea, but I don't think it's possible." When she was looking the other way, I snuck a peek at Miss Patterson. Worry still lurked under that brave face she wore. "What about hiring him to teach our other important guests how to behave?"

"You have anyone specific in mind?"

"The whole Hollywood crowd for starters," I said. "You'd think etiquette and class died with Fred Astaire."

"Frankly, I don't think Mr. Padilla wants to leave," Miss P noted.

Tiny Tortilla Padilla had been in residence in the Kasbah, our high-roller apartments, for a month now. I'd checked on him a couple of times, but he was amazingly maintenance-free.

"With a staff-to-guest ratio of five to one, I can understand his reluctance to return to the real world." I ducked into Miss Patterson's vestibule, then stepped behind the partition separating it from a miniscule kitchen area. My office had a wall of windows overlooking the lobby—I'm not shy, but I draw the line at stripping for the guests. "Doesn't he have a bunch of kids?" I raised my voice so it would carry to my office.

"Fifteen."

"Somebody ought to tell him what causes that," I said, but didn't get even a chuckle from my audience of one.

Keeping in mind I would be calling on Aunt Matilda after dinner, I chose a pair of tight suede pencil pants in a muted shade of olive, a silk tunic in peach and gold cut to the very edge of decency, and strappy, gold knock-me-down-and-fuck-me shoes.

Miss Patterson was suitably impressed when I reappeared. "Wow. What's the occasion? You and Teddie going partying at Babel?"

"I wish." Babel was our new lounge. Technically it had been open for six weeks, working out the kinks. Don't even ask me how much of a problem the clear retractable cover for the pool had been. Finally we had given up and turned the pool into a giant aquarium with a permanent clear cover that served as our dance floor. We'd stocked the thing with all manner of flesh-eating pretties from the deep—which, come to think of it, made it sort of creepy in light of the late Ms. Neidermeyer. Officially, the grand opening bash was this weekend, when the Hollywood crowd would be fully represented. "I have a date with your squeeze after dinner," I told her. "We're going on a fact-finding mission."

"Ms. Neidermeyer?" A little concern crept into Miss P's voice.

"Worried?" I shot her a lopsided grin.

"Don't be a dill."

THE Big Boss's apartment occupied the top floor—the fifty-second—of one wing of the hotel. My magic card, inserted in the appropriate slot, released the elevator to take me there. The doors opened, depositing me in the middle of the living room.

Teak flooring imported from somewhere in Indonesia and burnished to a rich sheen covered the entire three-thousand square feet. Hand-knotted rugs from the Middle East, each populated with a cluster of sturdy furniture made from the hides of different beasts and woods from different continents, dotted the expanse. Brass sconces cast a muted glow on leather-finished walls. Lesser original works by the Grand Masters, smaller pieces from the Big Boss's extensive art collection, hung reverently in appropriately lighted spots. A fire danced in the moveable fireplace, which tonight was placed next to the dining table—set for two.

The Big Boss stood at the bar, his profile outlined by the lights of the Strip shining through the windows behind him. A short man with salt and pepper hair, he wore his ubiquitous suit, perfectly tailored to his trim frame. Tonight's suit was gunmetal gray, his shirt white, his tie violet. Very old school, he secured his collar with a gold collar bar encrusted with pavé diamonds. "You want the usual?"

"Please." I watched him work—a maestro with various weird and wonderful healing waters. Frankly, I didn't need the usual,

Wild Turkey 101 neat. My stomach was already punishing me for two glasses of champagne in the hot tub. What I needed was food. But nobody, me included, said No to the Big Boss.

The world knew the Big Boss as Albert Rothstein, a Las Vegas legend. He hired me when I was fifteen and had lied about my age. At the time, I didn't know he was also my father. I didn't learn that little tidbit until a couple of months ago when he decided to come clean. It had taken a near-fatal heart condition and impending major surgery for him to find the need to tell me.

When I was very young, he and my mother had reluctantly parted ways—a golden boy in the casino business would never have been allowed to marry a hooker. The choice had been simple—a good career with infinite possibilities, or squalor with a former prostitute and an illegitimate kid. Since my parents had nothing, they made the obvious choice. And they'd carried a torch for each other ever since.

When I thought about it, it made me sad—all that time lost. However, from all appearances, now that the cat was out of the bag (at least among the family), they were making up for lost time. I really didn't want to know. I loved them both, but I didn't want the details of their sex life. Even at my age, the thought of my parents in flagrante delicto left me queasy.

After the Big Boss dropped the bombshell, my life had gone on pretty much the same. I insisted nobody be told about our familial ties—I just wanted to be the same Lucky I'd always been. I wanted my colleagues to treat me as they always had. I did not want to morph into "The Boss's Daughter." As far as I could tell, our secret was safe with the four of us—my parents, Teddie, and me.

As if my hunger had summoned him, the elevator dinged its arrival and a black-and-white-clad waiter stepped out, pushing a cart laden with covered dishes. I felt like attacking, but instead, like a shark circling its prey, I prowled the edge of the room pretending to be interested in the art on the walls, although I'd seen it all a million times.

On the verge of succumbing to my stomach's primal call and chasing the waiter into the kitchen, something caught my eye. Various small origami creatures frolicked on a small side table—a herd of tiny elephants, a couple of dogs, a cat, and a bird—all made out of folded one-hundred-dollar bills. Smiling, I picked up one I couldn't identify and held it aloft, turning it around.

"That's supposed to be a swan," the Big Boss said as he took a spot at my elbow. He handed me my drink—a Double Old Fashioned Glass filled with three fingers of amber liquid. "I haven't perfected the folds, yet. Damned arthritis isn't making it any easier."

Up until a few months ago, I didn't think any disease was bold enough to attack the Big Boss. Heart trouble had opened the door and apparently arthritis had charged through.

"Life's a bitch and then you die." I hid my grin behind my glass as I took a sip. Like molten lava, the bourbon scorched a path down my throat, making my eyes water.

"And to think I hoped a daughter would brighten my old age," he countered, his voice muted so only I could hear, as he placed a hand in the small of my back, urging me toward the table. "Hungry?"

"Famished." I let my father steer me to my appointed chair, which he pulled out for me.

He took the one opposite. An imperceptible nod from the Big Boss, and the waiter served us both the salad course, doffing the covers with a flourish. Baby spinach, pine nuts, goat cheese, avocado, and poached pears, all drizzled with balsamic vinaigrette—the salad was my favorite and a staple on the menu at Tigris, the Babylon's five-star eatery. The Big Boss didn't miss a trick.

The waiter repaired to the kitchen, leaving us alone.

I had just snagged two rolls from a silver basket in the middle of the table when my mother, Mona, dressed to kill in a tight blue suit, hot-pink lacy cami, and five-inch heels, charged out of the hallway leading from the private areas of the apartment. Her stilettos clacked on the hardwood as she hurried in our direction. She fiddled with an earring as she gave me the once-over.

"It's nice to see my daughter isn't suffering from an eating disorder." Her long brown hair was pulled tastefully back, a few tendrils softly framed her face, hiding remnants of her plastic surgery addiction. Her makeup, perfectly understated as usual, hid the rest. Tall and trim—a perfect size six—she looked twenty, if a day.

A pox on her.

"Eating disorders are all about control," I shot back, my mouth full of roll. "I traded the illusion of control for self-gratification years ago."

The Big Boss choked then reached for his water glass as his face turned red.

My mother leveled her sternest gaze on me—a look that used to terrify me. "Really, darling, carbs are the food of the Devil. Just wait, once you hit forty, your hips will be as big as a house."

"How sad you're not joining us, Mother. My well of guilt is getting kinda low."

"Tempting, dear, but I have a previous engagement. I'm holding a press conference."

"What?" My father and I said in unison.

"A young woman approached me last week. She is absolutely gorgeous, but her family is poor as church mice. And, the best thing . . . she's a virgin." My mother acted as if this were normal dinner conversation.

My father and I could only stare.

"And," my mother continued, clearly warming to the subject, "she wants me to auction her virginity."

"No way!" my father roared, as he jumped to his feet. "You are not going to—"

"Don't be silly." Mother put a slender hand in the middle of his chest and daintily pressed him back into his chair. "Of course I am! Think of the publicity. It'll hit the Internet like wildfire."

Mother had a point. "She's twenty-one?" I asked, the businesswoman in me overriding good taste.

"I have a certified birth certificate."

Unable to resist, I asked, "I assume you have a certified virgin certificate as well?"

She gave me a crisp nod and a do-you-think-I'm-stupid look. "Morris Feldman did the exam."

I shuddered. Dr. Feldman was the reason all of my doctors would now and for evermore be females. "You have it in writing?"

"Sworn, signed, and notarized."

Like a fan at a tennis match watching a rapid-fire rally, my father's head swiveled as he glowered first at one of us, then the other, then back again. After a few exchanges, he found his bellow. "Have you both lost your minds?"

My mother waved the fingers of one hand at us. "Ta-ta. Have a lovely dinner."

I grinned as she sashayed to the elevator and disappeared inside.

My grin vanished as I looked at my father across the table. His face bright red, he looked as if he might stroke out at any minute.

"I'm sorry. I know I shouldn't encourage her." I tried to adopt my most contrite expression, but my grin kept threatening to burst through. "I can't help myself—it's an ingrained habit."

"You and your mother are going to be the death of me." His mottled complexion faded a bit. He shook his head. "Why I even told you about your parentage! And I demanded Mona be a presence in my life again!"

"I don't know what you were thinking."

"I thought my days were over. I certainly wasn't considering the mess I was creating if I survived." A grin tugged at one corner of his mouth. His complexion was returning to normal.

"You *had* died once that day already," I noted. Satisfied I didn't need to call the paramedics, I again dove into my salad.

"Who can do anything about your mother?" he said aloud. "I don't know why I even try. She's going to do what she wants."

"She always has," I agreed. I mopped my empty salad plate with the last remnant of a roll. "So what did you call this meeting for?"

Seamlessly, the Big Boss shifted gears. "I've done as you asked—I've hired a new chef to develop a premier restaurant atop the Athena."

The Athena was an aging Las Vegas grande dame that had seen better times. The Big Boss and his money people had acquired her after Irv Gittings, the previous owner of the Athena, had conspired to frame the Big Boss for murder. The Big Boss was still licking his chops over that one. I had to admit, seeing Irv Gittings in an orange jumpsuit had done wonders for me as well.

"Tell me about him." I breathed deep as the waiter appeared from his hiding place behind closed doors in the kitchen. With a flourish, he delivered a plateful of roast duckling with Madeira sauce, asparagus with hollandaise, and herbed rice, setting it in front of me after removing the salad plate. I forced myself to wait until my father had been served and had taken his first bite, then I attacked my meal with relish.

The Big Boss had done his homework. As I ate, he regaled me with minutia about the Frenchman—where his parents were raised, where he attended *école maternelle*, *école primaire*, and *Lycée*. I had no idea the Big Boss knew so much French—either that or he was pretending, but you couldn't prove it by me.

Warming to the subject, he continued the story. However, when the Big Boss started telling about a pretty little au pair and the young Frenchman's subsequent loss of his virginity—clearly the Big Boss had split more than one bottle of wine with the guy or the Frenchman was more forthcoming than most men I knew, I drew the line.

"Boss," I interrupted. "We aren't hiring him for breeding purposes."

"What?" His face started getting splotchy again.

"Just his name and his cooking credentials will do."

"Insubordinate. Ungrateful," he muttered, while he concentrated on his dinner. A minute passed before he began again. "His name is Jean-Charles Bouclet. He's your age, give or take. He studied at La Sorbonne and Le Cordon Bleu in Paris, then apprenticed under several famous chefs—Daniel Boulud being one of them. After opening his own restaurant in New York last fall, he's the *gastronome extraordinaire* of the culinary world—the toast of those in the know. It's quite a coup for us to get his Vegas location."

"And what did you promise him?"

"I guaranteed him enough hotel comps that his restaurant will be successful even if not one customer opens their wallet."

"Pretty pricy bait." I dabbed at the corner of my mouth with my napkin as I wondered when the Vegas hotel business had quit being about good service and gambling. Now it was all about celebrities—Hollywood types and gastronomic types.

"He'll be worth it. The buzz is already starting." The Big Boss looked at me as if he read my thoughts.

"The reopening of the Athena is still a year or more away," I pointed out. "I've been more concerned with filling the restaurant space in the Bazaar." We'd recently closed an Italian place that wasn't pulling its weight in our retail area. Boarded-up space gave the wrong impression.

"That's the best part. Jean-Charles has agreed to take over that space—he's doing a high-end burger bar. He said he always wanted to play around with the American hamburger."

"As long as he understands horsemeat is illegal for human consumption in this country."

The Big Boss gave me The Look. "He said he could be open by Saturday with a limited menu."

"Really?"

"He's bringing a skeleton staff with him—enough to get started," my father said. "He'll handpick the rest from our employees. I want you to handle the transition and see that he has everything he needs."

"Sure." Hadn't my father ever heard about the straw and the camel's back? I wondered if cloning myself was a viable option.

"Is everything set for the opening of Babel on Saturday?" The

Big Boss pushed his plate away, then rose and stepped to the bar. "The headliner . . . remind me who she is again?" He poured us both a healthy snifter of Napoleon brandy.

"Reza Pashiri, an Indian import known the world over as simply Za. Apparently she has The Sound, whatever that is. Regardless, she's the hottest pop-tart on the planet right now." I sipped my brandy. From what I'd heard, little Miss Za was going to be a pain in za kaboodle. She liked handsome men or beautiful women, depending on her mood. Her suite had been feng shuied, the air ducts taped, the fridge stocked with Fiji water and Polish vodka, and the beds made with twelve-hundred-count cotton and goose down.

"I'm sending the plane to pick her up at the Ontario Airport Friday," I explained.

"Oh." The Boss was as clueless about these things as I was. "Is she the only one?"

"No. We also have engaged the hottest DJ and multiple lesser luminaries." I thought the fact that disc jockeys now rose to the ranks of stardom was the first sign of the apocalypse, but in a culture that could worship talent-free heiresses, why should I be surprised?

I joined the Big Boss at the window, where we both reveled in the light show of the Strip.

"I remember when we could get Frank and Dino and Sammy with a promise of a good time. Now that isn't enough." The Big Boss sounded tired. The doctors said his heart was healing, but it was a long road back.

"A serious six figures and you're in the ballpark."

His face wore a sad look. Frank Sinatra for nothing back then, versus the flavor of the month for serious green now. Somehow, pandering to the icons of pop culture felt demeaning.

THE rest of the evening with the Big Boss passed in pleasant conversation. Asking for my help with the new French guy hadn't required a meal, but lately my father had been looking for excuses to spend time with me. Frankly, I enjoyed our time together as much as he did and was grateful for the opportunities to get to know him in a slightly different way. Even though our relationship had always been comfortable and warm, I needed to adjust to the overlay of family.

Afterward, I had a few minutes to kill before leaving to meet the Beautiful Jeremy Whitlock, so I took a turn through the casino.

Casino design is a fine art, and the Big Boss had spent a cool million on the plans alone. If the size of the crowd now packing the space was a measure of success, the designer had hit this one out of the park. All shapes and sizes gathered around the tables and occupied the chairs in front of the slots. Drinks in hand, young men trolled, eyeing the ladies as if sizing up heifers at the state fair. The women pretended to be disinterested, but they couldn't resist casting furtive glances as well. Everyone had apparently gotten the memo that, when in Vegas, tacky attire was de rigueur.

Multicolored canvas looped from the ceiling, evoking an intimate Persian bazaar. Giant potted palms completed the theme. Flames burned at the end of bundles of faux reeds that were mounted on the walls under covered glass. Cocktail waitresses, clad in tiny, off-the-shoulder wraps, their waists cinched with gold braid, worked the crowd.

Occasional shouts arose from the tables. The slots sang out to passers-by, but the clattering of quarters signaling a winner was no more. All the casinos had converted to slots that accepted bills but no coins, then printed a receipt for any winnings, which the patron cashed at the window or at kiosks located strategically throughout the casino. Someone who studied these sorts of things had determined players spent more when stuffing in bills—apparently each quarter they put into the machine served as a visual reminder of how much they were spending. We deferred to the experts, but I missed the clank of metal money cascading through a metal tube. Exciting and exhilarating, the sound defined Vegas, as did the normal haze gathered about the crowd.

People smoked in Vegas as if the whole city had been declared a cancer-free zone.

As I passed the final row of slot machines, a man seated at the far end caught my eye. Lean and lanky, his eyes dark hollows in his angular face, the ubiquitous cigarette dangling from his lips, he stared as if mesmerized by the whirling wheels in front of him. Everything about him appeared normal—except for the pith helmet with a short antenna extending out of the top that adorned his head. I leaned against the machines and watched him for a moment. Without the clang of quarters, it was impossible to tell if he was winning. He didn't look twitchy or cast glances over his shoulder. Still, he warranted a look.

I grabbed my push-to-talk and keyed Security.

Jerry answered. "Whatcha got?"

"Are you at the monitors?"

Security had a wall of screens displaying live feeds from cameras watching all public areas of the property. "I can be. Give me a sec."

I waited while Jerry repositioned himself.

"Okay, shoot," he said when ready.

"You see the guy in the pith helmet in the last row of slots on the west side of the floor?"

"We've been watching him for about ten minutes, but we haven't seen anything weird."

"You mean beside the antenna?" I let a hint of sarcasm creep into my voice.

"There's an antenna?" Jerry's voice took on a hard tone.

"About an inch long—hard to see. He's probably just talking to aliens, but on the theory that the best place to hide something is in plain sight, why don't you have a couple of your guys check him out?"

"Are you thinking he might have an electronic transmitter in there?"

"A long shot, but we don't want him messing with our equipment—it's bad for the bottom line."

"I'll take care of it."

"Thanks." I started to rehook my phone in its cradle at my waist, then thought better of it. Instead, as I pushed myself upright and started toward the front of the hotel to retrieve my car from the valet, I hit number two on the speed-dial.

Teddie answered just as I thought his voicemail would pick up. "Hey, beautiful. Are you coming home?" He sounded excited and distracted at the same time—the perpetual emotional state of a composer.

I didn't have to ask what he was up to. "Jeremy and I have an errand to run, then I'll head your way. I can't imagine I'll be more than a couple of hours."

"Call me when you two are done, okay?"

"Sure." I started to ring-off, then remembered. "Hey, would you do me a favor?"

"Anything," he said, sounding like he meant it.

"Would you TIVO the eleven o'clock news? Mother's invited the media to her press conference." I gave the Hi sign to one of the valets, and he bolted into the darkness.

"Press conference? What is she announcing?"

"What? Me tell? And ruin it for you? No, you'll have to find out for yourself."

Chapter

THREE

♡

unt Matilda wasn't really my aunt at all.

And she shot anyone who called her by her given name.

Known far and wide as Darlin' Delacroix, she was my mother's best friend (a status that conferred honorary family membership over my objection), and had been a fixture in my life—and a pain in my ass—as far back as I could remember.

My dear aunt was a proud member of the leading family of Ely, Nevada. The Delacroixes had made their fortune in mining—silver, uranium, borax, molybdenum, and other sundry minor minerals. Minor minerals or not, the Delacroix stake was worth major money. When the old man died, Matilda had taken her share, fled to Vegas, changed her name, enlarged her bust, dyed her hair, and bought an off-strip casino. That had been years ago, when I was a little girl.

Now, on the downhill side of seventy, Darlin' reigned as the doyen of the French Quarter, the most successful local casino. The Quarter's largest drawing card besides loose slots was a slate of prizefights held every Friday night, which always attracted a huge, rabid crowd.

In an effort to avoid squandering even a single opportunity to separate patrons from their money, the Quarter also boasted a bowling alley, a twelve-screen movie extravaganza, and a kid zone where parents could deposit the scions of the clan while they gambled with the milk money. Darlin' had added a small theatre a couple of decades ago, which now hosted headliners who had passed their career apex in the 1970s. The ugly stepsister to the glittering Strip properties, the French Quarter made money hand-over-fist, much to the chagrin of the big dogs who had poured billions into their megacasinos.

One look at the jammed parking lot, and I headed for the valet. I pulled in behind a black Hummer. After taking a ticket from an out-of-breath kid, his shirttail hanging out, his hair wild, Jeremy stepped out of the Hummer. Apparently we ran on coordinated internal clocks.

Noise assaulted us as we pushed through the front doors. Dixieland jazz pumped through the sound system at a mind-numbing level. Ropes of cheap Mardi Gras beads circled the necks of most patrons, many of whom clutched tall glasses of hurricanes—the French Quarter's signature drink. Like too many fish in an aquarium, the jean-clad crowd filled every conceivable space.

An almost nauseating mixture of aromas filled the air—deep-fried beignets, strong Cajun spices, chickory coffee, stale beer, cigarette smoke. For a moment I even thought I could discern the stench of the previous night's excesses that coated the sidewalks of the real French Quarter. My imagination added the smell of the dirty water of Old Man River as it rolled through N'Awlins. At least I hoped it was my imagination.

An eardrum-shattering trumpet blast interrupted the revelry, announcing the aerial show. Every hour, on the hour, floats filled with costumed revelers tossing beaded trinkets into the crowd traversed a track hanging from the ceiling as carnival music blared. If a pretty young thing in the crowd flashed her cantaloupes, she was awarded special medallions from the King, who rode in his own regal raft.

What little movement there was within the packed crowd stopped as eyes turned skyward. The crowd whooped and hollered, trying to attract the attention of the bead-tossers. With me in the lead, Jeremy and I ducked down and wormed along. Before facing Matilda, I needed to make a stop at the lobby liquor store.

Aunt Matilda had two vices—handsome young men and cheap gin.

WITH a bottle of Admiral's firmly in hand, Jeremy and I again dove into the crowd and pushed and shoved our way to the elevators. The crowd there was six deep. Four elevators deposited their loads and took on another before we forced our way onto one.

Hands trapped at my side by the crush of people, I shouted, "Top floor, please." Matilda would be receiving in her parlor. I couldn't tell if anyone heard or responded. It didn't matter. Imprisoned, I was along for the ride.

After stopping at almost every intervening level, the elevator spit us out at the top. Jeremy and I walked the long corridor in silence. I know I was girding myself—I assumed Jeremy was also.

The man standing guard at the door nodded and ushered us inside.

With red flocked wallpaper, dainty Queen Anne couches covered in plush purple velvet, skirted end tables boasting lamps with fringed shades, and potted palms weeping in the corners,

Matilda's parlor had given me nightmares as a child. Now it just gave me the creeps. Especially when you added the bevy of beautiful young men who lounged on the couches as additional decoration and Rod Stewart warbling "I'm in the Mood for Love" from the speakers.

Sitting in the midst of this invitation to debauchery was my Aunt Matilda.

Four foot ten and eighty pounds dripping wet, she commanded attention from her perch on a raised chair, her legs stretched in front of her, her feet resting daintily on a footstool.

For a woman sliding toward eighty, she pushed the fashion envelope. Her hair long and blond, her lips a red slash across her face, she wore fishnet hose on her dancer's legs and red stilettos. A black Lycra mini, a beaded top, and her standard leather jacket that I knew had an image of Elvis in leather mosaic on the back completed the picture.

Like a black hole, Matilda sucked all the energy out of the room, leaving us to revolve around her like spent planets.

She bounced to her feet when she saw us. "Lucky!"

Hoping my pants had enough give in them, I half-squatted, then bent down to give her a hug—four foot ten is a long way down from my six feet. "Aunt—"

"None of that aunt stuff." She waggled a finger at me. "You're supposed to call me Darlin'."

"I am incapable of calling anyone Darlin'." I extended the bottle of gin. "But before you write me off as too big a disappointment, I brought you a present."

"Redeeming," she said, as she gripped the bottle in her red-tipped claws. "The handsome man doesn't hurt either." She flashed a coquettish look at Jeremy. "Good to see you, Aussie-boy."

"You, too, Darlin'." A hand under her elbow, he guided her back to her chair. "We've come on business."

With a dismissive wave, Darlin' cleared the room. She pointed to a couch on the far side of the parlor. "Lucky, make yourself comfortable over there. Jeremy, why don't you sit right here." She patted a stool next to her.

Then she turned her attention, capturing me from head to toe in a glance. "Honey, those clothes! You look cheap."

Some people set my teeth on edge without even trying—Matilda was their Queen. "You have no idea how much I paid to look this cheap."

"Just because that outfit is expensive doesn't mean it's not cheap," Darlin' opined, a serious expression on her face.

"Yeah, the cheaper it is, the more it costs," I agreed, having too much fun to stop now.

Darlin' stared at me, clearly at a loss for words.

I didn't know they still sold blue eye shadow.

She blinked, her eyes wide. Lined with two sets of false eyelashes, it was amazing she could blink at all.

Victory was in my grasp.

Jeremy had that semiamused, caught-in-the-crossfire look. "You two behave. We need her help, Darlin', so be nice."

"We do?" Darlin' asked, her doubt evident.

Matilda never read the papers—she preferred to live in her own world—so I waited while Jeremy filled her in on the recent developments regarding Fishbait Neidermeyer.

"Sounds like she had it coming." An old-timer, Darlin' couldn't understand why society frowned on someone ridding themselves of a menace.

Jeremy started to explain, then quit. I understood his frustration—I had the same conversation with the Big Boss time and time again.

"Darlin', I brought Lucky here so you could tell her what you told me." Jeremy put a hand on Darlin's knee. "I don't want to violate client confidentiality, so the decision is yours. But I think she can help."

She eyed me for a moment. "She did save Al's hotel from that frightful man and his murder scheme." She gave me an ironic smile. "And she is family."

I always suspected she knew I didn't cotton to the idea of us being "related"—now I knew for sure.

"I don't guess it could hurt," she said, then she launched in. "My Sports Book manager came to me with a problem a week or so ago. He'd noticed some trends in the betting. Betting is usually fairly random. When trends develop and repeat, they raise suspicions." Darlin' clapped her hands and magically a young man appeared with a glass pitcher of gin martinis, dirty, and three glasses.

When Matilda drank, everybody drank.

Cheap gin, dry vermouth, and olive brine—I'd rather sip battery acid—but I took my drink when offered and pretended to be delighted.

"We don't have any proof, just gut feelings, really." Darlin' took a big gulp of martini. "Big money would come in at the last minute, just before betting closed—before we had time to adjust the odds." She idly stirred two olives skewered on a toothpick around her glass.

"What kinds of bets are we talking about?" I asked.

"Local book only. Mainly our Friday night fight series."

"Did Numbers Neidermeyer set the odds?"

"On some of them, but not all. Even though she has . . . had . . . the reputation, I like to spread my business around." My aunt looked up from her drink. Her eyes locked with mine. "I've seen greed get to the best of them."

"Who was placing the action?"

"That's my girl, follow the money." This time my aunt looked pleased. Was this some kind of test and I'd missed it?

"Following the money, that's what I was doing." Jeremy joined the conversation. "Word on the street had it that someone was making private book."

"Ms. Neidermeyer?" I asked.

"I'd just started turning over rocks, but more than one snake writhed in her direction." Jeremy stood and started pacing. "I can't prove anything, of course."

"So, back to my original question: Nobody knows who places the action?" I asked.

"They don't send the same guy each time," Aunt Matilda said, choosing her words carefully. "But my manager thought he recognized Scully Winter as one of the carrier pigeons."

"Scully?" My eyebrows shot up. "Didn't he go underground after the State Bar yanked his license to practice law?"

"It appears he might have resurfaced." Aunt Matilda took a sip of her martini as she eyed me over the top of the glass.

"Did the security cameras get him?"

"If they did, the tapes were erased before we knew to start looking."

Unsure of what to do with my glass of witch's brew, I looked around for a resting place. Finally, I scooched the wide crystal flute onto the side table next to the couch and hoped my aunt wouldn't notice. Needing time to think, I leaned back. Scully! Single-handedly the slime had almost imploded the district attorney's office. Daniel had been on the brink of homicide when he learned one of his own had been making deals with the scum of the city. The police brought them in, and Scully pled them out and took a nice kickback for it.

After paying his debt to society, Scully had vanished. So why had he chosen now to reappear?

"You got any ideas?" Matilda's voice brought me back.

"What?" I sat up and looked at the two faces turned in my direction.

Jeremy and Matilda looked like believers waiting for words of wisdom from the Oracle of Delphi.

"I have ideas," I said. "But I need some time to work all the angles."

"Sure," my aunt said, her voice flat, devoid of any intonation that might hint at what she meant. Did she mean, *Sure, take the time you need*, or, *Sure, I don't think you have anything*?

"Lucky, you're picking me up on Friday, right?" Matilda shifted gears so seamlessly she left me in the dust.

I stared at my aunt, trying to think why I would ever do such a thing. "Friday?"

"For the virginity auction at your mother's place." Matilda held out her glass and Jeremy refreshed her drink from the pitcher as he looked at me with wide eyes. "She was supposed to talk to you about it."

"She's probably been too busy holding press conferences," I explained earnestly, then added, lying through my teeth, "I'll try to get away." Spending the afternoon with Matilda and Mona at a virginity auction was about as palatable as attending a weenie roast with a tribe of cannibals.

The three of us visited a little longer. When another unsuspecting victim arrived, Jeremy and I seized the opportunity and made our escape.

RIDING in Jeremy's Hummer, I could imagine what it felt like to cover ground in the belly of a Sherman Tank. Encased in metal, sitting high off the ground, the vehicle chewed up road with ease. I felt invincible. All we were lacking was a 105 mm howitzer and a turret bristling with machine guns, which would really be useful in traffic. Tonight the traffic was light, so I didn't really miss the weaponry.

"Want to tell me where we're going?" Jeremy asked, as he followed the directions I had given him.

"Summerlin."

He piloted his big black beast west on Tropicana, then south on Decatur. After a few blocks, we hit the 215, heading west, then north, around the city.

"A guy named Jimmy G has an Italian place there. He's had his fingers on the pulse of this city for fifty years. If there's even a hiccup, Jimmy hears about it."

"A hiccup like someone going rogue and making his own book?" Jeremy asked.

"Perhaps." My phone vibrated at my hip. Before I flipped it

open, I glanced at the number—it put a smile on my heart. "Hey. Still slaving over a hot piano?"

Teddie laughed. "No, I'm at the hotel. I wanted to catch the end of the show."

Once or twice a week, Teddie would watch his old show, the one he now produced. Quality control, he called it.

"How was it?" I asked. "Anything you need to fix?"

"Little things, but they can wait. Where are you?"

"On my way to Jimmy G's. I'm riding shotgun in Jeremy's Hummer, and I'm not properly accoutered—I need fatigues and an M16."

"I can see you on the cover of *Soldier of Fortune*," Teddie said, joining the game. "The Big Boss would be thrilled. His big-shot hotel executive and right-hand man turned to a life as a mercenary, helping despots and third-world dictators."

"If I'm ever forced to make a career move, I'll keep it in mind. In the meantime, we're on our way to see Jimmy G."

"Where's your car?"

"With the valet at the French Quarter."

He whistled. "You've had an exciting evening. How was dear old Aunt Matilda?"

"She told me I looked cheap. I took it as a compliment."

This bit of news elicited another laugh from Teddie. He had a nice laugh—of course, I was biased.

"You must be so proud," he teased. "Look, why don't I go get your car out of hock, then I'll swing up to Summerlin and pick you up."

"Deal. See you when you get here." I closed the phone and leaned my head back.

I must've had a goofy grin on my face or something because Jeremy took one look at me and said, "Man, the bigger they are, the harder they fall."

"That's the pot and the kettle."

"You have a point." He took a right onto Summerlin Parkway, heading east toward town again. From our vantage point as we traversed the foothills of the Spring Mountains, the valley stretched before us. Like a sparkling blanket, the city covered the low-lying areas—the clustered bright lights of the Strip, a small vessel in the glittering sea. "Who is Jimmy G?" he asked.

"One of the old guard." I pointed at the street sign announcing the next exit—Town Center. "Take the next exit, hang a right, you'll see it."

"I've been snooping around this burg for quite a while," Jeremy said. "How come I haven't heard of him?"

"You haven't been properly introduced."

"What?"

"The old guys don't talk to anybody who hasn't been vouched for by someone they trust," I explained.

Jeremy turned into the parking lot. "Who's going to vouch for me?"

"Me."

A quick tour and we found a parking space—actually we found two spaces—the city planners hadn't factored in Hummers when they approved the parking lot.

A neighborhood place, Jimmy G's was upscale yet casual, mirroring the fancy neighborhoods surrounding it. Summerlin was the high-rent district. The folks here had more money than God, but they didn't want to flaunt it . . . much. So Summerlin was an interesting island of attempted subtlety surrounded by a sea of gaudy excess.

This close to closing time, Jimmy's place was almost empty. The restaurant, with its mauves and grays accented with shiny brass, was spit-and-polished for a new day. Like boats torpedoed at the pier and now listing to port or starboard, a few hard-core drinkers were anchored to the bar. At least one bottle of almost every conceivable brand of booze occupied the rows of shelves behind the counter.

On the top shelf, next to the expensive stuff, Jimmy had placed a picture of his daughter. Wearing a very small bikini, a fake tan, and a butterfly tattoo on her shoulder—her muscles oiled and bulging—Glinda stood on a podium and held a pose for the camera. She looked ready to bite off someone's arm. Supposedly she was a natural bodybuilder, but I didn't see anything natural about it.

Jimmy G held court at a small square table tucked in the corner of the bar between the baby grand and the front window. A small wiry guy, with dancing eyes and a ready smile, Jimmy clutched his signature glass of Pinot Noir.

A couple of old-timers sat in rapt attention as the natural storyteller regaled them with a tale they likely had heard before—one about the old days when he had owned a place near the Strip where all the big names used to eat a late dinner after their shows. No matter how many times I'd heard Jimmy's stories, I'd gladly sit through them all again—there was an energy about him, an enthusiasm, that was impossible to resist.

A recent spate of bad health had doused his fire a bit, but from the looks of him, tonight was one of his better nights. I was flabbergasted when he jumped to his feet, dodged the table, and gave me a big bear hug. The last time I saw him, he'd needed help to stand—multiple sclerosis is a horrible disease. "Death by inches," Jimmy called it.

"Look at you!" I held the slight man at arm's length. "You look fantastic!"

"So do you." He gave me the once-over with a twinkling eye. "If I was twenty years younger . . ."

"If you were twenty years younger, you'd be the death of me and half the women in the Valley." I took a seat at the nearest table. "Seriously, you've been transformed. Do you have a new girlfriend or what?"

He colored. His cheeks hadn't held such a rosy glow in months. "It's this new stuff my daughter has me on. You know how she's into all this natural stuff. I don't know what's in it, and I don't care. It's a miracle, I can tell you that much"

I stepped aside and introduced Jeremy, who had been standing behind me.

Jeremy extended his hand. "Sir."

Jimmy G eyed the Aussie, sized him up, then he took his hand. "I heard about you."

"He's straight up, Jimmy," I said.

The older man let out a low whistle. "Son, if you got Lucky vouching for you . . . well, it don't come any higher than that." Jimmy motioned for us to sit at the nearest empty table. When we were seated and the bartender had put a fresh glass of wine in front of Jimmy, he continued. "Pretty late for a social visit."

Jeremy leaned back in his chair, arms crossed, as I took the lead. "You heard about Numbers Neidermeyer?"

"Yeah." Jimmy rolled the stem of his glass between his thumb and forefinger and pretended to be fascinated with the red liquid. "Can't say it was a shame." His head still tilted down, he glanced at me from under his eyebrows. "Mind you, I ain't being uncharitable or nothing."

"She had it coming," I said, stating the obvious. I didn't get any disagreement from the two men. "The street has it somebody was making private book—mainly on local fights," I continued. "You know anything about that?"

"I heard a whisper." The little man glanced at Jeremy, then his eyes drifted back to me. "I ain't saying who it was—don't know for a hundred percent—but there was big money in on it."

"Movers and shakers?" I asked.

He nodded.

"Could you find out who was running the show?"

"Now that's the sixty-four-thousand-dollar question." Jimmy G gave me a shrewd look—the look of a gambler setting his price. "You'll owe me."

"I've always paid my markers."

"That you have." The little negotiator drained his glass in one gulp, wiped his mouth with the back of his hand, and gave me a grin. "This one'll cost you big."

"Not so big. I heard Scully Winter was involved." I tossed off the line casually, as if I knew more than I did.

Jimmy's eyes grew hard, then he spit on the ground. "Yeah, that foul wind blew in my direction, too."

"I want to know who's pulling the strings, and why Scully?" I leaned back in my chair and crossed my arms across my chest. "Think you can handle that?"

Jimmy G snorted. "Piece a cake. But remember, you're gonna owe me."

BUSINESS done, Jimmy looked as if he wanted to tell stories. I asked Jeremy to go check on Miss P at the office, giving him an excuse to escape. After he'd said his good-byes, I settled back with a glass of very nice Zin, as Jimmy G started in. I let him talk. My mind wandered a bit as I watched him gesturing, his eyes alight with wonderful memories.

Teddie had sounded like he was in one of his I-want-to-talk moods. Was that a good thing or a bad thing? Who knew? Either way, I had a feeling we were going for a drive.

As if on cue and just as Jimmy ground to the end of his second story—or was it his third—I heard the familiar Porsche growl. Headlights flashed across the window. A car pulled up by the front door. Teddie didn't kill the engine so I took my leave.

Jimmy gave me another hug. This time he held tight. "You be careful," he said. "I don't gotta tell you this is a nest of rattlesnakes."

"I've waded around in the snake pit before."

The little man shrugged, but I could see the worry he was trying to hide. "It's your funeral."

I really wished he hadn't said that.

·   ·   ·

THANKFUL I didn't have to drive, I folded myself into the passenger seat. Teddie greeted me with a kiss, which I lingered in, testing his mood as much as enjoying the sensations. The heat of his kiss seeped into me, making me all hot and melty inside. If he was mad or worried, he hid it well, although I detected an undercurrent of something. I couldn't put my finger on it.

"I brought a blanket, a jacket for you, and a couple of cold Buds." He said as he maneuvered through the parking lot and onto the street. He didn't slow down as he hit the traffic circle. "How about we go up toward Red Rock?"

Now I knew for sure he had something on his mind. "Are you going to tell me what's bugging you, or are you going to make me wait?" I closed my eyes and leaned my head back as he accelerated up the ramp and onto Summerlin Parkway, heading west.

"Waiting will do you good."

No, waiting would just make me angry—I'm into immediate gratification—even when it comes to getting bad news.

Teddie knew that.

I got the distinct impression I was being punished.

MOST visitors to Vegas never think of renting a car, which is a shame. The Strip is but one Vegas Valley offering—Red Rock Canyon National Conservation Area is another. Just to the west of town, the thirteen-mile paved loop wanders through pristine desert with its yuccas and scrub, past breathtaking red rock monoliths, and two-thousand-foot cliffs. Here you can see wildlife of a different sort—herds of wild burros, and, if you are very lucky, an occasional wild mustang.

A developer, in his infinite arrogance, bought the top of the mountain just to the southeast of the park entrance. He planned a whole community with thousands of houses, retail shops, and commercial properties—the whole enchilada. When the fair citizens of Vegas got wind of it, Mr. Developer found himself unable to get the requisite permits. Imagine that! Eleven mil right down the slop chute. It put a song in my heart, I can tell you that.

Since then, tacky had been confined to the Strip.

Of course, Red Rock was closed at this hour, but that didn't matter. Teddie and I had a favorite place just outside the park. He turned off toward Calico Basin and bumped along on a fairly well-maintained oiled road for a half-mile or so. Finally he eased into the empty parking lot at the trailhead.

The night air had turned downright cold for a thin-blooded desert-dweller like me. I shrugged into the jacket, then we both scrambled up a boulder—a real challenge in my fuck-me shoes. Teddie spread the blanket, then settled in, his back propped against the rock behind. I felt the stored heat of the day still lingering in the hard surface as I curled in next to him, my head on his shoulder.

From the vantage point of our magical perch, we could see the whole of the Vegas Valley—a place of contrasts almost beyond comprehension. The city itself, blooming with life, glowed in the deep, lifeless void of the vast Mojave.

When I was a child and prone to fanciful imaginings, I thought Vegas was a lot like Berlin—each a city surrounded by its antithesis. I used to dream that I was an intrepid pilot flying a C-54, dropping essentials to the trapped citizenry of my fair city. I always saved them, each and every one. There was a reason I found my home in the customer relations office—now I saved people from their excesses and minor lapses in judgment.

Always the rescuer, never did I think *I* needed a line thrown to me . . . until Teddie came along with his rope.

Cuddled against him, his arms tight around me, I realized *I* had needed saving most of all.

Teddie rescued me from myself. Having left home at fifteen, I'd learned to rely on myself—trusting others didn't come easily. In fact, I avoided it at all costs. Teddie had delivered me from a self-imposed exile of loneliness. Most days I was really glad he did, but I had a feeling today was not going to be one of them.

"Here's your beer," he said, clearly intent on dragging this thing out.

I thought for a moment before answering. Let's see. The two glasses of champagne were so long ago they didn't count. A large tumbler of bourbon and a snifter of brandy with the Big Boss—those counted. A sip of a nasty martini? Didn't count. Then a glass of smooth Zin. That counted. How did the saying go? Liquor then wine, you'll be fine? So far, so good. But what about beer? I had no idea.

"Sure, why not?" If I was going before the firing squad, I needed liquid fortification.

After twisting off the cap, he handed me a longneck. "I got an interesting call this evening."

"Who from?"

"Dig-Me O'Dell."

"The music impresario?" I tried to keep my voice level, my curiosity appropriate. "The head of Smooth Sound Downtown Records?" I stuffed the bottle of beer in a crack in the rock. Then I worked my hand under his sweatshirt, splaying my fingers on his stomach. The heat of him radiated to my very core.

Teddie inhaled sharply; he felt it, too. Then he forced a laugh, the sound reverberating through his chest under my ear.

"You're good, O'Toole. Really good. I almost believe you're surprised." He pulled my hand from under his shirt, then held it against his chest.

Okay, he didn't want me touching him—not a good sign. I lifted my head and looked at him. In the dark, I couldn't see him clearly enough to get a good read on exactly how angry he was. "I am surprised. Truly. I just . . ."

"You just what?"

"Nothing." I returned my head to his shoulder. Lying would be so much easier if I didn't look at him.

"It's funny," he said after a moment. "I write a few songs, talk about my dream to be a legitimate singer, make a CD for you, and six weeks later I'm getting a call from one of the big boys in the business." Teddie must've felt me shiver because he reached across and pulled the blanket around me. "This has your fingerprints all over it."

"Why would you think that? Somebody could've heard you in the bar or even taken in your show. They could've put a bug in Mr. O'Dell's ear."

"But they didn't, did they?" His voice rode on an undercurrent of semicontained anger. "Sweetheart, the man had my music."

What in the heck was he mad about? "So? I really don't know how Mr. O'Dell got that disc." That was the truth. I had my suspicions, but I didn't *exactly* know.

"Quit prevaricating." Apparently Teddie's syllables multiplied when he was steamed. "Here's how I think it went down. You copied the CD I gave you and sent it to your buddy the music agent. What's her name?"

"One-Note Wylie." I slapped a hand over my mouth, but it was too late—I'd already inserted my foot up to my ankle.

"Right, Ms. One-Note." Teddie shifted, pulling me closer to him. "She passed the thing around L.A., and I ended up getting a call from Dig-Me O'Dell. How'm I doing?"

"Not bad." When push came to shove, even to save myself, I couldn't lie to Teddie. What I didn't get at all was why he wasn't doing handstands. Fool that I was, all of these revelations seemed like really good things. But what did I know? Not much, apparently. "What did Mr. O'Dell want?"

"He wants me on the first plane to L.A. in the morning to lay some tracks and play the rest of my stuff for him."

"That's terrific!" I pushed up to my elbow, narrowing my eyes at him, which I doubted he could see. "One would think you would be over the moon."

"I am." The words were flat, devoid of enthusiasm.

"Well, yippee. Alert the media." I ran a hand through my hair, swiping it out of my eyes. "I'm having a little problem here. You sound like you're ready to spit nails."

"You got that right." Teddie's voice rose. "I knew you were one tough broad, but I had no idea the cojones you swing."

"Don't be foul," I snapped, starting to see red. I would've pushed to my feet, but that didn't seem wise considering I was sitting in the pitch-black dark, on a rock, wearing six-inch stilettos. Fighting with myself, I resisted the urge to fight ugly—especially after that tough broad remark. "Let me get this straight. You've spent your life building the foundation for a career in music—legitimate music. You get an enthusiastic call from one of the bigs in the business. And you're pissed at me because I got the ball rolling?" Unable to control myself, I shouted the last bit.

"Damn right! You should've asked."

"Asked you what?" The ungrateful SOB! "You want me to get your permission to send *my* copy of your music to a friend in the business? And what would you have said?"

"No."

At least he was honest.

"Well then, at least it's a good thing one of us is swinging a set of cojones." Okay, that was a low blow, but, hey, I'm human. Trapped by the darkness, I sat there in a huff. Men! If God had wanted women to put up with the beasts, why hadn't he provided an owner's manual?

"You had no right."

"Look, Kowalski, you know well enough that helping people is what I do—I see a problem, I fix it. I admit, it's a horrible character flaw, but I can't help myself. And, like it or not, I am front and center in your life—you asked for it, you got it. Deal with it."

Teddie reached up and pulled me back into his embrace. I resisted for a fraction of a second to let him know I was steamed but hadn't quite reached blinding fury . . . yet.

"And what problem did you fix?" His voice still held the traces of his anger.

"I was the only one who got to hear your incredible songs."

He was silent for a moment, then he gave a resigned laugh. "You know just how to take the fight out of me."

Once again, I relaxed against him. Our first dust-up, and it looked like we'd make it through relatively unscathed.

"I guess I have a lot to learn about life by committee," I said, which was my way of apologizing.

"Lucky, we're just a committee of two."

"Double the number I'm used to working with."

"Point taken. Don't get me wrong, I appreciate what you did." He hesitated. "I'm just not sure I'm ready."

Now he was in my wheelhouse—I knew all about the courage it took to face the reality of your dreams. "It's one of the great ironies of life—just when you get comfortable, the cosmic powers pull the rug out from under you." Remembering my beer, I reached for it and took a long swallow.

"I think *you* pulled this rug out from under me." Teddie didn't sound mad anymore. He sounded half-amused.

I took that as a good sign.

"I don't have to go to L.A. The music can wait." He sounded as if he wanted me to agree with him.

"Yes, you do," I said. "And no, it can't." I sought strength from the warmth of Teddie next to me as I stared into the night sky, wishing I could divine the future from the alignment of the planets and stars. What did life have in store for us?

"You really think I'm ready?" Teddie tightened his arms around me.

"You don't have to take my word for it. Isn't that what Dig-Me O'Dell is trying to tell you?" I snuggled in close. Closing my eyes, I tried to capture the moment—the feel of his arms around me, the hint of his Old Spice, the warmth of his body next to mine. I had a feeling it might be awhile before we had another moment like this. Maybe the memory of this one would bridge the gap. . . . Who was I kidding?

Teddie was quiet for a moment. "Maybe I'm ready, but I'm a bit . . ."

"Scared? You wouldn't be human if you weren't. Dreams are damned scary things." I put my empty bottle down, then reached across Teddie, holding him tight. "Just remember, regret is ever so much more terrifying than fear." I should know.

Chapter

F O U R

eddie was gone.

Tangible and real, his absence throbbed like a deep wound.

Before I opened my eyes to the new day, and hoping I was wrong, I moved my hand under the covers to his side of the bed. The sheets were cold.

We'd decided to sleep at my place, which was all of one floor below Teddie's. I guess he'd thought it would be easier for me to wake up alone in my own bed. He was wrong.

The clock had rolled over to 2 A.M. just before I'd drifted to sleep with Teddie wrapped around me. Later, we'd made love. Slow and delicious, make-up sex was almost worth the irritation leading up to it. Almost.

I'd spent most of my life sleeping by myself, getting up by myself, eating alone—I even had a list of the finest restaurants in Vegas catering to a table of one. I could certainly function on my own. Yet, if I was so all-fired self-sufficient, why did Teddie's absence leave a hole in my heart?

Like a punch I never saw coming, the truth hammered home—I could never go back. Worse, along with my heart, I had sacrificed control. Love changed everything, and now my love was in California. He'd come back. Wouldn't he? But what if his dreams were bigger than me? Bigger than us?

My mother always told me that if I had a worry I couldn't do anything about, I should mentally lock it away and throw away the key. Closing my eyes, I tried her trick.

It didn't work.

A giant chasm of uncertainty, the day yawned in front of me.

I swung my feet to the floor then went in search of coffee. My apartment, a vast expanse of hardwood floors and whitewashed walls, wasn't nearly as grand as Teddie's place, but it was home. Huge floor-to-ceiling windows invited the bright desert sun inside. Pastels of the many moods of the Mojave hung on the walls. Clusters of furniture in bright colors broke the huge main room into definable areas, each with its own function—talking, eating, making love . . .

I clamped a lid on those memories—the whole visual thing was too much at this hour, especially without Teddie. God, I so needed to get my libido under control. If this is what I was like after a few hours of not even the remotest chance of meaningful sex, I'd be a blithering idiot by the time Teddie came home. Or I'd be really popular with the male half of the population. Or in jail.

I punched the button on the coffee machine, then grimaced as the grinder whirred like a jet engine at full power. On the theory fresh-ground coffee beans made better coffee than the stuff in hermetically sealed cans, I'd suffered the assault of the grinder each morning for months now. To be honest, I couldn't discern any difference in the coffee. One of these days the morning decibel overload would clash with a preceding night of liquid overindulgence and I'd fling the offending machine over the balcony. Coffee really wasn't my thing anyway—it was merely the most expedient caffeine delivery vehicle.

After cutting the dark brew with equal parts whole milk, I took my first sip. Like an addict savoring a hit, I sighed at the sheer physical delight of the caffeine jump-start. Good thing the drug was still legal or I'd be in serious need of a twelve-step program.

Scratching sounds from the corner reminded me I wasn't alone—I still had a roommate.

I might not have Teddie, but I had Newton.

As I pulled the cover from the large cage, Newton greeted me. "Asshole! Asshole! Asshole!" The macaw's head bobbed up and down as he scurried from one side of his perch to the other.

"Glad to see you, too." I pushed a piece of browned apple from the plate by his cage through the bars.

"Screw you!" Newton hurled at me, then grabbed the fruit.

"You're welcome." I changed the big bird's water while he worked on his treat. Newton and his foul mouth had found me a couple of years ago. Listening to his repertoire, I'd been appalled at the home he must've come from. Unable to send him back, I kept him despite the fact that pet ownership was inconsistent with my lifestyle.

Running back and forth from work to home to feed him and cover him for the night had lasted three days. Defeated, I hired a service to come twice a day—a good solution, so far.

Watching him, I drained my mug of coffee then refilled it, and headed off to the shower. Time to start the day. Romeo would be waiting.

THE bright yellow sign announced the Omelet House had been in business in the same location since 1979—a feat deserving of historical landmark status in Vegas, the town of constant renewal. The parking lot was almost full, but I managed to find two spaces to angle the Porsche across. For a moment I thought better of taking more than my share—I might avoid a door ding but get a fist to the hood for my efforts. In this neighborhood that was a possibility, but, after careful deliberation, I decided to take my chances.

I paused at the newspaper box. A minute of rooting in my Birkin and I'd found enough change to spring for this morning's *Review-Journal*. Numbers Neidermeyer had made the front page again. I scanned the article quickly—nothing really important other than the byline. "Flash" Gordon. A friend and ally. Today was looking up.

Behind solid-wood double doors surrounded by leaded glass, the Omelet House lurked in the back end of a strip center that had seen better days. I grabbed the handle of the right door and yanked—most of the time the left side was locked. With its dark wood paneling, dim lights, and floors stained with the passage of time, the interior did little to inspire confidence. Autographed pictures of celebrities competed for wall space with framed certificates from the annual "Best of Vegas" competition run by the *Review-Journal*. The Omelet House was a perennial winner in the Best Breakfast category. Kitschy knickknacks adorned the walls. Frank Sinatra crooned in the background.

Betty, the hostess, was as much an institution as the restaurant itself. A short woman with dark red hair, Betty wore an ever-present smile and so many gold bangles she was in serious danger of not being able to lift her arms. Each morning she corralled the patrons with a kind word and an iron hand—a good thing since the line often extended into the parking lot.

With a hint of her native Italy, she greeted me like an old friend. "How ya doin', Ms. O'Toole? Good to see ya."

"Good." I would've asked her how she was doing, but then I would have wanted to linger and chat and I didn't have the time. Romeo was waiting. "I'm meeting someone."

"Cute young fella?" She gave me a wink.

I nodded.

"Your secret's safe with me." She grabbed a menu and turned

on her heel. "He's waiting in your regular spot. It's not in Shirley's section today, but I'll let her know you're here."

I followed Betty up a small ramp to an elevated section of booths—my favorite was the last one on the right—don't ask me why. For some unfathomable reason, all of the booths had one side overstuffed like a built-in booster seat. I had a sneaky suspicion the carpenter who had built them must have been short, but I never could prove it—not that I'd tried.

Betty had put me on the high side . . . once. Now Romeo occupied that position. If he was uncomfortable, I couldn't tell from looking at him. Young and still wet behind the ears, Romeo had yet to adopt the jaded expression of a cop who'd seen it all, which made sense because he hadn't. In fact, he hadn't even seen a small fraction of the dirty side of the street.

His unruly sandy-blond hair, blue eyes, quick grin, and gee-whiz attitude reminded me more of a kid hoping for a Triple-A contract with the 51s than a future Columbo. Yet he was my best contact in Metro and, conveniently, he'd done the investigation up to this point on Shark-Bait Neidermeyer. A while ago I'd helped him score some points with the brass and now it was payback time. I needed to know what he knew.

"Sorry I'm late." I slid into the booth as Betty poured me a mug of coffee and freshened Romeo's. "I don't know if you've already made your decision, but their green chili is a religious experience."

The kid grabbed his menu. "Really? I didn't see that."

"They call it 'chili verde.'" I pushed my menu aside as I tried to open a creamer into my coffee. The white liquid squirted across the table. "Damn. These things always get me."

Romeo gave me the look a parent would give a helpless child. "Let me." He opened one and got all the white stuff into the mug with nary a squirt.

"Thanks. My skill set clearly excludes opening creamers." I took a sip of steaming coffee. I'd probably had enough already—the top of my head felt like it was going to explode—but lead this horse to caffeine, and you won't have a problem making her drink. "Order the number one," I instructed Romeo. "With scrambled eggs, pumpkin bread, crisp potatoes, and a small side of chili verde. You won't be disappointed."

My favorite waitress appeared as if summoned. A thin woman with dancing dark eyes and a ready smile, Shirley knew all the regulars. "Hey Lucky! You keepin' them in line at that hotel of yours?"

"They seem to be getting the better of me these days," I said, being more truthful than Shirley thought.

"And that cutie, Teddie, where is he today?" she asked, giving Romeo the eye. Teddie made fans wherever he went.

"He's in California. This is Detective Romeo."

Shirley looked relieved. Had she really thought I could handle Teddie and the kid? Or would want to? Clearly I was projecting the wrong image.

"I'll tell Teddie hello for you," I said.

"You do that." Shirley pulled her pencil from the mass of curls on top of her head. "I know you want your usual," she said to me, then looked at Romeo. "And young man, what'll it be?"

Romeo thought for a moment. "I'll have what she's having."

That settled, Shirley disappeared, then Romeo dove right in. "I know you didn't invite me to breakfast because you miss me. You want the skinny on the shark-tank lady." Under Romeo's Clark Kent exterior lurked a guy who could cut to the chase.

From the moment I'd met Romeo, I knew he had potential.

"She was no lady," I said with a scowl. "But yes, you're right."

"I don't know anything you don't know." Romeo kept his expression bland.

"Then why did you grill Jeremy Whitlock?"

Romeo's eyes grew a fraction wider. He had a thing or two to learn about bluffing. "The district attorney seemed to think your Mr. Whitlock knew more than he was letting on."

"I see." I said, although I didn't. Why was Lovie Lovato pushing so hard? "And did he?"

"Not that I could tell." Romeo's expression collapsed. He played with his fork and knife, knocking them together until I slapped a hand on them to silence the clanging. "It's the darndest thing. I think everybody in this town wanted that woman dead."

"That's a fair assessment, but only one somebody actually followed through." I held my mug out for freshening when a lady with the coffee pot passed by.

"Did you?"

"Did I what?" I asked, stalling for time.

"Want her dead?"

"Kid, I was probably on the list but way down toward the bottom. Anybody who had anything to do with Numbers Neidermeyer eventually found themselves praying for her to have an accident."

"So, where were you last night between four thirty and seven this morning?"

I narrowed my eyes at my young detective. "Don't mess with me, Romeo."

The kid's eyes skittered away from mine.

"So, exactly how did Ms. Neidermeyer become fish bait?" I asked casually.

"Somebody rigged a remote device to disable the cameras. The side door to Shark Reef was jimmied, but it's an internal door and not alarmed. They turned on all the lights, tossed her into the tank from the catwalk above, left her purse, and bolted. The sharks did their thing." The kid looked a little green around the gills as he finished. "The shark-keeper found what was left of her when he arrived at about seven."

"Turned on all the lights?"

"That's the signal to the sharks that it's feeding time. They get all excited and will eat anything tossed in front of them."

"Did the sharks kill her, or was she dead before she hit the tank?"

Romeo gave me a rueful smile. "The ME couldn't really tell. Nor could he pinpoint a time of death. He doesn't have much to go on—only a few pieces. I have some pictures here." The kid reached into the inner pocket of his jacket and pulled out a few glossies, which he spread on the table between us.

I scanned the photos, then was instantly sorry. 'Small pieces' was right. "May I keep these?"

"I probably shouldn't let you have them, but we're a team, right?"

"Team? Sure. Besides, you owe me." I picked up the photos and gave each one the once-over before I stowed them in my pocket.

Now I felt a little queasy—just in time for breakfast. Shirley silently set our plates in front of us. Romeo and I could only stare at the food.

I pushed at mine with my fork. "Anything of interest in her purse?"

Romeo rummaged in his pocket. Not finding what he wanted in that pocket, he started on another. This time he pulled out a crumpled bit of paper. He smoothed it on the table and pushed it to me. "Here's a list of the contents."

I raised an eyebrow at him.

"I knew you'd want it," he said, looking sheepish. "And, besides, I haven't won an argument with you, yet. This just saves time."

As I said, he had real potential. I scanned the list. Nothing jumped out at me. She had the usual—wallet with money and credit cards, two ticket stubs to last Friday's fights at the French Quarter, hairbrush, makeup kit with lipstick, eye shadow, mascara, a mirror, a box of Trojans, keys. "Can I keep this?"

He nodded. "See anything interesting?" The kid had finally found his appetite and was forking in the eggs and green chili.

"No, but you never know how things are going to play out. Something might become interesting later." I took a bite of the pumpkin bread. "How's your breakfast?"

"Awesome."

Another happy customer. I picked at the potatoes—they were my favorite part—but I had lost my appetite. "I know you said you couldn't pinpoint the time of death, but do you have an approximate?"

"She was last seen at your hotel at about four thirty in the morning—one of your cameras caught her crossing the casino by herself. And, no, she wasn't being followed—at least not overtly." This was bad, the kid knew what I was going to ask almost before I did.

"I assume you've looked at the tapes your boys seized. Did she talk to anybody?"

"Only your Jeremy Whitlock and that Tamale guy."

"Tamale?"

"Taco, Tamale, Enchilada—I'm from the North, I can't keep all that Mexican stuff straight." The kid reddened. "You know, the fighter guy."

"She talked to Tortilla Padilla?" I pushed my plate away and concentrated on my coffee.

"That's the one. Tortilla! What a name!"

"I don't think it's the one his mother picked. So Numbers talked to him right before she left or before that?"

"He was the last person we could see that she talked to."

"And they found her at seven?" I'd seen her between two thirty and three thirty arguing with Jeremy, then heading into the casino. Where she went between then and four thirty would be mighty interesting.

Romeo nodded, his mouth full. He swallowed then wiped his mouth with the napkin. His plate clean, he settled back with a contented sigh. "Good grub."

"If this place were all-you-can-eat, they'd lock the door whenever they saw you coming." I nibbled on the corner of one slice of potato—grease and starch, the breakfast of champions. "Are you following any other leads?"

"That's sorta why I'm here."

I raised an eyebrow at him.

Like an involuntary reflex, he reddened again—I liked that about him. "Look, you and I both know I'm new at this. But I'm smart enough to have figured out there are two sides to this city.

They taught me at the Academy how to deal with one side. For the other side, I need a guide."

Cradling my coffee mug in both hands, I leaned back and let the kid talk. Already he was smarter—by far—than most of the Metro higher-ups.

Romeo leaned forward. "That's where you come in. You got a foot in both worlds. You're my pipeline to the guys who've been here forever, and who know everything."

"They're not too keen on talking to cops."

"I know," he said, as he leaned toward me. "But they'll talk to you."

WHILE I waited for the bill, I sent Romeo off to start another day protecting the good citizens of Vegas from the evils of crime. Although I'd already planted a bug in Jimmy G's ear, I let the kid assume I would be doing the favor for him.

When the bill didn't materialize because Shirley was swamped, I slapped enough money to cover our tab on the table, added a twenty, and said my good-byes.

Still accustomed to the muted light of the interior, my eyes watered at the assault of the sun. Blinking furiously and shading my peepers, I almost missed the bit of paper stuck under one of the Porsche's wipers. I pulled it out, opened the car door, and squeezed inside. My eyes no longer under direct assault, I looked at the scrap.

It was a note.

In crayon.

Warning me off the Neidermeyer matter.

I laughed out loud. Who were they kidding? Somebody had been watching too many television cop shows. When I met the ass who had written it—and I had no doubt I would—I'd tell him that crayon really diminished the threatening tone.

Of course, Numbers Neidermeyer *had* ended up in pieces . . . I shrugged off the shiver that threatened to race down my spine.

The note might have been a bit dramatic, but it told me one

thing for sure—I had stepped on somebody's toes. I had no idea who or how, but I was wandering in the right direction.

Out of the corner of my eye, I caught Romeo maneuvering his sedan out of a tight space. Without too much public humiliation I flagged him down.

Looking like a kid taking the family station wagon out for a joyride, he eased the big car to a stop in front of me and rolled down the window. "What's up?"

I thrust the scrap of paper at him. "We've attracted somebody's attention."

Careful to handle the note as little as possible, he grabbed a corner and held it up. Tilting his head to match the angle of the paper dangling from his fingers, he quickly scanned down the page. "Sounds like they mean business."

I made a rude sound. "I found the crayon to be particularly threatening."

Romeo looked up at me, his eyes telegraphing his concern. "Lucky, this is serious stuff. Somebody's already been killed."

"Don't worry about me, I can take care of myself." I squinted against the sun as I glanced around. Nobody was taking any interest in us. "Let me know if you pull any interesting prints off of that, okay?"

"Sure." The kid set the note on the seat beside him. "I know you're pretty savvy, but watch your back, okay? Cocky can get you killed."

"I don't like being made the fool," I told him.

"Just the same, I really don't want to fish pieces of you out of the shark tank."

I seconded that.

THE office was empty when I showed up. I clicked on the lights, took the phone off call-forwarding, then headed for my little corner of the universe. I stowed my purse in the closet and settled myself behind a pile of paperwork on my desk. I was still staring at the pile trying to think of a way to get out of tackling it when I heard the outer office door burst open. A beat passed, then Miss Patterson appeared in my doorway. Today she wore black from head to toe, including the circles under her eyes.

She tugged on the fingers of one black glove, removed it, then started on the other. "I couldn't sleep. I felt useless at home. The walls were closing in."

She looked a mess, but I couldn't send her away. "If it's work you want . . ." I motioned to the pile of papers in front of me. "You can start with these."

After hanging her coat in the closet, she smoothed her blouse, then looked at me. "I've already been through them. That's your pile."

How easily she doused my tiny flame of hope. "Silly me, I thought as the boss, I could delegate the grunt work."

"You want me to forge your signature?"

"Probably not a good thing." Defeated, I leaned back in my chair. "Where's the Beautiful Jeremy Whitlock? Not getting into any more trouble, I hope?"

"He went to fill up the car. He'll be back in a bit." She didn't smile.

"When he shows up, I'd like a word with him."

WITH the stack of papers diminished by half, I was congratulating myself when my push-to-talk spoke my name. Excitement charged through me. I glanced at the number and frowned. My heart rate returned to normal. Security was calling. Ten thirty and I had yet to hear from Teddie. Out of sight and all of that, I guessed, but it still pricked.

"Hey, Jer. Don't they ever let you go home?"

"I'm keeping your kinda hours, these days." Jerry sounded as tired as I imagined he'd be. Security took the hit leading up to and during fight weekend—they had to clean up the messes.

I merely had to smooth things over enough so we didn't get

sued . . . or land on the front page of the paper. "Don't tell me the craziness is starting already."

"It's in the air. I got a call from one of my guys in the Bazaar. Your new chef has arrived and he's putting on quite a show."

THREE minutes later—a new record—I joined the throng in front of the future home of Burger Palais—or so said the sign above the doorway. I narrowed my eyes—Burger Palais? That was so not going to happen.

I muscled between two burly security guys. The crash of crockery punctuated an angry tirade of French streaming from the interior. I didn't need a translator to catch the drift—invectives sounded the same in every language.

Charging through the door, I didn't stop until I skidded into the kitchen. "What the hell is going on in here?"

All movement and sound stopped as heads swiveled in my direction. A man, presumably our chef, stared at me. The plate he'd been holding slipped though his fingers and shattered on the floor. Five of our kitchen staff, looking like rabbits cornered by a fox, huddled against the stove. Four other staff members stood by the prep table—they didn't look nearly as traumatized. Presumably they were the imported staff and, as such, were more accustomed to bad behavior from their boss.

I pointed to one of our staff. "Go take down that sign out front. It's tacky, and we do not do tacky at the Babylon." That was a bit of a fabrication, but it sounded good, so I went with it. Then I turned my attention to our new burger-meister.

I don't know what I was expecting—maybe Paul Prudhomme motoring his bulk around on a little cart—but I certainly wasn't expecting the incredibly good-looking man staring at me, his mouth set in a firm line.

Trim and fit, our new chef had the whole European thing going on. Looking not at all like a chef, he was dressed in creased slacks that could only have been Italian—they hugged his every curve and bulge but somehow avoided being obscene. His silk shirt draped over broad shoulders and tapered to a teenager's waist. A silk scarf knotted jauntily at his neck, his brown hair touching his collar, he looked like he'd stepped right off a yacht—except for the crimson complexion.

Disdain was written on his face in a language anyone could understand as he gave me the once-over. "You will leave," he announced in an imperious manner.

Oh God, another delicious accent infusing sexiness and seduction into every word.

"Leave. Now!"

Okay, maybe not *every* word. I resisted rolling my eyes. Was boorish behavior a required course in culinary school? I didn't know who he thought he was, but to me, he was just another in a long line of pompous Continental peacocks I'd had the misfortune to deal with.

Broken shards of crockery crunched beneath my feet as I closed the distance between us until we stood toe-to-toe, eye-to-eye. "I most certainly will *not* leave." My voice was low. "Get this straight. The Big Boss may have hired you, but it's me you have to go through."

Although clearly taken aback, the burger-man didn't give ground. "And you are?"

"Your worst nightmare if you continue to channel Gordon Ramsay playing to the cameras."

"Gordon Ramsay? Who is—"

I swept my arm, taking in the whole of the restaurant. "This restaurant belongs to the Babylon. The Babylon is my responsibility, and here are the rules." I poked him in the chest for emphasis. "First, you will treat my staff as the professionals they are. Second, you will clean up this mess. Each plate missing from the inventory will be billed to you." Our eyes locked. "And you *will* pay."

"Who are—" His face a mottled red, he looked ready to fillet me.

I felt the same about him. "Then you will get to work. You promised the Big Boss you would be open by Saturday. I'll have your head on a platter if you aren't."

"I have never—"

"You got it?"

His eyes broke the lock with mine. He gave a curt motion to his staff, who again fell to work, hiding smirks. He clamped his mouth shut, then spun on his heel. He didn't look back.

On my mental scorecard, I chalked one up for my team even though I knew from past experience the war was far from over. A pity, too. I cocked my head as I watched him stalk away. He had a nice ass.

Right then and there I realized trim-cut men's pants were Italy's legacy to womankind.

Hey, if I quit looking, I'm dead, right?

AS promised, the Beautiful Jeremy Whitlock perched in his normal position—one cheek on the corner of Miss P's desk—when I returned. A month ago, I had taken the liberty of having maintenance stencil his name in gold where one half of his butt now resided. Both he and his squeeze had been pleased.

Today, seeing them together made me feel alone. I felt a pity party of one coming on.

"Jeremy, I want you to go to Security," I said, pretending to be in charge. "See if you and Jerry can figure out where Ms. Neidermeyer went in this hotel between the time she was seen talking to you and four thirty, when she apparently left the hotel alone."

"So she didn't leave right after talking to me?" Jeremy followed me into my office.

I glanced at my phone . . . no missed calls. As I plopped myself on the couch against the window, I felt a black cloud settle over me. I redeposited the offending device in my pocket. "No. Romeo said the tapes showed her by herself, walking across the casino at four thirty."

"So that leaves a chunk of time unaccounted for."

"Right." I motioned to the chair across from me. "Another thing . . ." I waited while Jeremy turned the chair to face me, then took his place in it.

Today was the first day I'd ever seen him in blue jeans—although with their perfect crease and coupled with a starched button-down in a light shade of pink, they didn't detract from his GQ image. Loafers with no socks completed the picture.

"Who dressed you this morning? Ralph Lauren? Don't you know it's cold outside?"

"Pardon?" He flashed his dimples at me.

"Sorry." I shook my head and took a deep breath. Like sand through my fingers, I felt self-control slipping away. Teddie had really done a number on me. No. I'd really done a number on myself. "My brain has several channels. Apparently my mouth dialed in the wrong one."

"Might be fun listening to the nonpublic commentary."

"For you, maybe." I paled at the thought. "Trust me, the world is not ready."

He crossed one leg over the other, resting his ankle on the other knee. His foot bounced as he said, "So, you wanted to know . . . ?"

"Night before last, when you were arguing with Ms. Neidermeyer, you told me you were following hunches. What were they?"

"I was getting nowhere at the French Quarter, so I stepped back and looked at the big picture." He paused and closed his eyes for a moment as if trying to conjure that night. "The only two real facts I had were that the betting anomalies all centered around the Friday night fights, and Numbers Neidermeyer was the foremost authority and the premier oddsmaker in that venue."

"So you looked for connections."

"I hadn't even gotten that far. Like I do with everyone who shows up on my radar, I ran a background check on the cow." He shifted his legs, crossing the other one. "I've been in the business a good while—I've got damned good sources. But with Ms. Neider-meyer, I came up cold."

"Cold?"

"It's like she never existed until she showed up in Vegas ten years ago as Evelyn Wabash Neidermeyer."

That was a mouthful—no wonder she went by Numbers. "Didn't exist?"

Jeremy shook his head. "And here's the kicker. The real Evelyn Wabash Neidermeyer died in 1990."

Needing time for that little pearl to penetrate the gray matter, I leaned back and closed my eyes. "Could there have been more than one?"

"I've checked all of that. There was only one."

"So who was she if she wasn't a Neidermeyer?"

"I don't know. I've pulled every string I could reach trying to catch the scent. So far, I'm rolling craps."

"So you asked her?"

He snorted. "Don't be a stupid cow."

I raised my head and leveled my gaze on Jeremy. "I'm not the prettiest gal you'll come across and probably not the brightest by a good margin, but, I warn you, the last person to call me a stupid cow was Billy Watkins in the seventh grade. I broke his nose and at least one other appendage."

"Sorry. Would you believe something got lost in the transla-tion?"

"I'll buy that." I'd probably buy just about anything the Beauti-ful Jeremy Whitlock had to sell, but he didn't need to know that. "So what was she so steamed about?"

"She'd gotten wind I was asking around. She didn't like it."

"I can see why. She was hiding a pretty big secret." I gave Jer-emy a stern look. "Why didn't you tell me this last night?"

"I didn't know about the real Ms. Neidermeyer until a friend of mine called this morning. To be frank, when I came up cold, I thought I'd gotten some fact wrong or something. With computers, if you put garbage in, you get garbage out. It's happened before." He gave me a rueful shrug. "I'm good, but I'm not perfect."

That sounded like a reasonable explanation rather than an excuse, so I let the Beautiful Jeremy Whitlock off the hook. "Now that I think about it, why don't you leave the security tapes and the the unaccounted-for time to me."

"And what do you want me to do?"

"I want to know who Numbers Neidermeyer really was, and why she landed in my town."

MY little black cloud had morphed into a thumper of a headache behind my right eye, which did little to improve my mood. I listened to Jeremy say his good-byes to Miss P.

I eased my left eye open and took a gander at the clock. Noon and still no word from Teddie. I snapped the eye shut again.

"Are you okay?" Miss P asked, her voice emanating from the direction of the doorway.

"Yes. No." I stopped and regrouped. "Could you get me some aspirin, please?"

In a jiffy she was back. "Here."

I pushed myself upright and reluctantly opened my eyes. Three Extra Strengths should do the trick. I washed them down with a slug of bottled water—I'd had way too much caffeine already.

"You sure you're okay?"

"No." My heart still ached, along with my head. And worries niggled for attention. "Teddie's in California and I'm afraid he's not coming back." There, I'd said it.

"California?"

"He got a call late yesterday afternoon from Dig-Me O'Dell. Apparently, Teddie's music shook L.A. like a high-Richter earthquake. They wanted him on the next plane."

"I see." Miss P plopped down on the couch next to me. "No, I don't see. Isn't this what you wanted?"

"Yes. No." I sighed. "Okay, I clearly didn't think it through." I felt better with my eyes closed so I shut them again. "What if he doesn't come back?"

Miss Patterson knew me well enough to resist offering hollow assurances in an attempt to make me feel better. "We're a real pair. Both worried sick."

"Just two casualties on the rocky road to love." I felt a bit guilty wallowing in self-pity—my worries didn't include my love getting tossed into the slammer. "Can you and Brandy handle fight weekend by yourself? I'm seriously considering running away from home."

"You wouldn't throw us to the wolves," Miss P announced with conviction.

"You sound pretty sure about that." My assistant had a lot of faith in me, which I thought a bit misplaced. "Way back in my callow youth, before I became wedded to this job, when I actually used to have relationships, they were so much easier when I didn't care. The sex was good and the guy mildly amusing. When it was over, so what? Sex and amusement are fairly common commodities."

"You know what they say about risk and reward." Miss P might be above hollow assurances, but the same didn't hold true with platitudes.

"In every other aspect of life you can manage your risk," I said, answering politely. "In love, it's all or nothing—absolute bliss or total devastation—pretty scary stuff."

"Well then . . ." Miss P sat up and announced, "You know what they say about letting something go and, if it returns, it's yours forever."

"That is such a crock." I, too, sat up, but did so gingerly. My head didn't fall off, so I risked opening my eyes.

"I know, but it makes me feel better," she said blithely as she stood, then grabbed my hand and pulled me up as well.

"And what about the part of the saying that says if it doesn't come back, you hunt it down and kill it? Does that make you feel better, too?" I rubbed my temple trying to erase the lingering vestiges of my headache.

"Why do you think I have that Smith and Wesson by my bed?" she asked, smiling innocently.

"Because it precludes that tawdry moment where you have to negotiate the price before you have the sex?"

She gave me a look. "Come on. Let's go drown our worries with a Diet Coke and a good hamburger."

"Diet Coke I can handle, but not a hamburger. Definitely, not a hamburger."

Chapter

F I V E

wo bites into my tuna melt I was waylaid by my push-
to-talk. It was just going to be one of those days.
"O'Toole."

"Hey, Gorgeous, miss me?"

Teddie! The sound of his voice warmed me all over. "Miss you?
Why would you think that?"

"Because I started missing you the moment the elevator doors
closed behind me."

"I can work with that." Nodding to Miss Patterson, I excused
myself and stepped through the outer doors into an adjacent garden area where I could talk freely—and giggle without risking
ridicule. "How's the City of Angels?"

"The angels have fled. Sin is making a comeback." Teddie
laughed at either an unspoken observation or a private memory.

I didn't know which and didn't have the guts to ask. Of course, he'd only been there half a day. How much trouble could he have gotten into? I didn't have the guts to ask that, either. "I'm not surprised—Hollywood is the perfect confluence of too much money and too little sense."

"No kidding." This time, when Teddie laughed, I knew why. "Remind me to tell you about the new trend in recreational sex. They call them polyamorous parties."

"Do I really want to know? Casual sex gives me hives. And remember that whole visual thing I have going on?" Were we flirting or bantering? Never having had much experience with the former, I couldn't distinguish between the two. Maybe sleeping with someone turned banter into flirting? Who knew? Whatever it was, there was a comfort . . . an unanticipated feeling of connection. I liked it. "And, since we call the same address home, I have the right to ask how you came by this juicy tidbit."

"I was invited to one, but I respectfully declined."

"Wise fellow." I switched the phone to my other hand as I bent to retrieve a piece of trash from under a rose bush. "Monogamy will enhance your longevity."

"Then I will live to a ripe old age." He didn't try to hide the warmth in his voice.

"How's the music?" Half-oblivious to my surroundings, I wandered over to a trashcan and deposited my offering. "In contrast to their filmmaking cousins, do the jingle writers have any sense?"

"I don't know about sense, but they love my music." The excitement bubbled in Teddie's voice. "When I first got here, I wasn't sure how the whole thing was gonna go. Your Ms. One-Note met my plane and gave me the rundown. It seems it's easier to break into the business if you write songs for specific people or if you perform your own stuff. Apparently, crooners are considered one-trick ponies and are a ha'penny a dozen."

"So you got it covered either way." Teddie could certainly sing all his original songs, and I also knew he had composed some pieces with certain voices in mind.

"The response to my stuff was great when I sang it straight. But, when I started imitating certain celebs singing the songs I had written for them, man, the whole vibe changed. Magic happened. Dig-Me started calling in other folks to listen, then they called more people. Pretty soon I was playing to quite an audience. It's so much easier to feed off that energy than to try to create it with only a piano and a mike. It was amazing! I wish you'd been here."

I could picture it—Teddie channeling Mariah, Madonna, Ne-Yo, Akon, Tim McGraw, Streisand, Sinatra . . . he even did a pretty fair Johnny Mathis. And his Liberace would put you under the table. Of course, Liberace didn't really sing, but that didn't stop Teddie—he had the man down cold. My love had yet to realize he was a born performer—"the roar of the greasepaint, the smell of the crowd" was in his blood.

"I'm sure you wowed them."

"Don't know about that—they're pretty tough. But, they are bringing in Reza Pashiri this afternoon. She's looking for an opening act. Then there's some event tonight. They want me to run through a few numbers."

"Intoxicating."

"It's more than I could ever have hoped for." Teddie's voice sobered. "And I have you to thank."

Little did he know, but I was feeling real conflicted about that right now. "I opened a door, you stepped through and grabbed them by the throats," I said.

"I wish you were here," he said simply.

As a wave of nauseating jealousy roiled around in my stomach, I seconded that notion. "Teddie?"

"Yeah?"

"You *are* coming home, aren't you?" I hated myself the minute I said the words.

"Of course. That's where my stuff is."

His attempt at humor hit a sour note. "Break a leg, or whatever they say to ivory tinklers. Let me know how it goes."

"Lucky," he said, his voice no longer bantering, "I'll see you soon. Count on it."

The sad thing about all of this was the guy really got me. I wondered how much of me he would take when he left.

AN empty plate sat in front of Miss P when I returned.

"Sorry," I said as I plopped into my chair, fresh out of good humor. No longer hungry, I pushed my plate away as I settled back. I grabbed my glass of Diet Coke and stared into the murky depths trying to divine the future. If it works with tea leaves . . .

"Teddie's news wasn't good?"

I looked up from my Coke into the troubled eyes of my friend. "Ignore me, I'm just having a poor-pitiful-me attack. His news was great . . . for him. The Great Teddie Divine is cutting a wide swath through Hollywood. He's even being considered as the opening act for Reza Pashiri."

"Doesn't she go on tour for years at a time?"

I nodded, but refused to say the words. If I spoke them aloud, then all of this would be real.

Miss Patterson leaned back, a stunned look on her face as the ramifications hit home. Apparently she couldn't find an appropriate platitude, so she sat there in disbelief.

After a morose minute or two, which seemed like an eternity as I pondered my future long-distance bill, even I was getting tired of my act. I slapped my hands down on the table and pushed myself to my feet. "Enough of this. The future will take care of itself." I reached down and pulled Miss P to her feet. "In case you've forgotten, our job is the present, which is about to take off at a dead run. I suggest we get a head start."

GETTING a head start had been a good idea—unfortunately, we were too late. The day had galloped off without us. Brandy had a phone at each ear and a bland expression on her face when Miss P and I strolled through the door.

Young, tall, with brown hair, blue eyes, a wide smile that made you grin in spite of yourself, and a body that doubtlessly fired male fantasies, Brandy had seized her responsibilities as my second assistant like a mongrel grabbing a bone.

She'd been parking cars at the Athena when, by sheer luck, I'd found her. Our paths had crossed before—she had shown herself a diligent and clever student in a class I taught at the University of Nevada Las Vegas School of Hotel Management. I had admired her even more when I learned of her family life—her parents were both deaf and had never learned to read, making education a difficult and lonely path for their sole offspring. Due to her background as a cage dancer, Brandy had found it difficult to get a suit-and-tie job. I don't suffer from the heightened sensibilities that infect the management of other major hotel groups in town. Brandy was my kind of gal.

Like proud parents, Miss Patterson and I crossed our arms, leaned against the glass window separating our office from a plunge to certain death in the lobby below, and watched our protégé handle a sticky problem.

"Yessir. I understand, Sir. I am so sorry, Sir. Could you please hold?" Brandy said into one receiver then pressed the hold button. Into the other receiver she said, "Paolo, Mr. Hollywood Asshole is in the bar near the security entrance to concourses C and D. At least, that's where he thinks he is. He's not speaking in complete sentences and he's starting to sound like he has rocks in his mouth. I doubt if he can stand unassisted, much less walk. Is Filip with you?" Brandy nodded while she listened, then continued, "Good. Get your butts over there and get him out the back door before somebody with a camera finds him."

She took the first phone off Hold. "Sir, our staff is three minutes away. Again, I'm sorry for the mix-up. . . . Very good, Sir . . . Yes, we have a suite with a bar full of Patrón Añejo awaiting your arrival."

She paused for another moment, listening. "No, Sir, no female chasers. Those will be up to you." She slammed both receivers into their respective cradles, then gave us a grin.

"Impressive." I levered myself away from the window. "Which Hollywood asshole are we dealing with? An important orifice or a minor sphincter?"

"An important orifice—Spin Monkey Red, our DJ for Saturday night."

"I didn't think he was coming until Friday?"

"That was the plan, but he got his days mixed up and there was something about a bust-up with his girlfriend of the week." Brandy shook her head. "He really wasn't making much sense."

With a name like Spin Monkey Red, sense wasn't a trait I expected him to have, but my assistant apparently had a slightly higher expectation.

"When no one was at the airport to meet him, he headed for the bar. The bartender called us." Brandy blew a stray strand of hair out of her eyes. "We found him. Paolo is praying the guy doesn't lose his liquid lunch in the back of the limo."

"Hazards of his chosen profession."

My very naïve and inexperienced assistant grimaced. "I'm so glad it's not part of mine. Vomit makes me sick."

Miss Patterson shot me a grin. I gave her an almost imperceptible shake of the head in response. The young Miss Brandy Alexander had a rude awakening coming—the laws of biology dictated that when one overindulged, the body responded. If Vegas was about anything, it was about excesses of all kinds. And our job was to deal with the sometimes not-so-pretty ramifications. But now was not the time to dump reality into the girl's lap.

"He's Filip's problem now," Brandy said, and settled back in her chair, a look of self-satisfaction on her face.

Filip was one of our VIP hosts. Even though not terribly experienced, he had been around the block enough to know how to corral a shellacked miniluminary.

"But it's not even one o'clock," my new assistant said. "How can the guy be drunk already?"

"Not already. Still." I picked up a small pile of phone messages with my name scribbled at the top and said as I leafed through them, "If experience has taught me anything, the guy is still on last night's bender. Once here, he'll hit the hay until about midnight, then start all over again. Unless he gets arrested, I'm not sure he'll even notice he's not in L.A. anymore."

When the outer door opened, all three of us swiveled our heads to get a look at our visitor.

A young man slouched in. His hair stood from his head in a multicolored, foot-tall Mohawk that faded from black to shades of red and pink, with orange and purple thrown in for good measure. He wore numerous rings in each earlobe, a ring through his nose, and a look of youthful disdain on his face. Hollow-chested and wearing a dirty white muscle shirt with jeans slung low across his narrow hips, flip-flops, and brilliantly hued snakes and other reptiles tattooed from wrist to shoulder on each arm, he glanced at Brandy, gestured with his head toward the hallway, then left without saying a word. Rising from her chair, the young woman blushed as she rushed out the door.

"What was that about?" I asked.

Miss Patterson shrugged.

We made small talk while furtively glancing at the youngsters out in the hall. Their conversation animated, I couldn't imagine what the two of them would have in common—my designer-addicted assistant and her . . . my vocabulary failed me as to what the young man was or what he could do for a living. Or, for that matter, why such a brilliant, beautiful girl like the young Miss Alexander would come when so rudely summoned. So, I remained mute.

When Brandy returned, Miss P and I pretended to be knee-deep in work, without the slightest interest in the young man. But I couldn't pull it off. "Okay, who was that?"

Brandy moved some papers around on her desk so she wouldn't have to look at us. "Just a guy I know."

"Surprisingly, that much we could figure out on our own."

This time, she looked up. I sensed a bit of defiance there. "He's a nice guy, okay? We hang out sometimes, no big deal."

"What does he do?"

"He's in between jobs right now."

"No surprise there," I shot back. "Unless he's really good with Harleys, I'd say his prospects for gainful employment on this planet are slim."

Brandy frowned. "I would think you of all people wouldn't be judgmental."

"I'm not judging him, I'm merely pointing out the obvious. Look around you. How many of the guys working here look like your friend?"

"Not many," she mumbled.

"Try, none." I parked a hip on her desk. "Brandy, remember, you are in management at one of the premier resort properties in the world, and you earned it. You don't park cars anymore. When you move up, sometimes you leave people behind."

"I didn't know your influence extended to my choice of partners." Brandy's voice was hard. Foolish and young, she had spunk, and I liked that.

"It doesn't. I only own your soul. Your personal life is yours to keep. Believe me, I have enough trouble with my own." Levering myself back to my feet, I turned to Miss Patterson. "Take a run through Babel, will you? Make sure they've got the step-and-repeat where we want it and the red carpet is enough of a stroll that all the shutterbugs will have ample opportunity to capture the celeb of their choice."

The step-and-repeat was the banner with the names of all the sponsors of the opening night of Babel, our rooftop club/lounge. One of the games we played in Vegas was to make sure that the celebrities we had paid for were photographed only at our club and in front of the step-and-repeat. Heads would roll if one of our high-priced hosts ended up in the paper at a competitor's club—my head being at the top of the list.

"They were hanging the banner this morning." Miss P turned for the door. "I'll make sure it's the way you like it."

Brandy's face had cleared. Now she looked like a puppy ready for a bone, so I gave her one. "Get Mr. Padilla on the phone. I'd like to stop by to see him for a few minutes at his convenience, but preferably sooner rather than later."

I heard her pick up the phone and ask the operator to be connected as I strolled into my office. Already staggering under the burden of the impending weekend, I groaned at the mess of papers still covering the beautiful black walnut desk. As I rounded my desk, I saw one perfect red rose with a note attached lying across the seat of my chair. I picked it up, held it to my nose, and inhaled. Ah, the unmistakable scent of a fresh flower grown in the desert sun. No hothouse rose from this sender.

The message, in a flowing script I knew well, put a smile on my heart. "Think of me and know I'm thinking of you. Miss you more than you know."

The guy was definitely a keeper. If only keeping him was within my power.

Inhaling the strong scent again, I strolled back into the outer office. Brandy was off the phone. "How did this flower get into my chair?"

"I'm not at liberty to say." She grinned at me. "I caught Mr. Padilla having breakfast in his suite—apparently he's on a different schedule than the rest of us. He said now would be perfect."

"Great."

"Oh, and Jerry asked if you could swing by Security. Apparently he has some information you wanted. He said it would only take a minute."

"Call him. Tell him I'm on my way. Then tell Mr. Padilla I'll be there within the half hour." I took the efficient note out of my voice. "And, for future reference, while it might be true and somewhat appealing to refer to our guests as assholes, when you are on the phone with them there is a risk that you might not have gotten their call put properly on hold. If that happens . . . trust me, the ensuing fallout is not worth the momentary pleasure of calling a spade, a spade."

Brandy's face clouded.

I held up my hand. "No rebuke intended. And promise me you won't ask me how *I* learned that lesson." At her responding grin, I pushed through the outer door, leaving Teddie's rose on Miss P's desk.

AN intoxicating drug, the faint whiff of fight weekend craziness met me halfway down the stairs to the lobby. As I leaned on the crossbar to open the door at the bottom, I braced myself, but even I wasn't prepared as I pushed through into the throng. Riding on an undercurrent of excitement, a cacophony of raised voices hit me like a prizefighter's jab. Lit by the high-octane combination of liquid fuel and adrenaline, people mixed and mingled, shouting at friends, giving others an appreciative wolf-whistle, as they shrugged out of the strictures of their everyday lives.

Others waited near the front entrance, like a school of hungry piranhas, cameras at the ready, hoping to catch a glimpse of one of the current icons of pop culture, but they waited in vain. Eager to avoid the paparazzi, most recognizable faces arrived through the VIP entrance. Hidden and well guarded on the other side of the casino, that entrance led directly to the Kasbah suites and apartments—our celebrity enclave, and the current residence of Tortilla Padilla—my second stop this morning.

But first, a swing through Security—Jerry was waiting.

With the practiced moves of an NFL halfback, and thankful I had left the stilettos at home, I dodged our drink-wielding guests and made my way to the main bank of elevators. As I waited for the next car, I checked myself in the reflective surface of the metal doors—nary a drop of sloshed drink on my dark blue Dana Buchman trousers and cashmere sweater.

My hair was reasonably in place—I still fought with it every morning as I struggled to master my new style. Makeup highlighted my reluctant cheekbones, full lips, and blue eyes while hiding my facial flaws—too bad I couldn't find anything short of lipo to mask the flaws running rampant over my thighs.

All in all, my reflection was not the me I used to find so comfortable, and frankly, being well turned out was more trouble than it was worth. Personally, I liked it better when my hair was wild and my makeup nonexistent—it made me look more menacing. I'm not proud of it, but love had made me a pathetic slave to vanity. I hoped this was the low point. Balancing precariously on this slippery slope, I lived in fear that one day I would follow in my mother's footsteps—right through the revolving doors of a plastic surgery center.

A dim, formerly smoke-filled cave, Security was the command center, if not the beating heart, of the hotel. Like large mosaic tiles, video screens decorated every inch of the far wall, floor to ceiling. Security personnel were seated at intervals along a low counter in front of the monitors, where they scanned the feeds from the cameras scattered throughout the public areas of the hotel. Along an adjacent wall, also covered by monitors, gaming specialists watched the games currently in progress on the casino floor, looking for anomalies.

Jerry, a tall, trim black man (he never cared for the whole African American thing—I was white, he was black—distinctive, yet no different) was the captain of this starship. He stood with feet spread, his back to me, hands behind him, staring at the monitors as he gave each one his undivided attention for a few seconds. With his practiced eye, a few seconds was all he needed to subconsciously identify a problem in the making, if there was one.

The two of us had worked side by side for the Big Boss for as long as I could remember. Security and Customer Relations were halves of the same whole and the years had given Jerry and me an easy camaraderie and confidence—we guarded each other's backs, no questions asked.

Today Jerry wore a pair of casual slacks and a camel jacket in place of his usual suit and tie. Baby-soft Ferragamo loafers, a polo shirt, and a flash of gold at his wrist completed his ensemble. Comfortable, yet stylish, he was dressed for what we both knew would be a long weekend.

Sensing my presence, he turned. Nodding at me, he dispensed with the pleasantries. "We cobbled together some interesting footage from the tapes you asked me to review."

"You must've had your staff working overtime." Stepping in beside him, I pretended to be fascinated by the ever-changing show on the monitors. Watching others go about their business was too close to voyeurism for my comfort level.

"It didn't take as long as you might think. We used Jeremy's face-recognition software." Jerry rubbed a hand over his shiny pate—the hair was gone, but the habit remained. "That's pretty slick stuff."

"So I hear." I waited a moment. Jerry was lost in the movies playing in front of us. "You want to show me?"

"Oh, right." He shook his head as he turned away from the wall of screens. "Something's going on. I don't know what, but something doesn't feel right. Maybe it's just fight weekend—I don't know."

I followed him to a tiny cubicle in the back of the room. Two chairs had been placed in front of a computer screen for us. Jerry took the one in front of the video controls and punched a few buttons.

The screen came to life as I settled myself in the seat next to him.

Numbers Neidermeyer appeared on the screen. She looked as I remembered her—tailored suit, long hair, screw-you expression. Even though I knew she was dead, looking at her still set my blood simmering. Isn't it funny how love and hate both make you hot and bothered?

"Okay, I spliced all the footage together with the time imprints in the corner so you can keep track of the chronology," Jerry said, as he started the tape. "This is about two twenty yesterday morning. We got her coming into the hotel, apparently alone."

I watched as she marched across the lobby. Was that her normal gait or was she loaded for bear?

"There's Jeremy," I said, pointing as he appeared.

We both watched as the argument I had witnessed played out on the tape. Numbers disappeared into the casino, then after talking to me, Jeremy followed. My heart skipped a beat. "Don't tell me Jeremy followed her." I shifted my eyes to look at Jerry.

He shook his head. "No. Here's where it gets interesting. Your Ms. Neidermeyer was pretty clever. She knew where the cameras were, so we lost her for a bit, but we have some tricks of our own." He worked a few dials and buttons and again Numbers appeared on the screen. This time she stood in front of the bank of main elevators between the casino and the lobby. She had doubled back.

"I guess she knew we didn't have the manpower or the time to check all the tapes," Jerry said, grinning. "But she didn't know about Jeremy's face-recognition software, which cut our search time by a factor of ten."

Silence stretched between us as, on the screen, Numbers rode the elevator, then got off on the twelfth floor.

I raised my eyebrows at Jerry.

"I told you this is where it gets interesting."

Riveted, I turned my attention back to the screen. Numbers entered Room 12410—the Lovatos' room. Then, according to the time imprint on the tape, ten minutes later Daniel Lovato entered the room, swathed in his sheet and using the key I had given him. Twenty minutes later, a fully clothed Daniel, a hand shading his face, left. Numbers followed three minutes later and marched in the opposite direction. As she waited for the elevator to appear,

she rooted in her bag. She pulled something from her purse. As
the elevator doors opened and she entered, she sprayed first one
side of her neck then the other; the thing must've been a perfume
atomizer. Then she sprayed her wrists and rubbed them together.
She held them to her nose as the elevator doors closed.

"Who's this?" Jerry asked, as he pointed at the third player to
leave the room.

Small, blond, her muscles filling out a painted-on sheath of a
dress—I knew her without seeing her face, but when she glanced
over her shoulder toward the camera, that confirmed it. Glinda
Lovato, in all her glory. "That is the Mrs. District Attorney."

Jerry leaned back in his chair, a self-satisfied look on his face.
Reaching into his pants pocket, he extracted a silver cigarette
case. Flipping it open, he extended it toward me. "Want one?"

"You know that's not one of my vices."

"Lucky you. I've tried everything to quit. Nothing took." He
extracted a thin, unfiltered Gauloises, struck a match and held it
to the tip, inhaled deeply, then shook out the flame.

"Did the Big Boss give you special dispensation to ignore the
no smoking policy?"

"I had to threaten to go to work for the competition," Jerry said
smugly. "But he finally caved. I'm confined to my cubicle here, but
that's enough." Jerry took another hit, then blew a perfect circle
with the smoke. He nodded toward the screen. "Interesting mé-
nage à trois, wouldn't you say?"

Was it French Bon Mot Day and I missed it? "So they left sepa-
rately. Numbers and Mrs. Lovato leaving in the same direction,
Daniel in the other."

Jerry watched me as he enjoyed his cancer stick. He knew I
was thinking out loud.

"Can you go back to the part where Numbers left?"

"Sure." With the cigarette dangling from his lips, Jerry leaned
forward and worked his magic with the controls.

"There." I pointed at the image. "Numbers left with a purse. She didn't have it when she went in."

"Anytime you want to work in security, you've got a job." Jerry grinned at me, which dislodged the ash from the end of his cigarette. He brushed it away.

"She had been in that room before."

"She and the Mrs. arrived together yesterday afternoon. The check-in tapes show the Mrs. at Registration by herself, doing the paperwork and giving them her credit card, but we were able to capture Numbers in the background. They both went up to the room."

Terrific. The three of them came and went like the Keystone cops.

What was the connection between the district attorney, his wife, and pond scum like Numbers Neidermeyer? Who had tossed Numbers Neidermeyer to the sharks? Were the two related? Had Jeremy really just wandered into the whole thing? Too many questions, too few answers—actually, no answers at all. The whole thing made my head hurt. "So, what does all this mean?" I sagged back in my chair.

"That's for you to find out."

"Just my luck. I came here for answers, and all I get is more questions." I levered myself up as Jerry stuck another cigarette between his lips and lit it with the stub of the first. "I don't have to tell you those things will be the death of you," I scolded.

He cocked his head toward the screen and the last image of Numbers Neidermeyer. "There are worse ways to go."

IF Vegas was a temple to wealth, the Kasbah was its sanctuary. Built with the über-wealthy in mind, it oozed opulence, service, and comfort. A security guard at the tall hammered-bronze doors nodded at me as if I were entering the gates of Oz.

In stark contrast to the darkness of the casino, the Kasbah was well lit. Single, self-contained apartments surrounded an open courtyard with burbling waterfalls, a pond, and flowering vegetation. The sanctuary was so inviting that a pair of ducks returned every year to hatch their eggs and raise their young.

Tortilla Padilla had set up camp in Bungalow 7. The doors to each bungalow mimicked the door at the entrance to the Kasbah, only in a slightly smaller scale. As I stood before them, I felt like Indiana Jones on a harrowing hunt for some antiquity. My heart beat a staccato rhythm as I pondered what tests of courage and guile my quest would require. I'd checked on Tortilla Padilla before, but I'd never come face-to-face with the man himself. I imagined him to be a hulking blockade on my path to enlightenment.

Not only had I never met Mr. Padilla, I knew little about him—fights and fighters weren't my things. I never could understand the lure of watching two guys bludgeoning each other, blood flying, faces being turned to pulp, brains incurring irreversible damage . . . the whole thing turned my stomach. But, unfortunately, I wasn't paid to pass judgment or to cater to my own sensibilities, so there I was, ready to do battle with the former reigning middleweight champion of the world . . . or the universe . . . or whatever.

At my knock, the doors eased opened on well-oiled hinges.

"Ms. O'Toole?" It was Tiny Tortilla Padilla in the flesh. His thousand-watt smile, the very same one that graced all the posters around town, gave him away.

While he wasn't huge, he certainly wasn't tiny. Mr. Padilla fit the fighter mold—at least my version of it. Of average height, he sported a strong jaw, dancing dark eyes, a mop of tousled black hair, and a chiseled physique, which his chosen attire—workout pants and nothing else—showed to perfection. I tried not to stare, but one thing was certain—if I were his wife, fifteen children would be on the low side.

He stepped aside and motioned me into his bungalow.

I shook my head and stayed where I was. "I'm sorry to bother you. This won't take a minute."

"Suit yourself." With perfect balance he leaned against the

knife-edge of the door, crossed one leg over the other, and his arms across his chest.

If I'd tried that I would've fallen on my ass. God, he was distracting—I focused on his face. "Have you been reading about the woman who was found in the shark tank at Mandalay Bay?"

"Who hasn't?" Lifting one corner of his mouth into a wry smile, he shook his head. "Man, only in Vegas."

I felt like telling him that even by Vegas standards the demise of Numbers Neidermeyer was pretty spectacular, but I don't think he would've believed me. "Had you seen her around?"

"Only once," he said. "She cornered me in the casino one night—it may have been the night she died, I don't remember. It didn't seem important at the time."

"What did she want to know?"

"How was I feeling, what did I think my odds were . . . the usual." The fighter eyed me. "Why do you ask?"

"She set the odds for most of the fights in town," I explained, trying not to be unnerved by his glare. "Obviously, she'd stepped on somebody's toes. I just wondered if you'd gotten wind of anything unusual going down or if Ms. Neidermeyer had approached you at all." My eyes drifted from his. I never was very comfortable dancing around the real issue. As my mother said, both barrels blazing was more my kind of approach.

"You want to know if she was trying to buy me off or something?" His voice was hard. His eyes no longer danced. "Get me to throw the fight?"

"I didn't mean to suggest that." Well, maybe I did, but I was smart enough to deny it when the man I was busy insulting was considered by most to be the best all-around fighter in the world. "Why would you throw the fight? You've been promised a king's ransom, win or lose." My eyes locked onto his. "I just want to know anything you might know regarding Ms. Neidermeyer."

"Why do you care?" He still glared at me, not giving me an inch.

"Ms. Neidermeyer cast a wide net. She caught a good friend of mine—a P.I. who was sniffing in the wrong place at the wrong time."

As if he could see into my soul, Mr. Padilla stared at me with those inscrutable black eyes for a moment. Then he shouted over his shoulder, "Crash!"

We both waited. Nothing.

He shouted again. "Yo, Crash!"

"Yeah, yeah. I can hear, you know. Whatcha shoutin' for any-ways?" A huge black man wearing an apron and drying a dinner plate with a dishrag filled the doorway. One cauliflower ear, a nose mushed slightly to one side, an eye that didn't quite track, Crash had the look of a heavyweight who had fought past his prime. His hands shook a bit as he worked the rag around the dish.

Tortilla Padilla tilted his head toward the newcomer. "This is Crash Crawford, my trainer." Then he shifted his gaze to the big man. "Tell Ms. O'Toole here what you told me about the lady who got eaten by the sharks."

The big man gave me the once-over, then shrugged. "Not much to tell. She came sniffin' around the ring the other day asking all the normal questions about my man's preparations. You know, stuff like had he lost a step, and all that?"

I nodded, even though I only had the barest inkling as to what the 'normal' questions might be.

"But, you know, the weird thing was, she reminded me of somebody. I couldn't quite place her. But then, last night, I was eatin' pizza and it came to me, all of a sudden like."

He stopped. For some reason I got the distinct impression he was milking the limelight. So I gave him my best look of exagger-ated patience.

"Crash, quit jerking the lady's chain." Tortilla shot me a wink. "Don't mind him. He has a flair for the dramatic."

Not the least bit chagrined, Crash waited a moment longer then continued, "Ms. O'Toole, right?"

I nodded.

"Thought so. My brain isn't what it used to be."

"*Madre de Dios*, Crash." Tortilla Padilla rolled his eyes, but his grin was a mile wide. Unlike me, Mr. Padilla was apparently enjoying the show.

The big man shot a sideways glance at his boss. "Ms. O'Toole, I've been around the fight business a lotta years. I seen a bunch of things, know what I mean?"

"Only too well."

"There was this snot-nosed kid hanging around the ring when I was managing a fighter back in Atlantic City, maybe fifteen years ago. Maybe more. She was a slip of a girl, not over fourteen, with hair the color of a pale strawberry. She said she was writin' for her school paper. I don't know whether that was true or not, but she sure had a nose for the business."

"And you think that kid was Numbers Neidermeyer? There're a lot of people with strawberry blond hair." Hope flared in my chest—the timing would be about right . . .

"Yeah. It wasn't only the hair, though. It was her attitude. The way she asked questions like she was challenging you. And the questions she did ask—they were said in a way to make you believe she didn't know as much as she did." He looked at me with a questioning glance.

I nodded, encouraging him to continue.

"But she did know—a whole lot. That's why I remember her. Here was a flat-chested little scrap of a girl who knew the fight game. Only one I ever met who did."

"It sounds like Numbers Neidermeyer, all right."

"But it wasn't." Like a lion surveying the herd for his next meal, Crash swung his head slowly from side to side as his eyes shifted to focus on something over my shoulder. "Her name, I mean. Not back then. Not Numbers. Not Neidermeyer."

"No?" My pulse quickened. Oh God, he'd already given me

more than I thought he would, but now, let him give me something really good.

"Naw, the kid went by Shelly-Lynne Makepeace."

"You sure?" I tried to keep my voice even, my emotions under control.

He made a rude sound. "Like I said, the kid sorta stuck in your memory, know what I mean?"

I threw my arms around the big man's neck, surprising both of us. Self-control was never one of my stronger suits. "Brilliant! Absolutely brilliant!" Throwing caution to the wind, I kissed him on the cheek. Then I turned on my heel, leaving both men staring after me.

WHISTLING a jaunty tune I couldn't name—where was Teddie with his encyclopedic mastery of all things musical? I strode out of the Kasbah and once again immersed myself in the horde packing the casino. As this Wednesday afternoon marched resolutely toward evening, and our guests toward a big weekend, the energy would ratchet up one notch at a time until, like a spring wound too tightly, it would threaten to erupt at any minute.

Pausing for a moment, I closed my eyes and listened. While close to a fevered pitch, the throng had yet to reach the combustible stage. This was the calm before the storm. Add a few more minor luminaries, a bit more money wagered on the fight, and a few more gallons of liquid accelerant, and we'd be there.

Taking a deep breath, I opened my eyes. Surveying the crowd, I grabbed my phone from its perch on my hip, flipped it open, and dialed. My eyes wandered, looking for trouble in the making.

Jeremy answered before I even heard it ring. "Don't even ask. I've got zero, nothing, nada. It's like that woman materialized out of thin air." From his tone, I could picture him running a hand through that wonderful wavy hair of his, exasperation clouding those gold-flecked eyes. Try as he might, he couldn't keep the hint of worry out of his voice.

"Having a good day, are we?" I asked, as a couple of guys barreled into me from behind. One of them reached out to steady me as I staggered. Neither of them said they were sorry. "I might be able to make you feel better."

"You've got something?" In an instant, his voice sounded recharged.

"A name. Try Shelly-Lynne Makepeace. See if you can pick up a trail around Atlantic City, say fifteen to twenty years ago. Let me know what you find out."

"For sure."

I started to close the phone, but Jeremy's voice stopped me. "Lucky?"

"Yeah?"

"Atlantic City. That's New Jersey, right?"

"Right."

I had survived the casino and just entered the lobby when my phone rang again. With a practiced motion, I flipped it open with one hand. "O'Toole."

"Lucky?"

I recognized Jimmy G's distinctive voice.

He cleared his throat. "We gotta talk."

Chapter

S I X

Something was wrong—something big. And just when things had been going so swimmingly. Flat and lifeless, riding on an undercurrent of anger, the tone in Jimmy G's voice gave me a really bad feeling. He hadn't wanted to talk—not over the phone, anyway. I'd agreed to meet him at the Peppermill in thirty minutes. That gave me time to stop by the office as well as work myself into a lather waiting for the proverbial other shoe to fall.

On autopilot, I launched myself across the casino toward the lobby. Only half-aware, I dodged patrons with an ingrained ease as my thoughts tumbled. With a dread I tried to deny, I knew what had made Jimmy's voice brittle and hard, as if one blow would break it into a thousand daggers. Only one thing got to the old guard like that. Numbers Neidermeyer was no longer merely an interesting study in homicide.

Now it was personal.

I had no idea how or to whom, although I figured I was about to find out. And I so did not want to know. Genetically, I was only 50 percent old guard, but apparently that was enough to carry the taint—and the burden. One of us hurt, all of us felt the pain—and the responsibility to fix the problem.

Narrowing my eyes, I stopped mid-stride, turned around, and surveyed the path I had taken through the casino. Something had hit my muddled brain, bringing me back. What was it? With the practiced eye of experience, I scanned the crowd. Lost in thought, I jumped at the sound of a voice at my elbow.

"Looking for a good time?" The rich timber and subtle Texas drawl of Paxton Dane, our in-house rep from the Gaming Control Board.

Wavy brown hair worn a trifle long, piercing green eyes the color of Brazilian emeralds, a strong jaw, a warm smile, and broad in all the right places, Dane could have moonlighted as a cover model for bodice-ripper romance novels. For a nanosecond I let my mind wander there, picturing the open, flowing shirt, the tight pants—this was one of the times my whole visual thing was entertaining.

"Private joke?" Stepping in beside me, his eyes briefly met mine. A wry smile lifted the corner of his mouth, then he, too, cast his eyes over the crowd.

"What?" In addition to animal magnetism, was clairvoyance one of his gifts? I certainly hoped not. A flush warmed my cheeks.

"You had this weird grin. Sorta sexy, I might add." He clasped his hands behind his back, but didn't look at me.

Adopting a similar stance, I again turned my eyes back to the crowd, but I was having trouble making my mind follow. Not long ago, Dane had made a play for me, and I'd turned him down. We were still trying to find our way back to comfortable, neutral ground.

Teddie had stolen my heart, but I couldn't deny there was something between Dane and me. Something we'd have to deal with—eventually. I stuffed that thought, and the feelings niggling at the edge of my consciousness, deep down into what I hoped was an inaccessible place. A simple girl, I didn't need complications.

"What did you ask me?" I said, trying to refocus.

"I believe I asked if you were looking for a good time?" This time he gave me the full power of his megawatt grin as he glanced down at me.

"Is that what passes for a pickup line in West Texas?" I felt a little off-kilter, I didn't know exactly why. Of course I had a lot to be hot and bothered about: Teddie in L.A., Jimmy G and God knows what . . . Dane looking at me like that. Why did I seem to have a handle on everything, except my libido? Okay, maybe not *every-thing*—I was delusional—but even the illusion of control made me feel a bit better.

"I got a smile, didn't I?" Still Dane didn't look at me. "If you're not looking for a good time, what then?"

"Something that's not right, not normal."

Dane made a rude sound. "There ain't much about that crowd a boy from Lubbock would consider 'normal.'"

One more pass over the crowd and I had it.

"This one's easy." I nodded toward the far side of the casino. "When have you ever seen a queue to get into the men's restroom at a casino?"

A flicker of interest lit his voice. "Can't say I've ever waited in line to take a whizz."

"My point. Come with me. I may need your help." I started back across the casino.

"My help?" He was right on my heels. "With what?"

"A coming attraction."

I didn't even pause at the entrance to the men's room. Shouldering men aside, I worked my way up the line. One gallant young man, guilt reddening his features, even held the door open for me.

Dane grabbed my elbow from behind. "What are you doing? You can't go in there."

Pulling my arm from his grasp, I forged ahead. Explanations took time, and time was one of the things I didn't have much of. The other thing I found in short supply at the moment was control over my temper.

The absence of anyone standing at the long row of urinals, and the crowd of guys circling the last stall confirmed my hunch. A glance at me, and, like a flushed covey of quail, men scattered, then flew out the door. The few who had yet to register my presence, shifted anxiously from foot to foot in front of the closed door to the last stall. Eyes wide, they, too, drifted away as I pushed to the head of the line and into their consciousness, which I presumed was pre-occupied with our coming attraction.

Stopping in front of the last stall, I fisted my hand, and knocked sharply. "Open the door." My voice didn't betray my anger—as my mother said, one can catch more bees with honey.

"Yeah, yeah. I paid for the whole enchilada," a man said, sounding clearly agitated. "Some of us take longer than others." The latch grated as someone pushed it aside.

I didn't wait until he opened the door. Instead, I shoved it with my shoulder.

"Hey!" growled the same male voice.

Once inside the tiny space, I found myself face-to-face with a man with dark hair graying at the temples, and angry eyes, busily stuffing himself back into his designer jeans. A woman, her eyes wide, her expression guarded, sat on the closed lid of the toilet.

"What the hell do you think you're doing?" the man growled. As if he knew he couldn't hide the guilt in his eyes, his gaze drifted from mine as he focused on pulling up his fly. "My lady and I were just having some harmless fun. And, as far as I know, it's not illegal to have sex in here."

"Zip it," I said. That didn't come out quite the way I had planned, but I refused to smile. "It's illegal if you're paying for it. I'm sure a solicitation charge would make interesting reading in the paper back home."

For a moment I watched him war with himself, letting him stew in his own juices, then I said, "If I could offer you a piece of advice?"

This time, when his eyes met mine, the fight was gone, replaced by a look I knew well—self-preservation, one of the strongest primal emotions.

"Don't come looking for love in my hotel again." I stepped aside, and Dane followed my lead, clearing a path for retreat.

"You're going to let me go?" Surprise and disbelief washed across the john's face.

"You've just been given a get-out-of-jail-free card." I jerked my head toward the door. "Now, beat it, and don't let me catch you procuring sex in my hotel again. And, just to be clear, even though Bill Clinton doesn't think so, blow jobs are sex—in my book and in the Nevada Statutes."

His dignity carefully secured, the man glanced at the woman, gave her a rueful shrug, then bolted.

The woman rose from her throne, not a hint of embarrassment on her face. With blond hair, the dark roots showing, pasty skin, and cheap jewelry, she wore a nice suit, silk camisole, expensive-looking shoes, and a weary expression—the look of an out-of-towner. She'd probably bought her costume at a thrift shop as she hit town. Reaching around me, she gathered her purse from the hook on the back of the door—last season's Prada.

"I've made enough already. All you had to do was ask, and I'd have given you my gig," she said. Her voice held a hint of the Deep South in it. Pulling herself to her full height, which, even in heels was still a couple inches shy of mine, she moved to shoulder past me.

"I work for this hotel," I said, my voice flat as I let her move by me. She wasn't going far—Dane blocked her exit.

His eyes telegraphed his feelings, making it perfectly clear he thought I was an idiot for already letting one of them off with no consequences. At least Dane had the decency to keep his mouth shut and let me handle it my way—more than most men would do, so he got points for that. I gave him a curt nod then shifted my gaze back to the woman now trapped between us.

"You work for this hotel?" she whined, her voice heavy with defeat. "Aw geez, wouldn't you know it?"

She rooted around in her bag then came up with a wadded-up tissue. In the metal surface of the stall, she checked her reflection, then dabbed at her lipstick where it had smeared around the edges. Rubbing her lips together, she took one last look. Apparently satisfied, she shifted her attention to me, giving me the once-over.

"I shoulda known," she continued, as if we were really interested. "You see, I had this gypsy lady read my fortune last week." The woman glanced at me, her eyes the palest shade of blue. "Something about her didn't seem right—other than her being a gypsy and all— but I gave her the twenty bucks she charged, anyway. Now I know it was a waste—she said my luck was about to turn. Since it hadn't been so hot, you know, I figured she meant it would get better."

I gave Dane a wink over the woman's shoulder. "So what makes you think today isn't going your way? Your purse looks pretty fat. I don't know how long you've been in here, but if you were about to quit . . ."

"Yeah, it was goin' really good." The whine left the woman's voice as she relaxed a little. "But, when the guys start lining up like that, I learned they sorta attract attention—the wrong kind of attention."

"My kind of attention?"

"Yeah." She pulled a little box of tic tacs out of her purse, shook a couple into her hand, then popped them in her mouth as she nodded. "I'm real sorry you made me. This is a class joint; you got classy men here. But I'm not going to waste all my jack on a high-priced room, know what I mean?"

I nodded and thought about telling her that just because a guy had money for a good pipe cleaning didn't mean he was classy, but in her world it probably did. In my world, classy guys didn't pay for sex, but as my mother always told me, I'm way too picky.

"You going to give me up?" The woman tried to look disinterested, but her eyes darting between Dane and me betrayed her nervousness.

"Not this time. But, if you come back to this hotel to ply your trade, I'll have to." I smiled at the relief that washed over her face. "Let Mr. Dane escort you to the door."

Dane shot me a quizzical look as he extended his arm to her in a chivalrous gesture, and stepped aside. "Ma'am, would you allow me?"

Gazing up at him, her eyes wide with innocence, she grabbed his arm. "Why, Sir, I'd be delighted," she said, her voice dripping with enough honey to make a true Southern belle proud.

They left me there—alone in the men's room.

A stickler for manners, Jimmy G would be early. Not wanting to leave him waiting, I needed to hurry. Even though I didn't have it to spare, I had taken five minutes to swing by the office. Miss Patterson always liked me to transfer the reins of power personally when I was leaving the property.

Dane caught me as I burst out of the stairwell doors into the lobby. "I was coming to find you. You know, your remark about a 'coming attraction' was pretty clever."

"Clever killed the cat." I shouldered around him and kept moving toward the front entrance. I hoped he got the hint.

No such luck; he fell into step beside me. "No, curiosity killed the cat."

"Whatever." I pushed through the outer doors and headed down the drive. Thankfully, the Peppermill was only a short hike. "Look, I'm late for a meeting. Can this wait?"

"I just want to know one thing," he said, matching me stride for stride. "Then I won't bother you again . . . today."

"Don't make promises you can't keep." I turned north when I hit the Strip, and slowed. I was already bumping up against my thirty minutes—a couple more wouldn't kill Jimmy G. And, to be honest, a few more minutes of blissful ignorance wouldn't kill me, either. "What do you want to know so all-fired bad that you have to chase me halfway to downtown?"

"Downtown?" He raised one eyebrow at me. "Isn't that where we are?"

"Downtown." I pointed to the small mound of shorter buildings to the north. "This section of the Strip is the Center of the Universe."

"Weird. Back in Texas, the tallest buildings are in downtown."

"It's a common mistake." I turned to go. "Is that really what you wanted to ask me?"

"No." He put a hand on my arm, holding me there. "I want to know why you didn't have me turn that girl over to the police?"

I could feel the heat of his hand through the thin fabric of my sweater. Carefully, I removed my arm from his grasp. As the traffic snaked along the Strip behind Dane, and the swarm of people parted to move around us, I gave him the short course on what I'd learned growing up in a whorehouse and working in Vegas.

"Cowboy, folks come here from all over, for a million different reasons. Sometimes they do stuff I can't begin to understand." I squinted my eyes against the sun setting behind him, and shadowing his features. "I don't know anything about that girl—where she came from, why she's here. For all I know, her old man dumped her, leaving her with three kids at home, and she's trying to provide for them with no help and a high-school education."

"I see." His eyes, intense emerald lights piercing the shadow, captured me.

"Do you?" I ran my hand through my hair and tried to break his gaze, but couldn't.

"Yeah," he said, his voice heavy with an emotion I couldn't read. "Life's messy."

What do you know? He really did get it.

. . .

AS he had said he would, Dane left me, so I continued to the Peppermill alone. He hadn't even asked where I was going and what I would be doing there—so unlike him. This aberration might have worried me had I not already filled my quota of worries for the day.

A Vegas institution since the dawn of life as we know it, the Peppermill clung resolutely to what had been a prime Strip location just south of the Riviera Hotel and Casino, once the beating heart of the action. Now, with the growth of the megaresorts to the south, the little restaurant found itself barely clinging to the ragged edge of the excitement.

In what could only be described as an interesting effort to compete, the owners had converted the former fifties-style soda fountain by changing the décor to purple and pink with fluorescent lighting in the same color scheme. Then, they'd added a lounge—all purple and black—a beckoning cave of iniquity more reminiscent of a seventies nightclub than a place for serious sinners. One addition had been a fire pit where the flame leapt up through water. Patrons could sit on the circular couch surrounding it and watch embedded televisions when they weren't staring into the fire.

Of course, the hordes of local high-school kids crowding the booths out front did little to enhance the whole lounge thing. With precious few places to go in a city that catered to the over-twenty-one crowd, teens old enough to drive but too young to legally drink flocked to the Peppermill like pilgrims to Mecca. I'd done the same when I was their age.

For all of us raised in Sin City, the Peppermill was a comfortable blast from the past, a place where one could slide into a booth, order a shake, and be serenaded by Elvis, the Beatles, the Monkees—even Herman's Hermits—while we wallowed in memories.

As I pushed through the glass doors, the familiar smells of

hamburgers frying in their own grease, raw onions, and hot fat in the fryer rocketed me back to a simpler time. This had been a nice place to hang with friends, giggle at the first overtures of boys as they preened for my attention, and revel in the youthful assurance that the world held nothing but great things. Unlike my early impressions of the male of the species, I'd been right about my future—while perhaps not exactly as I'd planned it, life had turned out pretty great so far. I only hoped Jimmy G wouldn't stick too large a pin in my bubble.

Jimmie G waited in the last booth, the whole of the restaurant in front of him and no surprises behind him. He'd scrunched down low and, if I hadn't known where to look for him, I might have missed him all together.

"Sorry I'm late. Something came up," I said, as I slid in across from him. A double-thick chocolate shake sat in front of me, which immediately aroused my suspicions.

"Nothin' to cry about." The little man shrugged, not looking the least bit upset.

Okay, first the shake, now, not even a veiled hint of impatience . . . the guy was buttering me up for sure. "What's your angle, Mr. G?"

As if trying to martial his thoughts, he didn't answer right away. Instead, he stared over my shoulder as he crossed his hands on the table. They made a soft sound as he gently patted them, one on top of the other. For the first time, the realization hit me: The spry little man was probably almost as old as the Big Boss—two of a dying breed. And so much Vegas lore would pass with them—a huge loss that no one might notice. There was Mayor Goodman and his proposed Mob Museum . . . but that wasn't the history of Vegas I wanted—I wanted the magic. Jimmy G and the Big Boss knew the magic.

I took a sip of my shake and waited. Swirling the rich concoction over my tastebuds, I would have sighed with pleasure had my mouth not been full. How could a benevolent god make things so good for our souls, so bad for our health? If this were a divine test of the strength of my resolve, I would be found woefully lacking. I could live with that.

Finally Jimmy G moved. He tilted to the side, lifting one cheek off the seat, then reached in and tugged his wallet from his pocket. He pulled out a well-fondled picture and pushed it across the table to me. His granddaughter, Gabi.

How old was she now? Nine? Ten? I couldn't remember and couldn't tell from the photo. While truly magical, kids served as such harsh markers of the passage of time. It had been a year, no more, since I'd seen her but it seemed like last week. She'd been just a hardscrabble little girl then. Now, I could see the hint of the beauty she would become. Long black ringlets, olive skin, dark eyes that already held a sense of self-possession in their depths, a full mouth quick to grin—she was going to be a real ball-buster. I hoped her father and grandfather were prepared.

I looked up at Jimmy G, but didn't say anything. As the Big Boss had taught me, these guys get to their points in their own way, in their own time. However, this conversation had sure started down an alley I hadn't anticipated.

With one finger, he gently pulled the picture back then stared at it for a moment, a grin tickling his lips. "She's not at all like her mother, you know?" His eyes held a sadness as deep and enduring as a lifetime. They lit on mine, then fluttered back to the photo. "It's like the Creator gave Gabi not only her allotment of soft edges and feminine wiles, but the ones her mother should have gotten as well."

Warm and soft were not two adjectives anyone would use to describe Glinda Lovato, Gabi's mother and Jimmy G's daughter. In fact, most of the appropriate adjectives that sprang to mind weren't exactly complimentary, so I said nothing. The truth of the matter was, I knew Glinda by reputation only. Through the years I'd had a few minor social skirmishes with her, but nothing of any conse-quence and nothing unusual for two rather opinionated females.

The only real feeling I had for her was pity—pity because her hus-band's philandering provided the meat of many a joke about town.

"This little one . . ." Jimmy G touched the photo, ". . . is the apple of her father's eye. She has that man so hornswaggled. Everybody knows it, but the poor schnook has no clue." Jimmy smiled at the thought.

The picture he'd painted gave me warm fuzzies—I, too, was pretty partial to that special bond between fathers and daughters.

"You know she's not Daniel's real daughter?" Jimmy crinkled his brow as he continued examining his granddaughter's smiling face.

The product of Glinda's first marital misadventure, Gabi had been only one year old when her mother had married Daniel. "Just because she's not his biological child, doesn't mean she's not his real daughter, Jimmy."

For an instant, his eyes met mine. "Outta everyone, I knew you'd get it." He flashed me a sad smile that faded like a childhood memory, leaving only a hint of the good times. "The kid would be lost without him, you know? I don't even want to think about her life if something happened to Daniel."

"Jimmy, what's going to happen to Daniel?"

His hand shot across the table, grabbing mine in a viselike grip. Like an electric shock, his intensity, his emotion coursed be-tween us where our flesh met. "I love him like a son, you know." His voice was raw as his eyes filled with tears. "Glinda . . . she's so cold, so harsh—not the daughter a man hopes for. Daniel takes care of me . . . and Gabi."

"Jimmy, tell me about Daniel."

"Word on the street says he was into that oddsmaker big."

"Numbers Neidermeyer?"

He nodded once.

"So she *was* running an illegal book," I said. It wasn't a ques-tion; I already knew the answer. "How big?"

"Six figures big."

I made a noise my mother and her manners never would have

approved of. "That's ridiculous. Daniel's been the district attorney for what? Twenty-five years? All that time he's been so clean he squeaked."

"I'm tellin' ya, the street don't lie." The little man still gripped my hand so hard my fingers were going numb. "Word is he's in for 500K, maybe more."

From the looks of him, Jimmy clearly believed what he was telling me. The problem was, the whole thing sounded fantastical, like the script for a bad Al Pacino movie. "Okay, for argument's sake, let's assume you're right." I extracted my hand from his death grip and rubbed it to reestablish blood flow. "Why now? Why, after all these years, would he do something as stupid and self-destructive as not only placing action with an illegal book, but compounding his problem by allowing himself to get in deep?"

Jimmy, his hands in his lap, his eyes downcast, seemed to shrink into himself as he shook his head. "People do stupid stuff, you know?"

"Maybe so, but DAs with everything to lose and nothing to gain usually don't self-destruct—at least not quite so spectacularly. And not after twenty-five years on the job." I pointed to the photo. "*And not with a nine-year-old daughter in need of raising.*"

A group of kids caught my eye—laughing, the boys teased the girls who blushed, but bantered back. None of them could be older than sixteen or seventeen—such an innocent age, but one filled with self-doubt and angst. I wouldn't trade problems and emotions with any of those youngsters, not even with Jimmy's little stink bomb. However, I wouldn't mind trading skin tone.

"Lucky, girl. Help me. Help Daniel." Jimmy G's voice was just above a whisper.

I noticed Jimmy didn't tell me I owed him, which technically I didn't—yet. He just asked, friend to friend—the swine. He knew better than I did, nobody turns down a friend in need.

"You got anything to go on?" I asked.

"I can give you a line on Scully Winter."

. . .

APOLLO'S chariot had traversed the sky leaving only the lights of the Strip to hold the darkness at bay by the time Jimmy G and I had said our farewells. On my return trip to the Babylon, I didn't hurry. Like a rat in a cage, I was a creature of the air-conditioned world, rarely allowed to escape into the cool night air of the high desert. Adopting the same ambling gait of the crowds idling up and down the sidewalks, I soaked up their energy. In desperate need of an attitude adjustment, I tried to see Vegas through their eyes.

Fifteen minutes of moving with the crowd gave me the smile I had lost. Two buff young studs had asked for my number, which did wonders for my ego, if not for theirs when I turned them down. I'd learned the words to the fight song for some university in Texas, and I'd narrowly escaped wearing the dregs of one inebriated fellow's strawberry daiquiri, which he informed me I could buy by the gallon at a casino at the southern end of the Strip. From all appearances, he'd gone back for seconds . . . maybe thirds. I smiled at the couples holding hands as they watched the fountains at the Bellagio dance in time to the music.

Vegas *was* magic—and it was my job to keep it so.

And if our fearless district attorney had gone 'round the bend and tossed Ms. Neidermeyer into the fish tank over a gambling debt? We'd do what we always did: We'd throw him a hell of a send-off party on his way to the slammer.

That farewell gathering might even be better than usual—nobody in Vegas was going to miss Numbers Neidermeyer.

My smile dimmed a bit as I bid adieu to my drunken escorts and marched up the drive to the Babylon and back into the real world. Maybe no one would mourn Ms. Neidermeyer, but a whole city would miss District Attorney Daniel Lovato. And I shivered at the welcoming committee he would find in the State Pen—he or his office was responsible for almost all of its current residents.

Jimmy G was right about the word on the street usually being accurate. But I just didn't get it. I must be missing something—I kept adding two and two and getting zero. For the umpteenth time, I went over the facts as I knew them: the illegal bookmaking operation, Number's expertise in the fight game, Daniel naked in the laundry room, Daniel and the missus in the same room with the soon to be deceased, Jeremy's angry confrontation with the same future corpse, word on the street giving Daniel a possible motive . . . not much, and not nearly enough.

So far, all three of them, the Lovatos and Jeremy, had opportunity, but so far Daniel was the only one with a motive—unsubstantiated, but a motive nonetheless.

What were the three things the cops always looked for? Motive, opportunity . . . what was the other?

So far afield from my normal areas of expertise, I'd made it through the front doors, up the stairs, and to the door of my office before the third element hit me—means! Absent evidence to the contrary and with precious little to go on, we all, myself included, had been operating under the assumption that the sharks had done the dirty deed. But what if they hadn't? What if Numbers was the former Ms. Neidermeyer by the time she hit the water?

I burst through the door and came to a halt in front of Miss Patterson, who resolutely manned her desk even though the day had fled and night was gaining momentum. If she was startled by my arrival, she didn't show it. In fact, she looked dead on her feet. I pointed to her. "Call Romeo. If he's close, I'd like to see him."

Miss P nodded and reached for her phone.

"And I need to see or talk to Jeremy, pronto."

"He's asleep on your couch," Miss P said. Using one finger, she traced down her list of important numbers. When she'd found what she wanted, her finger stopped, holding her place on the list. Then she stuffed the receiver to her ear, using her shoulder to hold it there, and dialed with her free hand. Finally she glanced up at me. "He hadn't had any sleep to speak of, but he was intent on waiting until you got back. Something about a hot trail gone cold?"

Not what I wanted to hear, but I'd be damned before I let my fearless assistant see my deflation. "Put Romeo through when you get him on the line. Then I want you to scrape your hunk off my couch, after I talk to him of course, and both of you go home." I turned and tiptoed into my office.

As promised, the Beautiful Jeremy Whitlock was indeed fast asleep on my couch—all 6 feet plus a few inches and 225 well-muscled pounds of him.

I eased myself around him and into my desk chair, then leaned back and enjoyed the view. If my thoughts weren't lascivious—which they weren't—then no harm, no foul, right? Besides, I felt I deserved a moment of eye candy—the day had served up precious little to enjoy so far—if I excluded Dane.

And a moment was all I got. The phone rang. I jumped. Jeremy bolted to a seated postion.

Miss Patterson's calm voice announced, "Detective Romeo, line one."

Jeremy looked at me as I reached for the phone as if I had just been teleported from Mars. I watched him regain his surroundings then punched the button for the appropriate line.

"Romeo? Wherefore art thou?" I said, very pleased with myself.

With not even a chuckle, he gave me his location—two blocks away, which wasn't as close as it sounded given the traffic building on the strip. I guess he didn't think I was as cute as I thought I was.

"I need to ask you some questions. Should we do it over the phone or do you want to come by? Twenty minutes? Yeah, I'll be here." I nodded, which was stupid, but a habit. "Okay, make it thirty. See you then. Thanks." I cradled the phone, then looked at Jeremy.

Before I could drop a bon mot, he started in. "I'm sorry about racking on your couch. I was out of petrol." He ran a hand through his hair and shot me a dimple or two.

"Someone once told me a sofa in a woman's office was an invitation." I announced with a straight face. "Ever since, I've been leaving my office unlocked, hoping I'd catch a handsome guy."

"Sort of a casting couch in reverse?" he bantered back, joining the game. "Have much luck?"

"Not really. In fact, you're my first, but you've given me hope."

With a groan, Jeremy pushed himself to his feet, took two steps, then sagged into a chair across from me. He looked beat—unbelievably gorgeous, but beat. "Well, it's just a suggestion, mind you, but if you lose the wall of windows behind the couch, you might have more success."

"Good point." With a toe, I pulled out the bottom desk drawer then put both feet on it as I leaned back in my chair and shut my eyes. "I hear you don't have good news."

"Don't know whether it's good or bad. I haven't a clue what to make of it, actually. I've never run up against this before."

"Why don't you just start at the beginning?"

"Okay. I was skip-tracing the name you gave me, Shelley-Lynne Makepeace. She lived in New Jersey as your guy said, with her grandmother—."

"Grandmother? What about her parents?" My eyes still closed, I put my hands behind my head and let Jeremy's story wash over me.

"I couldn't find any mention of her parents, but I did find an uncle."

"Alive?"

"Amazingly enough, alive and kicking, and willing to talk, although I don't think he told me everything he knew." Jeremy's voice held a glimmer of hope. "I couldn't get him to open up about the father. But Shelly-Lynne's mother died when Shelly-Lynne was twelve. All he would tell me was her name was Mary Swearingen. Apparently Makepeace was the grandmother's second husband's name. Swearingen was the first husband, Shelly-Lynne's grandfather, who is dead, by the way, along with the grandmother and her second husband."

"Convenient." The way my luck was running, I'd better look twice before I crossed any streets and think seriously before making a commitment to green bananas. Maybe I should try a fortune-teller . . . "Did the uncle have anything else to offer?"

"He told me if I could find anything on the mother it would make pretty interesting reading." Jeremy stopped.

Dropping my arms, I raised my head and looked at him. "And?"

"I found her files, but apparently I didn't have the right clearances."

"What?" I shifted my feet to the floor and my butt to the edge of the chair, leaning toward him—he had my full attention now. "Clearances?"

"Apparently the FBI holds the key to the gate. They have sealed her files."

Chapter

S E V E N

The FBI? Time stopped. My brain function ground to a halt.

And they make solving murders look so easy on television.

Miss Patterson appeared in my doorway, interrupting my feeble attempts to marshal my scattered thoughts. "Did you know Jordan Marsh is on his way?"

"What?"

Miss Patterson tapped her pencil on her clipboard in irritation. "He's not on my list. How could you have overlooked telling me about him?"

An old friend, Jordan Marsh was a Hollywood icon and, if you believed the tabloids, the last of the red-hot lovers. We had bonded when his star was ascending and he'd made a rather embarrassing choice while booked into one of the Big Boss's lesser properties. I'd swept it under the rug, preserving his reputation. Jordan had continued on to bigger and better things and somehow I had ended up with a lifetime membership in the Jordan Marsh Fan and Functionary Club. He had the annoying habit of turning up unannounced, and at the worst possible time. At least the man was consistent.

"I didn't forget to tell you—this is news to me as well," I snapped, shooting her a dirty look. "Did he call?"

"Just now." Despite Jeremy's presence, Miss P couldn't quite disguise the awe in her voice. "His plane should just be lifting off from Ontario." She looked at me over the top of her readers. "He asked for the usual treatment. Do you care to explain what that means?"

"It means I am going to have a long night while you and Jeremy drag yourselves off for some shut-eye." I raised my hand, stopping her before she spoke. "No argument. You both are running on fumes, and I'm afraid I'm the only one who can handle Mr. Marsh."

AFTER Jeremy and Miss P had gathered themselves and their things and had done as I asked, I shut my office door behind them and again took my place in the chair behind my desk. Pushing the mounting paperwork aside, I put my elbows on the smooth black walnut surface and my face in my hands. Shutting the world out, I set aside thoughts of Jordan Marsh and let my brain play word association.

I mothballed Jimmy G's line on Scully Winter. It was way too early in the game to flush a player like Scully—I couldn't run the risk of scaring him away before I knew what I needed him for. Right now I needed answers.

Okay, concentrate, O'Toole.

Mary Swearingen Makepeace. Vegas. The fight game. Gambling. The district attorney. Sealed FBI files. I lifted my head from my hands as the light dawned. The Witness Protection Program. Of course!

Energy pulsed through me. However, I was fresh out of contacts at the FBI. We'd have to do an end-run—not ideal, but definitely doable. And I knew just the person for the job.

Flash Gordon, ace investigative reporter for the local paper, answered after the second ring with her customary cordiality. "Whatcha got?"

We'd met at UNLV our freshman year. Soul mates on sight, we had shared all the usual stupid freshman hijinks—and then some. She had kept me out of the newspapers, and I had kept her out of jail. An old Vegas adage defined real friends as those you knew well enough to blackmail. Flash and I were real friends.

"As usual, I don't know what I got," I said, adopting Flash's businesslike tone. "I need your help to figure it out."

She recognized my voice. "Hey, Lucky."

"How hard would it be for you to search editions of the *Review-Journal* back twenty-five years?" I asked.

"It wouldn't be easy. They're all on microfiche. Nothing's digital past the last couple of years."

"Then I'll rephrase the question: How hard would you work to help me break open the Numbers Neidermeyer case?"

She whistled low. "I'd work myself blind."

I heard my outer office door open, then a tentative knock at my door—Romeo. Cupping my hand over the receiver, I shouted, "Just a minute."

"Who's that?" Flash asked.

"Romeo. I need him to work another angle. But you, I need you to try to find out all you can about somebody by the name of Mary Swearingen Makepeace. Search partial names, anything you can think of."

Scuffling noises came over the phone as I assumed Flash switched her phone to the other ear, then held it there with her shoulder. I could picture her rooting between her double denvers for the stub of a pencil she always stuck there, then flipping open a notepad and taking notes in her own special shorthand. Keep her notes on a PDA or a computer where anyone could read them? Not Flash Gordon. Not in a million years.

"Can you narrow my search any?" she asked, her voice still all business.

"Focus on reports of criminal trials no older than twenty-five years."

If memory served, that was about the time Daniel started as an assistant DA. However, I wasn't going to tell Flash that. Even though a person was innocent until proven guilty, the press didn't always see it that way. And once an accusation, or even the hint of a misdeed, leaked into the public consciousness, it remained permanently embedded like a fossil in stone. When I stood before St. Peter at the Pearly Gates, I did not want to answer for jumping the gun and ruining a perfectly adequate district attorney.

"You got it," she clipped, then the line went dead.

I smiled as I cradled the phone. If Mary Swearingen Makepeace had a story, Flash would stick to it. Like a tick on a dog, she'd suck it dry.

I rose to go greet Romeo.

The young detective jumped as I threw open the door. He'd been standing, legs spread, arms behind his back, at my wall of windows, staring down at the throng in the lobby. "I like your view."

"Really?" I joined him at the window. "It makes me feel like an ant in a kid's ant farm." I slapped a hand to my head. "Shoot, what time is it?"

"Seven thirty. Why?"

I grabbed him by his coat sleeve and led him toward the door. "Come with me. I've got to start killing two birds with one stone or I'm going to be covered in bird sh . . . *guano*."

"What?" He let me pull him along.

When I was sure he was following, I let go of his sleeve. "I've got to check on the entomologists. Their program kicks off at eight."

"Entomologists?"

I waved away his question as we trotted down the stairs. "Do you have the ME's report on the shark-tank lady yet?"

"Just the basics." He had to shout to be heard as we pushed into the crowd in the lobby. "Toxicology will take another day or two."

"What did he list as cause of death?"

"Shark attack."

"I bet that's a first for Clark County." I worked my way toward the casino. Another hour or two and the people would be packed in so tight the fire department would have a cow. "Is the ME willing to go to the mat with that?"

"No." Romeo had to trot to keep up with me as I headed through the casino toward the convention area. "He tested the oxygen profusion of the . . . corpse. It was low, but there was so much degradation and contamination, he couldn't certify the results. And since the lungs had been eaten . . ."

"Got it," I said, wanting to cut short that line of conversation. "So you really have no way to determine time of death?"

"Not conclusively."

Geoffrey David-Williston stood in a group huddled in front of a large display filled with what was left of our bee population. Gesturing energetically, he addressed the small crowd.

I couldn't hear exactly what he was talking about but it likely had to do with too few bees—his current passion. As I rubbed the lingering red welts on my neck, I thought fewer bees would be a good thing. Romeo and I waited on the fringe as Dr. Williston wound down.

When he had finished, I pushed my way to the front. "Geoffrey."

"Lucky! I thought you'd forgotten us!" He actually seemed happy to see me, which was amazing. The last time we'd spoken I had held the undisguised opinion that a speedy demise would be too good for him. I felt certain he held me in equally low esteem.

"What do you think of our display?" He waved his arm at the curved wall of Lucite separating us from a rather large bee population. "Even though we lost most of our bees, it still looks pretty good, don't you think?"

"Impressive." For once I wasn't blowing smoke—the exhibit's concave surface created the illusion we had stepped inside an active hive.

"A bit dramatic, but we're trying to get people alarmed over the declining honeybee population, or Colony Collapse Disorder. The numbers are dwindling at an increasing rate. Most people think this is due to the Africanized bees migrating north out of Mexico, but that's only part of the cause. We can't identify the other part."

I nodded as I felt my eyes glazing over.

"I know you think this is just an interesting little problem for PhDs, but it has very real ramifications. The California almond crop alone requires 1.3 million individuals for annual pollination. Without them—no almonds."

The lack of bees impacted our food supply? Now he had my attention.

A man walked through the crowd ringing a bell signaling ten minutes until the start of the presentation; people began drifting toward the banquet room. Geoffrey glanced at them over his shoulder. "I would love to tell you more, but I better find my seat. I'm introducing the speaker tonight, an expert in the growing field of alternative uses for bee venom."

"You wouldn't want to miss that." I flashed him a benign smile. "I won't keep you, but tell me, are the arrangements for your conference satisfactory? Is there anything I can do? Anything you need?"

"No, everything is fabulous, as usual." He turned to go, then stopped and turned back around, placing a hand on my arm. "I'm really sorry about the whole . . . fiasco last night. I was upset, and I behaved badly."

"Understandable. Apology accepted."

With that, he disappeared, leaving Romeo and me alone in the emptying vestibule.

"You hang out with the most interesting people," Romeo dead-panned.

I couldn't tell if the kid was needling me or not—I sorta hoped he was. "Got anything else on the other matter?" I didn't want to spell it out—our conversation wouldn't be hidden by the noise of the crowd as before. And, as my mother used to say, in Vegas, even the walls had ears.

"One thing I think you should know." He glanced around as if looking to see if anyone was taking an interest in us. Satisfied, he lowered his voice and stepped near. "I'm getting pressure to put the squeeze on your buddy."

"Jeremy?" I whispered. "Who from?"

"Higher up than I can see." His brows crinkled. "If I didn't know better, I'd almost say it was coming from outside the department."

He may not know better, but I did. I knew who, outside Metro, had not only the interest but also that kind of stroke. A trip to visit our district attorney was numero uno on my morning to-do list. Until then, I'd play clueless. "Really? If you get wind of where the pressure is coming from, will you let me know?"

He nodded but didn't make any promises, which made me feel less like a creep withholding suspicions from my cohort in crime.

"Anything for me?" he asked.

"I've got some lines out but haven't reeled in a fish. Soon, though."

"I'd be worried about landing a shark or two, if I were you." His eyes skittered from mine as he developed a fascination with his shoes. "I got something else to ask you. Off the record, okay?"

"I've forgotten it already."

"Huh?"

"Off the record," I said. "Give it to me."

"Is your new assistant, Brandy, hooking up with anyone?"

Hooking up, what did that mean? Dating? Screwing? I had only the vaguest idea. "Carrying a torch for the beautiful Miss Alexander, are we?"

Red crept up his cheeks. He still refused to meet my eyes.

"You have impeccable taste."

"She's prime for sure."

Prime? This certainly wasn't one of my fluent dialects. "I don't know about her personal life, but why don't you ask her out? What's the worst that could happen?"

"She could laugh."

I threw my arm around my young friend's shoulder as we walked back the way we had come. "Romeo, love makes fools out of us all. Get used to it."

I said good-bye to the detective at the garage elevators. A glance at my watch told me *tempus* really did *fugit* when you were having fun—Jordan Marsh would be arriving at the Executive Terminal in a half hour or less and I'd better be there to meet him. That didn't give me long to figure out what I was going to do with him when he got here.

I dove into the lobby crowd, which was clearly gaining momentum. Arriving guests waited in queues, most of which were at least five deep, in front of individual registration bays. One line, though, was considerably longer than the others, and patience appeared to be running thin as Tommy Bahama–clad new arrivals craned around each other, shooting exasperated looks toward the front desk.

Sergio Fabiano, our front desk manager, a smile plastered on his face, stood at attention next to the exasperated young lady helping an older gentleman at the head of the line.

"May I help?" I asked, as I stepped in next to the man causing the holdup.

"Only if you speak Spanish," Sergio replied. "Mr. Garza is from Madrid and speaks fluent Castilian Spanish, but very little English. Unfortunately, his Italian isn't very good either, or I would have had no problem." Sergio gave me a weak smile. "Ms. Rodriguez is busy with another guest from Mexico right now, so I have no one who can speak with Mr. Garza. He is trying to register the thirty people in his party into the twenty rooms he has booked. You know the regulations—we need to put names with room numbers. He doesn't understand."

"Easy enough." I turned to Mr. Garza and greeted him in his native language.

A grin split his face as he wrapped me in a big hug, his relief almost palpable, as he began his tale.

"Esperaté un momentito, por favor," I said, interrupting his staccato torrent of Spanish. "Sergio, can you open the desk on the end? Take the next five parties in this line with you." I glanced at the name tag on the reservation agent. "Miss Shakova and I will take care of Mr. Garza and his party."

With a crisp nod and the assured gestures of a conductor leading a symphony, Sergio clapped his hands for attention, then motioned to the guests behind us, as he moved to the end of the registration desk, taking half of the line behind us with him.

The look on Miss Shakova's face told me she was clearly in over her head. "Where're you from?" I asked.

"Georgia," she replied, in a thick Slavic accent.

Ah, she wasn't referring to one of the original Thirteen Colonies. We had so many different nationalities represented on our staff, even I was amazed communication didn't completely grind to a halt more often—or minor wars didn't break out.

"Long way from home?"

Her shy smile hinted she was starting to relax.

"Here's what we're going to do. First, please write all of Mr. Garza's room numbers in a column down one side of a sheet of paper, indicating the type of accommodation next to each. I will ask him to write the names of the guests beside the number of the room they will be staying in. If we get that information, can you take it from there?"

"Yes."

"Good. Then, while Mr. Garza is filling in the names, why don't you call the Bell Desk? Ask them to send anyone who speaks

Spanish, even a valet will do. If they put you off—and they might, everyone is maxed-out right now—tell them I'm the one who is asking."

"Yes, Ms. O'Toole. Thank you."

Ten minutes later, we had the registration gridlock eliminated and the line of guests flowing once again, I'd been anointed an honorary member of the Emilio Garza family, and now had only five minutes to lock up the office and beat feet to the airport. Since the airport was right down the street—piece of cake. But if the idiots who were talking about moving it twenty miles down the Interstate got their way, I'd be screwed.

Halfway across the lobby, I caught my parents walking arm in arm toward me. Still an unusual sight, I couldn't resist stopping to watch them. A few tourists stopped to take their picture, but, as minor royalty in a world where one's Q score was king, they didn't attract a lot of attention.

My mother, dressed to the nines in an Escada suit and her South Sea pearls, had forsaken her ubiquitous heels for a pair of flats. Still a few inches taller than my father, she tilted her head to the side to catch something he was saying. A smile on her face, she glowed.

With her on his arm, the Big Boss's chest puffed with pride. Bathed in the light of love, they both looked like kids. Their faces lit when they saw me.

Even at my advanced age, parental affection still warmed my heart. "Where are you two off to?"

"First dinner, then we're going to a show!" My mother beamed.

"A date?"

"Just a couple of old romantics," said the Big Boss, looking quite thrilled with the whole thing.

"He's being modest." Mother squeezed her man's arm. "Do you know what this guy did? He booked us a table by the window at Prime, so we can watch the fountains while we eat that seafood tower thing they have."

"Really? The Bellagio?" I raised an eyebrow at my father. "Giving the competition some business?"

"Industrial espionage." He winked at me. "We needed to keep track of what they're up to."

"Going undercover, are we?"

"No, we're not going undercover," my mother said, adopting the same tone of exaggerated patience she used when I was a child.

That attitude used to punch my buttons. Now it just made me smile.

"He's taking me to see *Mystère*." Mother's excitement oozed from every pore. "This old softie even stood in line for the tickets. Just like a normal person!"

Normal wasn't a classification either of my parents was in danger of earning, but I wasn't about to disillusion my mother, not when she was having so much fun. Who wanted to be normal anyway? "Why *Mystère*? I thought *O* was the show to see."

"Honey, you should see all the male acrobats." Mother's voice drooled in anticipation. "Those muscles! Do you know they're naked from the waist up and only wear tights down below?"

"So you like the men. No real surprise there." I nodded toward my father. "What, if anything, does your escort like?"

Mother leaned into me, her voice lowered to a whisper. "The whole thing makes me horny."

I gave her a look, then glanced at my father. "I walked into that one, didn't I?"

He shrugged, then gave me a wicked grin, one I don't ever recall seeing on his face before. "One thing about your mother, she keeps life interesting."

To anyone else, my response would've been, "So you'll be up all night, then?" But, somehow, saying that to my father would've given me the willies.

STILL shell-shocked by my mother's blithe announcement—a traumatizing tidbit to this very visual offspring—I bounded up the stairs two at a time. A minute later, with purse over my shoulder, the office locked behind me, the phones forwarded to Security, I was headed back down. Bursting through the doors at a dead run, I collided with a solid body.

"So sorry." Steadying myself, I kept going.

A familiar, dreaded voice stopped me. "I was hoping I would run into you, *cherie*."

I stopped, closed my eyes, and took a deep breath before I turned around. I so did not need this right now. Opening my eyes, one glance confirmed my worst fears—our new chef stood in front of me in all of his Gallic glory, wearing insouciance like a comfortable old coat. Clearly unruffled, Jean-Charles still looked scrumptious, but the memory of the bad taste he'd left in my mouth lingered. "Not now. I'm in a hurry and I have no time for skirmishing."

Putting a hand to his chest, he adopted a wounded look. "I am French. We do not fight."

"As evidenced by the last world war." Reshouldering my Birkin, I turned to go. "However, right now, I don't even have time to accept a white flag."

He walked with me. "Could you accept an invitation instead?"

"To what?" I only half-listened as I pushed through the throng of paparazzi and casual onlookers. I'd rather join the Foreign Legion than put up with Chef Bouclet's act any more than I absolutely had to. Stepping to the curb, I waved at Paolo, who waited off to the side with the limo.

"I am having a tasting party tomorrow night. I'd like your approval of the new menu."

"What time?" As the limo eased to a stop in front of me, I opened the passenger door.

"Seven o'clock. At the restaurant."

I couldn't tell whether the Frenchman was offering me an olive branch or luring me into his lair for the next battle, but the Big Boss *had* made him my responsibility . . . and, if the menu wasn't up to snuff I'd never hear the end of it. "I'll be there, but I can't guarantee how much time I'll have."

Shutting the door, I cut off his reply. "Paolo, how fast can you make it to the Executive Terminal?"

"My record is a touch under five minutes."

"Let's see if we can break it—preferably without killing anyone. If we start mowing down the tourists, you and I will be out of work."

"Yes ma'am." Paolo pulled his cap down low, then hunched over the wheel as he maneuvered the big car away from the curb. Heading for the rear entrance, he glanced at me in the rearview mirror. "Are you watching the news back there?"

"I'm not sure I can handle any more 'news' today." I leaned my head back and shut my eyes. God I was tired. All I wanted to do was climb into bed, wrap Teddie around me, and stay there for the next week. A pipe dream if ever there was one—still, a girl could dream, couldn't she?

As if they had conspired to give me a miserable evening, my stomach and head bookended me with pain. On top of that I felt a little woozy, definitely not on top of my game.

As Paolo turned the car south on Koval, he hit the gas; the acceleration pressed me back into the seat. "Our luck is holding—green lights all the way. I'll patch the television feed through—you need to see this."

That wasn't what I needed at all, but I didn't have the energy to argue.

Keeping my eyes closed, I thought I recognized the voice of the talking head, Anderson Cooper. "All hell has broken loose in Pahrump, Nevada—a small town sixty miles outside of Las Vegas that many have dubbed ground zero in the attack on American morality. I'm standing in front of Mona's Place, the self-described 'Best Whorehouse in Nevada,' where day after tomorrow, a young woman will auction her virginity to the highest bidder."

My eyes snapped open and riveted on the screen as Mr. Cooper continued his explanation of Mother's upcoming event. Behind him, people carried signs denouncing prostitution, perversion, and seemingly sex in general, as they marched in front of the unmistakable purple and pink of Mona's establishment. A man in black, wielding a Bible, urged them on.

I pressed the intercom button. "Is CNN the only station covering this story?"

"Geraldo Rivera is on site for FOX." Paolo turned left on Tropicana, then swung right into the Executive Terminal. "I'm sure the local stations will all have something on the late-night news, but that won't be on for a half hour or so."

"Turn it off, will you? I've seen enough." Again, I closed my eyes and rested my head on the soft cushion behind me. Anderson Cooper had hit the nail on the head—all hell *had* broken loose in Pahrump—and Mother was out on a date. Briefly, I wondered if she knew about all the attention she had garnered, then laughed at my stupidity. If she knew, she'd be there, front and center.

Well, it looked like she was going to get her fifteen minutes of fame, and I couldn't wait to watch the show.

OUR timing perfect, we arrived just as Jordan Marsh's plane taxied onto the tarmac. Paolo and I waited in the limo until the sleek silver jet came to a stop in a remote corner, far from prying eyes, and the pilots had opened the door and unfolded the stairs. Then Paolo eased the big car onto the loading area, positioning it next to the aircraft. He jumped, and grabbed a bag from one of the pilots, and stowed it in the trunk while I stepped out to greet our guest.

With a finely honed sense of timing, Jordan Marsh waited until the expectation of those of us in attendance—the two pilots, Paolo, the line boys chocking the wheels, and me—had reached a crescendo, before ducking through the doorway and stepping to the top of the stairs. Buttoning his jacket, he paused for a moment—he never could resist playing to an audience, no matter how small.

One of the line boys nudged the other, then whispered something.

Pretending he had just caught sight of me, Jordan flashed his famous smile—the one that could make a thousand women faint, or so the story went—then bounded down the steps . . . all three of them.

Sweeping me into an embrace, he kissed me dramatically. His lips still only inches from mine, he said, "Thanks for coming to get me."

I eased myself out of his grasp. "My pleasure. Next time, if you'd give me a bit of warning, I could make good money auctioning the opportunity to receive that greeting from the Great Jordan Marsh."

We both knew I was joking, but with his matinée idol looks—jet-black hair graying at the temples, hazel eyes that changed colors with his moods, high cheekbones, a Kirk Douglas divot in his chin, chiseled physique—and his reputation as a bit of a bad boy, most women would pay a king's ransom for the opportunity I'd just had.

But they didn't know what I knew: Jordan Marsh was gay.

He was also the reigning Hollywood romantic lead. If it became public knowledge, the truth about his sexual orientation would break female hearts the world over . . . and it would terminate his career.

In true Hollywood style, Jordan Marsh was an act—a carefully created, zealously guarded fantasy. And, in an ironic twist we both appreciated, he came to my little fantasyland to live his truth.

Jordan's soul mate, Rudy Gillespi, was an entertainment lawyer in town. When I set them up three years ago, I had no idea theirs would be a love story like none other, nor that I had signed a contract to run interference for them until the end of time. As they say, no good deed goes unpunished.

Jordan and I slid into the back of the limo through the door Paolo held open for us. As the door shut, the light dimmed, and prying eyes could no longer see us behind the heavily tinted glass, we were momentarily alone and invisible. Jordan's smile vanished. A very serious expression replaced it.

A chill washed over me. "Don't tell me you and Rudy broke up?"

"Don't be silly." Jordan half turned so he faced me. Grabbing my hand, he squeezed hard. "Rudy and I want to get married, and we want you to help us."

THE next thing that registered on my consciousness was the face of Forrest, the security guard for the condo-tower I called home, inches from my own, but upside-down. How did he get here? Or how did I get to where he was? And why was I lying down in the back of the limo?

"Should we call the paramedics?" he asked, his brows crinkled in concern.

"That won't be necessary," Jordan said, in his best doctor impersonation. "She's just had a shock. She'll get over it."

"I will not," I mumbled, more than a little peeved at him. How did he know the pounding of my heart and the cold sweat popping out all over, chilling me to the bone, weren't harbingers of a major health event?

His face swam into view—his was right-side up.

Nose to nose, I looked up into his hazel eyes that now appeared more blue than anything—and not the least bit concerned. Of course, he was probably used to women swooning in his presence. "Jordan, you could do me a favor, though."

"Anything."

"Check me into one of those nice sanatoriums where they park the sane people. Three meals a day, eight hours of restful sleep, room service . . . and no crazy people wanting my help." I glared at him as I pushed myself to my elbow—stars swirled around me, then faded. Not willing to admit I needed time to pull myself together, I made a show of exasperated patience as Jordan crawled off of me.

Thank God there wasn't anyone with a camera around—photos

of Jordan Marsh on top of anyone in the back of a limo would create a feeding frenzy. I didn't want that person to be me. A résumé line item entitled "caught in a compromising position with Jordan Marsh" would not enhance my resulting job search.

"A sane person's sanatorium? Isn't that an oxymoron?" Jordan looked quizzical for a moment, then a lightbulb went off. "Oh! You mean like the Ritz-Carlton?" Not looking the least bit worried, he grinned as he backed out of the car, and extended his hand to me.

"A nice long stay at the Ritz on the Place Vendôme in Paris sounds about right." I let him help me out of the car. "In a suite."

He raised his eyebrows at that part, but he didn't refuse. He knew I was grandstanding.

I brushed down my pants and tried to locate my dignity . . . and my bearings—I was still seeing stars. I had fainted. How humiliating! The last time I'd done something like that had been ages ago when Mother had sliced open her thumb while attempting to cut frozen meat. "Forrest, I think I'm fine now. Thank you."

The big man looked at me over the top of the car. "Man, you both sound like fruit loops. I have no idea what you're talking about." As he headed back to his post he muttered, "Sanatoriums for sane people. Who ever heard of such a thing?"

Steadying myself with a hand on the car, I took stock of my surroundings. Jordan watched me, a trace of concern leaking into his bemused expression. Peeking out from behind him, Paolo wrung his hands as he looked at me with eyes as big as saucers.

"Woman, you're pale as a ghost." Jordan leaned in for a closer look. "When did you last eat?"

"Eat?" That gave me pause. I tried to reconstruct the day—I'd picked at my breakfast with Romeo and talked to Teddie through lunch with Miss P. I'd only been able to swallow two gulps of my shake at the Peppermill. "Dinner. Last night." And to think, I'd always thought I'd keel over if I missed a meal—now I knew it took three missed meals for that to happen.

"Well, no wonder you feel faint."

"My lack of sustenance may have weakened me, but you provided the knockout punch, and I'm not done with you. You're not going to get off that easily." No longer seeing stars, I was now starting to see red. Not only did my good friend want to throw himself in front of the train, he wanted to pull me along with him—or leave me to take the fall. I didn't know which would be worse. "However, first things first. Do you have another mission for Paolo?"

"I've already given him the address."

"Good." I turned to my diminutive chauffeur. "On your way back with Mr. Gillespi, will you swing through In-N-Out? Buy enough animal-style burgers and fries to give us all coronaries."

He slapped his hat on his head and turned to go.

"Oh, and some Diet Coke."

He waved as he climbed into the car, then fired up the engine and roared away.

"Hamburgers and French fries, manna from Heaven," Jordan said, with the slightest hint of disdain.

"Don't give me that sanctimonious, your-body-is-a-temple BS. *My* body has had enough of a shock already, and I have no intention of denying it the usual dose of saturated fat. I need my strength."

"For what?" Jordan asked, looking like a man with a clean conscience.

"For wringing your neck, that's what." I whirled on him. "Are you batshit insane?"

Chapter

E I G H T

♡

"You, sit," Jordan ordered, once the elevator deposited us in the middle of my apartment. "First a drink, then you can take a bite out of my ass."

Still feeling a bit sub-par, I didn't put up a fight—alcohol on an empty stomach, why not? It's not as if the day could get any worse. I wedged myself into the corner of a couch. Kicking off my shoes, I crossed my legs under me. Then, feeling the need for a shield, I pulled a pillow over my lap.

Jordan handed me a tumbler of Wild Turkey, keeping another for himself, then sat in the other corner of my couch so he faced me. In this light I could see the strain on his face. He'd told me once that living a lie took a lot of energy. Each erg expended through the years had engraved his face, leaving a visible accounting of the toll it had taken. At this moment, he looked every inch the fifty-year-old man he was.

"I don't want to take a chunk out of your ass." I reached over and squeezed his hand, but he looked so sad, I felt I should be wrapping him in a bear hug instead. "I only want to know one thing."

"One? This is my lucky day." He gave me a weak smile. "Fire away."

"Is Rudy pushing you to do this?"

"He would never." Jordan's anger flashed. "That's not the kind of choice you put a person to, especially when you love him."

"I didn't think so, but I needed to hear it from you." Against my better judgment, I took a sip of the witch's brew in my hand. My folly rewarded me with a trail of fire down my throat that burned a raw hole in my hollow stomach. However, the pain was worth the reward—a relaxing warmth to mask the cold dread. "Then why now? Look at you . . . well, not right now . . . but normally you're a hunk and a half with at least a decade of good roles in front of you."

"Thank you, I think." He gave me a dirty look, then took a long pull on his drink as he visibly transported himself back in time. "I've known I was gay since I was fourteen. It's not a lifestyle any-one chooses, you know?"

"I wouldn't think." No one in his right mind would pick a ho-mosexual lifestyle in a heterosexual world. I mean, why climb the sheer face of the mountain when there's an easy trail to the top?

"That's a long damned time to hide such a vital part of me, I can tell you that. It was like trying to run with only one leg— something integral was missing." He stared over my shoulder, the hint of a smile lifting the corner of his mouth. "And then, thanks to you, I met Rudy, and I was whole. Happy . . . no, ecstatic, for the first time in my life."

The pain, raw and visceral, that filled his eyes as he once again looked at me, stole my breath. Like stars overwhelmed by the in-tensity of the sun, words paled. There truly was nothing to say.

Knowing Jordan, he had thought his decision through from

every angle, analyzed every sacrifice against its gain, so I wouldn't insult him by asking if he had. Trapped not only by the choices we made, but the hand we were dealt, the cards in the game of life sometimes ran cold. The only way out was to fold the hand.

With nothing to add, I sat with him as he talked, hoping the comfort of friendship was enough.

"The last movie I starred in has been out on DVD for almost a year, so when my sex appeal tanks, I won't be taking any investors with me. My production company is going strong. We have a film up for consideration by the Academy this year, two more in the can, and options on a couple of novels, neither of which are vehicles for me." He jumped as the elevator whirred to life—someone had called the car we had ridden up in. "I enjoy being a producer and would like to concentrate on that. Since we can now afford him, Rudy is going to be the company's general counsel."

"You've worked this all out." His was a good plan, and it didn't sound like justification at all. It sounded like the truth.

"It's not like news of my sexual orientation is really going to come out of left field, anyway." Jordan swirled the amber liquid in his glass as he talked. He seemed at peace. "The tabloids have been speculating for years. I'm fifty, never married, never sired any children—either I'm gay or I'm the shallowest, most superficial man on the planet."

"When you put it that way, being gay doesn't sound so bad."

He gave me a shocked look. "I never said it was. However, the choice that little complication put me to . . . that was living Hell." He glanced over the rim of his glass at me as he took another sip of fortification. "Will you help us?"

"Was there ever any doubt?"

EVEN though it was almost two in the morning, juiced on fat, starch, caffeine, and true love, I knew trying to sleep now would be futile. Filled with enough hamburgers and French fries to fortify even the weakest soul, and after hours of chatter, funny stories, and wedding

plans, Rudy and Jordan had repaired to the largest of my guestrooms, leaving me alone with my thoughts. I checked to make sure
the service had fed the bird—they had—and cloaked his cage for
the night, then made a mental note to move the bird to Teddie's
for the duration of Jordan's stay.

I swapped my day-clothes for one of Teddie's shirts, poured
myself another drink—limiting it to one finger of bourbon—and
settled into the big chair by the window. The lights of the Strip
stretched before me. Usually I found the view and my surroundings comforting—my home was my sanctuary. But not tonight.

Like a ballroom after the band had packed up and the last guest
had gone, my apartment was nothing but a hollow shell, echoes of
the party magnifying the emptiness. All the joy had left. The guests
had gone to bed . . . and my heart had tripped off to California.

Sipping my drink, I tucked my bare feet under me, and wondered where Teddie was. What was he doing right now? Was he
asleep? Was he looking out his window like me? Were we looking
at the same moon hanging in the night sky?

He'd said something about a party tonight where they wanted
him to play a set, so I hadn't expected a call. But not talking to
him, not telling him about my day, not hearing about his . . . didn't
seem right somehow.

Sipping my drink, I fiddled with a button on his shirt. Hanging
by a thread, it needed fixing, but, if I owned a needle and thread, I
didn't have a clue where I might have hidden them. I was always a
failure at the girl stuff. Thank God Teddie didn't see that as a major shortcoming; his take on women was broader than that.

I took another sip of anesthetizing bourbon.

God, what a day! Beginning with Teddie leaving, not to return
until I-don't-know-when, segueing into a breakfast over photos of
the inedible parts of Numbers Neidermeyer, and ending with being invited to preside over the destruction of a legendary Hollywood career, the last twenty-four hours really took the cake. Add a
district attorney up to his ass in alligators who was trying to rush

a murder indictment against the Beautiful Jeremy Whitlock, and my humiliation over that little weak spell in the limo—in front of witnesses no less—and this day was truly one for the record books.

I needed to talk to Teddie.

Reaching for my phone, I flipped it open and hit number two on the speed-dial before I talked myself out of it.

After five or six rings, I thought my call would be kicked to voicemail.

At the last minute a voice answered—a female voice. A young, giggly female voice. "Theodore is busy right now. He can't come to the phone."

Music thumped in the background as I thought I heard Teddie say, "What are you doing? Give me that thing."

"Theodore, quit that. That tickles." The female voice again, dissolving into a fit of laughter.

I heard scuffling noises, more laughter, then finally Teddie's voice. "Hello?"

"I guess this isn't a good time for some phone sex." I kept my voice neutral even though my heart raced.

"Lucky! I'm so glad you called. This day has been fucking amazing!"

Scuffling noises came over the line, as if he'd covered the microphone. But he didn't cover it fully and I heard him say, presumably to the young woman "Quit that. Go away. I'll be right there." Then back to me. "God, honey, they loved my stuff!" He sounded half looped, riding on an incendiary mix of euphoria and too little sleep. He wasn't drunk, that much I knew—he never mixed business and alcohol. However, the rest of what he was up to was a bit murky.

"I'd love to hear about it, but you sound busy."

"I've got so much to tell you! But I gotta go. They want me to play some more."

Play some more, I bet.

"Can I hit you back later?" he asked.

I heard the girl in the background pleading with Teddie to quit talking. "If that's music-speak for call me later, sure."

First Romeo, now Teddie—everybody was speaking Martian and I felt old. And even more alone than before, if that was possible.

I folded the phone, disconnecting the call, thought for a moment, then flipped it open again and punched the red button until the thing powered off. Even though I felt like flinging it across the room, I set it carefully on the side table. Since I had refused to spring for a landline, if I shattered my cell off the far wall, I'd effectively cut off contact with the outside world—not that I wanted any right now—but tomorrow was another day.

Curling up in a ball in the big chair, I pulled an afghan over me and hugged myself tight as I stared out at the lights of the Strip.

Well, *that* call had certainly made me feel better.

A hand on my shoulder gently shook me.

"Lucky? Did you sleep in this chair?"

A male voice. Not Teddie's. I tried to concentrate. Last night. Images, soft and blurry, hiding behind the veil of a screaming headache.

"Honey," the voice seemed to be attached to the hand that shook me harder, more insistent now.

I eased one eye open. Light—an arrow of pain. I snapped it shut again. Then I remembered—Jordan, Rudy, bourbon, Teddie . . . more bourbon.

"Lucky, are you okay? Why did you sleep in the chair?" Jordan sounded horrified.

"My bed was too big and empty." My voice sounded whiney, like it didn't belong to me. Putting my feet on the floor, I bent over. Elbows on my knees, I buried my face in my hands, as the world whirled, then slowly righted itself. "The sheets were cold, and Teddie was off at some party in L.A. with some giggly female." One eye shut, the other a slit, I looked up at Jordan. "Giggling is so . . . unattractive."

"No, so female." Reaching down, he grabbed my arm and tried to pull me to my feet. "Most men find women who giggle alluring."

"So said the world's authority on male/female attraction," I groused, as I stood and let him lead me toward the kitchen, then instantly regretted my harsh assessment. "Sorry, that was uncalled for."

Patting a stool at the counter, he smiled. "I still find women attractive, you know. However, right now, you look a bit worse for wear."

"Worse for wear? You're being kind."

"Maybe, but I love you enough to try to hide the truth." He helped me onto the stool, then satisfied I wasn't going to keel over, he moved around to the kitchen side of the counter "So, what is this about Theodore?"

Why do I have this annoying habit of opening my mouth before engaging my brain?

"Don't look at me with owl eyes," Jordan said.

Clothed in one of the thick white Turkish robes from the Babylon, his hair tousled, and a shit-eating grin on his face, he looked good enough to eat.

"Come on, give it up," he said. "If you do, I'll fix you my famous hangover cure—time-tested, it's one hundred percent guaranteed."

"You play dirty." Still excruciating, my headache reduced my field of vision to a small circle of clarity. I felt half-sick—no, more than half. Absolute misery, that's what I felt, in both body and soul. "Start working on your concoction. I'll tell you anything you want to know."

Jordan fell to work. He grabbed apples and lemons from the fridge, sugar from the pantry, and a bottle of Napoleon from my secret hiding place in the back of the cupboard beside the sink. "Teddie? Don't tell me you finally took pity on the boy and gave him a tumble?"

"You knew, too?"

He snorted as he squeezed the lemons, then tossed all his

gatherings into a blender with some ice. Then he hit the switch, and almost dropped me to the floor.

Reflexively, my hands flew to my ears.

"Sorry," he shouted over the noise, looking far happier than I thought he should. After an interminable time, he cut the switch and poured some of the thick concoction into a mug. "Honey, everybody knew but you. Drink up. Hair of the dog and all of that."

I took a tentative sip, igniting a craving on some visceral level. Draining the whole thing in one long session, I thrust the empty mug toward him. "More."

Jordan complied and I sipped, more slowly this time, as I filled him in on my recent adventures in love.

When I had finished, he didn't comment immediately. Instead, he looked at me for a moment as if trying to find the right words. When he finally spoke, his words weren't the ones I expected to hear. "Quit fighting yourself, Lucky. Let it happen. Life's like Disneyland and love is the best ride in the park."

"The one that snaps your head around, then breaks your back?"

I set my empty glass on the counter and pushed myself to my feet. Thankfully, the world had stopped spinning.

"Well, if I'm not going to get any sympathy, it's time to get a move on. The circus awaits."

Chapter

N I N E

s promised, Jordan's concoction proved to be a miracle cure—I actually felt half-human, which was better than I felt yesterday. Forrest again manned his post—he worked almost as many hours as I did—and he gave me a questioning look as I stepped out of the elevator.

I waggled my fingers at him as I strolled by. "Beautiful day, isn't it?"

"Yes, Ma'am."

I couldn't read his expression, but it didn't matter. We paid Forrest a lot of money to pretend to be deaf, dumb, and blind.

Today was the perfect day to walk to work. Breathing deep, I drank my fill of the cool morning air as I stepped out of the building and started on my way. The warmth of the sun felt good on my face. I felt like Goldilocks and her porridge—this day was just right. If I picked up the pace, I would be shucking my sweater soon.

The Babylon loomed in front of me, a ten-minute walk, no more. Putting my brain on autopilot, I relaxed and enjoyed being outside, in the real world. I had no idea what to think about Teddie, so I didn't. Even a condemned man is entitled to last words.

A lone hawk circled high above, riding a thermal. A dog of indeterminate breeding whined at me as I passed, but didn't bark. One of my neighbors in a blue pickup pulled out of the parking lot in front of his apartment building and waved. Life stirred, but the streets were quiet—it was still early.

At the next corner, I turned left, heading for the Strip. Curiously, the street was named Albert Rothstein Way—I'd never noticed that before. Was the sign new?

Cutting across an old construction staging area to my left would save me a minute or two. Whistling "I'm Gonna Wash That Man Right Outa My Hair" and swinging my Birkin to the rhythm, I headed that way.

Halfway across the sand lot, I heard an engine rev as a car turned the corner behind me and accelerated. The street was short and dead-ended into the back of the Babylon. What idiot would gun his ride on this tiny stretch of asphalt? Curious, I turned and glanced back.

The car jumped the curb and headed straight for me! For a fraction of a second I could only stare at it, unable to process what I saw as it barreled down on me. Finally, adrenaline kicked in and jump-started the whole fight-or-flight thing.

I turned tail and ran.

I knew it was futile, but I ran anyway. In the vast field of sand, there was nowhere to hide. I could hear the car right behind me. I didn't look. I kept running until I thought my lungs would burst.

At the last minute, the car veered and raced by me. A cloud of choking sand enveloped me, stinging my eyes. Breathing was out of the question. Gasping for air, I stopped. The car raced away. I could see the dim red of its taillights through the sand, but nothing more.

Damn! I hadn't even gotten a good look at the driver. Male or female, I couldn't be sure. And the car? Something small, nondescript. Yellow, maybe. Sort of a cream color.

That was *really* going to narrow it down. Brilliant, my dear Watson, absolutely brilliant.

Searching for a shoe I had lost, I retraced my steps and berated myself. What an eyewitness I was! I found the shoe and slapped it on my foot, then stalked toward work.

The perfect day shattered, I was more than a little bit steamed. Running me down would've been child's play. So, the driver hadn't wanted to kill me.

He wanted to deliver a warning. And this one wasn't written in crayon.

Well, consider me warned . . . and really, really pissed.

Reaching pavement, I kicked off my favorite Ferragamo flats, dumping out the sand before reinstalling them. I brushed myself down, then shook the sand from my hair. God knows what I looked like, but it would have to do until I made it to civilization and running water.

Unfortunately, the reporters saw me before I saw them. They swarmed me halfway up the entrance to the Babylon. My eyes grew slitty, and I kept walking, even as one brazen young thing stuck a mike in my face.

"Ms. O'Toole, first, according to Norm Clarke's column in the R-J this morning, you sneaked into the airport and whisked away Jordan Marsh, who hasn't surfaced since. Then Mr. Kowalski is seen doing a hot and heavy with Reza Pashiri at a music industry shindig in West Hollywood last night. Is there trouble in paradise?"

Her words hit me like a punch to the solar plexus. "You guys are here because of me? *I'm* the news?" Man, if the Big Boss got wind of this, my ass was a grape. He paid me big bucks to keep stuff *out* of the papers, not make headlines myself.

"Honey," I continued, "If I'm what you think passes for news in this town, then you better start looking for another line of work. Go bark up another tree." I pushed past her, and tried to force my way through the throng that seemed to be growing exponentially.

I hadn't made much progress and was starting to panic a bit as people pressed all around me, firing questions, when I heard a strong male voice shout, "Everyone, back off. If you don't leave now, you will be thrown off the property and not welcomed back." Dane!

Like Moses parting the Red Sea, the Texan strode toward me, the reporters and other gadflies clearing out of his way. "Well, you certainly made a splash today, Ms O'Toole." He grabbed my elbow and led me toward the front entrance.

"You have no idea."

Escorting me across the lobby, he deposited me in an open elevator. Reaching in, he pushed the button for the mezzanine. "Call if you need rescuing again." He stepped back as the doors closed.

Sticking a hand out, I held them open for a moment. "Dane?"

"Yeah?" His eyes, now the deepest shade of emerald, held me spellbound.

"Thank you."

He pretended to tip a hat, breaking the spell. "In cowboy school, I aced the course on rescuing damsels in distress."

GIVING my office doorknob a twist, then an angry shove, I threw the thing open. It banged off the wall. On the bounce-back, I shoved it again.

Not looking the least bit alarmed, Miss Patterson gazed at me over the top of her reading glasses.

"Where is it?" I growled, as I glowered at her.

"On your chair. I circled the best parts," she chirped.

As I read through the good Mr. Clarke's column, I marveled at his pipeline—something happens and five minutes later he knows about it. Of course the lineboys had put the bug in his ear about

Jordan and me. But I couldn't fathom where he got the photo of Teddie and Reza Pashiri. And so fast, too.

There is nothing like seeing your lover in the paper kissing someone else to jump-start your day.

Add that to the car thing, and being accused of cheating with a Hollywood Hottie, and today was already worse than yesterday. And it was only eight o'clock in the morning! The day was still young! What else could go wrong?

"Lucky, your mother is on line one. She doesn't sound happy."

MY life flashed before my eyes as I sagged into my desk chair. The light for line one blinked at me, challenging me, goading me. In one angry swipe, I hit the button, grabbed the receiver, and pressed it to my ear.

"Mother, did you have a good time last night?" I tried to sound chipper—I don't think I succeeded.

"Don't patronize me, Lucky." Her voice was as hard as tempered steel.

"Patronize? What are you talking—"

"Where have you been?" she shouted. I had to hold the phone away from my ear. "I've left a million messages."

"I've been home, sleeping with Jordan Marsh. That is, if you believe the newspapers." Putting my feet on my desk, I settled back in my chair. "And, since I was in the throes of unbridled lust, I turned my cell phone off. Any other questions?"

Silence greeted that announcement. Score one for the home team.

"I have no idea what you're talking about," Mother huffed. "But something must be done. Right now! All these people are out front and they're running off my business."

"Having fun getting to know the network affiliates up close and personal?" I couldn't keep the smirk out of my voice. "One could have predicted that the prospect of appearing on the national news would have a chilling effect on your clientele."

"This is not funny."

"From where I sit, it is. Remember, Mother, you wouldn't talk this adventure over with the Big Boss. You dove in headfirst without checking for rocks."

"You don't have to gloat." Her voice had lost its fight. "I admit, I didn't think it through. This whole thing hasn't turned out quite the way I planned."

"Nothing ever does, Mother."

"I need your help. We can't get a moment's peace as long as our virgin is in residence. People are climbing the trellises to catch a glimpse. I need you to come get her."

"What do you propose I do with her?"

"I don't know—keep her at your place or something."

If I didn't know better, I would say my mother sounded harried. I sorta liked it—Mona the control freak, suddenly out of control. "My condo is booked solid. Any other ideas?"

"You'll think of something. You always do."

Before I could answer, Mona rang off.

EIGHT fifteen on a Thursday morning and I was already shell-shocked. I had completely lost my edge and life was spinning out of control. Even though the line was dead, I still held the receiver.

Miss Patterson found me like that, staring into space. "What happened to you? Are you all right?"

"You *are* kidding, right?" Slowly, I replaced the receiver. "How about you?"

She shrugged. "About the same."

I took my feet off the desk, then pushed myself upright. "You know what they say . . ."

"If you're not moving forward, they're gaining on you."

I slapped her on the back. "Precisely!" I grabbed my Birkin from the couch where I had thrown it, then stepped into my private restroom for some much needed repair. "I need to make a surgical strike on Pahrump."

"Do you want me to call downstairs for a car?"

"I don't have time to drive. See if the helicopter is available. Oh, and find some place to stash mother's virgin, someplace secure." My reflection staring back at me wasn't as bad as I feared, nor as good as I hoped—not that it ever was. "Then, call the district attorney's office—I need to talk with our dear friend, Mr. Lovato."

"Anything else?"

"Yes, I need to talk to Delphinia."

"Delphinia, the wedding planner, from the chapel downstairs?"

"How many Delphinias do you know?" My trip to Pahrump shouldn't take more than an hour, then another hour to fit in the DA and thirty minutes of wiggle room. "Tell her I'd like to stop by at eleven, if that's convenient."

"Is there a wedding I don't know about?"

Repairs made, I brushed down my sweater and slacks one more time in a futile attempt to establish some sense of order. Yesterday's events had started me pinging around like a pinball. Today, the game played on. At some point, I sure wished whoever was playing me would tilt the game and drop me into a hole.

"Are you going to make those calls?" I asked, as I breezed out of the bathroom on my way out the door.

"Are you going to answer my question?" She followed me into the front office.

I paused with my hand on the doorknob. "Do you really expect me to?"

"Call me a cockeyed optimist." She moved around her desk. "There were several messages from Teddie on the voicemail. Something about your phone not working."

"It works fine . . . when I turn it on." I reached into my pocket and extracted the thing, then handed it to her. "You keep it for now. Get the messages off. If anyone calls, tell them I've gone over the fence."

"Okay." She looked at me a moment, weighing her words. "Is Jordan Marsh really staying at your place?"

"Yes. I have him handcuffed to the bed. Can you hold down the fort while I'm gone?"

She gave me an exasperated look. "Brandy will be in at ten. There won't be anything the two of us can't handle."

"Don't bet on it."

"Lucky?" She paused, looking uncomfortable. "The picture in the paper—the one of Teddie and the singer? Well, I don't think it's what it appears to be."

"Nothing ever is." I opened the door to leave. "Remember that."

THE helicopter was already spooling-up when I arrived at the helipad perched atop one wing of the hotel. Crouching, I ran under the whirling blades, and ducked into the copilot seat. Headset on, Dane grinned back at me from the pilot's position.

"What are you doing here?" I shouted over the whine of the engine and the whap of the accelerating blades as I wrestled with the door. Finally, the lock dropped, securing it in place.

He shook his head and pointed to his headset. Thrusting an identical set toward me, he then gave the thumbs-up to an attendant on the helipad who scurried out of the way. Once I had my headset in place, the noise level dropped to a tolerable roar and I could hear Dane's voice clearly.

"Fasten your seat belt." He waited while I complied. "Temps are up and everything's in the green. Are you all set?"

"You *do* know how to fly this thing, don't you?" Dane wasn't one of our regular pilots. "I didn't know your job description for the Gaming Control Board included flying hotel execs around."

"I'm moonlighting. It's good practice." Gently pulling on the collective, he eased the flying machine into the air, glancing around as he did so. Once clear of the hotel, he pushed the stick forward, lowering the nose and starting us in forward flight. With a grin at me, he threw us hard into a bank toward Pahrump.

Somehow I resisted grabbing for a handhold. While I didn't find flying terrifying, it wasn't exactly as comfortable as terra firma.

But it was exhilarating . . . and liberating. Up here, my problems couldn't follow me. For a brief few moments I was free. "So this is practice for you? I can't tell you how much better *that* makes me feel. When are you going to get good at it?"

He scoffed. "Is that a challenge?"

The man thought I was joking. "Show me what you got, rotor-head."

Once we cleared McCarran airspace and the bounds of civilization, he dropped us down until we skimmed no more than twenty feet above the ground, which whizzed underneath us at dizzying speed. With a flick of his wrist, Dane popped us around a tall Joshua tree. Another tree, another flick of the wrist as we raced toward the Spring Mountains. When the mountains filled the windscreen, Dane jerked on the collective and yanked the stick back, sending us skyrocketing into the air. The Gs forced me back and down into the seat. Up and over we went, then back down to the desert floor on the other side. As the negative Gs worked on my stomach, I was glad I hadn't had much breakfast.

Racing along, nose down, the ground so close I felt I could reach out and touch it, we scared a herd of burros. The creatures ran in front of us, then scattered.

My worries fell away, leaving only the here and now. Both Dane and I had stupid grins on our faces.

Too soon, the sobering silhouette of Mona's Place appeared in front of us.

"You want to go around the patch some more? I know this dry lakebed west of here. We could really put this puppy through its paces," Dane said.

"I would like that, but today I don't have the time."

"Perhaps another time?"

I looked at him and saw the unspoken question in his eyes. I guessed he'd seen Norm Clarke's column as well. Boy, bad news sure traveled fast. "Perhaps."

As we closed in, the full extent of the media circus Mother had created became apparent. An invading horde of television crews, reporters, picketers, and curious onlookers amassed in the parking lot in front of Mona's. Behind them, on the other side of the street, a dozen or more television trucks sat side by side. Their relay booms extended, the vehicles looked like catapults, cocked and ready to throw digitized news to the world.

"Out of the frying pan and into the fire," I said, to no one in particular as Dane lowered us to the landing pad, a scoured rectangle of desert behind the main building.

"What is our mission?" Dane asked, looking out the side door at the ground.

"Rescue a virgin in distress."

As the skids settled on solid ground, he whipped his head around. "You *are* shitting me, aren't you?"

"Unfortunately not." I opened my door. "Keep the thing running, okay? We're going to have to make a quick getaway." I ripped off my headset before he could reply, jumped down, and bolted for the back door. Where the heck was everybody?

I found Trudi, mother's chief cook, bottle washer, right-hand man—and my surrogate parent—nervously smoking a cigarette in the kitchen. A trim woman with an overabundance of nervous energy, she started in the minute she spied me. "Your mother has really gone and done it now." She took a long drag, then stuck the butt under the faucet and doused it with a burst of water. "The girls are in their rooms. Some of them are hiding. Others are hanging out the windows showing everything they got to the cameras. Business has evaporated like a stream in the summer sun. What was your mother thinking?"

"I don't know why you're surprised," I replied. "It's not like this is the first time she has leapt before she looked." I shot the woman a grin. "Remember the time she and the girls had a bake sale at the elementary school to benefit the Girl Scouts? I thought the members of the PTA were going to burn her at the stake."

We both smiled at the memory.

Trudi lowered her voice as if she were telling me a secret, "The sheriff told all those crazies out front he'd shoot anyone who sets foot on the porch. I tell ya, that man means business. He peppered one guy who was climbing up the gutter pipe."

"He shot a reporter?" Why did he get to have all the fun?

"With rock salt—probably stung like hell, but didn't hurt him none." She flicked the butt. We both watched as it traced a perfect arc, then landed in the trashcan near the door—a center shot. "So far he has them scared. Don't know how long that'll last."

"Where's Mother?"

"She and that poor girl have barricaded themselves in your mother's suite on the top floor."

As I turned and ran for the stairs, Trudi's voice trailed after me. "Be careful, she has her twenty-gauge and it's loaded for bear. If you don't announce yourself, she'll perforate you for sure."

In the foyer, I paused for a moment. Opening the front door a couple of inches, I stood behind it so no one would see me, and stuck my face to the opening.

A shotgun across his lap, his hat pulled low, the sheriff sat in one of mother's Queen Anne chairs. His feet crossed on the porch railing, he balanced on the rear legs, his bulk straining the delicate chair. If he broke the thing, he'd better start running and not look back—Mother was armed. And we all knew she was dangerous.

"Sheriff, it's me, Lucky," I whispered, loud but not too.

He turned his head toward me.

"Don't look at me."

He snapped his head back to neutral. "How'd you get here?" he asked, out of the side of his mouth.

"Didn't you hear the helicopter?" The guy must've been tail-end Charlie in sheriff school. "We're parked out back. I'm going to take the girl with me, but I need you to provide cover—keep the sharks at bay. Can you do that?"

"Yes, Ma'am."

"Remember, I'm one of the good guys—don't shoot me and, if

you want to live until lunchtime, don't even think about aiming toward the helicopter. Got it?"

"What? You think I'm stupid?"

He really didn't want me to answer that question, so I pretended it was rhetorical. "You work your way around back. I'll go get the girl."

"That ought to take some of the fuel off the fire." He stood, hitched his pants up, belched, then ambled toward the south end of the house.

I lost sight of him as he turned the corner, heading around back.

Mother's suite occupied the attic level, four flights up. At the top of the stairs, out of breath and short on patience, I fisted my hand and banged on Mother's door. "Don't shoot, Mother. The cavalry has arrived."

I heard Mother chamber a round in her pump-action. I stepped to the side in case she had a twitchy trigger finger. The bolt hit the stops with a bang, the door opened a couple of inches, then the barrel poked out. I almost peed my pants.

Mother's face appeared, then the door opened wider.

"I had to make sure it was you," she said matter-of-factly, glancing along the hallway to ensure I was alone.

"Who else calls you *Mother*? And, for God's sake, don't stick the gun out where someone could grab it." I pushed the shotgun's barrel aside as I stepped into the room.

"Someone could pretend to be you." She pulled herself to her full height—I still had a few inches on her. "And, for the record, you're being insulting—I only have one illegitimate child—and that would be you."

"I should get that in writing, but I don't have the time. And, for the record, no one in their right mind would pretend to be me." I glanced over her shoulder, scanning the room. "Now, where is the prisoner I'm supposed to break out of this loony bin?"

Motioning toward her bed, she stepped aside.

I followed her gesture. My breath caught in my throat.

From her perch on the edge of Mother's four-poster, an exquisitely beautiful young woman stared at me with luminous brown eyes. Her olive skin was a soft, smooth canvas stretched over high cheekbones. Her eyes tilted up at the corners, enhancing her exotic aura. Full lips softened the angles of her face. A shiny cascade of golden brown hair fell over her shoulders. Fragile and trim like a delicate porcelain doll, she appeared as if she would shatter at the slightest touch.

Dressed in a khaki skirt and a starched white shirt, her hands tucked under her thighs, her long brown legs dangling over the edge of the elevated bed, she stared at me. Her eyes held the terror of the hunted, not the cold-blooded calculation of the hunter.

"Mother, what have you done?" I whispered half to myself as I motioned to the young woman. "Come," I said to her. "Let's get you out of here."

THE heartwarming thumping of the helicopter at full rpm greeted us as I eased open the back door. Her birdlike hand clutched lightly in mine, I led the young girl outside.

The sheriff, his several deputies, and most of Mother's staff formed a phalanx, keeping the reporters and photographers well away from our path to the helicopter.

"We'll have to run for it," I shouted as I took off, pulling my charge in tow.

Dane had opened both of the doors facing us, and we dove in, me in the front, the girl in the back. Once he had us, Dane lifted the bird and headed for home.

As I buckled the young girl in, she started to cry—tears tracing a sad trail down her cheeks. My heart threatened to break as I placed a headset over her ears and adjusted the mike close to her lips.

Once I settled myself, I said, "Sweetheart, what's your name?"

"Arrianna."

"Well, Arrianna, relax. I'm Lucky." I hooked a thumb at our pi-lot. "And this is Mr. Dane. We've got a nice safe place for you to rest."

"I think I've made a big mistake," she choked, her voice a tor-tured whisper.

"The deed isn't done, yet." I reached around and squeezed her hand. "You still have time to change your mind. I'll help you, whatever you decide."

She looked at me with those mesmerizing eyes, now red with tears.

The trip back to the Babylon wasn't nearly as much fun as the trip out.

Dane and I sat in silence as Arrianna quietly cried.

IF I didn't know better, I would've said Miss Patterson was showing her passive-aggressive side. In my absence, she had reserved the second largest bungalow in the Kasbah, Bungalow Two, for Arri-anna, and had charged it to me. Right now, I wasn't in the mood to quibble.

As I bustled about, pointing out the various features of one of our finest rooms to Arrianna, it occurred to me I was talking to myself. She wasn't listening. Not only that, she wasn't following me, either. Retracing my steps, I found her standing in the main room of the suite looking like a lost puppy caught in the middle of rush-hour traffic.

"This is amazing," she said, her eyes as big and bright as a har-vest moon. "How much does this cost a night?"

"With staff, twenty grand."

"That's more than my father makes in a year." Her shock evident, she walked over to a wingback chair near the window. Her fingers traced the heavy brocade. She looked afraid to sit in it.

"What does your father do?"

"This and that—whatever he can get. He and my mother emi-grated from India when they both were in their twenties. My mother was Muslim, my father Hindu. He defied his family, renounced his religion, and married her anyway. With no family, no dowry, no nothing, they've had a tough road. They're living proof that true love doesn't put food on the table or a roof over your head." Her back to me, she stared out the window at the fountain burbling in the garden and cascading into the private pool.

"And what do they think about you auctioning yourself to the highest bidder?"

"They are very disappointed." Her shoulders sagged under the burden of expectation. "This is not what they wanted for me, but I will make it up to them. Next semester, I will join my boyfriend at Stanford Medical School. I'm going to be a pediatrician."

"Your boyfriend?"

"I know what you're thinking—Charles and I decided to stay pure until we both were absolutely ready."

"I see," I said, although the logic of her story was as convoluted as a mountain road. "No, I don't see, at all."

"Do you know how much it costs to attend a private medical school? Even with scholarships we will be buried under debt by the time we can actually earn a living. And we both won't earn much where we're going."

"Where is that?"

"Home to India, where the children die like flies and the world doesn't seem to care." Some of her fight came back as she talked. "What does it say about a world that sacrifices its children?"

As I looked at her I wondered, what indeed? I don't think my young friend saw the irony at all. Of course, I doubted she saw herself as the child she was.

"And Charles, what does he think?"

She deflated. "At first, he was okay with it. I mean, he's going to marry me because he loves me, right? Not because I'm a virgin."

"If he loves you, who came before is irrelevant."

She nodded as if I had confirmed a belief she held, but those close to her did not.

"What about now? Is he still gung ho?"

"He says so, but I think he's lying."

"Pragmatism is no match for love. Nobody wants to see their loved one in someone else's arms." Even thinking about Teddie and Reza Pashiri made my heart crack a little. With nothing else to add and at a loss as to how to comfort the girl, I turned to go. "I'll have someone bring you a change of clothes. You're about a size two, right?"

She nodded.

"Stay put, don't go wandering around. Since we picked you up in a hot pink helicopter with Babylon stenciled in chartreuse on the side, I think even reporters can put two and two together. Room service has anything you want. Don't be afraid to indulge. Eat, drink, and be merry."

"For tomorrow I die?"

"Poor proverb, sorry." I shrugged. "But hey, it's better than 'best laid plans,' don't you think?"

She just stared at me, her eyes blinking furiously. Then a grin split her face—it was breathtaking.

"That's better." I gave her a gentle hug. "Remember, the choice is yours."

"But your mother . . ."

I made a rude sound. "My mother is using you for publicity. I'd say she's gotten her money's worth already."

Chapter

T E N

eeling a bit guilty, I swung by my office to rescue my phone before I headed out for a tête-à-tête with Daniel Lovato. I could run, but it wasn't fair for me to hide, leaving my staff holding the bag.

Both my assistants were sitting behind their respective desks when I walked in. The clock read nine forty-five, yet Miss Alexander appeared hard at work. She'd come in early—good for her.

They both glanced up at my arrival, but it was Miss Patterson who started in. "The district attorney can give you from ten fifteen to ten thirty. Today he's at the civil division. That makes your eleven o'clock with Delphinia doable." She looked up from her notes and gave me a scowl. "Teddie has left ten messages. And your mother—"

The phone rang, interrupting her. She motioned for Brandy to

let it ring, then waited through the second ring. "That's probably
her now. She's positively apoplectic. She's certain your helicopter
went down somewhere in the desert. Last time she called she
wanted to alert the Civil Air Patrol and Search and Rescue."

"Glad to see things were pretty much same ol' same ol' while I
was gone."

That got a smirk from Brandy. Miss Patterson looked daggers
at her, and Brandy fell back to work.

"I'll take the call in my office." As I disappeared into my inner
sanctum, I said, "And I'll take my phone when you're done with it."
Kicking the door shut behind me, I reached across the desk,
grabbed the receiver, and hit the lit button. "Customer Relations,
Lucky O'Toole speaking."

"Lucky! Thank God!" Mona, as expected.

All my frustration focused into one white-hot needle between
my shoulder blades. "Mother, I've had enough of your act today. Do
you want to know how *my* morning started? Well, it started with a
hangover and went downhill from there. My virtue, or lack thereof,
was dissected in the morning papers, right under a picture of
Teddie in a lip-lock with a sweet young thing in California. Someone tried to run me over on the way to work, then you summoned
me to save your ass." I took a deep breath.

"Lucky, I—"

"Oh no, I'm just getting started." I was sure my voice could be
heard in Pahrump without the benefit of the phone line, but I
didn't care—yelling felt good, really good. "Do you know anything
about the young lady you're going to put on the block tomorrow?
Don't answer—the question was rhetorical. Seeing only a goose to
lay a golden egg, you jumped right in, didn't you? Did you know
she has a boyfriend?"

"Boyfriend?"

"They agreed to remain chaste until they both were ready."

"An archaic bit of romantic drivel."

Like spurs to the flank of a wild-eyed racehorse, mother's snotty remark shot me into orbit. The anger settled me down. My vision cleared, my voice lowered—I only shout when I am frustrated. When I am really mad, I tend to mix metaphors, my eyes get all slitty, and my words sharpen to a razor's edge. Mother couldn't see my eyes, but she could darn well hear the deadly tone to my voice. "Really? I find it refreshing. And I know you don't mean that—you of all people."

"Lucky, sweetheart, you have every right to be angry."

"Angry? I'm beyond anger. I'm disgusted—with you *and* with myself for not stopping you the other night. Now, that sweet young girl's first sexual experience will not be the gentle stroke of a lover, but a cold deflowering at the hands of the highest bidder."

"It was her choice . . ."

"Choice? My God, Mother! She's twenty-one. Making good choices at her age is a hit-or-miss thing. That's why the youngsters let us old people live—they count on us for good advice."

"Legally, she's an adult."

"Mother, if you value your life, steer clear of me for a while." With that I slammed down the receiver. God, that felt good! I took a deep breath then threw back my shoulders. I was back. Bring it on, world!

I burst out of my office door. "Okay, let's kick some ass and solve some of these problems. First, give me my phone. Second, I need a ride."

"Ferrari? Or will mine do?" Miss Patterson handed me my phone and extended her car keys.

I grabbed both. "Yours is perfect. Brandy, in the Bazaar there is a clothing store for tiny people like you. Find it and buy an outfit for our guest in Bungalow Two. She's about your size and age. Charge it to our office. Then, when we have the final tally on the costs being incurred for that same guest, apply the employee discount and send the whole tab to my mother—including the helicopter round-trip."

Miss Patterson raised her eyebrows, then grinned like a fool.

"What?" I asked.

"She's had this coming for a long time."

"See that?" I said to Brandy. "That's loyalty. You can earn your way to Heaven with that attitude."

Her eyes alight, Brandy reached under her desk, pulled out three perfect long-stem roses, one white, one yellow, and one red—each with little notes attached—and extended them to me. "From the same admirer," she said. "With the same message."

Grabbing them, I buried my nose in their heady aroma. Were these an act of passion or an act of contrition? Either way, they put a smile on my heart. "Could you put them in some water?" I handed the flowers back to Brandy, who nodded then set off to find a vase.

When she returned, I was hunched over her desk scribbling a note. I thrust it at her. "Hope you can read my chicken scratch. See if you can track that name down."

She nodded, her brows crinkled in thought, as she glanced at the name I'd written.

"Someone tried to run you over this morning?" Miss Patterson asked in a poorly disguised attempt to catch me off guard. "I couldn't help but overhear."

"It was a warning, nothing more. Don't worry about me."

"Actually, I was worried about my car."

MISS Patterson's ungainly little car squatted in its normal parking space, the one assigned to me on the executive level of the garage. I folded myself into the machine and piloted it out of the cavernous building and off toward the local government center, where the civil division of the district attorney's office had its new home.

With one hand, I flipped my phone open then pressed Teddie's number on the speed-dial with my thumb.

He answered on the first ring. "I am so sorry. Are you really mad?"

"Should I be?" Since I had no idea how to find the right balance between doormat and shrew, I kept my voice light, but noncommittal.

"Miss P told me about the picture in the paper. It was nothing. Really. We'd just finished a song on stage. You know the one that goes like this . . ." He hummed a few bars.

"One of my favorites."

"Reza joined me for the chorus. The next thing I knew she kissed me. I don't know, I guess she was carried away by the music or something."

Or something. I doubted there were too many women immune to Ted Kowalski in full entertainer mode. If he decided to go on the road, I had no idea how to reconcile myself to that. But that was a problem for another day.

"It didn't mean anything. But after the phone conversation, I can see where you might have gotten the wrong impression." Chagrin tinged his voice, but I couldn't detect a hint of guilt.

The thought had crossed my mind that the picture in the paper could just as easily have been of Jordan Marsh kissing me at the airport. That kiss hadn't meant anything either, but the papers would have had a field day regardless. The old proverb about throwing stones and glass houses leapt to mind. "So the roses were a peace offering?"

"Hell no. They were because I love you."

He said it so easily, with such graceful ease. Why couldn't I? "They're beautiful by the way. Thank you. So, things are going well in California?"

"They offered me a recording contract."

I let out a war whoop. "That's wonderful!"

"We're still working out the details. I'll tell you all about it when I see you. You wouldn't happen to know where Rudy Gillespi is, would you? I could use his expertise in finalizing the contract."

I went all still. Had someone let the cat out of the bag? "I don't keep tabs on Rudy. Why would you think I would know where he is?"

"With you guys being friends and all, I just thought you might know if he's in town."

I knew better than that—he was in my guestroom in bed with Jordan Marsh, but I didn't tell Teddie that, either. "I'm pretty sure he's in Vegas. Want me to make an appointment for you?"

"Thanks, but I can do it. So, how's your life? It must be a real humdinger if you left your phone at the office. Anything I can do?"

That simple question broke the dam, releasing a torrent. I started with the emptiness I felt at him being gone and finished with Mona's little foray into the legal slave trade. Of course I edited my story somewhat—Jordan Marsh and Rudy Gillespi ended up on the cutting room floor. Their story was not mine to tell.

Teddie listened through it all without interrupting. When I had finished, he waited, then, his voice quiet and still with a hint of menace in it, he asked, "Somebody tried to run you over?"

"It was just a warning. If the guy had wanted to kill me, he would have."

"*That* makes me feel better." Teddie's voice sounded harsh and protective at the same time. "Was this the first warning?"

"Yesterday I found a note in crayon on my windshield."

"So, he's escalating. I'm coming home."

"To do what? Put me under armed guard? It's fight weekend and I'm already drowning. There's nothing you can do." As I pulled up to the kiosk at the government center parking garage, I lowered my window. Barely able to reach the button, I managed to punch it and claim my ticket. "Finish your work in California, then come home. When do you think that might be, anyway?"

"Maybe Friday, late, but for sure Saturday, if you're positive you'll be okay. We have a couple of studio sessions the next two days; then I need to meet with my new agent. Your Ms. One-Note Wylie agreed to represent me."

"Two days? I guess I can survive."

"You damned well better. I'd be lost without you." Teddie sounded like he meant it, making my heart soar. "I know it's futile to ask you to back off this Neidermeyer thing, but couldn't you keep Jeremy or Romeo close by at least until I get there? It would make me feel better."

"I'll try," I fudged. The last thing I needed was to be put on a leash. "But I promise, I won't be stupid." Having someone care about me wasn't the burden I'd always envisioned. This being-in-love was heady stuff.

"I guess that will have to do. So you're not mad?"

"No." After circling the garage several times, I found a parking place and swung into it with five minutes to spare. "I needed some time to find my footing."

"We're cool, then?"

"Totally." I grabbed my Birkin and levered myself out of the car. "But promise me one thing. If you ever want someone else, if you fall out of love with me, let me be the first to know about it."

"If you promise me the same."

"Scout's honor."

GOVERNMENT buildings the world over have the same feel, as if there's one uninspired architect responsible for them all. Daniel Lovato's office was no different. Decorated in what could only be described as upscale institutional (the furniture was made from wood rather than metal, and carpet rather than linoleum graced the floors), with a large rendition of the seal of the state of Nevada looming ominously over the waiting area, the place felt foreboding and tragic. Nothing good happened here. Oh, the citizens of the Silver State were protected and life as we knew it was preserved, but this was not a happy place.

I didn't envy Daniel his job—I don't know how lawyers stay sane, dealing with all the ugliness life has to offer day-in and day-out. Of course, that assumed a great deal about their mental health to start with . . .

Daniel rose when I entered his office, leaned across his desk, and extended his hand. "Lucky."

Attired differently than the last time I'd seen him, today he wore a tailored blue suit, his hair was slicked straight back, and a bright purple and green shiner surrounded his left eye, which was still swollen half-shut.

I took his hand then seated myself in the chair he indicated. "I hope you won."

"What?" He stepped around his desk and took the chair next to mine, shifting slightly so he faced me.

"You look as if you've been moonlighting as Tortilla Padilla's sparring partner."

"Oh, a mishap in the dark. It's nothing." Anger flashed across his face then disappeared.

There was a story there, I thought. I wondered what it was.

"What can I do for you?" One elbow on the arm of his chair, his hands clasped, Daniel leaned slightly toward me.

"You can tell me why you're pushing so hard on Jeremy Whitlock."

"He had opportunity and means."

"So did you and your wife."

Daniel raised his eyebrows, but he didn't look surprised.

"What's Jeremy's motive?" I asked.

"That's why we're pushing." Daniel leaned back in his chair and crossed his arms in front of him. "What motive would Glinda or myself have?"

"I've heard whispers of a gambling debt."

"That's absurd!" Daniel launched himself out of the chair and began pacing. "You and I have known each other for a long time. Does that ring true to you?"

"No, but frankly, none of this makes any sense."

"Somebody hated Ms. Neidermeyer enough to kill her—pretty simple." His back to me, Daniel stared out the window behind his desk.

"Yeah, but it's the *who* and the *why* that are a bit confusing."

Before Daniel could reply, Glinda Lovato, sheathed in bright orange, flew into the room, unannounced and apparently unrepentant. "Daniel, you have to pick up Gabi from school this afternoon."

The district attorney whirled around at the sound of his wife's voice. He took refuge behind his desk as Glinda advanced on him.

Her purse over her arm, she tugged at the fingers of a peach glove. Once uncovered, she waggled her hand under his nose. "I'm in desperate need of a manicure and the only time open was three o'clock."

Daniel's eyebrows lowered, forming a dark line. "Glinda, I'm busy." He motioned toward me.

"Oh." Glinda gave me a haughty look. "What are you doing here? Trying to keep one of your friends out of jail?"

"Occupational hazard."

She gave me a quizzical look—no one had ever accused Glinda Lovato of holding aces high—three syllables was about her max. "Okay. Well, gotta scoot. Oh, and Daniel, remember I'll be late. Don't forget the kid. And try to cook something edible this time, would you?"

Daniel eased himself into his chair as his wife breezed out. While his face was devoid of expression, his eyes—well the one nonswollen eye anyway—held hatred.

"I don't know what they're going to put on my headstone, but it won't be that I married well." For a moment a window to his soul opened, then, when he realized what he'd said, it slammed shut. "O'Toole, what exactly did you come here for today?"

"Like you said, we've known each other a long time. And in all that time, I've never known you to go out on a limb. But that's what you're doing with Jeremy Whitlock. You don't have anything on him that would get you over the beyond-a-reasonable-doubt hurdle. If you go forward with what you've got, his lawyer will shred your case in court—assuming you get that far."

"Is that a threat?"

"No, it's the truth. You're not stupid, Daniel. I shouldn't have to spell it out for you. All your pushing does nothing but arouse suspicion."

"Whose?"

"Mine, for starters." I rose to go. "And I won't stop digging until I find the buried treasure."

MY thoughts bouncing and tumbling like a barrel plunging over Niagara Falls, I returned to the Babylon on autopilot—unaware of my surroundings. I don't know how long I sat, engine idling, in my original parking space, before my focus returned.

I hated when I did that.

Not really remembering anything about the drive, I always worried I had run over somebody and not even noticed. I would never admit to it, but, on the off chance something horrible had happened, I made a circuit around the car just to make sure there weren't any dents or blood—or someone clinging for their life to a fender.

Luck was with me—the car was clean and I had three minutes to get to the Temple of Love.

I saw Rudy pacing nervously in front of the wedding chapel as I passed Samson's Salon—the Babylon's purveyor of beauty. It was housed in its own ziggurat, complete with huge wooden doors to ward off an invading horde, a waterfall in the reception area, and a multitude of flowering plants cascading from its stepped exterior—all of which I'm sure the women found mildly interesting. But it was the herd of Samson look-alikes, beefy, buff, and beautiful—and waiting to do their bidding—that the women found most appealing. Resisting the urge to take a peek inside, I kept motoring toward Rudy, who hadn't noticed me, yet.

An absolute Greek God, the man always took my breath away. Jet-black curls, tan, flashing robin's-egg eyes, a soft smile, and a body like Michelangelo's David—at least the parts I was privy to matched up pretty well—he caused heads to turn everywhere he went.

One time I had remarked to Jordan that two such beautiful men not being interested in the female of the species was such a waste. Quick as a rattler, he'd fired back a line from our favorite movie, *Victor-Victoria*: "Honey, I can assure you it's not wasted."

Well, maybe not to him, but as a card-carrying member of the World Association of Red-Blooded Women, I mourned the loss of two gorgeous hunks from the gene pool so much that, every time I saw the two of them, I felt like holding a candlelight vigil.

"Have you been waiting long?" I asked, as I skidded to a stop beside Rudy.

He gave me a look I'd last seen on a kid's face when he was stumped in the last round of the National Spelling Bee. I had no idea such a simple question could be as hard as spelling *appoggiatura* or *serrefine* or *gallinazo*—or some other ridiculous word never used in polite conversation.

Grabbing my arm, he pulled me into the mouth of a nearby hallway. "We need to talk." He didn't stop until we were at the very end, far from eavesdroppers, my arm still clutched tightly in his grasp. "I can't do this."

Squelching my rising panic, I kept my face calm, my voice casual. "Can't do what?"

"This!" He gestured back toward the Temple of Love. "I can't go through with it. I can't let Jordan ruin his life for me."

So the great cosmic joker had appointed me the Swami of Love. Me, of all people! An emotional cripple who couldn't tell the man who had stolen my heart that I loved him. I felt like an imposter pretending to be a surgeon, scalpel poised over the patient . . .

I took my time choosing my words. "Seems to me that's Jordan's choice to make."

"But he's giving up everything." Rudy's voice cracked.

"No, he's giving up a career. In exchange, he's getting everything he's ever wanted—the chance to live openly with you, the person he loves."

"You think?"

I nodded.

"How do you know?" Rudy asked, his voice a whisper.

"He told me so. Right after I asked him if he was batshit insane."

That got a fleeting grin from the nervous bride.

"Rudy, what I know about love wouldn't fill an index card . . . if you write big . . . in crayon. So keep that in mind when weighing what I tell you." I pried his fingers from my arm, then put my arm around his shoulders as I led him back to civilization. "The people in our lives, our relationships, are the only things that really matter. Get those right, you get life right. The rest of the stuff is just details."

He'd calmed down a bit by the time we reached the doors to the Temple of Love, but his eyes still looked troubled.

"You look like you could use a drink, relax a little."

"It's eleven o'clock in the morning. And what about our meeting?"

"It's five o'clock somewhere, and Delphinia will wait." My arm still around his shoulders, I steered him further into the Babylon's mall of shops and straight to the counter at the Daiquiri Den. "Let me buy you something fruity and sinful." I kept my face passive.

He narrowed his eyes at me, then grinned. "You're lucky we've been friends forever or I'd have to spank you."

"Promises, promises." I surveyed the drink menu even though I knew it by heart. "Pick your poison."

He chose a frozen piña colada.

"The same, but make mine a virgin," I said to the girl behind the counter. "I always like saying that—I don't know why."

"I'm not even going to think about what that says about your sexual fantasies," Rudy said, as he took his drink from the young woman. She gave him a shy smile.

"Charge them to me, Gloria," I said, when she handed me my drink.

"You got it, Ms. O'Toole."

Rudy took a long gulp of his colada as we wandered back to the Temple of Love. "Everybody here knows who you are. What's that like?" Rudy asked.

"You'll find out for yourself soon enough."

"Now there's a sobering thought." Forgoing the straw, Rudy tilted the glass and began chugging.

IN designing our wedding chapel, the Big Boss had hoped to re-create a true Babylonian temple, which I thought ill-advised. After all, the Babylonians were pagans and had a nasty habit of sacrific-ing women and small children. Waving away my concerns, the Big Boss reasoned that since most folks were a little unclear as to the identities of the first four presidents of our great country, they wouldn't have a clue as to some of the less savory Babylonian reli-gious practices. I couldn't argue with him there, but the whole thing gave me the creeps. Each time I stepped through the door into the cool interior, I had to stifle the urge to look over my shoulder for a guy with a knife. Was that Freudian? Who knew?

Built out of huge rectangular blocks of sandstone, The Temple of Love reminded me of that Egyptian temple someone had recon-structed at the Metropolitan Museum of Art in New York, The Temple of Dendur. Massive in exterior appearance, both temples were small and intimate inside. Open flame sconces lined the walls, casting a warm glow. Urns of reeds softened the corners. Empty by design, the center of the room was a blank canvas to be painted with the desires of the marrying couple.

A bundle of energy and discretion, Delphinia rushed to greet us. "Ms. O'Toole, good to see you."

Of medium height and weight, with limp brown hair brushing her shoulders, sensible shoes, and uninspired attire, Delphinia blended into the background and did little to inspire confidence—until she looked at you. The clearest violet, her eyes were the eyes of an old soul.

"This is Mr. Gillespi." I motioned to Rudy at my side, who was draining the last of his drink. "He'll be making all of the arrangements."

Her pad at the ready, her pen poised, Delphinia asked, "So this is to be Sunday afternoon, correct?"

Rudy nodded. "Five o'clock, if that's possible."

"Of course." Delphinia wrote the time on her pad. "And what is the name of the bride?"

Rudy and I looked at each other. "That will remain confidential for now, but the paperwork will all be in order," I said.

The wedding planner didn't miss a beat. "Okay, do you know what kind of wedding you would like? Elvis impersonator? Thematic? Lately, for some odd reason, vampires have been popular." She looked at us over the rim of her glasses with those mesmerizing eyes. "I can tell you, you haven't lived until you've seen a minister dressed as Dracula, complete with fake blood and fangs, trying to say, 'Dearly Beloved, we are gathered here today . . .'"

Rudy swallowed hard, then cleared his throat. "It won't actually be a wedding . . ." He trailed off, looking uncomfortable.

"A commitment ceremony, perhaps?" Delphinia asked, her eyes full of understanding.

"Yes, that's it." Rudy seemed to find his footing. "Since Nevada has constitutionally banned marriage between members of the same gender, we will have a ceremony here, then a legal union when and wherever it might actually be possible."

"That sounds wonderful." Delphinia scratched a few notes. "And would you like your ceremony to be held here in the temple?"

"No," I interjected. "We'll be having it in Mr. Rothstein's apartment."

"I see." If she was surprised, she didn't show it.

Out of the corner of his mouth, Rudy said, "The Big Boss agreed to that?"

I shook my head. "He doesn't know about it yet."

Both Delphinia and Rudy looked at me with owl eyes.

"Oh ye of little faith," I intoned. "Let me handle the *where,* you guys work on the *when* and the *how.*"

The two of them fell deep into conversation about flowers.

I set forth to nail down the Big Boss.

AFTER looking in all the usual places, querying his assistant, and rejecting the idea of calling my mother, I finally located my father in the Spa, finishing one of his thrice-weekly workouts with his personal trainer.

His face red, he gave me a nod as he pounded out the last few reps of shoulder presses, then dropped the weights, which bounced off the rubber floor. Struggling to catch his breath, he wiped his face with a towel.

"I can't remember ever seeing you in here," he said, squinting one eye as he looked up at me. He looked vigorous and alive—taut and tight in all the right places with not even the hint of a paunch. He could have passed for a man twenty years younger, in the prime of life—if you overlooked the angry red scar peeking out of the top of his shirt. Only a couple of months from open-heart surgery and the guy was throwing iron around like Arnold Schwarzenegger.

Had the doctor cleared him to exercise or was my father blithely ignoring medical wisdom? Since there wasn't anything I could do about it, I really didn't want to know. Problems I can't fix make me as twitchy as a drunk with a bottle he can't open.

"Exercise makes me itch," I said. I took his outstretched hand and pulled him to his feet. "Besides, one time, just for giggles, Miss Patterson strapped a pedometer on me. Fifteen miles—that's what I cover in an average day."

"That's activity, not exercise. You've got to get your heart rate up."

Thinking of Teddie, I said, "Oh, I get my heart pumping."

He shot me a sideways glance. "Sex doesn't count."

"Where's the justice in that?" I walked with him as he thanked his trainer, then pushed through the doors to the elevator. "Do you have a few minutes? I need to talk to you privately."

"Come on up with me. I have a massage scheduled, but the masseuse won't be there until twelve. That gives us fifteen minutes. Is that enough?"

"Sure."

He held the elevator door for me, then followed me inside, put his card in the slot and punched the button. "I heard you took a chunk out of your mother's ass this morning."

I could see the reflection of his scowl as the doors closed. "She had it coming."

"Maybe so, but are you sure you weren't a bit harsh?"

Well-intentioned or not, I didn't need my recently found father trying to broker peace between my mother and me. We'd been firing salvos across each other's bows for a long time now. "Look," I said, "let me save you the breath. I know Mother has a heart as big as all outdoors—she rescues everything and everybody—or at least tries to. However, she has an annoying habit of leaping without looking, and then expects me to clean up the mess. I'm trying to get her to pause before she takes that last step off the cliff, okay?"

"Okay."

"And, to be honest, I'm almost as mad at myself as I am at her," my reflection said to his. Talking in an elevator was always uncomfortable—too close to turn and look at the person, but awkward talking to a mirror image.

"Do you really think either of us could have stopped her?" The elevator dinged and he motioned for me to walk ahead.

"Probably not. She had the bit in her teeth."

"Your mother can handle herself; it's the girl I'm worried about." That's my father, hard-boiled exterior, gooey middle.

"Don't be. I have it under control." I cringed as I said it. Announcing control invited the Fates to throw curveballs.

"I also caught Norm Clarke's column," my father said, deftly conceding defeat. "Are you and Teddie okay?"

"Far as I know. I need more evidence than a picture taken in a public place, in front of a crowd, to convict him. Besides, people kiss me all the time. That doesn't mean I'm groping them in the cloakroom. Teddie deserves the same latitude."

"I hope that boy knows what he's got."

"If he doesn't, he's not the right guy for me." The words were true, but as I said them, my heart cracked a little. I'm not sure I could handle Teddie disappointing me.

"I also caught an innuendo in Norm's column about you." He pulled the towel from his neck and a bottle of water from the fridge in the bar. "Want one?"

I shook my head.

"Want to tell me about Jordan Marsh?"

"That's why I'm here, actually. I need your apartment for a wedding this Sunday afternoon."

His eyes grew wide as he tipped back his head, drained the water bottle, then wiped his mouth on the towel he still held in his other hand. "You and Teddie?"

"No, Jordan Marsh."

He blinked at me a few times. "You and Jordan Marsh?"

"No." I paused before I let the cat out of the bag. Jordan had asked me to do this, but still . . . I was intensely aware that I was teetering at the point of no return. "Jordan Marsh and Rudy Gillespi."

"For real?" My father couldn't hide his surprise.

I nodded, then shrugged. "In a way, I'm responsible. Three years ago I introduced them and have been running cover ever since. It was nothing new—I'd been doing the same for Jordan long before that."

"And here I thought you'd been shagging the biggest heartthrob on the planet off and on for years."

"Really?" It was my turn to be surprised.

"Everybody thought so," he assured me.

"I had no idea." The blood drained from my head and I felt woozy. "My sex life is a topic of conversation?"

"It is for your mother and me. I was speaking a bit broadly, but I doubt we were the only ones."

Oh, happy day.

"Come. Sit." He motioned to the couch in front of his wall of windows. He shook his head. "Jordan Marsh, gay? Who would have believed it?"

MY story complete and the Big Boss's complicity gained with a promise to join him for cocktails later, I made my escape as the masseuse arrived. Blond, willowy, and young, she didn't know it yet, but when my mother got a look at her she was as good as gone.

I reviewed my morning as I rode down in the elevator. So far I'd rescued a virgin, threatened the district attorney, and set in motion events that would derail a stellar career—and the day wasn't even half-over. Rather depressing, all things considered.

There was only one thing to do—eat.

The lunch crowd had yet to arrive in full force when I stepped in line at Nebuchadnezzar's, the Babylon's renowned buffet. I flashed my employee badge, grabbed a tray and plate, and then, like a kid in a candy store, made a reconnaissance of all the offerings. Never one to make snap decisions when it came to food, I loaded my plate with gustatory delights from five different continents, then took a seat at a two-top by the window.

The fall day in full bloom, I watched golfers do what golfers do on the Babylon's championship course as I tried to decide what foodstuff to attack first.

My phone rang, catching me with a mouth full of ribs. I wiped one hand then flipped the thing open. "O'Toole."

Flash Gordon lived by the motto, "Why waste time being cordial when you can be efficient?" "I'm in your office, why aren't you here?"

"My office is just a front where I enslave others to do my work so I can shirk my duties and hide out in Nebuchadnezzar's. Want some lunch?"

"You're buying," she said, then the line went dead.

.   .   .

FLASH made it, well . . . in a flash. I had barely plowed through three ribs and had a fork poised over the potato salad when she arrived.

She tossed her bag at my feet. "I found your Mary Swearingen Makepeace. You are *so* not gonna like it." She pointed at my plate. "But first, I've gotta get me one of those. I'm wasting away standing here."

As she sashayed away, I narrowed my eyes at her full-sized behind. She didn't seem in imminent danger of emaciation to me.

Stuffed into a pair of painted-on jeans, she balanced on towering hot pink stilettos. Her lush figure cinched in by a tight belt, her double denvers threatening to bust loose from her tight white tee shirt with Bob Marley stenciled on the front, Flash turned every male head in the place.

Like her wardrobe, everything about Flash Gordon was overstated, from her red hair to her full lips painted a pouty pink to her in-your-face personality. Hanging out with her was like being strapped to the back of a honeybee—exhilarating, nauseating, terrifying—and sometimes life-threatening. That girl had a nose for trouble.

God knew what she'd dug up on Mary Swearingen Makepeace. Milking me like this meant she'd found something good. Her stonewalling would normally light my short fuse, but since I had food to keep me happy, I let her have her fun.

I was busy stuffing a Chinese egg roll in my mouth when she returned. Two continents down, three to go, and I was already full. I couldn't remember being this much off my feed before—except for that time I got food poisoning and darn near died.

Flash plopped two fully laden plates on the table, then her heinie in the chair. "I'm a two-fisted eater. So sue me."

"I didn't say anything."

"Not out loud." She took a huge bite out of a hamburger, oozing cheese and mayo—a little splotch dribbled on her chin, but she didn't notice—or, if she did, she didn't care. With her mouth full, she leaned over and grabbed an egg roll off my plate, adding it to the pile on her's, then gave me a grin—hard to do with her mouth full.

I narrowed my eyes at her—she knew I considered swiping other people's food a capital offense.

She swallowed the bite of hamburger, then grabbed a cube of watermelon off my plate and popped it into her mouth, her eyes dancing with glee as they challenged me.

Pushing my plate out of her easy reach, I cleared the table in front of me.

"Is that all you're going to eat? Are you pregnant or something?" She eyed me, a look of horror on her face.

Crossing my arms, I raised one eyebrow at her. When I pointed to her chin, she dabbed at it with her napkin.

"Okay, okay." She wolfed another bite of burger then started paraphrasing the notes she kept in her head, her mind like a steel trap. "Do you remember a guy named Joseph Ferenti?"

"The name doesn't strike a chord."

"He was a fight promoter out of Atlantic City—strictly small-time. Twenty-five years ago he was put on trial here in Vegas on what the general consensus seemed to think were trumped-up charges."

"Charges of what?"

"Fight-fixing and some gambling anomalies—the paper didn't spell out the exact charges, but it sounded like he was making his own book, although I'm not sure. Does it matter?" She reached for my plate then yanked her hand back with a yowl when I slapped it. Shrugging, she wolfed another bite of burger while waiting for me to answer.

"I can get someone to search the court files if we need the particulars. Right now I don't think they matter."

Flash paused a minute, thinking. "Where was I . . . oh yes, anyway, many thought a wet-behind-the-ears assistant DA was trying to make a big splash. You won't believe who it was."

"Daniel Lovato."

She looked crestfallen. "Man, how'd you know?"

"I'm clairvoyant." I took a sip of water, then grimaced. Taste-less beverages are not my thing. I wondered, could taste-free bev-erages be an acquired taste? How would that work? The strangest details sidetracked me—should I be worried? "What happened to Mr. Ferenti?"

"Twenty years in the Big House."

I whistled. "Major time for a minor crook. So what does any of this have to do with Ms. Makepeace?"

"She was his squeeze. Apparently, Mr. Ferenti had some not-so-minor business associates. Lovato got the Feds to promise her im-munity and a spot in the witness protection program for her and her kid if she rolled on everyone. Since she and Mr. Ferenti weren't married, he couldn't block her testimony against him, so he got the book."

"And Daniel used her to clean house of all the other vermin."

Flash grabbed a glass of wine from the waiter before he had time to set it on the table and took a slurp. "Yup. It made his career."

"And Mary and her kid—Mr. Ferenti's child—disappeared," I said, thinking out loud.

"Now it's your turn." Flash leaned back, a satisfied look on her face. "What does this have to do with anything?"

"The Ferenti kid?" I raised my eyebrows at her and waited.

Flash thought for a moment—I could almost see the wheels spinning. Then she looked up, her eyes bright. "Numbers Neider-meyer?"

"We can't prove it . . . yet. But from what we have, and what you've given, we're pretty close to connecting some of the dots." I took a sip of my wine, swirling it around in my mouth before I swallowed. "What happened to Mr. Ferenti?"

"About five years after he was sent up, he lapsed into a coma and died. Apparently he had developed diabetes—he'd been com-plaining to the medical staff for months, but they ignored him,"

Flash said, as she eyed the now cold food on my plate. "Here's the interesting part—at the funeral, everybody said his kid was inconsolable—totally beside herself."

"And Ms. Makepeace?"

"She never really got back on her feet. Funny thing though, she died about the same time as her husband."

"Anything unusual about her death?" I said, as my thoughts whirled.

"You mean other than one shot to the head and her body found floating in the Hudson?" Flash polished off her burger then licked each finger, savoring the last tastes.

"Was anyone ever charged?"

Flash shook her head. "No. Obviously it reeked of a Mob hit, but that's as far as it went."

"And the grandmother? Don't tell me she was whacked, too?"

"No, heart attack. Not too long after her daughter's body was found."

First Numbers lost her father, then her mother, then her grand-mother—a chain of sorrow started by Daniel Lovato. Even though I couldn't prove it, I knew in my heart I had my first answer:

Numbers Neidermeyer had come to town for revenge.

Chapter

E L E V E N

Thankfully, the rest of our lunch passed in idle, more benign, conversation. Flash regaled me with her latest romantic conquest, while I sipped my wine and pretended not to be horrified. The woman left broken hearts scattered in her wake—a plethora of men used, abused, and totally ruined.

"One day you are going to meet a guy who can give as good as he gets." I shook my head, then drained the last drop of wine. "Paybacks are hell, girlfriend."

"My problem is I'm always hooking up with second-stringers—bottom-feeders looking for a meal ticket. I seem to scare away the quality meat."

"You do come on a bit strong. My mother used to tell me that, while men like a challenge, they don't want to be bludgeoned until they're on the ropes." I had no idea why I was spouting life-according-to-Mona-isms. After all, she wasn't the most reliable authority on men who didn't expect to pay for sex.

"What are you suggesting?"

Despite the challenge in Flash's voice, I waded into battle. "Tone down that effusive personality and dim the lightbulb. Sorta ease them into it—like putting a lobster in a pot of cold water, then turning up the heat. By the time they realize something's wrong, they're cooked."

"Subterfuge, I like it." She gave me an evil grin and waggled her eyebrows at me.

"Mother always told me I was smart enough to play dumb. While that is overstating, you do need to learn the benefits of the soft-sell."

"Is that how you got Teddie? He's totally a keeper."

"Unfortunately, I'm not very good at playing games—that's why I spent decades alone." I eyed my plate, the food now cold, and thought about snaking another egg roll—I didn't want a repeat performance of yesterday's swoon. But I couldn't work myself up to fried food that had gone soft, oozing grease. "With Teddie, I went the straightforward route: I hit him with a club, then dragged him back to my lair, and chained him to my bed."

"Bold."

"And a lie," I admitted with a sigh. "It was actually Teddie who used the straightforward method. First, he was my best friend, then he kissed me in Delilah's Bar and proceeded to show me he loved me. I couldn't resist."

"Jeez, who would want to?" Flash bounced to her feet, gave her mouth a swipe with her napkin, then threw it back on the table. "Are you finished? I gotta run—Tortilla Padilla is putting on a show for the press. Fighters aren't my normal gig, but he's such a tasty morsel, I can't resist a chance to catch him without his shirt."

"I'm headed there myself." We walked to the front counter, where I added a tip to the bill and paid it. "And, for the record," I said. "He's married with fifteen children."

Flash stared at me, momentarily speechless. "Fifteen?"

I nodded, and shrugged.

"Heck of a price to pay—guess he must be prime meat," Flash reasoned.

"Maybe so, but it doesn't sound like he spends much time on the hoof, so to speak."

Flash shot me an appreciative grin as she hooked her arm through mine. "So he's taken. That doesn't mean we can't drool."

The girl had a point.

THE Babylon's Grand Arena, Las Vegas's largest venue with seating for over thirty thousand fans, had hosted performers of every persuasion, from aging rockers to flamenco guitarists, from circus performers to Cirque du Soleil traveling shows, from exhibition basketball to bull riders. Patrons entered on the highest level, then filtered down to seats sloping to a sunken floor. Suspended from the ceiling high overhead, a latticework of scaffolding and walkways dangled like a net over the crowd. Depending on the show, lights, speakers, backdrops, stage sets, and the occasional warbler riding a crescent moon could be permanently affixed or raised and lowered using a series of cables and high-torque motors. Fights didn't require much staging—only lights, so the walkways above were empty.

A huge screen had been erected at the far end of the arena so the patrons who had paid several hundred dollars apiece to sit in the nosebleed section could actually see the fight. Standing at one of the entrances, I realized the screen wasn't superfluous, it was essential—the ring, erected on a raised platform in the middle of the floor, looked tiny from up here. And the boxers bouncing around in it looked more like toy figures ready for a game of sandbox war than grown men doing battle.

Standing in what would be the VIP section on Saturday night, a throng encircled the ring. Flash bounded down the stairs, taking two at a time—a feat in her stilettos—and pushed her way to ringside. As I took a more prudent journey to the floor, Flash squeezed in next to Paxton Dane. Apparently she greeted him, because I saw him turn and grin in response. Flash and Dane? Now that would be a pair. Was the world ready?

Ever the showman, Tortilla Padilla seemed to expand in front of a crowd, becoming larger-than-life. With each *ooohh* or *aaahh* from his admiring onlookers, he taunted his sparring partner, egging him on. The man would throw a punch, Tortilla would dodge then counter, punishing the hapless fellow. At the nauseating whump of his well-landed punch, Tortilla would raise his arms, urging the crowd to show its appreciation.

Leaning back against the railing in front of the first raised section, I crossed my arms, and closed my eyes. With two nights of iffy sleep and the morning I had had, I was running on fumes, too tired to even eat, which for me was a sign of impending death. Maybe I could catch a couple of winks this afternoon.

Lost in thought, I wasn't aware that Jerry had sidled in next to me until he spoke.

"You look like crap."

I didn't move, but opened one eye. "I keep wondering why I keep you as a friend. It must be because you're so good at brightening my day. What are you doing here?"

"I'm running security checks for the fight," he said. "And you?"

"In theory, I'm here to solve any problems that might arise during this punch-fest for the press."

"So you're not a fight fan?"

"Fighters are a bunch of overblown egos sacrificing their brains, what little they have, for the almighty dollar." That came out a bit harsher than I intended, so I elaborated. "I find the whole thing barbaric." I'm not sure that softened my response any.

Jerry gave me a sardonic grin. "I'll take that as a *no*."

Something flashed across the few synapses of mine that were actually firing. "Do you have a minute?"

"Sure, what's up?" Jerry looked interested.

"Let's find a couple of seats, then I'll tell you."

We trooped halfway up the stairs, then out into one of the empty sections where I chose two spots. Once settled, I said, "Remember the tape from the other night—the one of the twelfth floor."

"Yeah, I was the one who actually spliced that one together, so I remember it well."

"When Daniel left the room, he shielded his face. Do you remember which side?"

Jerry closed his eyes, and sat stock still, as if rewinding, then reviewing the tape in his head. "The left. Why?"

"One of those two women hit him."

Jerry looked at me as if I'd grown a second head. "No way."

"He didn't have a problem with his eye when I saw him in the laundry room. Then, a short while later, he shields his face as he leaves. And this morning he has a well-advanced shiner." I looked square at Jerry. "Daniel wasn't hiding his identity—we already knew that—he was hiding his eye. I'm sure of it."

"Somebody could have punched him later, after he left."

"If that was the case, why would he shield it from the cameras?"

Jerry thought for a moment. "I have no idea. Let's assume you're right, for argument's sake only. Why would either of them hit him?"

I could think of a couple of reasons, none of which I felt compelled to share right now.

"Beats me," I said, proud of myself. "And even if neither of them hit him, and he got his shiner later that night . . . well, that looks a bit suspicious, don't you think? He could've gotten it in a struggle."

"Or he could have walked into the bathroom door." Jerry put his feet up on the back of the seat in front of him and relaxed back. "There's just one tiny problem with your scenario."

"Proof. I know." The air escaped from my balloon of enthusiasm, leaving me flat. I felt defeated. There was a reason I wasn't a detective—I sucked at it.

All of a sudden I got this prickly feeling at the nape of my neck. I looked behind me. Seeing no one, I scanned the crowd below.

Not a face turned our way. Everyone seemed engrossed in Tortilla Padilla's antics. Then I saw her, hiding in the shadows of a doorway—a hint of orange.

Glinda Lovato. Staring straight at me.

She stepped out into the light. A defiant tilt to her chin, she held my eye. Then she disappeared.

THERE were so many ways the tortured little trio of the Lovatos and Numbers Neidermeyer could've gone down. Did Glinda kill Numbers in a fit of jealousy? Doubtful since Daniel had slept with half the female population of Vegas and they were still walking and talking. Did Numbers want to kill Daniel, and he did it to her first? How did the gambling debt rumor play into all of this? And the private book? And, come to think of it, why did the murderer dispose of the body in the shark tank, a very public venue where Numbers, or what was left of her, was sure to be found? Didn't a murderer usually try to conceal his crime? And, how the heck was I going to prove any of this?

Why was I trying? Oh yeah . . . Jeremy.

All these questions pinged around my brain as I wandered from the Arena back to the main hotel. All speculation and conjecture— no proof. My head hurt. I might have totally despaired and given up if it wasn't for someone trying to run me down this morning. I may not have any idea where this path would lead, but I sure was making someone nervous. Unwittingly, that someone's attempts to put me off the chase had fortified my resolve.

Lost in thought, I didn't see the hurtling body until it had crashed into my knees, bringing us both down.

Stunned, I rolled to a seated position and tried to reorient myself. A young girl untangled herself from my legs and jumped to her feet, ready to bolt.

"Whoa, there." I grabbed the tiny human torpedo by the hand, bringing her up short. "Not so fast."

As delicate as a hummingbird, her hand was cold and clammy.

Her dark eyes wild with fear, she looked like a cornered animal as she struggled to pull away from me.

Thin as a rail and not more than five years old, she had long dark hair, one side corralled with a pretty red bow. Her olive skin was flawless except for a fresh scar, still purple, running from her nose through her upper lip. Dressed in a smocked white dress, the front of which was embroidered over tiny pleats, thin white socks fastidiously turned down, and a pair of bright red Mary Janes that reminded me of the pair that took Dorothy home to Kansas, my tiny captive didn't seem like she was on the run—she must have family close by.

Surrounded by knees and thighs and still sitting on the ground, I felt as if I had fallen into a canyon of humanity. Looking up, I scanned the crowd streaming around us for a face that held the panic-stricken look of a parent who had lost a child. Nothing. No raised voices calling, either.

"What's your name?" I asked. Still gripping her hand, I pushed myself to my feet.

She looked up at me with those big eyes, now blinking in surprise, but said nothing.

Her stare gave me insight into how Gulliver felt in Lilliput, or how the giant felt talking to Jack after he'd climbed the beanstalk. "Your mother or father? Where are they?"

Big alligator tears leaked out of the girl's eyes. She swiped at them with the back of her free hand.

Yes, I have a knack with kids.

Clearly *that* was the wrong question. I narrowed my eyes at her. Or the wrong language.

"*¿Como se llama?*" What is your name?

Her eyes brightened, losing that wild animal look. "Maria José." Her voice soft and low, I had to bend down to catch her words.

"*Encantada*, Maria José. *¿Cual es tu apellido?*" What is your last name?

She gave me a blank look. Terrific. She didn't know her last name. *"Me llamo . . ."* My name . . . Now I was stumped. What *was* my name in Spanish? I knew the word for *luck*. But there was no really good translation for *lucky*—not for use as a name anyway. I settled for the appellation I abhorred. *"Me llamo Señorita O'Toole."*

A flicker of interest flashed across her features, but she still looked stricken. *"No puedo hablar con estranjeras."* I'm not supposed to talk to strangers.

"Ni yo, tampoco." Me neither.

That got a shy smile.

I proceeded to tell her that I wasn't a stranger—well, not much of one anyway—and I worked for the hotel, sort of like a policeman. She watched in amazement as I pulled out my phone, keyed Security, and asked if anyone had reported a missing child. No one had. Making a calculated guess, I bet the youngster had sneaked out of a room and gone exploring. I left her description with Security and told them she would be with me at the gelato stand.

"¿Gelado?" Maria José asked, brightening considerably.

"Si." As I lead her into the Bazaar, I told her I would help her find her family, but she was going to have to help me.

My untrained ear and her slight speech impediment made clear understanding of her rapid colloquial Spanish a bit of a stretch, but I listened intently as she told me her story. There was a plane ride with her mother and multiple siblings, and a very big car. Then a house with many rooms, a garden with birds in it, and her very own swimming pool.

The Kasbah. Now we were narrowing things down.

Suddenly the light dawned. *"¿Y tu padre, donde esta?"* And your father, where is he?

Another torrent of Spanish and my suspicions were confirmed. Young Maria Josè belonged to Tortilla Padilla.

Again I called Security and asked them to alert the Padilla family that I had found their wayward daughter and would be bringing her back in a bit. Mystery solved and crisis averted, I let Maria José linger over her strawberry gelato cone.

Hand in hand we strolled past the shops, the youngster gasping in delight at the riches in the window of the toy store. A beautiful little doll with long black hair and a lacy white dress caught her eye. Of course she was going home with it—my life had a shortage of little girls to spoil. I paid for our purchase and, when I presented the doll to her, she clutched it to her chest and gave me a million-watt smile. That smile was like an arrow to my heart—she totally had me.

Feeling slightly guilty that my joy was coming at the expense of a placated, but probably still slightly frantic, parent I moved us along through the casino into the quiet of the Kasbah.

Even through the solid wooden doors of Bungalow Seven, I could hear the raised voices of excited children. I started to ring the bell then decided that was pointless, so I knocked loudly.

I heard several shouts back and forth then the door flew open.

"Yes." A petite woman, long dark hair and laughing dark eyes, clad in blue jeans and a halter-top, looked at me. When her eyes trickled down to the child, they widened in surprise. "Oh! You've brought Maria José!"

I could see the woman's anger building, overriding her concern as she gave her daughter one of those parental looks my mother was so fond of when I was that age.

"Don't be angry. My name is Lucky O'Toole; I work for the Babylon. Your daughter asked my assistance in helping her find her father. He was just finishing his press conference, so I brought her back here."

The woman pushed her dark hair out of her eyes, and sighed as she looked at the little girl. "It's been quite a day," she said, to no one in particular. Then she bent and gave her daughter a hug and a pretend swat on the butt.

Straightening, she gave me a good look. "Thank you for bringing her back. My name is Carmen. Torti is my husband." She opened the door wider, sweeping an arm to the interior as she did so. "And these are our children."

Clutching her doll, Maria José darted around her mother and threw her body into the fray. Children cascaded from every piece of furniture and seemed to cover every square foot of floor space. Through the French doors, several more were visible doing cannonballs into the pool, then scrambling out to try it again.

Carmen had to shout to be heard as she grabbed my arm and dragged me inside. "Maria José is my Daddy's girl. I thought I had all the doors and windows locked, but she must have found one." Carmen shook her head then barked at a couple of the boys she thought were getting too rough.

They snapped to attention.

"I had put her down for a nap. She's the baby, and it's been a long, exciting day for her—a day of many firsts. Her first airplane ride, her first limo, her first time in Vegas. I love her dearly, but she has enough energy to light the Strip for a year! That girl will be the death of me. I turn my back and she disappears."

"So this is what fifteen children looks like?" I said, totally overwhelmed by the hurtling bodies and the cacophony of laughing voices.

"Sixteen, actually. We just got another six weeks ago." With a practiced dip, Carmen bent and grabbed a piece of discarded clothing from the floor. A quick command, and a sheepish boy, his head bowed, stopped his play. He took the garment from her outstretched hand, then disappeared toward the bedrooms to put it away as she had asked.

"Sixteen children? And you just got a new one? I thought you said Maria Jose is the youngest? I stood in the middle of the pandemonium, young bodies darting like bees around me, voices raised in excitement.

"Our children find us," Carmen said as she watched them, her arms crossed, her eyes alight, a smile tugging at her lips. "They are magic, no?"

Before I could answer, the front door opened with a bang, and another, larger body, added itself to the chaos. Tortilla Padilla, minus the gloves, but still dressed for the ring, shouted, "*¡Hijos!*" Kids!

Heads swiveled, voices shouted, children launched through the air like living missiles, as they flung their bodies at their father. With feet spread, he absorbed each one, grabbing them to him. Grinning from ear to ear, he looked lit from within.

Carmen watched it all, a bit misty-eyed. Finally, after Torti had hugged and spoken with each child, he turned toward his wife. The look he gave her . . . well, if a man looked at me like that, my life would be complete.

Carmen gave a subtle nod to her husband, who turned in the direction she had indicated.

A young boy, no more than eight, dripping wet from the pool, hobbled into the room, then stopped by the door. His foot was badly twisted underneath itself. Clutching the heavy drapes for support, he watched the other children. The young boy's face was serious; doubt clouded his black eyes. Unsure and self-aware, he hung back even though he practically vibrated with need.

Torti set the other children down. The man said nothing to the boy. Instead he knelt down in front of him, leaving a space between them, then opened his arms and waited.

For a moment the room fell quiet, still.

Then, with a smile that could soften even the most hardened heart, the boy fell into his father's arms. Flinging his own reed-thin arms around his father's neck, the boy clung to him like a survivor gripping a life raft tossed on the stormy seas of life.

Torti clutched the small body to him and rose.

Completely caught up, I'd been holding my breath. I let it out with a whoosh.

"Tomás is our newest," Carmen said. "We found him begging

on the streets of Juárez. Starving, sick, regularly beaten by the other street kids or the drug traffickers, or the police, he would not have made it much longer. After we leave here, we are taking him to see a surgeon in L.A. who specializes in his sort of deformity."

Pandemonium again reigned. The other children grasped for any handhold they could get on their father as he staggered over to his wife. Even fully festooned with children, he managed to give her the most incredible kiss I think I have ever seen.

Then he gave me that trademark grin. "I see you have met my family, Ms. O'Toole. They are fabulous, don't you think?"

"Beyond words."

Dancing around their father, the kids begged for a game of Hop on Pop. He shrugged at me, set Tomás down, then fell to the floor. Kids leapt on him until they had built a tower of love six kids high. Under it all, Tiny Tortilla Padilla laughed as he tickled the nearest tummy.

"Tell me about the kids," I said to Carmen, as we watched, both of us cringing when another kid landed on his father's stomach.

"Come, let's have some tea and leave the children to their play."

We took refuge in the kitchen, where Carmen poured iced tea into tall glasses, a fresh sprig of mint in each. Setting a small plate of Mexican Wedding Cookies on the table, she motioned me to sit. "The children were abandoned for some reason or another. Some were deformed. Some were sick. Some just came at the wrong time for their families—a burden that could not be borne."

"And you go looking for them?" I took a sip of the tea—peach mango from Teavana—yummy. I resisted the siren song of the cookies.

"Not really. We keep our hearts open and they find us." Carmen's face clouded. "That's why my husband is fighting one more time . . . for the children. Not just for our family, but for the ones we can't help—especially for them. We have a foundation, it is small, but we hope not for long. There are so many children, you see."

I saw it all very clearly. A guarantee of sixty-four million would go a long way . . . "You don't want him to fight?"

"He's not so young anymore, for a fighter. It's a risky business. You never know."

THE noise in the casino, building toward evening, paled in comparison to sixteen children at full throttle. After saying good-bye to the Padillas, and getting a tight squeeze from Maria José, I hadn't made it halfway to my office before a thought had me retracing my steps. This time, I rapped on the door of Bungalow Two.

Arrianna, dressed in cutoffs and the top of a bikini, her feet bare, answered. Her eyes clear and bright, a smile split her face when she saw me. "Hey! Good to see you. I was getting lonely."

Brandy really was a wonder—I had no idea the shops in the Bazaar carried something as mundane as a pair of cutoffs.

"A cage, even though gilded, is still a cage. What do you say I spring you?"

"Sure!" Her grin grew wider, then faded. "What about the media? I'm not up for another circus."

"Me, neither." I stepped aside as she pulled the door behind her. "We're not going far."

ANOTHER young man, tattooed and pierced, a studded collar around his neck, was perched on the corner of Brandy's desk when I returned to my office. Dressed in dirty jeans, a faded black tee shirt with the arms and neck ripped out and the remnants of a stenciled skull and crossbones below the word *poison* still visible, he held a cigarette in his left hand, which dangled down beside his leg. Periodically, he would flick the ashes to the floor.

Miss Patterson glowered at me, her shoulders hunched, her distaste evident.

Brandy didn't look happy, either.

"You." I pointed to the young man. "Are you a guest in this hotel?"

He turned his head, giving me the once-over before his eyes met mine. "What's it to you, lady?"

I took that as a *no*. "Out!" I pointed to the door. "Now!"

"Don't have a hernia." He stood then. His eyes never leaving mine, he dropped his cigarette on the carpet and ground it out with a booted foot.

My anger spiked as he sauntered out. "Brandy. My office. Now!"

A stricken look on her face, the girl jumped at my bark and followed me into my office.

"Shut the door."

Brandy did as I asked then planted herself in front of my desk as I took my chair. "I'm really sorry . . ." At the look on my face, she trailed off.

I let her stew as I counted to ten. Then to twenty. Finally, with my anger somewhat contained, I looked at my clueless young assistant. "Didn't your mother ever tell you we are known by the company we keep?"

The girl bowed her head. "Yes, ma'am."

"You and I have already established that your personal life is your own and you do not want my input. However, this is my office and you are my assistant." Placing my elbows on my desk, I steepled my fingers. "And we represent this hotel. Do you think your young friend there is consistent with the image we are expected to uphold?"

"No, ma'am."

"Make better choices, okay?"

She mustered the courage to glance at me. "Am I fired?"

"Of course not." I leaned back in my chair. "What would make you think that?"

"I screwed up and embarrassed you."

"If you embarrassed anyone, it was yourself." I let that sink in for a moment. "And I don't think there's a mistake you could make that I haven't already made. Strange as it may seem, I was once your age."

"I promise I won't let it happen again." The girl, looking a bit less panicked and properly chastised, still wrung her hands.

"I don't expect perfection, but I want you to do me a favor," I said.

"Anything."

"I want you to take a good hard look at yourself. Are those guys really what you want? Or do you deserve better?"

AFTER Brandy left, I pushed around the papers on my desk and flipped through my phone messages, then buzzed Miss P. "Got a minute?"

"Be right there."

When she appeared in the doorway, I motioned for her to shut the door.

"You need to give Brandy some advice on men," she said, as she took a seat across from me.

"Me? That's rare." I gave her a dirty look. "Not only am I uniquely unqualified, but our Miss Alexander wouldn't recognize a good thing if it bit her on the ass."

"She *is* only twenty-one," Miss P stated, as if I needed reminding.

"Youth, an impediment to discernment," I said, taking a quick tour through my own memories. Had I ever been that young? I ran my fingers through my hair. I couldn't remember the last time I'd been this beat—lack of sleep and lack of food, a killer combination. "Why don't you take Brandy and check on the preparations at Babel, and anything else you think needs tending to?"

"Good idea."

"Before you go could you call Romeo and get him over here. I know I should quit summoning him like a dog, but I'm practically nonfunctional."

"Late night?" she groused, not even attempting to mask her irritation at me.

"Look, I know you want the skinny on Jordan Marsh, but there isn't anything to tell. We've been friends for a long time."

"He is so dreamy. Is he everything he seems to be?"

"And so much more."

MISS Patterson left with Brandy in tow. My couch called my name—twenty winks sounded like a good use of the thirty minutes I had before Romeo said he'd be here.

Prostrate, I was just falling asleep when I heard the outer office door open. Today was not my day.

"Anybody here?" The Beautiful Jeremy Whitlock.

"In here." One forearm over my eyes, I didn't bother to move. Whatever he had to say, he could darn well deliver it while I kept my current position.

"Man, since you didn't get a nibble with the couch alone, now you're baiting the thing. I don't mind telling you, that has a whiff of desperation."

"I'm getting there. Teddie's in California."

"So I heard." He grabbed my feet, lifted them, and slid in underneath. My feet in his lap, he shucked my shoes and started rubbing one foot.

Removing my arm, I raised my head and looked at him.

"Inappropriate, I know. But I'm good at this and you look totally knackered."

I didn't have the energy to resist—and he was as advertised. I had to stifle a groan of absolute pleasure as he went to work.

"I don't mean anything by it. Hope you don't mind."

"Mind? I'd pay you good money to never stop." I relaxed back and again covered my eyes. A foot rub was the next best thing to a back rub and one of the top five most pleasurable things to do fully clothed. "Did you come by for Miss P or do you have anything else to report?"

"I've been pressing a bloke I know at the FBI. Once Mary Makepeace died, the FBI terminated the protection. The kid wasn't in danger and the mother was dead, so case closed." Finished with one foot, Jeremy started on the other.

"So we've reached a dead end there?"

"Pretty much, but I did get a bit of interesting information. My friend checked the Makepeace kid's birth date on her original birth certificate. The one in the sealed files before they issued her a new name and new papers."

"Oh god, right there. For some reason that foot hurts more than the other," I said, momentarily distracted. "What about the birth date?"

"It matches the one Numbers was using. I know that's not definitive, but it seems to indicate we might be on to something."

"When folks enter into the Witness Protection Program, are they fingerprinted?"

Jeremy was quiet for a moment as he worked his thumbs into the sole of my foot just below my toes. "Sure, but where are we going to get a copy of Ms. Neidermeyer's fingerprints? As I recall, taking a set directly isn't an option—no fingers, no prints."

"I bet Romeo can help us. I'm sure the police dusted her house and car. And, if we're lucky, the Gaming Control Board might have a set on file. They keep gaming professionals on a pretty short leash." I swung my feet to the floor and sat up. "Thanks, that was medicinal, just what the doctor ordered."

I had just plopped myself back into my desk chair, when the outer door again opened and Romeo rushed in.

"Ask and ye shall receive," I said, in response to Jeremy's startled expression. "Take a seat, Romeo, the party's just getting started.

They both sat in rapt attention as I regaled them with all I knew up to this point. Of course, I left out the part about someone trying to run me over. That was my problem and I'd handle it my own way.

"So, you think the district attorney is in on this?" Romeo asked, his eyes wide.

"It should be painfully obvious, and it bears emphasizing: I can't prove anything!" I looked at both of them. "If you two can match fingerprints then we'd have Number's identity nailed down.

And a motive for revenge. After that, we can speculate, but any evidence we have now is purely circumstantial."

"I can get a set of fingerprints for you," Romeo said.

"I don't need to tell you that you must keep all of this under your hat. The district attorney's reach extends far and wide. He already knows I'm pushing, but let's let him worry a bit, okay?"

Romeo nodded. "Agreed."

"You two work the fingerprint angle," I said, as I rose—a subtle sign the party was over. "I've got to see a man about some rock."

Chapter

T W E L V E

♡

aiting for the valet to bring a car around, I stood just inside the front entrance watching people parade past. A river of humanity streamed through the doors, some with drinks, some without, all laughing, joking, pointing to the glass hummingbirds and butterflies covering the ceiling or the skiers testing their skills on our indoor mountain.

The energy level in the lobby was almost palpable, a living, breathing beast that grabbed me in its jaws and shook me until all my worries fell away. Like a wave hitting the shoals, the race to the weekend was building, higher and higher, carrying me along.

Paxton Dane grabbed me by the elbow. "Looking for something?"

"Perspective." I glanced at him—yup, still a hunk and a half. "And you?"

"I've been watching the women," he said, his face a picture of innocence.

"Honesty! Completely unexpected."

"I think this hotel has a real hooker problem."

I started to laugh, but he sounded serious. "How so?"

He swept his arm in an arc. "Just look. I'll bet you most of these females are charging for it."

"You can pick out the hookers by just looking?"

He made a rude noise, and rolled those incredible emerald eyes. "Who couldn't?"

"Okay, show me one."

We both cast our eyes around the lobby, which was full of tall, thin, surgically enhanced women, dressed to show their assets to the best advantage.

"There." Dane pointed. "See the blond woman standing with the other two?"

I followed his finger, then stifled a grin. "You have just pointed out the wife of a prominent casino executive. The woman on her left is her sister. I don't know the other one, but I really should go over and say hello. That would be nice, don't you think?"

Dane narrowed his eyes at me. "Seriously?"

"I can introduce you if you'd like." I was telling the truth, even if he had a hard time believing me. "Give me another."

Again, we scanned the lobby.

"See that old guy with the dolly on his arm. Bet she's hooking."

"I don't know her, and you may be right. What do you want me to do? Should I stop him and say, Sir, that gorgeous young thing couldn't possibly be with you, unless money was involved?"

Dane laughed. "Sarcasm becomes you."

"You are the only one who thinks so, but I'll take that as a compliment."

A bright red Ferrari eased to the curb out front, and a valet stepped out and motioned to me. Borrowing a ride from our in-house Ferrari dealer was one of the perks of my job.

"I like a lady who rides in style," Dane said, his admiration for the car evident.

"Want to come with me? To be honest I could use your help." I pushed through the front doors, with Dane close behind.

"You want my help? And I thought it was my sparkling personality."

"That, too." I thanked the valet and paused, looking back at Dane. "Ever since someone tried to run me over this morning, I've been a little jumpy. And now, I've got to go see a guy at a rock quarry. Somehow, going by myself is losing its luster. Want to ride shotgun?"

"Being a knight in shining armor is my best thing." Dane folded himself into the passenger seat. "Get a move on, woman. What are you waiting for? Show me what this thing can do"

ACCORDING to Jimmy G, Scully Winter was the day foreman at a quarry on the west side of town.

The top down, the cool afternoon breeze tempering the warmth of the sun, Dane and I rode in silence, satisfied grins on our faces, as we savored the dwindling day, the fast car, a returning ease between us. Feeling no need to hurry, I took the long way around to the west side. With rush hour imminent, traffic was building, but it thinned as we merged from the 95 onto Summerlin Parkway. Quickly working through the top gears, I let the Ferrari's horses run a bit.

Speed distilled the senses and outran conscious thought, leaving only the visceral punch of the world ripping past. If only life were that elemental, that simple.

Dane's fingers brushing the back of my hand startled me back to real time. "I hope you're paying more attention to driving than you appear to be." He didn't move his hand.

"Not really. Sorry." His skin on mine felt warm, nice. That's the trouble with picking a partner in the dance of love—you turn your back on all the other possibilities.

"Teddie on your mind?"

I shot him a sideways glance.

"I saw the paper." Dane's eyes shone with an intensity absent from his voice. "You okay?"

"Never better." I really wished he'd take his hand off of mine, but I didn't move either.

"Liar."

At the 215, I turned left, heading south, then hit the gas. The increased Gs pressed me back into the seat.

"You can't outrun this, Lucky. Not Teddie. And not me."

"I can't deal with this now." Easing the Ferrari down, I shifted my hand from under Dane's. "I trust Teddie—I've entrusted him with all I've got."

"I understand, but I'm not quitting the game, not until there's a ring on your finger and you've pled your troth in front of God and country." He stuck his arms up through the open top into the air streaming past.

I couldn't deny there was definitely something appealing about a guy who wanted me. I had no idea what to do about that . . . or about him. "You say you read Norm Clarke's column today?"

"Yeah."

"Don't you want to ask me what Jordan Marsh is like in bed?"

"That part was so ludicrous it made me laugh."

For some reason his pronouncement frosted me a little. "What, you don't think I can land a guy like that?" Downshifting, I whipped the car onto the off-ramp at Flamingo and braked to a stop at the red light.

Dane shifted in his seat, angling to look at me. "On the contrary, if he had any sense he'd be pressing you as hard as he could, but you're not the type to move a guy in through the back door as one is leaving through the front."

The guy was earning points hand over fist. If I didn't get him out of the car fast, I was going to back myself into a corner. I reminded myself over and over—I'm a simple girl, I don't want complications.

And then there was that whole "trust is a two-way street" thing.

Dane fell silent as I eased the car through the residential streets.

A frontier town in both mind and spirit, Las Vegas had grown in size and number before anyone really knew it had happened. Like mud flowing along, engulfing everything in its path, the city limits had crawled across the valley floor, incorporating tiny hamlets, spring-fed watering holes, and a rock quarry. Once so far from civilization that visitors swore they needed to pack provisions to get there, a very deep and very active quarry was now surrounded by neighborhoods of single-family homes and sidewalks filled with kids on bicycles.

The miners and the residents kept a fragile peace, which I found amazing since Ralph Nader strong-armed Congress into mandating that commercial vehicles all be equipped with shrill beepers that signaled when the truck was put into reverse. At a quarry, trucks in reverse happened regularly. At this particular quarry it happened around the clock. Incessant beeping was not exactly the lullaby I would like to hear at four in the morning.

The guard stepped out of a small shack at the entrance—a gravel road cut through the chain-link perimeter fence—and gave the car an admiring glance.

Nothing like being shown up by my wheels.

"You guys slumming today?"

"Scully Winter?" I asked, a hint of frost in my voice.

The guard shrugged in the direction of a single-wide that looked as if it had ridden through a couple of tornado seasons in Texas, then had been unceremoniously dropped where it sat.

Out of habit, I angled the Ferrari across several loosely drawn spaces in front of a sign that read PETERSON QUARRY—ROCK AROUND THE CLOCK. Let's hope Scully shared his employer's sense of humor.

As always, Jimmy G's info was golden. Through a grimy window, I could see the bullet-shaped head of Scully Winter bent over papers spread on a table in front of him.

The door, rusty and dented, with a padlock dangling open from the lock, didn't look like it would be much of an impediment to anyone bent on getting in. Maybe that was the point.

I didn't knock.

Scully didn't look up when we entered. "Whaddya want?"

"A moment of your time." Our presence may not have generated any interest, but my voice sure did.

Scully's head snapped up; his eyes narrowed. "What do you want?" His voice was a low growl. "How'd you find me?"

"Despite its size, Vegas is still a small town."

Dane shut the door behind him then leaned back against it, his arms crossed, his expression flat.

Scully glanced at Dane, a smile lifting a corner of his mouth. "You brought muscle. This must be good."

Scully Winter had fallen a long way since his days as the heir apparent in the district attorney's office, and it showed. Dirty jeans, work boots, and a white tee shirt with yellow stains circling under each arm had replaced the tailored wool suit, silk tie, and starched cotton shirt. Resignation bowed his shoulders, which were once broad and strong with promise. Suspicion had replaced confidence. Soft rolls of fat hid a body that had once been carved with pride. But the mean slash of his mouth and the flat, emotionless eyes of a predator? Those were the same.

"I want you to tell me about Numbers Neidermeyer, her private bookmaking operation, and your buddy Daniel Lovato." Since there was nowhere to sit, I remained standing. I preferred it that way—I'd found my height could be intimidating to shorter men, and I wasn't above using that advantage.

Scully laughed. "You got some guts, traipsing in here, asking questions. 'Course you always did have more balls than sense."

Dane stirred behind me.

I shook my head.

"How sweet, he likes you," Scully leered. "I heard you were hooking up with the queer boy in the dresses. That surprised me—Cowboy here seems more your type. I always had you pegged as a gal who liked it rough."

The fact that Scully Winter had ever considered my sexual preferences chased a chill down my spine. "You gonna tell me what I want to know?"

"Why should I?" Scully let his eyes travel lazily down my body, pausing at points of interest.

"I have you on tape placing action at the French Quarter." I lied. Those flat eyes found mine. "So."

"Well, there's that pesky little probation problem. I don't think your probation officer would be thrilled to know you'd jumped back into the game in violation of your parole."

Scully thought that over for a moment. Despite his outward appearance, he still had the calculating mind of a shyster lawyer—to the extent those two words were not synonymous. "What do you want to know?"

"I want to know how Daniel Lovato was involved in the whole thing."

Sully cocked his head and squinted one eye at me. "He wasn't."

"I heard he was into Numbers big time—five hundred grand or so."

"Not him. Her."

"Her?"

"Mrs. Lovato. Glinda," he said with a distasteful sneer, as if he'd gotten a mouthful of something vile.

"Glinda?" Well, well, another brick in the wall.

"Yeah, I don't know what the Neidermeyer broad and that bitch had goin', if you get my drift. You women have weird relationships, you know?" He tapped a pencil on the table while he talked. "Anyway, the Neidermeyer broad had some axe to grind with our fearless district attorney. She used Glinda, got her to place the bets and make it look like Daniel did it. Funny thing was, Neidermeyer was screwing the DA behind his wife's back all along. Always liked a gal who could ride both sides of the fence."

"Did Glinda ever get wise to it?"

Scully whistled. "I'll say. That little stink bomb exploded a couple of days before Numbers got fed to the sharks."

DANE and I made the return trip to the Babylon in silence—we seemed to be making a habit of that. I turned the car back over to the valet and ambled into the hotel, lost in thought. In the lobby, I turned to Dane, who was looking at me with an unreadable expression. "That was a wee bit too easy, don't you think?" I asked, voicing my reservations.

"Either that or you're very lucky," Dane answered, his face a blank canvas.

"Cute." I turned to go. "Thanks for being my muscle."

His hand on my arm stopped me. "Dinner?"

"I can't. I'm having cocktails with the Big Boss, then I've been invited to a hamburger tasting."

For a moment he looked at me. "I'm not even going to ask." With that, he turned and walked away.

I watched until he disappeared into the crowd.

ROMEO jumped from his perch on the edge of Brandy's desk when I returned to the office, his face reddening when his eyes met mine. He and my young assistant were alone.

"I'm assuming Miss Patterson left?"

"She took Jeremy home—both of them were totally wrung-out," Brandy said. "She said if you needed anything, just send up a flare."

"Romeo, are you here on business or pleasure?" I stuck my head into my office, took a glance around, then flipped off the light.

"A bit of both. We got a positive ID on Numbers Neidermeyer. You were right."

"What do you know, I finally got an answer instead of more questions." I shouldered my Birkin. "Why don't you two knock off for the day? Brandy, forward the phones to my cell. I'll handle it from here."

"I can stay." Brandy offered, but she didn't look too enthusiastic as she cast furtive glances at Romeo.

"Go on. Turn out the lights and lock the door. I'll be having drinks with the Big Boss in the Garden Bar."

IN creating a special experience for the Babylon's sun-worshipers, the Big Boss attempted to duplicate the hanging gardens of ancient Babylon—one of the seven wonders of the ancient world—and he'd outdone himself. Huge tropical trees draped over three separate pools which were connected by a river with grottos and caves. Roses, gardenias, and other flowering plants grew in riotous abandon on both sides of meandering paths that widened occasionally into larger areas for lounging. Trailing vegetation dripped from the balconies of the overlooking rooms. Water burbled over rock formations on its way to the pools.

Curiously enough, the Garden Bar actually overlooked the gardens. And, in my opinion, it was misnamed. A series of platforms suspended above one end of our pool area, the bar was more reminiscent of the Swiss Family Robinson than ancient Babylon.

But in Vegas most folks overlook a little creative license.

Rope bridges connected the platforms to each other, and a larger, more stable bridge connected the bar to the hotel's mezzanine floor. Sometimes, very early in the morning, I enjoyed watching the heavy drinkers attempting to traverse the bridges.

Like the king overlooking his kingdom, the Big Boss waited at a table at the edge of the highest platform. He'd ordered us both bourbon, neat, and sat staring off into space. As his eyes surveyed the activity below, his fingers were busy with what I knew to be a hundred dollar bill. Following a remembered pattern, he worked the paper bill, folding, rotating, folding again.

I slipped into the chair next to his. "You thinking about something in particular or everything in general?"

His eyes flicked to me then returned to stare into the distance. "I was thinking about your mother's little fracas."

"She's made quite a splash."

"You have a flair for the sarcastic understatement." This time, when his eyes shifted to mine, they stayed.

"This is news?" I took a sip of the strong brew then took a deep breath, relishing the warmth spreading through me. Every now and then the thought that I might like bourbon more than I should tried to get my attention, but I pushed it away. Distilled spirits and fine wine were two of life's pleasures and I had no intention of depriving myself of either. Besides, the word *should* was not part of my vocabulary.

"I'm finding the media attention your mother is garnering fairly disconcerting." My father glanced at me and shrugged sheepishly. "I don't think she appreciates how squeaky-clean my image has to be." He finished the tiny origami figure and set it on the table for my inspection.

I smiled at the tiny work of art—an elephant, its trunk raised. For as long as I'd known him, the Big Boss had turned to origami when his stress level rose.

"Mother doesn't understand the shadow her profession casts, or, if she does, she chooses to ignore it."

"The Gaming Commission takes a dim view of it, I can tell you that—and they won't look the other way. Even a hint of scandal, and they'll review my gaming license. Without it, I'm done."

"Does Mother know that?"

"I'm not sure she's thought about it." My father looked out over the hanging gardens, his eyes troubled. "To be honest, I haven't wanted to mention it, but this little auction of hers may have forced my hand."

"What are you going to say?" My heart leapt into my throat. Just once, couldn't these two people I loved have everything they wanted?

"If the Gaming Commission holds my feet to the fire . . ." He shrugged. "One of us is going to have to choose."

"Choose?"

"Between who we are and who we want to be with."

"Are you sure that's the only way out?" Boy, talk about the cards of life going cold. First life forced Jordan Marsh to finally fold his hand. Were my parents next?

"I don't see any peas-and-carrots kind of ending here. That's been the problem all along." As he lifted his glass to his lips, ice clinking in his glass betrayed his shaking hand.

I grasped his hand, squeezing hard.

"I do love her so," he whispered, shooting an arrow of pain through my heart.

Life was nothing more than a series of choices, some easy, some difficult . . . some impossible. And love complicated everything. This day, already depressing enough, had taken a turn straight toward abysmal.

The Big Boss drained his drink, then motioned for another. "Do you think we can get her to understand the concept of subtlety?"

"Ah, the sweep-it-under-the-rug-and-maybe-nobody-will-notice approach. That's like trying to lasso a shooting star."

"I was afraid you'd say that." He took his fresh drink from the waiter as he handed him the empty.

Each of us lost in our own thoughts, we sat for a few moments soaking in the last warm rays of a brilliant day. A hummingbird darted among the flowers, undeterred by the crowd gathering in the bar. Birds winged high above, waiting for the bugs to come out as the day faded to dusk.

"Do you remember a guy named Joseph Ferenti?" I asked.

"Jabbin' JoJo Ferenti?" A cloud crossed my father's face. "Why?"

"Looking for connections."

"Connections? You don't want to dig too hard on that one. The wounds are deep; the scabs thin." The Big Boss stretched his mouth into a thin, stern line.

"A certain oddsmaker was Jabbin' JoJo Ferenti's daughter."

He took a deep breath, held it for a moment, then let it out slowly. "That answers a few questions."

"Answers? Really? All she's done for me is raise questions."

"It's over now," he announced, resignation flattening his voice.

And maybe a hint of relief? Or was I imagining that? "What's over?"

"A string of bad luck." His eyes flashed as if he had spoken out of turn, then he shook his head. "None of us could ever prove anything, but everyone involved in JoJo's take-down has died of unnatural causes. We always thought the kid had a hand in it. I heard some guys looked for her, but she had disappeared. All the old guys are gone now, anyway."

"The kid did it?" My eybrows almost shot off my face. "You think she killed her mother? One bullet to the head, execution style? Pretty coldhearted for a kid of twelve."

"Sociopaths are born, honey. Age is irrelevant." My father sipped his drink as he stared in the distance. "She got them all."

"All but one."

A flicker of understanding lit in the Big Boss's eyes. "Daniel. Do you think he killed her?"

It was my turn to stare into the distance. "I don't know. Everything is pointing toward his wife rather than him. Numbers had set up an elaborate scheme to discredit Daniel, ruin his life, so he'd lose everything. She used Glinda to put some of it in place."

"He was the big fish," my father explained. "If Ferenti's kid was that hell-bent on revenge, then a shot to the head would be too good for Daniel. She'd want to watch him dangle on the line while she bled the life out of him." When my father's eyes met mine, they were serious black dots in a hard face. "If Daniel killed her, good for him."

I didn't want to think of our district attorney being capable of murder. Of course, I guess we all have it in us if the price is right.

"Tell me about Mr. Ferenti."

"JoJo got caught up in an extermination. Back then, the Mob was on the way out, their influence all but gone. Everyone knew that for Las Vegas to become what it is today, the Mob had to go. Fortunes were involved; the future of the city depended on cleaning house." My father threw down the last of his drink. He looked like he wanted a third, but thought better of it. "JoJo was a bit player. He did some stupid stuff, cultivated the wrong friends. Daniel made sure the book was thrown at him when a slap on the wrist would have been appropriate."

I saw the faraway look in my father's eyes, so I waited while he worked through his memories.

"I can't really describe what it was like then—sorta like McCarthyism Vegas-style." He ran a finger under the collar of his shirt as if it suddenly had become a noose, tightening until he couldn't breathe. "Hell, I wasn't part of the Family, but even I was scared to death the Feds would come after me for doing business with them."

"I don't guess the Feds worried about throwing out some of the wheat with the chaff."

"A small sacrifice in their eyes. But when they threw the book at JoJo . . ." A brief flash of anger colored the Big Boss's cheeks. "I thought Daniel had signed his own death warrant. Everybody loved JoJo. He wasn't the brightest guy, but people sorta adopted him, you know what I mean?"

"Yeah." I reached over and squeezed his hand. "Were you there at Mr. Ferenti's trial?"

"You don't abandon friends just because they've gotten their ass in a crack."

Of course he was there.

The Big Boss stared into space before continuing. "Every day, his girl, Mary, I think her name was, and their kid sat in the front row. Cute kid, strawberry blonde pigtails, big, scared eyes."

"Every day?"

His brows crinkled. "Every day but one."

"What happened that day?"

"I'm trying to remember. It was a lifetime ago." My father looked at me and I could see the hurt in his eyes. "JoJo's daughter was sick . . . real sick. I think she was in the hospital." My father shook his head in frustration. "I haven't thought about this in a long time."

I pushed my unfinished drink toward him. He looked like he could use it.

"JoJo flipped out when the judge wouldn't grant a recess. They drug the poor bastard from the courtroom in cuffs and shackles."

"Why?"

He took a sip of his drink, a dreamy, lost look in his eyes. Then he slapped the table. "I remember. The kid had had an allergic reaction—anaphylactic shock, I think they called it."

"Really? What to?"

"Bees. She was stung by a bee and damned near died."

I don't know how many seconds passed as I stared at my father. Bees. My mind reached for a connection . . . there was something there . . . and I couldn't quite put it together.

"Lucky, are you with me? What's wrong?" my father asked, his voice barely penetrating my haze of confusion.

My phone rang, scaring me back to the present.

"Shit." I grabbed the thing, flipped it open, and said, "What?"

Static filled the air before a voice I didn't recognize filtered over the open connection. "Is this the Customer Relations Department at the Babylon in Las Vegas?" It was a woman's voice, an interesting accent I couldn't quite place.

"I apologize for my rudeness." I'd completely forgotten I'd asked for the phones to be forwarded to my cell. "This is Lucky O'Toole, Head of Customer Relations for the Babylon, I am embarrassed to say. What may I do for you?"

"This is Reza Pashiri. And you are the woman I was looking for."

My emotions tumbled. The young woman who'd been caught in a lip-lock with Teddie—I had no idea what to say, how to act. So, I took the high road—I bailed. "Yes, Ms. Pashiri, what can I do for you?"

"First I'd like to thank you for sharing Theodore with us—he's amazing."

"Amazing is one adjective that fits." I didn't want to elaborate as to the others.

She giggled as if she found me funny.

Ah, the voice on the phone last night—I recognized the giggle. Teddie had some explaining to do.

"I'm sorry to bother you so late in the game, but I have a favor to ask." The young woman continued, her voice warm, melodious . . . irritating.

"I'll do what I can." Even I couldn't find a hint of warmth in my voice. I didn't care.

"I know my band and I weren't scheduled to come to Vegas until tomorrow, but we've finished our business here and everyone's ready to blow town. Can you arrange it? Are our accommodations available?"

"Bungalow One is ready for you, but I'll need to rework your transportation. When and where would you like to be met?" Was there any worse humiliation than having to be a step-and-fetch-it for this particular woman? I doubted it. A dozen years younger, beautiful, thin, and she connected with my man through music—a connection I didn't share. Life was trying to teach me something, but damned if I could figure out what it was.

We worked out the details. I confirmed them with the air charter service, then reconfirmed them with Ms. Pashiri. The upshot of it all was I would personally meet them at McCarran Executive Terminal at ten thirty.

Right now I was late for an appointment with the hamburger man.

AFTER a hasty good-bye to my father, I charged in the direction of the Bazaar and Jean-Charles's little burger stand. Oblivious, my mind elsewhere, I worked my phone as I dodged the crowds gathering in the lobby and the casino.

First Romeo.

He answered on the first ring. "Hey."

I could hear laughter in the background, and music. I hoped he was still with Brandy, but as her personal life was none of my business, I didn't ask. "Has the toxicology report come back?"

"Why?" His voice turned serious, I had his attention.

"If they haven't done so already, ask them to run a tox screen for bee venom."

"Bee venom?"

"Yeah, and if the test comes back positive, I want to know the levels as well." I slapped my phone closed without waiting for his reply.

The noose was tightening.

AS I stood, mouth open, in the middle of what had been a fairly pedestrian Italian joint, I realized Jean-Charles Bouclet couldn't be the Devil incarnate, as I had believed him to be. Divine intervention was the only explanation for the transformation that surrounded me. Gone were the tacky red and green crown moldings, the Italian signs on the walls, and the baskets filled with silk flowers.

The moldings, now returned to their original bare wood, lustered with a light coat of natural finish. The brick walls with the original drippy mortar were adorned only with burnished brass sconces, shining a soft, diffused light. Green leather banquet seating lined one wall, dotted with two-tops at appropriate intervals. Four-tops, with red-and-white checkered tablecloths filled the rest of the space. Irregularly milled wood, stained a warm brown, replaced the former black-and-white linoleum. A wall of glass had replaced the opaque wall separating the kitchen from the rest of the restaurant. Soft French bistro music playing in the background completed the overall atmosphere of cultured casualness.

The place lacked only one thing—a crowd.

Empty as a bank after Bonnie and Clyde had blown through town, this was clearly not the location for the tasting party. But, if it wasn't here, where would it be? What had I screwed up? Time? Location? Day? Probably all three.

"Ah, Lucky!" Jean-Charles emerged from the kitchen, wiping his hands on a towel that hung from his waist. Attired today in a pristine, white chef's coat over creased blue jeans, casual shoes, and an irritated frown, Jean-Charles still looked as yummy as a soufflé. A nice piece of eye candy who could cook? The stuff female fantasies are made of.

He frowned at me. "You are late. That is very rude."

But that personality was a deal-breaker.

"With my life, tardiness is unavoidable." I crossed my arms and leveled a serious gaze on him. "You said a party, but we are the only ones here."

"Two is a party, *oui*?" His eyes were the perfect color of blue, not too dark, but not too pale. When he smiled, as he did now, the smile made his eyes shimmer.

"Yes. I mean, no." I would not let his Gallic charms fluster me. "I didn't agree to a party of two. That is a date."

He shrugged as only the French can do. "My English is not so good. Party? Date? It's not important."

Oh yes, it was important—very, very important. Do they take little French boys aside and give them charm pills or something? Whatever it was, it put the rest of us at a distinct disadvantage.

"You are here," he said. "While I am cooking you will drink a wine I picked especially for you." He took my hand and pulled me with him into the kitchen.

I sat on the stool he indicated in front of a small round table, pulled close to the grill. "Look, I want to get something straight," I said, needing to clear the air. My thoughts were still muddled, my emotions raw, I didn't need our resident French stud making things worse.

He poured wine the color of blood into a large rounded wine glass from a crystal decanter that had been set out to breathe, then extended the glass to me.

Not wanting to be rude, I took it.

"Yes?" he asked, as he poured himself a glass.

"What am I doing here?" I took a sip of wine and thankfully stopped myself before I groaned in delight. A fine French Bordeaux— nectar of the gods.

"We must work together. We are friends, no?"

"No."

"We will be." Again, he gave me one of those shrugs, then a knowing look. "Thanks to your Big Boss, we are, how do you say, like partners. You are a formidable woman—perhaps the first woman who has spoken so harshly to me since I was but a boy and my beloved *mère* scolded me."

"So I'm here because you like to be manhandled?" I hid a grin behind my glass. "Or I remind you of your mother?"

"I am intrigued, that is all." Jean-Charles pulled trays of small beef patties and other ingredients from the walk-in as he talked. The charcoal in the massive grill glowed white-hot. He tossed fat slabs of hand-cut bacon on the griddle. "And we must work together. This restaurant your Big Boss has promised, my career rides on its success."

"It's pretty important to mine as well."

He grabbed the end of the cloth hanging from his waist and used it to protect his hand as he grabbed various skillet handles, jostling the contents of the pans as they sizzled over gas flames. "Yes, but if it fails, you . . . how do you say it? Eat bird?"

"Crow."

"Ah yes! Crow!" He gestured toward me with the spatula. "I have never discovered a good way to make crow pleasing to the palate, by the way." He flipped the bacon then the tiny burgers, which he had placed over the open coals.

That probably meant crow wouldn't appear on the menu, which I took to be a good thing.

"So you eat crow," Jean-Charles continued. "Then you find another chef and try again. But me, I am left in disgrace—out in the cold." He made it sound like we'd give him a one-way ticket to Siberia.

As he cooked, mouth-watering smells filled the kitchen, making my stomach dance in anticipation.

"So I'm here for you to butter up." I gazed in rapture at the plate of tiny tasting burgers he set in front of me. "And you want to let me know in that subtle, charming French manner that you have no intention of letting some demanding female stand in your way?"

After wiping his hands on his towel, he pointed to the various delicacies in front of me. "That one is American Kobe beef, grilled Vidalia onions, thick smoke-cured bacon, and fresh guacamole on an onion kaiser roll. The second is my version of a turkey burger, with a few surprises. You tell me what secret ingredient is in the third."

He watched as I took a bite of the Kobe burger. Apparently satisfied at my groan of pleasure, he turned back to the stove. "We are on the same team, no?"

"We have the same goal, but we manage two different sides of the operation. I hold the purse strings, you control the quality—conflict is inevitable." Moist and full of flavor, the turkey burger melted in my mouth.

A smile lit his eyes as he spread his arms wide. "So this is why you are here."

"Looking for common ground, are you?" I polished off the turkey burger and stuffed a couple of hot fries into my mouth, after dipping them in ketchup. Grabbing more fries, I used them to point to the tub of ketchup. "That's not homemade. That's Heinz."

His back to me, he said, "Very good. Nobody does it better than Heinz, so why try?"

Who would've thought our common ground would be built on a shared opinion of American tomato sauce?

This time he set two plates on the table, one in front of me, the other in front of the stool across from me. He poured himself another glass of wine as he took a seat. "You haven't tried the third. Tell me what's in it."

Under the gun, I took a tentative taste. Chewing slowly, I focused on the individual flavors caressing my taste buds. "Kobe beef, but this time perhaps the Japanese version."

"Good."

"Fennel, coriander? Something with a hint of anise?"

"Anise seed. Good, continue."

"A touch of fresh basil, and finished with a thin layer of paté on the top. Wait . . ." I held up my hand, then wrinkled my nose. "And truffles . . . white truffles."

"Bravo." He raised his glass in salute. "But why did you make that face?"

"I'm not a big fan of truffles. They taste like dirt after a rain, or like the moldy stuff you pull out of the back of the refrigerator."

He shot me the perfect look of French disdain. "You have a palate, but not a very cultured one."

"Nobody's perfect."

"I will have to educate you." Jean-Charles tilted his head, his face inscrutable.

"My *palate*, you mean?"

"But of course," he said, though his eyes said something else.

I was not going to open that door, not tonight. Bantering with him was bad enough—I refused to cross the line into flirting with him.

"Here, try this." He held out a small burger from his plate. "You will like."

I took a small bite, then he popped the rest into his mouth. "Mmmm, crabmeat with a bit of Old Bay's. All it needs is a genuine French remoulade and thick onion rings."

"You have read my mind."

"What about milkshakes?"

"Thick with various liqueurs for adults, the basics for the kids."

"And desserts?"

Pressing a hand to his chest in mock dismay, he gave me a wounded look. "I am French! Your words cut me."

I took a bite of another little burger he held out for me. Delicious, I couldn't place it. "That one I don't know."

Again Jean-Charles finished it off, which I found intimate in an uncomfortable way. "That is a veggie burger, for those who don't eat meat."

"Amazing." I tipped my glass to him. "To the chef."

He dipped his head in acknowledgment, then he squeezed my hand. Holding it, he asked, "So we can work together, *oui*?"

I eased my hand from his. "Of course, but I will hold your feet to the fire. You will have to justify every expense, but your budget will be quite generous."

Common ground established, I settled back with a full glass of wine and listened to our new French charmer talk of his plans and his dreams. His eyes dancing, he regaled me with stories of his youth in France, his various positions as he worked his way up the culinary food chain. Particularly hilarious was a stint as the head chef at a European hotel in Moscow.

"I have talked so much," he said as he filled my glass again, despite my protests. "What about you?"

Never willing to share much, I gave him the short version.

When I finished, he was momentarily at a loss for words—not uncommon. "Most interesting," he finally said. "So you are an expert on Las Vegas."

That was not what I expected. "As much as anyone is, I guess. I've been here a long time and seen a lot."

"Then you will help me tailor my restaurant for this market." A self-satisfied grin split his face. "I knew you were perfect when I met you." Again, his eyes held something more than his words. This guy was good, really good.

"Of course I will help you. That's my job."

"So we will be working closely together, *oui?*"

"That's how it's normally done." I dismounted my stool. "But now I have to go. I have a plane to meet."

Jean-Charles took my hand in his and raised it briefly to his lips, his eyes warm as he looked up at me. "I should warn you, I am very demanding," he said, his lips grazing my hand as he spoke.

"You've met your match," I countered without conviction. Had he really? Time would tell, but one thing I knew for certain: I didn't trust him any farther than I could throw him.

I wasn't so sure I could trust myself, either.

Without even a hint of suck-up left in me, now I had to go make nice with Reza Pashiri.

Reading my mood, Paolo let me ride in silence as he navigated one more time to the Executive Terminal. He could probably get there with his eyes closed, although I sincerely hoped he didn't try.

With a few minutes to kill, Paolo parked on the tarmac and killed the engine and the lights.

Putting my head back and closing my eyes, I surrendered.

The next thing I knew, Paolo was gently shaking my shoulder. "Ms. O'Toole. The plane is here."

Like a yoke over my shoulders, fatigue weighed on me until I was sure my legs would buckle.

Unable to summon even a modicum of enthusiasm, I waited by the car.

Reza Pashiri appeared at the top of the stairs. When she caught sight of me, she gave me a wave and bounded in my direction. Had I ever had that much energy at this hour? If I had, I didn't remember . . . and they say the second thing to go is the memory. . . .

Breathless, Ms. Pashiri arrived at my side.

Tall and skeletal, she embodied the whole unkempt-pop-star thing. Her embroidered shirt, tied at the neckline, hung off one shoulder and ended at her belly button, which sported the ubiquitous navel ring. Grungy-like Salvation Army rejects, her jeans clung to nonexistent hips and were slung so low I doubted they were legal in most towns in Middle America. Barefoot, with dark hair that hung in a limp curtain down her back, flat, dark eyes, and a sallow complexion, she was less than I expected. Fairly unexceptional—a living testament to the magic of makeup and good lighting. And, swine that I am, I took a bit of delight in that.

"Ms. O'Toole?" she asked in her melodious voice.

"Welcome to Vegas." I motioned to the car. "Paolo will take you to the hotel. I will wait for the van that should be here any minute. If your band could help load the equipment, that would be wonderful."

Wide-eyed, she nodded and made this uh-huh noise at every word I uttered. "That's way cool. You are so trippin'."

"Is that a good thing?"

She giggled as if I wasn't serious. "Theodore said you were one of a kind."

I was pretty sure *that* was a good thing.

"Do you know what he told me when I asked him why he kept brushing off the ladies?"

"I have no idea." If Teddie sent her to run interference for him, he'd picked a good front man—if she was blowing smoke, I couldn't tell.

"He asked me why he would want hamburger when he had steak at home."

Teddie often trotted out that Paul Newman quote. Maybe she wasn't blowing smoke after all. It warmed the cockles of my heart: My man thought I was steak! Of course Jean-Charles had just educated me as to the merits of ground beef . . .

"I really appreciate you juggling your schedule to meet us," Reza said, as she twirled a strand of hair around an index finger. She looked at me with an interesting expression I couldn't quite place. "I hope we weren't too much trouble."

"Of course not. We are honored that you have agreed to host the opening on Saturday. Anything I can do to make your stay more pleasurable, let me know." Wonder of wonders, I *did* a have a teensy bit of suck-up left.

A smile tugged at her thin lips. For a moment she looked older than twentysomething. "To thank you for your trouble, I brought you a present."

"I assure you, that was not necessary."

"Oh, yes it was." Her grin broke through in full force. "As much for my sanity as for yours."

She motioned toward the plane. Her crew was busy unloading instruments and other equipment with the help of the two pilots and several lineboys.

A figure stepped to the open doorway, ducked through, then stood to his full height.

My heart leapt in my chest.

Teddie!

"He was driving us nuts. You were all he ever talked about."

"Me?" I asked, my eyes never leaving Teddie's.

"That man has it bad. I know enough about you to be your sister."

A look of unconditional adoration on his face, Teddie stepped slowly down the steps as I rushed to meet him.

My life was complete.

I didn't care how I looked. I didn't care about playing it cool. Three strides and I launched myself into his arms. Looping my arms around him, I buried my face in his neck.

He grabbed me and held me tight. "Nothing was the same without you," he whispered.

Simple words that stole my breath away.

I pulled back so I could see him. I brushed my fingers across his cheek then lost myself in his kiss. God, he lit every nerve ending on fire.

I don't know how long we were lost in each other, but long enough for the natives to get restless.

Reza politely cleared her throat. "Man, when you dudes read the Book of True Love, you didn't just look at the pictures— you must've read the instructions. I need to find me some of that."

Teddie and I broke our kiss, but neither of us let go.

"Want to go home?" I asked.

"I've been dreaming of home since the moment I left."

HIS hand gripping mine, Teddie stayed with me while I made sure that Reza and her crew were settled and had everything they needed. Finally, we headed for home. A beautiful night—actually an exquisite night with his hand in mine—we decided to walk.

The night air had a bite to it—a cool harbinger of change. In the cloudless sky, the stars shone so brightly they seemed to hang over our heads, just out of reach. A sliver of moon smiled down on us. All was right in my little corner of the world.

Teddie shucked his jacket and draped it around my shoulders, then pulled me tight against him.

I snaked an arm around his waist, then worked my other hand under his shirt. An intoxicating sensation, his skin on mine generated a frisson of energy, a spark of connection that shot through me to my soul.

When my flesh met his, he took a deep, savoring breath. "I don't know what you've done to me or how you did it. You're like a drug I can't live without." He kissed me on the temple, his lips lingering there.

"I know the feeling." Nobody affected me the way Teddie did.

"Tonight, I was supposed to go out with Dig-Me O'Dell and a bunch of the record company suits. They wanted to celebrate our future collaborations."

"Why didn't you go?" I rested my head on his shoulder as we strolled.

"It wouldn't have been a celebration without you." He stopped. Pulling me in front of him, he framed my face in his hands then kissed me.

I couldn't imagine a more perfect kiss. Murmuring against his lips, I said, "You keep that up, and we won't make it home."

Reluctantly, he relented and we continued on our way, this time with more urgency, which made me smile. We walked in silence, drinking in the nearness of each other. There would be time for catching up later . . . much later.

Forrest still manned his post when we pushed through the front doors. His eyebrows shot skyward when he saw Teddie. "Mr. Kowalski. Ms. O'Toole."

Teddie nodded. I waved.

"Let's stay at your place, but I need to stop at home to get some clothes for tomorrow," I said, when Teddie's hand hovered over the elevator buttons. "Oh, and you'll find the bird in your kitchen. I needed a place to stash him for a few days."

"What for?"

"It's complicated. I have a houseguest and the service traipsing in twice a day would've been inconvenient."

"Suits me." His mouth covered mine, and I lost myself.

Teddie was working through the buttons on my blouse when we staggered out of the elevator.

"Would you wait?" I slapped at his hands without much conviction. "I'd really like to take this upstairs."

Before Teddie could reply, a male voice, seductive and filled with innuendo, rang out. "Honey? Is that you? I've been waiting up for you."

Teddie went rigid as Jordan appeared in the doorway dressed only in a pair of gym shorts.

The wicked grin on his face vanished when he caught sight of us. "Oh, sorry. I didn't . . . you're not . . ."

"I'm not what?" Teddie's voice was lethal. "Not the person you expected?"

Jordan looked at me and shrugged. "Do you want to explain, or should I?"

I laughed as I disengaged myself from Teddie. "Better let me. Jordan's been hiding out here for a few days."

"Really? How nice for you." Venom dripped from Teddie's every word.

"Nice?" His tone threw me off. "I do enjoy his visits, but this time we haven't had much time to catch up. It's been sort of crazy."

"Catch up? Never heard it referred to that way." His eyes narrowed as he looked at Jordan over my shoulder. "So I leave and you move an old boyfriend in?" He emphasized "old" which I thought was unnecessary.

In fact, this whole scene was unnecessary. "No need to be rude."

"Rude? You want me to be polite to the man who has been keeping my bed warm and my lover satisfied in my absence." Teddie ripped into me, sarcasm dripping from every word. "You take the cake, O'Toole, you really do."

"Me?" Like a punch to the stomach, Teddie's words finally registered, taking my breath away. At least Norm Clarke had had the kindness to insinuate. But not once in a million years would I have thought Teddie would accuse me of such superficiality, such callousness. The ultimate betrayal!

With the shake of my head, I stopped Jordan from entering the fray. This was my fight. Sucking in lungfuls of air, it took me a moment before I could speak again. "So, Jordan and I have been fucking like rabbits while you were gone? Like, what's a little casual sex among friends? Is that what you think?"

"What am I supposed to think?" He glared at me, his anger not quite covering the hurt. "Everybody knows you've been sleeping with him for years."

"Everybody knows that, do they?" My eyes had gone all slitty, my voice deadly.

"It's common knowledge."

"Really?"

At least Teddie knew me well enough to know when he'd pushed me across the line—he started retreating. "If you didn't have something to hide, why didn't you tell me?"

"It didn't seem like a big deal." I advanced on him, not sure exactly what I would do. "Although, had I known that I lack the moral fiber to reign in my galloping nympho tendencies, I might have thought otherwise."

"So, you want me, but you want the old guy, too?" Teddie's voice had dropped an octave. Clearly he had blown right by the sarcasm. "That won't work for me. And, for the record, this is a big deal, a very big deal."

"Apparently." A lot of verbal missiles shot through my brain as I stood looking at him, my heart crushed. I could've thrown his picture with the young Ms. Pashiri in his face. I could've asked him, if that's the opinion he truly held of me, why would he want to be with me? I could've asked him what was love without trust? I could've told him that I had never slept with Jordan Marsh and certainly wasn't going to take a place in his bed now. But I didn't. I shouldn't have to . . . if Teddie was the right guy for me.

"You need to leave." My voice was soft, defeated.

"Lucky! I need an explanation."

"You already got one, but apparently it wasn't good enough. If the truth won't do, what will? Now, go away."

He grabbed my arm as I turned to go.

My face must've conveyed everything I didn't say because he let go.

As I ran into my bedroom I heard Jordan say, "Theodore, you are sooooo going to regret this."

. . .

FOR some reason, I didn't cry. My chest felt empty, as if my heart had been ripped out, but I was too angry to give in to tears. Instead, I stood at my window, which looked south toward the airport. Planes taxied out, then launched themselves into the sky bound for points unknown. Climbing aboard one of them right now was an almost irresistible notion. It would be easy—throw a few things in my bag and boogie.

Running was always easy—it was the staying that was hard.

Jordan stuck his head through the door. "You okay?"

I gave him a look.

"Okay, stupid question." He'd put on a shirt, but that was too little, too late. "Why didn't you let me explain?"

"I had already explained—you were hiding out here for a few days. That was the truth, and it should've been enough."

"Don't be too hard on him, he's really vulnerable right now. New love can do that to you."

I gave Jordan a disgusted look. "You guys always stick up for each other. Right now, I'm thinking shooting him would be too merciful."

"Then it's a good thing he took himself out of the line of fire." He glanced around the room. "Just in case your homicidal tendencies get the better of you, all the weapons are locked up, aren't they?"

"All except the butcher knives."

"Then we'll stay out of the kitchen." Jordan extended a hand to me. "Come, let's have a drink or something. For the record, you *do* know I thought you were Rudy when the elevator opened? I wasn't trying to jerk you around."

"Of course." I took his hand and walked with him into the great room. "Where is your boy toy, by the way?"

"He just called. He has clients in town and dinner is running later than expected. They hadn't even had dessert yet, so he'll be awhile." Jordan stepped to the bar. "Do you want a drink?"

I shook my head. The memory of this morning's hangover was still too fresh. Besides, I'd consumed my annual quota of alcohol in the last few days alone. Not like me. And not a good sign.

"Then dance with me?" Jordan asked.

"What?"

He fiddled with the stereo for a few moments. As the first strains of "Trust in Me" played, he threw open the French doors, then folded me into his arms. "Music, a wonderful salve for the soul."

I buried my face in his shoulder as we swayed to the music. Reza Pashiri could definitely sing.

When she swung into a heartfelt rendition of "At Last," the tears finally came.

A true friend, Jordan held me until I couldn't cry anymore. Then I crawled into my empty bed. But sleep wouldn't come.

Through the open windows, music drifted in on the breeze. Teddie always turned to the piano when he was hurting. Staring at the ceiling, I lay on my back, feeling wrung-out, lifeless. My eyes closed, I pushed everything aside, forcing my brain into idle. This problem would work itself out, one way or the other. I had no control—either he trusted me, or he didn't.

As I listened to Teddie play "Smoke Gets in Your Eyes," a single tear trickled out of each eye, and I took a ragged breath.

Homecomings totally suck.

And for a smart woman, I was totally clueless. Testosterone-fueled jealousies were mythic. I'd walked into the middle of one, but I'd be damned if I was going to tolerate the insults.

What a great couple of days the last two had been.

The last thing I remembered hearing was Teddie's voice as he sang, "How I knew, my true love was true . . ."

Like I said, the guy had a song for every occasion.

SOMETHING jarred me out of a sound sleep. A noise? I sat up in bed and listened. Someone was in the den.

"Jordan?" I called out.

"Lucky?" Teddie's voice, but not his voice. "Woman, get your ass out here." Definitely Teddie, but not the Teddie I knew. His words were slurred, his voice too loud. "I swear, if you don't get out here, I'm coming in there and that would be emb . . . embar . . . awkward for all of us."

All of us? I guess thinking clearly hadn't been high on his priority list since I'd last seen him. Hastily, I wrapped a robe around me.

An empty bourbon bottle clutched in one hand, the back of the couch in the other, Teddie wobbled where he stood. "There you are," he slurred, when he caught sight of me.

"Shhh." I held a finger to my lips. I didn't know whether to laugh or cry. "How much have you had to drink?"

"Not enough. It still hurts." He let go of the couch and took a tentative step in my direction. He staggered, then grabbed the couch before he fell.

"It does, doesn't it?"

A quizzical look on his face, he squinted at me as if he was trying to understand what I meant by the question—or bring me into focus. Either way, with his brain cells awash in alcohol and dying like flies, he was fighting a losing battle. "We need to talk."

"I'm not sure now is the right time." I stood where I was. No way was I going to rescue him.

"I said NOW!" he bellowed.

That shout brought Jordan skidding into the room.

"You!" Teddie pointed at him. "You caused all of this."

"Afraid it was you, old buddy." With one look, Jordan sized up the situation.

Rudy, clad only in a pair of boxer briefs, skidded in next to him.

Teddie's eyes flew open, then he blinked as if trying to process what he saw. "Hey, Rudy. What're you doing here?" Then Teddie looked at me, his bloodshot eyes as big as saucers. "One wasn't enough? You needed two?"

In the silence that followed that remark, I said, "They're together, you ass."

"Wha . . . ?" Teddie looked first at Jordan, then to Rudy, then back again. "Together? Like . . ." Teddie pantomimed the sex act.

Jordan nodded and gave him a pained smile. "I told you, you would really regret making a horse's butt out of yourself."

"Whoa!" With that, Teddie let go of the couch, staggered, then landed in a heap on his butt. He held his head in his hands. "Man, I feel like I'm on the Tilt-A-Whirl—I wish you guys would stand still."

Jordan elbowed Rudy. "Come on. Let's take care of the poor sot. I think we owe Lucky at least that."

The two men each grabbed an arm and pulled Teddie from the room.

"Make sure he's sober for his studio session tomorrow at two with Reza Pashiri at the Palms," I hollered after them.

Jordan gave me a wave as the three of them disappeared toward the guestrooms.

Knowing slumber was over for the night, I went in search of coffee.

THE sky still dark, I thought I could see a very faint brightening in the east, although it might have been my imagination. I had no idea what time it was, and I didn't care. Showered and caffeinated, I started my day. This time, I called for a limo to come get me and take me to work.

Nose to the grindstone, head down, I powered through the paperwork on my desk. Down to the last few items, like a racehorse charging to the finish, I didn't even look up when the outer office door opened.

"Who died?" Miss Patterson asked from the doorway.

I held up one finger then signed my name on the last paper, finishing with a flourish. Placing it on the top of the stack in my out basket, I looked at her. "What?"

"You're looking a bit worse for wear and positively funereal in black. Who died?"

"Innocence? Good sense? Me?"

Her mouth set in a thin line, she stared at me for a moment. "You're not going to tell me what you mean by that, are you? Or why you look like death warmed over?"

"Let's just say, it was an interesting evening." I glanced at the clock. Nine A.M., time to get a move on if I was going to deliver a virgin for sacrifice.

I handed her my phone, then ducked into the closet for my purse. "Can I borrow your car? I need a car that holds more than two, and yours is the most convenient."

"Today's the virginity auction, isn't it? I'd almost forgotten." Miss Patterson rooted in her purse, extracted the keys, then dropped them into my outstretched hand. "I'm going to have to start charging you rental."

"Add it to the list of everything else I owe you." I pocketed the keys. "What do you imagine people will think when I show up at a virginity auction in a politically correct car?"

"That you're schizophrenic?"

"Or that I'm not committed?" We grinned at each other. "Thanks for the car. In case you want me, you'll have to use the pager. I'm killing my phone when I get to Mother's. I won't be able to do much from there—if the place is anything like it was yesterday, we'll be lucky to get out alive."

THE door to Bungalow Two stood open, so I walked in. "Arrianna?"

Like a virginal vision, the girl materialized before me, dressed in a white sundress and white sandals—both of which had probably been charged to my office. Mona's bill was climbing into serious five figures.

Motioning to my own attire, I said, "We clearly have divergent views of the day."

That elicited a wobbly smile from the girl, but nothing more. "So, are you ready?"

AUNT Matilda tottered out of the French Quarter, balancing on a cane and four-inch heels, as I pulled up. A valet opened the door and helped her settle herself in the passenger seat. She didn't tip him.

"I thought you'd never get here," she groused. "What if your mother starts without us?"

I hooked my thumb toward the backseat. "She can't. We're bringing the sacrificial lamb." I made the appropriate introductions, then motored out of the parking lot.

Like an auctioneer sizing up a rare gem, Aunt Matilda gave the girl a long stare. "You ought to bring a pretty penny."

Why did she sound exactly like the Wicked Witch of the West to me? *I'll get you my pretty, and your little dog, too. . . .* A shiver chased down my spine. "What is it with you and Mother?" I snarled. "When did you decide everything had a price? Including sex and innocence?"

Aunt Matilda turned her rheumy eyes on me. "Sex always made you uncomfortable."

"Not sex. *Casual* sex." I turned onto the on-ramp for the 215, pressed the accelerator, then waited for something to happen. And waited. Actually, I expected anemic performance from a car with less horsepower than a lawnmower, but this was ridiculous—I could run faster. At this rate, we'd hit highway speed about the time we reached Pahrump.

"What's so bad about casual sex? You should climb off that high horse, before someone knocks you off—learn to enjoy some of the baser pleasures of life."

"If nothing has value, then what can you hope for? Without hope, I would be like you . . . or Mother." Out of the corner of my eye, I saw my words hit her like a slap. I didn't feel bad—she'd made her choices, I'd made mine, and we both had to live with the paths we'd taken. "When did you two become so jaded?"

"You always thought you were better than us."

"Not hardly." I gripped the steering wheel and cringed as I saw an eighteen-wheeler barreling down on us in the rearview mirror. "You ladies did an impressive job carving out the lives you did. I wanted something different, though." I wanted different all right, and I sure got it—I didn't add that part. I shut my mind to Teddie— I didn't know what to think about all of that, so I didn't.

With a tug on the horn, the driver eased the big truck into the outer lane and charged past. One near-death experience averted, I had the sinking feeling it wouldn't be our last. "Call me crazy, but I still believe in true love—even in this town."

Aunt Matilda stared out the side window. All was quiet in the backseat.

True love? Who was I kidding? The words sounded hollow, even to me.

THE traffic jam started about five miles outside of town. Lucky for me, I was a native, and knew all the burro paths that would get us around the worst of it. As we bumped over rutted dirt roads, I was glad I hadn't brought the Porsche or a Ferrari. Of course, Miss Patterson might be less than pleased when she saw her car, but I'd think of some way to make it up to her.

Pulling the Beautiful Jeremy Whitlock out from under Metro's microscope would go a long way in that direction. For most of the drive, I had pushed possible scenarios around in my mind, trying to find a connection.

Of course, pretty early on, it had dawned on me that Numbers could have been stung by one of our millions of bees on the loose that night and simply died. The one fly in that ointment was, if she died like that, why the shark tank? Which raised another question: Who tossed her in? And wouldn't she have one of those epinephrine pens all the highly allergic folks carried, just in case? So where was that?

I had a sneaking suspicion it wasn't just one bee, but Romeo would tell me for sure.

One of the sheriff's deputies manned a roadblock at the entrance to an alleyway leading behind Mona's. In his green uniform shirt, beige pants, combat boots, and flat-brimmed hat, he looked like a kid playing dress-up. Was the sheriff's office recruiting them right out of middle school now? I bet he only had to shave once a week, if that. When did the whole world get so much younger? And when did we start giving them sidearms?

I rolled down the window and stuck my head out as I eased to a stop.

Before I could say anything, the child pretending to be a deputy tipped his hat at me. "Ma'am," he said, making my day.

"I'm the delivery service." I motioned with my head toward the backseat. "She's the center ring attraction in today's circus."

"Ma'am?"

If he said that one more time, I'd show him what his gun was for. I felt like I had one foot in the grave already—I didn't need him to give me a shove. "I'm Lucky O'Toole, Mona's daughter. The young lady in the back is the one being auctioned today."

"Really?" The kid bent down and stared at Arrianna, then recognition dawned. "Hey, Ari! I haven't seen you since high school." Then he turned to me. "We went to school together."

"So I gathered."

The boy whistled. "Man, I didn't know it was you that's got the town in such a dither, but I should have known. You always could get 'em all lathered up."

"Thank you for that insight," I said. "Could we go now?" Clearly I had left my sunny disposition at home.

He patted my windowsill then stepped back. "Good luck. It's a feeding frenzy up the road a piece."

I left him in a cloud of dust.

As Mona's came into view, I realized that, along with being really irritating, our young deputy was prone to gross understatement. Yesterday's mob had multiplied overnight and now filled not only the front parking lot but also the side yards. A few intrepid souls even filtered around the back.

Ignoring all of them, I positioned the car so Arrianna would have the shortest run to the backdoor, then called Mother's cell number. "We're out back," I said, when she answered.

The sheriff and a couple of deputies appeared and ushered the main attraction into the house. They left Aunt Matilda and me to fend for ourselves. Once I had her settled in the front sitting room with an appropriate beverage, I made a circuit of the house to assess the situation.

Obviously, access was carefully controlled—I was the only living creature patrolling the common areas of the ground floor. Pots clanged behind the door to the kitchen and snippets of music filtered down from the upper floors, so I wasn't alone in the house, but you couldn't prove it by me.

I peeked through the lace curtains on the front window. Like a pack of rabid dogs, various reporters with cameramen in tow patrolled the front lawn looking for fresh meat. A scrum of men knotted in front of a large screen off to the side of the house—either Mother had been busy or I'd been particularly unobservant, but I didn't recall seeing it yesterday. Reminding me of the stock exchange ticker, real-time bid information marched across the screen. Men waited in line at computer terminals, which sprouted in the yard like electronic weeds.

People of all shapes and sizes packed the parking lot. Some of them I recognized as locals. Off to the side, a group of women and men marched—the same group of thumpers I had seen yesterday. The same black-clad man, holding a Bible aloft, spurred them on.

One enterprising fellow served food and refreshments from his weenie wagon, which he had wedged in between the news trucks

across the street. His sign advertised homemade tamales and fun‐
nel cakes—an interesting combination. My stomach growled at the
thought. I would pay for it, but tamales were definitely in my im‐
mediate future.

A door slammed upstairs and I heard the telltale clacking of
Mona's stilettos on the stairs.

At the same time, a middle-aged man, his jeans hanging low
under his burgeoning belly, darted from the parlor. He stopped in
front of me, tilted his head back, and looked at me through a pair
of reading glasses perched on the end of his nose. I guess I must've
been blurry because he lowered his head, then gazed at me over
the top of the glasses. "Do I know you?" he asked.

"No."

He looked relieved—I didn't know what that meant. "Do you
know where Mona is? The servers are overloaded. We've blown a
fuse!" He ran an unsteady hand through his thinning hair as his
eyes darted around the room. "I can't keep up with the volume of
bids coming in."

"The fuse box is in a panel in the laundry room off the kitchen.
Does that help?"

With a scowl at me, he darted through the door to the back of
the house.

I met Mother in the foyer, at the bottom of the stairs.

Smartly dressed in a black suit with a gold lamé sweater un‐
derneath, black hose with a gold seam down the back of each leg,
and black leather Ferragamos with gold buckles, she was the pic‐
ture of calm, cool, and collected—if you overlooked the sheen of
perspiration above her upper lip. She fixed me with a cold stare.
"Where's our girl?"

"Upstairs, preparing herself." The tone of my voice matched
hers. "And you're welcome."

With a nod, she dismissed me as she strode to the front door
and opened it a few inches. "Send in the next one," she said through
the crack.

The door opened to admit a reporter and cameraman.

"Over here," Mona ordered, as she took a stance in the curve of the staircase. "Any time you're ready."

The cameraman set up the shot, the lights came on. "We're rolling," he said, his eye glued to the eyepiece.

The reporter stepped in next to Mother, thrust a mike in her face, and said, "Mona, as owner of this establishment, how do feel about being called the leader of the attack on American morality?"

This ought to be good. I crossed my arms and leaned against the front door.

Mother gave the camera an elegant smile. "Morality is a luxury of the middle class. It's all well and good when you have food on the table and a roof over your head."

Whoo boy. Talk about biting the hand that feeds you . . . I hoped the Big Boss wasn't watching.

If Mother was counting on me to ride to her rescue again, she had a rude fall coming. She could stew in her own juice for all I cared. Maybe the scorching would teach her a lesson—doubtful, but I'm a bit of a Pollyanna, so hope springs eternal.

Glancing at my watch, I opened the front door and eased outside. I still had fifteen minutes, and those tamales were calling my name.

Call me shallow, but, as I wandered through the crowd listening to snippets of conversation, I was sorta enjoying the comeuppance I saw in Mother's future.

I nodded at two men I recognized as locals. "Mr. Beckwith. Mr. Perkins."

Mr. Beckwith had been caught with his pants down in the girl's bathroom at the local high school. Mr. Perkins was caught doin' a cute little redhead at the local Dairy Queen. When his wife had gotten word of his shenanigans she'd chased him around the kitchen with a butcher knife until the law had arrived.

As I eased past them, the two men glared at me as if I had a scarlet letter tattooed on my forehead. "Your mother gives prostitution a bad name," one of them hissed at me.

Explanations would be futile—those two didn't think with the heads above their shoulders. I resisted pointing out the obvious—they weren't exactly stellar examples of the Y chromosome set either.

And they weren't entirely accurate. Mother was one of the white hats in a black business. This virginity auction was an anomaly for her. Rescuing young women from their bad choices was more her style. I don't know how many she'd taken off the street, cleaned up, provided with an education, and sent on their way. Throwing this one to the wolves . . . well, I couldn't figure it out at all. I wondered what was going on. Did I really want to know? Probably not.

Pausing next to the sheriff, I watched as his deputies herded the picketers across the street. "I'm glad you're taking them out of Mona's range," I said. "That could get ugly."

A day's stubble dotting his cheeks, his uniform wilted, the sheriff looked ready to crumple where he stood. "I had to threaten to shoot them before they finally moved," he said. "It's some outfit from somewhere in Kentucky. They travel around the country sticking their noses into other people's business."

This was tantamount to a felony in Nevada—a mind-your-own-damned-business state. "Remember the guy that railed against the sex trade by day, then availed himself by night?" I asked the sheriff, who smiled at the memory.

He had a bit of chewing tobacco stuck in his front teeth. "As I recall," he said, "the dude liked men, which made it even better." He pulled a bandana out of his back pocket, doffed his hat, then dabbed at his brow. "Do you happen to know what the high bid is now?"

"Haven't a clue," I said curtly.

The sheriff didn't take the hint. "My daughter buys stuff on eBay all the time," he said. "She told me it's best to wait until the very last few seconds, then throw in your bid. What do you think?"

This man was going to have to stop asking me what I thought. Any minute I might lose control and give him both barrels. "I'd defer to experience," I said, gravely.

He chewed his lip as he tried to muster a thought.

Shoulder to shoulder, we stood for a moment watching the throng as they jostled to place bids at the terminals. The chanting of the picketers provided an interesting soundtrack.

Finally, the sheriff broke our silence. "So, what do you think about all of this?"

"Personally, I'm against prostitution," I deadpanned. "I don't think anybody ought to have to pay for sex."

Chapter

FOURTEEN

J had wolfed down two tamales when I felt a hand on my elbow.

"Ms. O'Toole?"

One finger to my lips as I worked to finish a bite, I nodded.

"I thought that was you," the young man said. "I'm Charles. After your call last night, I raced to the airport. You know the Bay Area—the fog was rolling in fast. I wouldn't be surprised if my plane was the last one out."

"You're here; that's all that matters."

Of medium height and slight build, Charles had the slouchy, approachable look of a doctor; kindness surrounded him like an aura. His soft brown puppy-dog eyes were filled with concern. His close-cropped blond hair reminded me of Teddie's—a thought that daggered my heart, momentarily stealing my breath.

Tracking him down had given Brandy a bit of trouble. Since he was a first-year medical student, reaching him by phone had taken me so long that I had almost gotten on a plane to look for him in person, like Diogenes with his lantern searching for an honest man.

After wiping my hand with a napkin, I shook his. "Nice to meet you."

"I tried to stay out of this," he said. "I mean, it's really her decision, isn't it?" He jammed his hands into the pockets of his jeans as he cast furtive glances toward the house. "Besides, she's not taking my calls. Last time we talked, she said she didn't want to hear from me until it was over."

"Understandable. If I were in her position, I wouldn't discuss sleeping with someone else—even just for money—with the man I loved." On occasion Vegas could be weirder than other times— this was one of the truly odd moments. "I know you think this is all Arrianna's decision, but it's not. First, we all need the advice of loved ones—especially when we wander off the path. Second, she's going to be your wife. I'd say you have a right to weigh in."

For some reason, I'd lost my appetite. I offered the remaining tamale to Charles. He shook his head, so I wandered to a nearby can and pitched it.

"If she goes through with this, I don't know how we're going to move on," he said as he followed me. "I'm afraid it's going to hang between us forever." He looked at me with hound-dog eyes. "Like that movie, you know?"

"*Indecent Proposal?*" Movie nights with Teddie brought perspective at the oddest times. "With Robert Redford and Demi Moore?"

"That's the one—damned depressing show." His face held the look of a condemned man. "I feel like a creep letting the woman I love sell herself—for us. I don't think I could live with myself if I didn't try to stop her."

I liked this guy—oh, I liked him a lot.

"As I said on the phone, I can get you inside and I can keep Mona occupied for a bit. The rest is up to you."

. . .

TRUDI hadn't been hard to bribe, although her price had been higher than I'd anticipated—a spa weekend at the Babylon. At my knock, she opened the backdoor. "Mona's still preening for the cameras. Take the service stairs." Trudi smiled at us and thumped Charles on the back. Just another sucker for love.

I pushed Charles ahead of me up the narrow staircase. "All the way to the top, then turn right. Mother's suite is the only room up there. You'll see the door."

Like a gazelle, he bounded up the stairs two at a time. I darn near herniated myself trying to keep up—I should have known better. I arrived at the top landing in time to see him disappear through Mona's door.

A voice behind me turned me to stone. "Why your mother won't put in an elevator! I've been telling her to do it for decades."

Aunt Matilda! I'd forgotten about that particular fly in the ointment.

Hoping my face wasn't as red as a hothouse tomato, I collected myself and turned to face her. "The stairs are Mother's final assurance her clients are healthy enough for sexual activity." God, I sounded like one of those horrid commercials. "Ask your doctor if you're healthy enough . . . and seek immediate medical attention for an erection lasting more than four hours." Like every female I knew, I had been traumatized by that last part. Four hours! I'd be dead . . . or in need of immediate medical attention myself.

"Move aside." Matilda tried to move me with her cane. Who was she kidding? I could take her with one hand behind my back, although she looked pretty scrappy. "That was the boyfriend, wasn't it?"

"Leave them alone, okay?" I said, as I stood my ground. *If he talks her out of it* . . . from the look on her face, it was clear elaboration would be redundant. And I wanted her out of the way, but short of throwing her over my shoulder and toting her downstairs, I was fresh out of ideas.

"I've been thinking about what you said in the car." For a moment Matilda looked almost human, fragile.

"That money is no compensation for a life poorly lived?"

"Is that what you said?"

"I'm paraphrasing, but that was the nut of it."

She gave me a shrewd, appraising look. "I always knew you were smart, but I never realized you were wise."

Well, knock me over with a feather boa.

Without giving too much away, and gaining an ally in the process. I was able to negotiate our return to the ground floor.

Melancholy washed over my aunt as I deposited her in an overstuffed chair in the corner of the parlor. "The best part of life had passed me by before I figured out the important parts," she said. "I refused to let the same thing happen to your mother. I wasn't entirely successful, as you know. But now, she's still young enough to have her bite of the apple."

"Perhaps she's bitten off more than she can chew," I stated, as I motioned to one of the extra staff Mother had engaged for the big event. "A gin martini, for the lady here. Make it dirty, please."

"I heard she had taken up with your Big Boss," Matilda stated matter-of-factly. Neither her tone nor her expression gave any hint as to what she knew.

"Yeah, it's sort of a new twist on a old theme. Instead of sleeping with the boss myself, I sent my mother. Do you think that was wise?"

"You know, don't you?" Matilda's eyes fixed on mine.

"Know what?" I asked with a wink.

"He's very sad that you won't let him crow to the world."

"I know." I pulled a throw from the couch and tucked it around her bird legs. "In time. Life's coming at me pretty fast right now; I'm having a hard time keeping up."

WITH her dirty martini and studly waiter, Matilda was happy. I left her there and repositioned myself by the front door, where I could watch Mother's series of interviews. She worked through the last of the lot as I arrived. When finished, she deigned to grace me with her attention. "I can talk to you now."

"Am I lucky, or what?"

She gave me a stare, but, for once, she didn't launch a return salvo.

"Remember, I'm not talking to you," I said, as I took a good look at her.

A little ragged around the edges, Mona's mask was slipping. "No, I didn't remember. Apparently you didn't either."

"Good point." Pulling the curtains aside, I looked out the window. The crowd pulsed with excitement. This was the biggest thing to happen to Pahrump since Mabel Jenkins ran down Highway 160 through the middle of town buck-naked in a desperate attempt to get her husband's attention. I don't know whether Mr. Jenkins noticed, but the rest of the town sat up and saluted. "Is this all you hoped it would be?"

"Are you giving me a hard time again?" Mona dabbed at the corner of an eye with a knuckle.

"Probably."

"What time is it?"

"Ten minutes until the stroke of the axe."

"Lucky, I swear!" She gave me a dirty look. "Time to go get our—"

"Sacrificial lamb?" Rubbing salt in the wound, I know. Sometimes shallow feels really good.

With a groan of frustration, Mother started up the stairs. As she disappeared around the first landing, I threw a look at my aunt over my shoulder. She gave me the thumbs-up sign. We'd put all our money on Charles—the dark horse in this race. I couldn't wait for the big payoff.

I didn't have to wait long.

A scream echoed down the stairs. "She's gone!"

I pumped my fists in the air and did a happy dance.

Mona clacked furiously down the stairs. Like a jet on a strafing run, the noise grew louder and louder until she appeared in front of me waving a piece of paper. "She left a note!"

"Really?" I widened my eyes in feigned innocence.

Tapping one stilettoed foot, she ripped the letter into tiny pieces in front of my face, then let them drift to the floor. "This was all your fault, wasn't it?"

"I sincerely hope so."

"You called the boyfriend, didn't you?" A smile tugged at the corner of her lips.

"I'm a sucker for love."

Then my mother did the darndest thing. She hugged me.

AS I piloted Miss P's car back toward Vegas—which was now looking positively mundane compared to Pahrump—I marveled at my friends and family and their unusual behavior of late. First, Jordan wanting to marry Rudy, thereby shooting his livelihood through the heart, then Teddie and his little trust issue, and then Matilda and Mother.

It seemed they all were playing musical personalities and I'd been tossed from the game. Was I the only sane person left? Or maybe they were all sane and I'd finally lost it? Who knew? Either way, I was clearly out of synch. Perhaps I'd better keep my distance in case there really was something to the whole insanity-by-association thing.

Tortilla Padilla's weigh-in lit off at four o'clock. I'd better hurry if I was to make it back, check in with the office, then be there to watch two buff males parade around in their underwear.

Stomping on the accelerator, then being underwhelmed, I remembered. Fast was not possible unless I could spur the squirrels under the hood to peddle faster.

MY office was empty when I breezed through the door, tossed Miss Patterson's keys on the desk, then deposited my Birkin in the closet.

I had just settled a hip on the corner of my desk and was rifling through my messages when the outer door burst open and Miss P appeared in my doorway.

"How'd the auction go?" she asked, looking at me over the top of her cheaters as she handed me my phone.

"True love carried the day." I pocketed my phone, then pulled a message from Romeo out of the stack. It read simply, "Nothing yet."

"What does that mean?" Miss P asked.

"Hunh?" I crumpled the paper and launched it toward the can. I missed. "Sorry. The auction was . . . interesting."

Her eyes grew wider and wider as I regaled her with the Cliffs-Notes version of my morning. "So the girl bolted, leaving your mother holding the bag? And you set the whole thing in motion?" Admiration shone in her eyes.

I basked in her fleeting hero worship. "Very occasionally, I do something right."

"I bet somebody sues your mother."

"On what grounds? Raised . . . expectations?" I moved to perch in my chair. "And what would they sue for? Specific performance? I've met some interesting judges in my time, but I can't see one ordering a young lady to sacrifice her virginity."

"So you left your mother to clean up the mess?"

"It was hers to deal with, and besides, she had Aunt Matilda to help." I pushed at a new pile of papers propagating on my desk.

"There is a God." Miss P grinned at me.

"Any major fires I should know about?"

"I put Brandy in charge of our DJ—apparently he has some issues with the equipment setup." Miss P consulted her clipboard. "Bakker Rutan, the actress, is coming but she must be flown in after dark, just prior to the party, then flown home again so she can see the sunrise in Malibu."

I raised my eyebrows.

"Apparently she finds Vegas depressing in the daylight."

I couldn't fault her there. "Have you made the appropriate arrangements?"

"I'll meet her plane, then Brandy is going to do the return."

"Anything else?"

"You've been invited to an ice-cream social."

"An ice-cream social?" I hadn't been to one of those since I was a very little girl, and even then they were few and far between for the daughter of a madam. "By whom?"

"Miss Maria José Padilla. Tonight at seven thirty in the Padilla's bungalow."

"Please tell her I am honored and will most certainly be there."

Miss Patterson looked surprised. "You will?"

"Of course. Now, if you don't have anything else for me, I've got to go ogle a couple of middleweights in their skivvies."

A stage, bathed in the otherworldly glow of klieg lights, sat in the middle of one of our larger ballrooms. A large scale occupied the center of the stage and was the demarcation between Tortilla Padilla's camp on the left and the European's on the right. A tuxedo-clad man with a radio voice presided over the festivities. Both fighters bounced on their toes, jabbing the air. As expected, each of them wore next to nothing.

Television cameras recorded the event for posterity as a large crowd gathered in front. My eyes needed a moment to adjust to the darkness. Sidling out of the doorway, my shoulder collided with another. "Sorry."

"O'Toole?" A familiar male voice.

"Daniel?" I squinted in the darkness.

The district attorney leaned against the back wall, clutching his daughter, Gabi, who rested against him.

"Hey, Gabi. What are you two doing here?"

"Glinda is one of the Round Card Girls for the fight. Gabi's too young for the main event, so I brought her today to see her mother in action."

As if on cue, Glinda, her figure beautifully displayed in an orange bikini and matching high heels, appeared on stage to numerous catcalls.

Gabi gasped, then she grabbed her father's hand. "Isn't she pretty, Daddy?" She didn't seem to notice that her father didn't answer.

The three of us watched as the fighters were each weighed and measured, then pretended to argue for the crowd. Periodically, Glinda would stroll across the stage with a sign igniting the crowd to a particular activity: boo, applause, cheer. All went swimmingly until one of the European's handlers decided to take on Crash. With one punch, the big man flattened him. Security stepped in to restrain the rest of the group, who postured and preened, making a big show of their collective manliness.

Daniel, Gabi, and I walked out together.

The girl tugged her father's hand. "Take me to the park. You promised. Remember?"

Daniel grinned like a fool. In his daughter's presence, he looked ten years younger—if you ignored the black eye that had faded to greens and yellows and the new gash, closed with two butterfly bandages, on his left cheekbone. "She loves the new kid's park in Summerlin. We go every Sunday after church."

"You promised," Gabi whined, playing her father as only young girls can.

"Go wait for me by the door. I need to talk to Ms. O'Toole for a minute."

Gabi groaned and gave him an exaggerated eye roll, but did as he asked.

Daniel stepped in close to me, grasping my arm in a viselike grip. "If I were you, I'd quit digging into the Neidermeyer matter."

Taken aback at his tone, I managed to hold my ground. "Why?"

"These sorts of things can be dangerous—not only to you but to the ones you love. A father, for instance." His eyes, dark and fathomless, held mine.

"Is that a threat, Daniel?" I jerked my arm from his grasp in what I hoped was a show of strength—strength I didn't feel as my stomach roiled. "You know as well as I, I don't have a father."

"You were warned, O'Toole." He stepped away, his usual mask falling into place. "Be careful. Be very careful."

NERVOUS energy pulsed through me, thoughts rattled my brain, feelings battered my heart. In short, I was a wreck.

I needed to walk—or have sex, but sex didn't seem to be in the cards right now, so walking it was. After two circuits of the casino, the only thing I had accomplished was to add my feet to the long list of body parts that ached. On the verge of surrender, I heard a voice shout my name.

"Lucky!"

I turned and scanned the crowd.

"Ms. O'Toole, wait."

Arrianna, her face flushed, Charles's hand clutched in hers as she pulled him along, broke through the crowd. Out of breath, the two of them arrived in front of me.

"Hey, you two. I am not going to ask you what you've been doing." I gave them a group hug.

"We've been looking for you!"

"Really? What for?"

Charles, looking equally as giddy as his girl, stepped forward. "She said *yes!*" He proffered her left hand and the ring on her finger for my inspection.

I whistled appropriately. "Congratulations. And best wishes to you, Arrianna. What a day, huh?"

"It's not over," she said. "We're getting married."

"So I gathered."

"*Now!* We're getting married *now,* but we couldn't do it without you."

"Now? Me?" My heart filled to overflowing. I'd never been a required member at a wedding before.

She grabbed my hand and I raced along with the youngsters,

high on the adrenaline spike of love . . . and youthful lust. True love was alive and well!

The personification of patience, Delphinia waited in front of the Temple of Love. A smile split her face when she saw us. "Fabulous! I was beginning to despair."

As she ushered us inside, I drew Arrianna aside. "What about your parents?"

"They asked that you stand in, then we can have a full Indian wedding this summer between semesters."

"I'm a poor substitute for parents—this isn't one of my areas of expertise, but let's see what we can do."

Still dressed in her white sundress and sandals, Arrianna looked every inch the blushing bride.

"How does that ditty go? Something old, something new?" I said.

"My dress is new—my underwear is old."

I gave her a look. "Old underwear is not what I had in mind." I unscrewed my square-cut diamond earrings and handed them to her. "For luck."

As she inserted them, she glanced over her shoulder at Charles and gave him a shy smile. His eyes shone with love as he looked at his bride-to-be. This was way more fun than I thought.

"What's the rest of it? Something old, something new. Something borrowed, something blue."

"So the earrings are old and borrowed," Arrianna said. "That leaves blue."

Delphinia came to our rescue with a blue ribbon, which the girl tied into her hair. With only the blush of love tinting her skin, her simple dress, and flowing hair, Arrianna was the most beautiful bride I had ever seen. I had to choke back tears as she moved to take her intended's hand and they turned to face the minister.

The ceremony was simple, elegant, and over too fast. We all played our parts, and Arrianna and Charles were one.

· · ·

AFTER celebrating with a bottle of champagne I pilfered from Samson's, the newlyweds wandered off, hand in hand, toward Bungalow Two. I'd made sure it remained theirs through the weekend.

Buzzed on life, I strolled through the Bazaar toward the hotel. With over an hour to kill before the ice-cream social, I didn't want to puncture my good mood by showing up in any of the usual places. If a real problem cropped up, I had no doubt someone would find me. Until then, I intended to float on my cloud of good feelings.

I had just tucked into another virgin frozen piña colada, and was drooling over the new Louis Vuitton designs, when I caught a familiar face reflected in the window.

Teddie.

My heart rolled over and died. Terrific. I set my glass on the window ledge then turned to face him.

His eyes red, his complexion green, he looked like he'd just crawled out from under a rock. Apparently he'd slept in his clothes.

"I've been looking for you everywhere."

"My office can always find me." I kept the hope out of my voice. He'd already disappointed me once.

"I wanted to say my piece in person, man to man," Teddie said. "Besides, it's very hard to eat crow over the phone." He gave me a rueful shrug.

For a moment neither of us moved—the space between us yawning wide—an unbridgeable chasm.

"There's no excuse for the things I said." He held his arms toward me, imploring.

"Nor for the things I haven't." I stepped into him. With one hand behind his head, I pulled him to me, and kissed him deep and long, with everything I had.

He grabbed me tight and kissed me back.

When I found the strength, I pulled back just far enough so I could look him right in the eye, but I kept my body pressed to his. "Look, here's the way it is. No matter how much I want to deny it, there's something strong between us. Nobody affects me the way you do. I'd write it off to hormones or lust or . . . well, you get my point. But I know better. This isn't any of that."

His eyes widened slightly.

"I didn't want to fall in love. I don't want to be in love. For all its giddy pleasures, love exacts a toll. I don't want to pay it. But, as usual, I didn't get what I wanted."

"You'd turn your back on love?" Teddie's voice was quiet, hollow with defeat.

"Of course not. Just because I didn't ask for it, and it scares me to death, doesn't mean I won't try for the brass ring. I mean, people have written odes to love, they've given their lives for love. Look at Romeo and Juliet, for chrissake! And Odysseus, what about him? He sailed twenty years, braving the world's worst dangers. And why? To get home to the woman he loved! There must be something to this love thing. So, when given my shot, why would I turn tail and run? What do you think I am, an idiot?"

"Well, you're not making a whole lot of sense," Teddie said, his pinched expression relaxing a little.

"I know I'm babbling." I resisted the urge to nibble his ear—I was hopeless, a doormat. "But I can't decide whether I'm being a putz"

"A putz?"

"My head tells me I should be reaming you out for last night. But my heart tells me to make you suffer a bit, then let it go."

"Which way are you leaning?"

"I'm sitting on the fence." I stepped back, putting a little distance between us. With his body pressed to mine, clearly my ability to form a coherent, concise thought was trickling away. Heart overriding head. If I let that happen, I wouldn't like myself in the morning. "Perhaps you ought to have a go?"

"I only have an explanation—no excuses." He ran a hand through his hair, which lacked its normal spikes—crestfallen like the look on its owner's face. "You and Jordan Marsh have been grist for the rumor mill for a long time. At first, I didn't believe it.

But you hear something often enough you figure there's a grain of truth."

"So you condemned me based on unfounded rumor and innuendo?"

He pressed his lips together then shook his head slowly. "No, I think it was finding the man himself in your apartment dressed only in a pair of gym shorts and looking like a guy's worst nightmare, doing the whole 'Honey, I'm home' thing."

"Well, there was that."

"And it hit me, like a punch I never saw coming—losing you . . . I can't imagine anything worse. Should you choose to, you could rip my heart out and I'd be powerless to stop you. I guess I got defensive."

"You guess?"

"Okay, I acted like a total jerk. I admit it. I'm not trying to be smarmy here, but I really don't know what I would do if I lost you." He brushed the back of his fingers across my cheek. "Lucky, you're in every melody I hear, every lyric I write. You fill my heart and feed my soul."

"Steak in a hamburger world?" I quit fighting and let the hint of a grin curl my lips.

"Precisely!" Teddie didn't look quite so green now. "Reza told you?"

"Yes. And you owe her one—that little admission from a disinterested party paved a whole section of your road to redemption."

"Can you forgive me?"

"If you promise me one thing," I said, enjoying the mix of emotions surging across his face.

"Anything."

I grabbed him by the shirt and brought his face close to mine. "Later, when the day is done, I want you to open a bottle of very expensive brandy." I kept my voice low.

His eyes widened as I ran a finger along his jaw. One corner of his mouth lifted. "Okay."

"Then . . ." I nipped at his lower lip. "Warm me a snifter."

"Jesus, woman," he groaned. "What then?"

"Then, very slowly, very deliberately, I want you to show me just how much you love me."

"I'll make you beg."

"Even better," I whispered against his lips just before they captured mine.

The shoppers around us applauded.

AWARE only of my hand in Teddie's, his shoulder touching mine as we sat on the bench in front of the piano in Delilah's Bar, I thought about love—a gossamer, silken thread of joy. With a tensile strength to pull even the most stubborn, the most fearful of us through the quicksand of our own insecurities and stupidities, love was truly the tie that binds, a rare gift.

I relinquished Teddie's hand. "Play something and tell me about your trip to California."

"It was a whirlwind. Reza and I finished laying some tracks this afternoon at the Palms, so that should be done. I'll work with her team on the mixing next week." Without obvious thought, Teddie began to play a nice melody, one I didn't recognize.

I watched his hands as they moved fluidly, lightly. Long-fingered, his hands were the hands of an artist, the keyboard his palette.

"Mr. O'Dell offered me a nice contract. He's signed it, but before I did, I wanted Rudy to go over it. My knowledge of recording contracts is just enough to get me into trouble." Unable to resist the call of the music, Teddie closed his eyes and swayed to the rhythm.

"Music feeds your soul, doesn't it." I said.

"Always has. I'd never found anything else that put me so at peace until I found you."

"Where did you learn how to steal my breath away?"

"Simple words, spoken from the heart." He finished his song with a flourish then looked at me. "Who's your favorite singer?

Give me someone romantic, okay? I'm in that kind of mood, don't know why."

"Let's go with an oldie, then. How about Tony Bennett?"

"Perfect," he said. "Now shut your eyes."

I did as I was told and rested my head on his shoulders.

Teddie began the intro to "The Very Thought of You." When he began to sing, I got chills—if I didn't know better, I would swear Mr. Bennett himself was singing. Teddie's impersonations always amazed me.

I sneaked one eye open and glanced at the other patrons in the bar. Most had stopped talking and were watching Teddie. When he finished, the bar erupted into applause.

Pulling me to my feet, Teddie gave a bow then moved me toward the steps. "Can we go home now?" he asked. The poor man looked dead on his feet.

"Unfortunately I'm so far from home, I can't even see it from here." At the bottom of the steps I steered him in the direction of the Kasbah. "Right now, my presence is required at a party. Want to come?"

"I'm not dressed for a party." He hung back.

I took in his jeans, his crumpled shirt. "You're perfect. In every way."

THE door to Bungalow Seven was open when we got there, the party in full swing. Kids ricocheted off the furniture, the walls, each other.

Tortilla Padilla, half hidden behind a table overloaded with five-gallon tubs of ice cream, waved a scoop at us. "Welcome!" He gestured to his youngest daughter. "Maria José, your guest is here and she's brought a friend."

The young girl launched herself in my direction. Arms open wide, I squatted down then caught her as she jumped. Clutching her to me, I stood and laughed—a laugh that bubbled up unexpectedly from some happy place deep inside. Unable to resist, I whirled her around until she giggled uncontrollably.

When she sobered, she cast her dark eyes on Teddie. *"¿Quien es?"* Who is that?

"Es mi amor. Se llama, Teo." *He is my love. His name is Teo.* That's the closest I could come to Ted.

"Teo," the young girl whispered dreamily. I knew how she felt.

Maria José shimmied down my body, grabbed Teddie's hand in one of hers, my hand with the other, and led us into the fray.

Teddie, his eyes warm, shot me a grin over the girl's head. "This is some party, *mi amor*!"

I knew he'd like it.

A shout from the door turned heads. Arrianna and Charles strolled in. Like bees to verdant flowers, the kids swarmed around them. When I'd introduced Arrianna to them yesterday, I figured the chemistry would work. She and Charles both knelt as the children each shouted for attention.

"Interesting way to spend your wedding evening," I said, then smiled as they blushed.

"The night's still young," Charles countered with a grin. "But we had to be with the children, even if only for a little while. Arrianna . . ." He glanced at the young woman at his side, love in his eyes. "My *wife* has told me so much about them." Happiness radiated off the two of them like heat off asphalt.

Young love, nothing like it. I felt like the Grinch when he realized he couldn't steal Christmas and his heart grew three sizes.

"Sixteen children are a force to be reckoned with," I said, as Maria José gave Arrianna a big hug.

"The Padillas have asked us to spend the summer in Mexico working with them," Charles continued. "Apparently their foundation funds a children's clinic. We can work alongside the doctors."

The kids chattered in Spanish, and I helped bridge the language barrier.

As bellies filled with ice cream, the energy level and the decibel level rose. Somewhere along the way I lost track of Teddie. Before I could go look for him, Carmen motioned to me from the doorway, and I followed her down a hallway into the salon.

Seated at the grand piano, Teddie played, a bevy of children circled on the floor and Tomás sat next to him.

Teddie, a constant surprise, played and sang the theme song to Barney, sounding just like the purple dinosaur. Enraptured, not one of the kids so much as wiggled as they stared at him in awe.

Swaying slightly, Tomás watched Teddie's hands as they moved over the keys.

When Teddie finished, he put his hands in his lap, then said to Carmen, "Watch this." He nodded to the boy next to him.

With a little encouragement, Tomás began to play, his deformed foot swinging in time to the music, a smile playing with his lips, his brow furrowed in concentration.

Next to me, Carmen gasped.

When the boy faltered, Teddie was quick to show him the keys. Two passes through the music, the youngster had mastered the melody and started chording by ear. Periodically Teddie would show him what he was reaching for, but there was no doubt music resonated in the boy's soul.

Carmen left, returning quickly with her husband and the other children. We all gathered around, witnesses to the magic.

There wasn't a dry eye in the house.

Chapter

FIFTEEN

♡

So, Ms. O'Toole, do you have any more surprises for me this evening?" Teddie asked, as we opened the door to my empty office and stepped inside. Our good-byes to the children had taken over an hour, and we each wore various flavors of ice cream by the time we were able to disengage.

I grabbed him by the front of his shirt, pulling him to me. "I can think of one or two."

"Here?" Teddie looked intrigued, but a little dubious at the same time. "What about all these windows?"

Leaving the lights off, I pulled him into my inner office and kicked the door shut behind us, locking it. "This couch has been yearning for a shake-down cruise."

Pulling my shirttail from my pants, he started on the buttons, taking his time. A smile worked the corner of his mouth as his eyes shone. "I like this side of you—a bit unexpected."

Stopping him, I grabbed a clicker from my desk drawer, hit a button, and—like magic—window shades descended from a recessed track in the ceiling. "This is a private show."

While he watched, I finished the buttons on my shirt, letting it drop to the floor. Kicking off my shoes, I stepped out of my slacks. At the look on his face, I was glad I'd picked the matching red-lace bra and bikini briefs with gartered stockings.

Running his hands down my arms, he lit a fire.

Hurrying now, I worked through the buttons on his shirt and pushed it over his shoulders, letting my hands wander over his chest.

With one hand he unhooked my bra then crushed me to him.

"Remember what you promised," I whispered against his lips.

"To make you beg."

WITH Teddie collapsed on top of me, my heart beating a staccato rhythm, I ran a shaky hand through my hair as I tried to catch my breath. Mr. Kowalski had indeed delivered on his promise . . . in spades. And the titillation of perhaps being interrupted had added a bit of unexpected spice. Who knew getting in touch with my naughty-girl side could be so . . . incendiary.

Echoes of an earthquake of pleasure shockwaves still pulsed through me. Excitement sparked where his skin touched mine. Office sex had to be right up there with make-up sex.

"Woman, if that was my penance, I'm going to sin more often," Teddie groaned, as he pushed himself to an elbow, his body still covering mine.

"If that's what it takes, I might be willing to put up with it, but I wouldn't push your luck." I didn't want to move, not ever.

He gave me a long, lingering kiss. I worked one leg from under him, looping it over his as he deepened his kiss.

Finally, I came up for air. "You better quit that, unless you're ready for round two."

The torn look on his face made me laugh. "I'm willing to risk death, if you are," he murmured against my lips.

Finding strength I didn't know I had, I put my hands on his chest and pushed. "I think we've stretched our luck far enough already. Sooner rather than later, someone is going to bang on that door."

As if on cue, I heard keys in the outer door.

With a sigh, he rolled off me then pulled me to my feet. Hugging me against him for a moment, he nuzzled my neck then let me go. Gathering our clothing a piece at a time we helped each other. Dressing Teddie was almost as much fun as working the other way—almost. We'd at least covered the essentials when a knock sounded on the door.

"Lucky? Are you in there?" Brandy asked, as she tried the knob.

"Give me a sec." I lingered in a last kiss.

When I threw open the door, Brandy stood, arm raised, hand poised to knock again.

"Come in," I said.

As she slowly lowered her arm, she narrowed her eyes, giving me a quizzical look. Then she looked around me, and her eyebrows shot up.

Shirtless, Teddie worked his belt back through the loops in his jeans. "Hey," he said, as he shot her a grin.

A smile spread across her face as she looked from him to me and back again. "I've heard office nookie can be mind blowing." She must've realized she was talking to the boss because she flushed crimson. "Sorry. That was inappropriate."

I looped an arm around her shoulders and escorted her to a chair. "This job is a bitch; we all develop our own coping skills," I rationalized.

"When I grow up, I want to be you." My awestruck assistant looked at me, her eyes wide.

"Fine, but you'll have to find your own man."

She looked at Teddie. "Bummer."

"Sorry, I'm totally taken," he said with a wink.

"Enough banter," I said, shutting them down. I'm the jealous type. You guys do not want to bait me." I plopped into my desk chair. "So, where's the fire?"

"Our DJ, he's not happy with the setup in Babel. I used to date one of our local DJs so I have a working knowledge of the equipment requirements."

"I'm glad one of us is conversant." Having a youngster on the staff was paying unexpected dividends. "And what's your take on his demands?"

"He's blowing smoke up my ass."

"Where is he now?"

"He's taken his prima donna act up to Babel, where he's, and I quote, 'Waiting for the Customer Relations bitch to get off her ass and solve this problem.'" Brandy leaned back as if there was truth to the old adage about shooting the messenger.

"I see. I'm assuming he has recovered from his bender the other day?" I pushed to my feet and girded myself for battle.

"He appears to be sober and none the worse for wear, although, with him, it's hard to tell."

I stepped around the desk and headed for the door. "Let's go handle the cocky Mr. Spin Monkey Red, shall we?"

Teddie nudged Brandy as they fell in step behind me. "I just love it when she gets her back up like this. Sexy as hell."

"Really," Brandy said. "I guess that shows how much I have to learn about men."

Maybe she'd listened after all—scary thought. The blind leading the blind.

IN Vegas, most nightclubs don't open until 10:30 P.M. and the crowd doesn't arrive until midnight. Babel was no exception—a fact I was glad for if I was going to have to face down a minor celebrity who'd been reading too much of his own press. As if dating heiresses and compiling playlists anointed him king! Each day the world made less and less sense. Either I was getting old or losing my mind.

Under the twinkling lights strung overhead, Mr. Spin Monkey Red paced back and forth across the Lucite-covered aquarium. Short and stocky, he wore a white muscle shirt with a larger flannel one tied around his neck. Bedecked in chains, his jeans clung resolutely to his hips, defying gravity and most of the other rules of physics. Tattoos chased down both arms from shoulder to wrist. His wiry black hair cut short, his lips thick, his chin recessed, he wasn't even attractive. A tiny fedora perched on the top of his head, reminding me of Charlie Chaplin or one of the Three Stooges—not the look I'd bet he was hoping for.

Staring down at the marine life swimming leisurely below him, the DJ didn't notice me until I stepped in front of him, bringing his pacing to an abrupt halt. He looked up at me through tiny dark eyes set too close together.

"Who're you? This place is closed," he growled, as he stepped around me.

"I'm the Customer Relations bitch."

As he turned around, he threw a dirty look toward Brandy, who had taken refuge on a stool at the bar next to Teddie.

She smiled.

"I didn't mean that literally. I was just doing the big-shot thing—it's expected, you know." His voice was high-pitched, childish in its whine. He was the very personification of 'the less you have, the more you pretend.'

"No, I didn't know." I easily had six inches on him. I stepped in closer, so he had to look up to see my face. "I understand you have some concerns about the equipment?"

Citing decibels and ohms and other terms I didn't have even a passing familiarity with, he started in on all the deficiencies. Pretending to be interested, I let him rant. He'd worked himself into quite a lather by the time I'd had enough—and had seen through his little charade.

I held up my hand, stopping him mid-tirade. "You faxed us your requirements when you accepted this engagement. Our technicians adhered strictly to your every request. The setup has been thoroughly tested and has been in play for the last week. The best local DJs have all thrown several sets. No one has complained."

His face flushed crimson. "You're not going to throw out this trash?" He gestured toward the stage. "You're not going to get me the stuff I deserve?" His voice cracked.

I leaned down, my mouth next to his ear. "This setup is more than you deserve. We have done as you asked. I expect you to do the same."

"I don't need this shit." He backed away from me.

Kids, they missed the point even when it stared them in the face—especially when they were scared. And under all that swagger and bluster, this kid looked terrified. I couldn't blame him—the Big Boss had made sure the grand opening of Babel was going to be the biggest extravaganza the Strip had ever seen. The thought sorta made me queasy as well, impossible to control, these events had a way of taking on a life of their own. If this one got out of hand and headed in the wrong direction, I'd be left holding the bag.

When I was sure I had his attention, I gave him my spiel. "Since Bugsy Siegel opened the Flamingo on a wing and a prayer, Vegas has been the center of the entertainment universe. The best in the business have begged to play Vegas. A gig here can make a career." I gestured toward the buildings of the Strip, bright beacons in the night. "This place is pure magic. The Hollywood crowd flocks here to be seen. Sinatra came here to revive a sagging career and became a legend in the process. So, yes you do need this shit, as you so eloquently put it. You need Vegas."

He hitched up his pants as he chewed on his lip. I could see his inner conflict—the truth versus his fear.

"The funny thing is, Vegas doesn't need you."

"So what are you saying?" Cocking his head to the side, he squinted one eye at me.

Unattractive, untalented, and dim . . . the ultimate American pop culture creation.

"You can walk. I could care. I'll get a replacement and sue your ass for breach of contract. Your call."

"That simple, huh?"

"That simple." I stared him down.

Finally, he shrugged. "Okay. You win. I'll do it, but I won't be happy."

"No, you'll do it, *and* you'll be happy."

Finally a smile tugged at the corner of his mouth. "You're one tough bitch, man."

At least he managed to get one point without me beating him over the head with it.

I stood at the edge of the roof, drinking in the view. Like Mesmer's mirror, the lights of the Strip held me in their spell—they always had. Under all the glitz and glamour, under the explicit in-your-face attitude, under the make-it-or-break-it mentality, Vegas celebrated people in all their weird and wonderful uniqueness. The city not only tolerated individuality, it threw a party to it each and every day. No judgments were passed, no looks of disdain thrown. All of us—misfits from all walks of life—were not only tolerated, we were appreciated.

That was the magic of Vegas.

I felt Teddie's presence at my side. Hooking my arm through his, I rested my head on his shoulder.

"It's our town," he murmured against my hair. "We fit here."

I knew he understood. Two peas in a pod.

With all the craziness whirling around me, with my mother and the Big Boss heading for a rough patch, with Tortilla Padilla putting his life on the line tomorrow night for the kids, with a murderer still wandering loose and a DA trying to frame Jeremy, with Jordan and his upcoming train wreck . . . with all of that, I still couldn't imagine life could get any better than it was right at this moment in time, with Teddie by my side and Vegas at my feet.

So, if life was so perfect, why did I get the feeling the prover-bial axe was about to lop off my head? Probably nothing more than the dark side of my Pollyanna personality, but something was niggling for my attention, I just couldn't put my finger on it.

"Everything smoothed over with your song-and-dance man?" Teddie asked.

My negative thoughts dissipated like a cloud under assault from the midday sun. "For now, but he's scared to death. He understands this is going to be a big stage and the world will be watching." I worked my hand into Teddie's as I led him away from the edge and back toward the dance floor. "I need you to do me a favor."

"Name it." He looped an arm around my waist, twirled me around, then gathered me to him.

With his body pressed to mine, it took all of my self-control to keep my mind . . . and my hands . . . from wandering. "The crowd tomorrow night will be a bit older than our DJ is used to, so the music will need to be adjusted accordingly. You're a music man, could you saunter over there and casually offer to help. The kid is at sea."

"You got it." He nuzzled my neck then gave me a parting kiss, jangling every nerve.

Still seated at the bar, Brandy had been watching the goings-on with a bemused expression, an expression she still wore.

Straddling the stool next to hers, I motioned to the bartender who was busy wiping down a glass at the far end of the bar. "Two Kir Royales, please."

"Even though I couldn't hear what you said to him, from the looks of things I'd say you got our boy lined out," Brandy said, once I got myself settled.

"Sometimes the biggest bullies are the most scared, so I threat-ened him to keep him on the job—which I doubt he would have walked away from anyway. Then I sent Teddie to help with the music and to calm frayed nerves, nerves our DJ never would have let you see."

"So I wasn't one to fix the problem?" Brandy took the fluted glasses from the bartender, then handed one to me.

"No. You'll get a feel for this as you go. Sometimes a problem needs a brawny guy from Security, sometimes it needs the delicate smile of a young, beautiful woman, sometimes it needs Miss P's motherly touch, and sometimes it needs the Customer Relations bitch." I clinked my glass to hers. "To teamwork."

"To teamwork," she replied, then we both took a drink, savoring the black raspberry and champagne bubbles. "It doesn't make you mad that he called you a bitch?"

"He can anoint me the personification of Lucifer himself as long as he does his job."

Teddie and our DJ had their heads together as Teddie pointed and punched keys. Every now and then he would nudge the kid in the ribs and they would nod and smile. The magic was working.

My phone vibrated in my pocket. Glancing at the number before I flipped it open, I smiled. "Jordan! Where are you?"

Brandy's eyes grew wide when she realized who I was talking to, then she glanced between me and Teddie, her brow creased into a frown. I tried to ignore her.

"I was going to ask you the same thing. I've been worried sick all day." Jordan's voice resonated with concern. "What happened with you and Teddie? Per your instructions, Rudy and I deposited him at the recording studio at the Palms at two this afternoon and that's the last I've heard."

"Everything's great. We're in Babel. Teddie's working through the dance sets with the DJ, Brandy and I are floating on champagne bubbles. Want to join us?"

"Rudy and I are in the lobby. We'll be right there."

"I'll have Security release the elevator—the club isn't open yet."

After I called Security, I flipped my phone shut and stuffed it back in my pocket.

Brandy was scrutinizing me, her face a mask. "Jordan Marsh and Teddie, here? Together? That doesn't seem very wise."

I sipped my champagne and leaned back against the bar. "Child, you should never believe everything you hear."

LIKE fireworks shot into the night sky, Jordan and Rudy burst from the elevator, the force of their personalities igniting the air around them.

Catching sight of me, Jordan headed toward us with Rudy two steps behind.

"Holy cow," Brandy muttered under her breath.

"They take your breath away, don't they?"

"They are the hottest, most gorgeous . . . well, I'm finding it hard to resist ripping my clothes off right here and now."

"My mother used to tell me not to do anything in public that I wouldn't want to read about on the front page of the morning paper," I remarked. "That might be an appropriate thought to cling to at a time like this."

I set my drink on the bar, then stood and braced myself for Jordan's greeting. He didn't disappoint.

Bending me backward over a knee, he kissed me long and fervently. "You look happy," he whispered, before he set me back on my feet.

"Who wouldn't be with that kind of greeting from Jordan Marsh," Brandy opined, the raw jealousy in her voice only casually concealed.

"Jordan, this is my assistant, Brandy Alexander. She's a bit starstruck at the moment."

With a wink to me, Jordan swooped and captured Brandy, giving her the same treatment he'd given me. When he set her back upright, I didn't have much confidence she would stay that way. As she swooned a bit, I pushed her back down on her stool.

Never one to miss an opportunity, Teddie stepped in. "Where's the line? Am I next, Jordan?"

"Hell, the last time I saw you, you were puking into a toilet," he shot back. "I don't want to kiss you. I'll leave that to Lucky; she's less discerning than I am."

"Apparently," I agreed.

Everybody laughed as the music started.

Teddie pulled my hand. "Come on. Dance with me."

He led me to the dance floor and folded me into his arms. Relaxing against him, I knew what it felt like to finally make it home after a long, tough journey. A lifetime spent in Teddie's arms would never be enough.

A pounding beat with a danceable melody, the music swirled around us as Teddie spun me around the floor. Jordan and Brandy joined in while Rudy waited his turn. At the next song, we traded partners—Teddie with Brandy, me with Rudy, and Jordan at the bar, sipping a drink at the bar that Rudy had ordered for him.

The music slowed and Rudy pulled me closer.

"Are you doing okay?" I asked.

"Much better, thanks to you. I don't know how you do it, but you manage to say just the right thing."

"Sheer dumb luck, but I'm happy for you," I said, and I meant it.

He pushed me away, twirling me under his arm, then he pulled me back.

"Thanks for taking care of Teddie last night."

"He's a good guy, Lucky. The best. And he loves you so bad he doesn't know how to handle it."

"I know the feeling." I watched Teddie dancing with Brandy—just the sight of him warmed my heart. He caught me looking and gave me a big grin.

"Go with your heart, even when it scares the hell out of you." Rudy's eyes, an intense deep blue, caught and held mine. I saw truth in them.

The music changed, and it was time to switch partners, again.

This time I waltzed into Jordan's arms. He looked happier, more at peace, than I'd ever seen him.

"You look like you won the Powerball," I said as he held me tight, swaying slowly despite the beat of the music.

"Rudy's my soul mate. You're the best friend a guy could ever hope for. I got money in the bank and an interesting job. I have everything life has to offer."

"Even better than the Powerball." I pressed my cheek to his.

"How about you? Is Theodore the one?"

"How do you know who's the one? I've never been able to figure that out."

The music thumped a danceable beat, but Jordan still held me close, swaying to his own rhythm. "You don't recognize your soul mate with your head, Lucky. You recognize him with your heart."

Ignoring the beat of the music, I matched my rhythm to Jordan's, letting him lead me in a dance only he heard. "There's something special about Teddie, something I can't describe. Just the thought of him makes my heart soar. And when he touches me . . . it's mind-blowing. Even when I'm furious with him, I don't want to be with anybody else. I know he's fighting with himself about going on tour with Reza Pashiri. He thinks I want him to stay."

"Don't you?"

"For me, yes. But not for him. I want him to chase his dreams—I'd feel terrible if he gave them up for me." Just saying the words scared the hell out of me, but I knew in my heart they were true. I leaned back so I could look Jordan in the eyes. "What would you call that?"

"Love with a capital L." With a finger, he gently pushed a strand of hair out of my eye. "This is sort of a stupid analogy, but treat each other like a cherished kite—hang tightly to the string. Reel each other in when the weather turns bad, but let each other fly."

"What a soft heart you have, Mr. Marsh. Too bad you're gay."

He threw back his head and laughed.

Once again the music changed and I found myself back in

Teddie's arms, exactly where I had started. This time the music settled into a slow, sensuous rhythm. I closed my eyes trying to memorize every moment as Teddie held me tightly, swaying to the music.

Very softly, in his rich tenor, he began to sing—words of love and hope and a life filled with promise. A beautiful song, heartfelt and romantic.

Too soon the music ended. Unwilling to move from his arms, I kept my head on his shoulder. "What a fabulous song."

"It's called 'Lucky for Me.'" He stepped back, forcing me to look into his eyes. "I wrote it for you." Then his mouth captured mine, and my heart melted.

Our friends gathered around and began clapping and whistling until finally Teddie let me up for air.

Then we finished off the evening with a rousing rendition of "YMCA" by the Village People, complete with the physical effects, as the doors to Babel opened, admitting the public to our little corner of paradise.

JORDAN and Rudy decided to stay at Babel, Jordan playing movie star, with Rudy admiring from the sidelines. Wishing fervently I could stay with them, I instead heeded the call of the real world. Brandy and Teddie left with me. When the doors of the elevator opened at the casino level, we almost staggered back as the noise pummeled us.

Fight weekend had arrived.

People of all shapes and sizes occupied every available spot at a table or machine. If music played in the background, the party drowned it out. Excited chatter, punctuated by the occasional shout, filled the air. The machines, muted by the collective wisdom of "gaming experts," whispered their come-on song—the upscaling of Vegas. I missed the clanking coins, the whirring slot reels, and the shouts of "wheel of fortune"—the last ubiquitous theme before the machines were silenced.

I filled my lungs with the smoky air—ah Vegas! Home sweet home.

Halfway across the casino, I pulled Teddie in front of me. Unable to help myself, I caressed his cheek with the back on one hand. "You look beat. I've got to stay for a few hours more—Brandy and I are the roustabouts riding herd on this crowd tonight. Why don't you go home? Get some sleep."

"Sleep? What's that?" He pressed my hand against his cheek then kissed my fingers. "Are you sure you'll be okay? You haven't had much more sleep than me."

"I can't leave, but that's no reason for both of us to be catatonic. Go on. I'll come home when I can."

"My place or yours?"

"Yours. My guests can have their privacy."

Teddie pulled me to him; he seemed reluctant to leave. "A kiss before I go?"

I complied. Kissing Teddie was the second best part of my day.

"Promise me you won't walk home. Get Paolo to drive you, or steal a car. Anything. Just don't walk by yourself."

"I promise." Admiring his rear view, I watched until the crowd closed around him like the curtain around a stage after the play was over.

Without Teddie, the night had lost its spark. I hooked my arm through Brandy's, "Okay, Tonto, it's you and me," I said, trying to put on a happy face.

Before Brandy could think up a witty reply, a big, burly guy lunged out of the crowd, grabbing her by the arm and spinning her around. "If you gals are giving it away, I want some," he slurred. He wrapped his thick arms around her.

I grabbed his arm. "Hey, back off."

Like a bull dislodging a fly, he shook me off.

Quick as a snake, Brandy leaned into him, throwing him off balance. She stuck a foot behind his leg, and pushed. He tumbled back like a felled tree. Instinctively he loosened his grip on her and put a hand out behind him to break his fall.

Brandy moved in, pressing her advantage. She threw an elbow. With a meaty thunk, it connected with his jaw. Out cold, the guy dropped and splattered like a sack of rotten fruit.

Slack jawed, I stared at Brandy.

Her eyes little slits, she stared down at the man lying at her feet. Then, her anger fled and realization dawned. Wide-eyed, she looked at me, then her hand flew to her mouth. "Oh my God! I'm so sorry! I promised I wouldn't do that. Oh brother, now I've really gone and done it."

The big man groaned as he stirred on the floor.

I put a foot in his chest. "Don't move," I growled at him. Then to Brandy I said, "Call Security."

She had just opened her phone, when two security guys came running. They helped me pull the guy to his feet as he tried to shake the cobwebs out of his head.

"I'm gonna sue you and your hotel," our drunk managed to bark, but most of his bite was gone.

"Be my guest." I poked him in the chest for emphasis. "You assaulted one of my staff. I'll not stand for that." I leaned in close to him, my mouth next to his ear. "Touch her again, and I'll let her break your arm."

With a casual wave, I dismissed him and his security escort. The rest of the night in the drunk tank downstairs might educate our tough guy, if Brandy hadn't already.

"Are you going to fire me?" Brandy asked, her voice small and pained.

"Not if you teach me how to do that."

"For real?"

I threw my arm around her shoulder. "Honey, your job description does not include being mauled by drunk patrons. You are free to defend yourself. Do me a favor though . . ."

"Name it."

"Just don't kill anyone, okay?"

AFTER dealing with several more rowdies, a woman offended when one of our dealers wouldn't accept her favors in exchange for more chips, a young guy using his iPhone to count cards at the black-jack table, and a newlywed couple who had decided they couldn't wait until they got upstairs, I sent Brandy home.

My second wind kicked in as I tidied up my office before calling it a day myself. I'd rolled the phones to Security and checked out, when my door opened. Peering through the door, I caught sight of a rumpled Romeo, sagging under the weight of a long day as well.

"You keep this up," I told him, "and you'll either be dead or anointed the Second Coming of Columbo by the time you're thirty." Kicking off my shoes, I put my feet on my desk and leaned back.

Romeo staggered in then lay on the couch, his hands behind his head. "I'll be cold in the ground before anyone in the department thinks of giving me a raise."

"Is this a social call or are you just looking for a place to catch forty winks, because I'm on my way home. It's almost one and to-morrow starts early."

"I got something you might want to see." He extracted a crum-pled sheet of paper from his inside jacket pocket and held it out to me. "You owe me big time, even though I don't think it's what you were looking for."

Another bit of disappointing news—just what I needed. "I'm too tired to move, can you just give it to me?"

"I sat on a friend of mine who works in the state lab up in Reno."

"And?"

"Bee venom. Too much to have gotten from bee stings, but not enough to kill a normal person. So, you were right, but that's not what killed her. Sorry."

His words jolted me like a cattle prod. I leapt to my feet, then planted a big one on the kid's forehead. "Sorry? You've made my day!"

"I'm not following." Romeo pushed himself to a seated position. He still looked ready to keel over.

"Maybe it wasn't enough to kill a normal person, but our Ms. Neidermeyer was far from normal. She was highly allergic." I stepped into my shoes. "A little bee venom without an almost immediate dose of epinephrine would kill her. Only a few people knew that."

Renewed, Romeo scanned the toxicology report again. "There's enough here to kill her several times over then."

"Once was sufficient."

"Where would somebody get something like that? And how would they get it into her system without her knowing it?" Romeo rubbed his eyes. "And of course, there's the pesky little question as to *who* would do such a thing."

"One at a time, my friend. One at a time." I grabbed Romeo's hand and pulled him to his feet. "I know who can help us with your first two questions, but we have to hurry."

On my last pass through the hotel I'd seen Geoffrey David-Williston holding forth in Delilah's. I only hoped he was still there.

oday was my lucky day.

Geoffrey motioned to us when we reached the top of the steps into Delilah's Bar. "Lucky! And friend! Come join us." He gestured to his colleagues to make room for us. After much skooching of chairs, he pulled two more around the tiny circular table. "A libation?"

"No, thanks," I said and introduced Romeo to the group. "I've had enough already today to preserve my liver for generations of medical students." I took my place at the table, then pulled the detective into the chair beside mine.

"That never stopped us," said one of Geoffrey's colleagues, who I thought had been asleep. The lady raised her glass, drained it, then fell back, her eyes once again closed.

Entomologists—no one had ever accused them of being wild and crazy party animals.

"Geoffrey, I need your help. I need to know about honeybees."

He gave me a half-amused, half-sardonic smile. "Really? What do you want to know? It's a fairly broad subject, and I don't want to run the risk of boring you . . . again."

If he read me that easily the other evening, then my poker face was in need of a tune-up. "Specifically, I want to know about bee venom: Where would one acquire it, for what purpose, and how is it administered?"

He waved a slender hand as he sipped from a dainty flute—champagne, and I had no doubt, expensive. "That's easy. First, why bee venom? As you may know, it contains a mild neurotoxin. Before attending the lecture the other night on alternative uses, I thought this was the important factor. I was wrong."

Geoffrey didn't really know how to have a conversation—he gave lectures. I settled back in my chair to wait for him to get to the point. Past experience had taught me prodding him only made him mad.

"Bee venom actually is used as an anti-inflammatory agent in a therapy called apitherapy. It's very cutting-edge, and no scientifically valid trials have been performed. However, the volume of anecdotal support is garnering interest from the medical community." He glanced around the group to see who was listening—apparently only Romeo and I, so he fixed us with his gaze. "The venom of bees contains melittin, which some scientists claim is much more powerful than cortisone."

"What's it used for?"

"To ease the symptoms of diseases ranging from diabetes to lupus." He motioned to the waitress to refill his glass.

"Would it have any effect on multiple sclerosis?"

Geoffrey nodded, his aroused interest showed in his eyes. "Yes, but it's a bit murkier there. Although there have been some pretty strong testimonials supporting apitherapy for MS, clinical trials, admittedly very small trials, have been unable to support that finding."

"But people with the disease have reported easing of their symptoms?" I asked, leaning forward. Pieces of the puzzle were falling into place.

"Some even dramatically improved."

Romeo sat like a statue next to me. "Where would someone get it?" I pressed, the questions coming faster now. "Would they need a prescription?"

"Anyone can buy it over the Internet. All you need is a credit card."

Several of Geoffrey's colleagues had nodded off now, and the man himself looked well on his way.

"One more question, how would one apply or ingest the venom?"

Geoffrey set his empty glass on the table. "Multiple ways, but if it were me, I'd just order the stuff in a topical solution and put it on my skin."

Leaning back in my chair, I tried to grab the thoughts racing through my head. "So, just apply it to the skin?"

"Sure, doctors use transdermal delivery methods for a huge number of drugs—hormone therapy is a great example."

"Would the bee venom hurt when applied?"

"It could, but mixing it with lidocaine or a similar topical analgesic would solve that problem."

"Are there any dangers?"

"The obvious one—the possibility of allergic reaction increases with the increase in dosage."

"And what if the patient is already highly allergic."

"It would be deadly."

HOT on the trail of missing connections, I dragged Romeo down to the valet and into the waiting Ferrari.

"You want to tell me where we're going at this hour?" Romeo strapped himself in. "And what we're looking for?"

Adrenaline coursed through me as I whipped the car from the

curb, turned north on the Strip, and gunned it. "We're looking for the last piece of the puzzle."

Romeo listened while I told him about Numbers and her allergy, Jimmy G and his MS, and his miraculous recent improvement.

"So you think Mrs. Lovato knew about Numbers's allergy, bought the venom for her father as a cover, then figured a way to put some on the woman's skin and wait for the inevitable?"

"That's a good scenario," I said, as I whipped the car up the ramp and onto the 15, then took the 95 toward Reno. We hit one hundred and thirty by the time we reached the Summerlin Parkway exit. Romeo didn't appear to be bothered by the speed, so I kept my foot to the pedal.

"How'd she know about the bee allergy?"

"Her husband knew, and I have a feeling her father knew as well—he's been around a long time. Either of them could have told her. For that matter, Numbers could have told her herself—it's not like it's inherently a big deal."

"Say you're right," Romeo said, as he glanced at the speedometer and grinned. "Why would Mrs. Lovato want to kill Numbers Neidermeyer?"

"A number of reasons." I smiled despite the topic of conversation—a pun is a thing of beauty. "A love affair gone bad. Or she discovered that not only was our fair Ms. Neidermeyer using her to bring down our illustrious district attorney, but, on top of it, she was also sleeping with him." I was on a roll.

"All good motives." Romeo stuck his arms up into the slipstream, just as Dane had done. It must be a Y-chromosome thing—at these speeds my two X chromosomes cautioned me against bodily harm.

"So how'd she do it?" Romeo asked, a smile tickling his lips—boys and their toys.

"This is pure conjecture, but in the security video of the two women leaving the hotel the night Numbers bit the big one, she is seen spraying an atomizer—presumably of perfume—on her neck and on her wrists, then rubbing her wrists together." I slowed at the exit for Town Center, not because I wanted to, but because I'm a firm believer in the hard-and-fast rules of physics, and even Ferraris can't make a ninety-degree turn at over a hundred miles an hour. "But, if I remember correctly," I continued, "the atomizer wasn't among the items found in her purse at the scene—at least it wasn't on the list you showed me at breakfast."

"Correct. The killer must've taken it," Romeo added unnecessarily.

"Romeo, if you find that atomizer, you've got your smoking gun."

The lights still burned in the café when I wheeled to a stop out front. The door was locked when I tried it. Cupping my hands around my face, I pressed my nose to the window and peered inside.

Antonio, Jimmy G's right-hand man, spied us. Twisting the keys hanging from the lock, he opened the door and motioned us inside. "What are you doing here, Ms. O'Toole?"

"I need to see Jimmy."

"He ain't here."

"What do you mean he isn't here?" Two steps through the doorway, I stopped and whirled around. "He's always here. I've known him twenty years and in all that time, if his place was open, he was here."

Romeo, who was behind me, nimbly ducked to the side

Antonio gave an indifferent shrug, but I could see the worry in his eyes. "Yeah, I know. I never knowed him not to run his place, you know?"

"Did he call?"

"I talked to him myself. He didn't sound right, you know? Worried like."

"What did he say?" A cold ball of dread settled in my stomach.

"He said he had somethin' important to take care of."

The ball of dread exploded into icy fingers of fear. "Did he say what?"

"He said it was personal."

· · ·

JIMMY G had disappeared.

I'd called every number I had for him, to no avail. His house was dark, his car gone. And I had to find him before he did anything stupid.

After dropping Romeo back at the hotel, then debating with myself long and hard as I drove the few short blocks home, I called in reinforcements.

Even at this ungodly hour, the Beautiful Jeremy Whitlock answered on the second ring, sounding wide awake. "Whitlock Investigations."

"Jimmy G has gone AWOL. I'm worried."

"Hang on." Jeremy whispered something I couldn't quite make out—presumably an explanation to Miss P. "Tell me what you got."

I heard the beep as he unlocked his car. Did the guy sleep fully clothed? Or was he just getting home when I caught him? I didn't want to know—I felt guilty enough already. I filled him in on what I knew so far, including the bee angle, then I gave him Mr. G's address, and the Lovatos' and Numbers's for good measure.

"Do you think he's on his own?" Jeremy's Bluetooth captured the call—now he sounded like he was talking out of a barrel.

"Either that or the killer has figured out he's a pretty good link in the chain of evidence—if all my theories pan out."

"Damn!"

"Do you need my help?" I asked, praying he said no. Dead on my feet, I doubted I'd be anything other than an impediment.

"I can work faster on my own—besides, if I bend the laws a little bit, I don't want you around."

I seconded that. "Find him, Jeremy. Find him fast, before anything happens."

TEDDIE had left a light on for me. All week I'd been dreaming of slipping into bed and wrapping my man around me. Shucking clothes, I made a beeline for the master bedroom. A soft light glowed on the nightstand. I doused it, then lifted one corner of the duvet, and eased in next to him, my front to his back.

"Mmmmm," he said, his voice husky with sleep. "I've been waiting for you to get home."

Wrapping an arm over him, I pulled him against me, luxuriating in the feel of naked man against my skin. Was there anything better? "I thought you were asleep."

"Not fully. Not without you," he said, as he gathered my hand to him, tucking it to his chest.

I kissed the back of his neck just because I felt like it.

"Are you tired?" he asked, as he rolled over and wrapped me in his arms.

"Tired?" I put my head on his chest, taking comfort in its rhythmic rise and fall. "No. Catatonic? Yes."

"It's been a heck of a few days."

I tried to muster a chuckle at his gross understatement, but I was too exhausted. "Just hold me," I whispered.

"For the rest of your life," he whispered against my hair, then he kissed my forehead.

I relinquished myself to sleep.

SUNLIGHT streamed through the windows, and the smell of coffee wafted in on a breeze when I returned to the land of the living. Since I didn't have to be at work until eleven—Miss P had volunteered for the early shift—I hadn't set the alarm. I'd forgotten how nice it was to leisurely awaken rather than be jangled out of a deep sleep.

With the coffee calling my name, I put my feet on the floor, wrapped myself in a blanket, and went in search of caffeine and a hug.

"Good morning," Teddie said when he met me halfway to the kitchen wearing pajama pants and a grin, a steaming mug of my favorite brew in his hand. "I was just coming to wake you up—I was looking forward to it."

Deborah Coonts

"I could jump back in and pretend I was asleep." Cupping my hands around the mug, I breathed deep, then took a sip. Like an addict anticipating the first hit, my body danced in joy. For too long now I'd been running on a high-octane mix of caffeine and alcohol. Cleaning up my act was in my near future—either that or the crash and burn was going to be spectacular.

"Come here," Teddie said gently as he took my mug, setting it on a side table, then wrapped me in a bear hug.

Before we'd even slept together, Teddie had told me the waking-up part could be almost as good as the going to bed part. He was right.

I nuzzled his neck. Warm and prickly with a day's growth of beard, he smelled masculine, sensual—full of promise. This time I didn't resist nibbling his ear.

"Keep that up, you are going to be late for work—very late," Teddie groaned, as he slipped my blanket from around my shoulders then dropped it to the floor. Swooping down, he scooped me up and headed toward the bedroom.

I looped my arms around his shoulders. "What time is it?" I asked, not really concerned—it couldn't be that late.

"Almost eleven."

"What?" I wiggled to get free. "Put me down. I don't have time to play."

Dropping my legs, he held me against him so my toes barely touched the ground, then he kissed me. Long and deep, it took my breath away. "You sure?" he asked.

I groaned as he kissed me again. "I've got to go. Any other weekend and I'd leave Miss P to hold them off, but not this one—I can't."

"Okay." He set me fully on my feet. "You go take a shower; I'll work on breakfast."

Humming snatches of tunes from last night, I stepped into the cascade of water Teddie called a shower. Large enough for the two of us—and several of our closest friends—I delighted in the stuff of

302

a man's shower. Who knew they still sold soap-on-a-rope? And this back scrubber thing? Was this part of the normal routine or was it wishful thinking? Since there was only one kind of shampoo and no conditioner, I had no choices to make, so that part was easy.

My eyes squeezed tight to keep the shampoo out, I reached for the soap. I found the dish, but the bar was missing. Drat. I felt a blast of cool air as the shower door opened.

"Allow me," Teddie said, as he stepped in beside me.

Quickly, I washed the shampoo out of my hair. Opening my eyes, I took in all of him—shit-eating grin, a bar of soap, and . . . all.

I was *so* going to be late for work.

EVEN though I practically ran, I was still an hour late. Miss Patterson seemed nonplussed when I arrived, out of breath and out of gas—while incredible, sex in the shower was no Breakfast of Champions—I needed food.

"Where have you been? I've been calling like crazy. I started to think they might have run you over for real this time." Although she tried to sound angry, she couldn't.

"I'm sorry." I sagged into a chair across from her, my legs stuck out in front of me. How to explain? "Teddie's home," I said, unable and unwilling to elaborate.

"In that case, you are forgiven." A huge grin split her face. "How is Mr. Kowalski?"

"Exhausting." I said, but couldn't hide my smile.

"You're a lucky girl."

She managed to keep a straight face even when I rolled my eyes and groaned.

"I've fired people for saying that," I said starchily.

"Promises, promises." Miss P looked very professional in a herringbone black and white blazer and hot-pink sweater. She'd broken out her zebra cheaters, but even the matching accessories and her smart manner couldn't hide her distress. She hadn't been sleeping—fatigue worried her edges.

"Has Jeremy called in?" I asked.

She gave me a stern look. "Why don't you check your phone?"

I did. Seven missed calls—all from Miss P except for two from Jeremy, the last one was an hour ago. "He's helping me chase some leads; I can't tell you all of it—the last bit I don't know yet, but we've pretty much got this Neidermeyer thing nailed down."

"For real?" Miss P's voice was quiet, pregnant with hope.

"We've narrowed it down to two suspects—Jeremy isn't one of them," I said, which was more than I should have said. I know full well the perils of raising false hope—but I couldn't stand another moment of seeing her so miserable.

With a deep sigh, she sagged back in her chair. "Thank you."

"Don't break out the party favors just yet. Soon, though. I get the feeling things are coming to a head." I glanced in my office and groaned. The paper fairy had visited again—my desk was covered. Somebody ought to shoot that damned fairy. "Have I missed anything important today?"

"I've got it under control," Miss P fired back, her manner brusque. "Except for the Big Boss."

"What's up with him?"

"I couldn't tell you, but he's got his knickers in a twist for sure." Miss P looked at me over the top of her cheaters. "He's been calling down here every half hour since I got here."

I jumped to my feet. "Why didn't you tell me?" As I leapt for the door, someone opened it from the outside.

The Big Boss. "Lucky, where the hell have you been?" he snarled.

I live my life on the theory that the best defense is a good offense. "On my few free hours away from this loony bin," I said. "I've actually been trying to get some shut-eye and some meaningful sex. Do you have any idea how hard it is to have sex in the shower without killing yourself?"

That stopped him mid-bluster, proving my theory.

"Oh, well. In that case . . ." He ground to a halt, staring at me.

Impassively, I held his gaze.

My father was the first to look away. "If I said good for you, would that be appropriate?" he asked, clearly at a loss.

"Works for me," I said blithely, as I gave him a lopsided grin.

He grabbed me by the arm and pulled me into the hall. Ever the gentleman, he threw a "please excuse us" over his shoulder to Miss P. "I know what hard wires you to the pissed-off position— you need food," he said, turning his attention back to me.

The man always could read me like a book—I guess we had that whole genetic-empathy thing going on.

"So where's the fire, anyway?" I asked, as I let him lead me along.

"It's your mother."

Why did I know that?

I ran down the usual list. "Is she sick? Dying? Have the citizens of Pahrump hung her in effigy? Are they calling for her blood?"

My father threw me a shocked look. "Of course not."

"Then food first. Mother can wait."

EVEN though I wanted breakfast, Nebuchadnezzar had the lunch buffet out. Quickly I heaped my plate—I didn't really care with what—then took the chair across from the Big Boss at our usual table by the window. Before I took a bite, I asked my father, "Will you excuse me a moment. I need to make a call. It's important."

At his nod, I stepped outside into the garden and dialed Jeremy.

"I came up zeros," Jeremy said without pretense, when he answered. "I checked his place a couple of times—no car, no lights. If he was there he was hiding. I swung by Neidermeyer's place— nobody there, inside or out."

"Isn't her house in a gated community?" I asked.

"Yes." Jeremy's flat tone didn't invite any more conversation on that topic.

I didn't need to become an unwitting accomplice, so I let that one alone. "What about the Lovatos'?" I asked.

"On a hunch, I staked out their place for the rest of the night. My hunch didn't pan out—Jimmy G didn't show up, but neither did the Mrs. I gather the Lovatos are not a happy couple?"

"From what I've seen, I would say that was accurate," I said, as I glanced at my father through the window. He was waiting to eat until I returned. "Glinda's a tough cookie."

"I've seen her. Many guys I know would be proud to have her biceps. I wouldn't want to meet her in a dark alley, that's for sure." Jeremy sounded half grossed out and half in awe.

Personally, I thought Glinda Lovato only inspired fear. "How do you know she wasn't at the house?"

"A car was missing from the garage, then Daniel left alone to take his daughter to school." Jeremy's voice dropped. "After he left, I thought the house was empty. I was right."

"Okay, well then," I said, stalling for time. I had no idea what to say in response to his insinuation that he'd done a little recreational breaking and entering. "Are you going to keep looking for Jimmy G?" I finally managed.

"Of course. I'll keep an eye on his restaurant, and I've got some other lookouts combing the city. I'll let you know if we find him, but what about Mrs. Lovato? Her absence is . . . timely." Jeremy sounded worn out. I tried not to feel guilty.

"If we don't find her beforehand, Glinda has a job at Tortilla Padilla's fight tonight," I said. "How do you feel about trying to shake her down?"

"And risk serious injury? Did you know that not only is our lovely Mrs. Lovato a bodybuilder, but she's a rising star in the world of cage-fighting?"

"I'll bring a Taser."

THE Big Boss eyed me over a tumbler of whiskey as he took a big gulp.

"Drinking at noon, not a good sign," I said, as I settled in across from him and gazed at my plate, the food now cold.

"I needed something to settle my nerves."

"What's Mother done this time?" I asked, bracing myself as I picked at my salad.

"She's acting very strange." Apparently worry didn't affect my father's appetite—he dove into his plate of food. All those calories and they never seemed to show up in any of the usual places. Too bad that trait didn't trickle down the genome.

"How can you tell?" I pushed my salad away and eyed the other offerings on my plate. Cold pizza would have to do. "Strange is her MO."

"Okay," my father said through a mouthful. "She's acting stranger than usual. She won't take my calls and, according to Trudi, she's barricaded herself in her room and won't come out."

"Wouldn't be the first time." Cold pizza was as bad as it looked, so I stabbed a piece of cantaloupe. "Remember when she brought my whole class to Mona's Place on take-your-child-to-work day?"

My father choked, then grabbed for his glass of water. After he'd fought some air into his lungs, he said, "I'd forgotten that! Half the mothers in town canvassed the neighborhoods to get sig-natures on their petition to fire the principal and to kick you and your mother out of the county."

"She stayed in her room a whole week that time," I reminded him. I waved my fork with the cantaloupe for emphasis. "She could hide. I wasn't so lucky—I had to go to school and face the music. My first real lesson in life." I popped the bite of fruit in my mouth for emphasis.

"You think that's what she's doing? Hiding?" Still at least two fingers of bourbon in his glass, he pushed it away.

"Or licking her wounds," I said. "Give her a day or two; I bet she'll come around."

THE Big Boss opened my office door with a flourish and a grin. Riding on a high of familial warmth, I stepped through. The fran-tic look on Miss Patterson's face brought me up short.

"The Ferrari you checked out last night? It's gone missing. They can't find it anywhere!"

I slapped a hand to my forehead. "Shoot! I forgot the damned car!"

"You forgot a quarter of a million dollar car?" Her eyes, large and round . . . and amused . . . looked at me over the top of her glasses.

"With all I have on my plate and with as little sleep as I get, I'd forget my head if it wasn't attached," I groused. It was a car, for chrissake! It's not like I ran off all our whales or alienated the Hollywood crowd, or something truly catastrophic. "Your precious hunk of Italian machinery is snuggled safe and sound in the garage at the Presidio."

"And the keys?" Miss Patterson asked, apparently unwilling to let me off the hook that easily.

I waved my hand airily. "Somewhere at home . . . at Teddie's. I'll call him, perhaps he can bring the car around."

My father chuckled behind me. I whirled on him. "And how many cars have you . . . misplaced? I seem to recall a gull-wing and a blonde . . ."

That wiped the grin off his face . . . almost. "Are you going to introduce me?" he asked, effortlessly changing the subject.

"What?"

He tilted his head toward Brandy, who, to be honest, I hadn't noticed until he drew my attention to her.

With the look of the devout in the presence of the Pope, she stood at attention by her desk. I didn't know what I would do if she dropped to her knees and asked to kiss the Big Boss's ring. Shoot her maybe . . .

"Sir," I said, extending my arm toward my new assistant. "May I present Brandy Alexander, this office's newest addition?"

The Big Boss held out his hand. "Young lady, I'm Albert Rothstein."

Her voice having flown, Brandy nodded then wiped her hand on her pants before reaching for his.

"This is my boss," I added, probably unnecessarily.

"I hope you have as wonderful a boss as I do," Brandy said to me, finding her voice, as she grasped the Big Boss's hand.

Boy, I could use some of her suck-up. And she was wise enough to suck up to the right person. Clever girl.

"Nice to meet you, Sir," Brandy said to the Big Boss.

"You take good care of my—"

I cleared my throat, interrupting him.

"Our Head of Customer Relations," he said, recovering nicely. "She's the grease that keeps the wheels moving around here."

"Yessir." Brandy retreated back to her desk.

Miss Patterson, her face a mask, said nothing.

Before I thought about it, I squeezed my father's arm and gave him a peck on the cheek. "Mona willl be fine. Give her some space."

He nodded, then left, leaving me with both of my assistants staring at me.

"What?" I asked. "He's dating my mother. I've worked for him since I was fifteen. The lines get blurry, okay?" Not waiting for any editorial comments, I retreated into my office.

TEDDIE answered his phone on the third ring. "Hey! You caught me just getting out of the shower."

"Two showers in one morning?"

"Just reliving wonderful memories," he said. "And, as I recall, we didn't do a whole lot of . . . showering . . . before."

"No. And we were lucky we didn't break something." I fell into the whole flirting thing with unexpected ease, proving once and for all you can teach an old dog new tricks. For some reason that made me feel better.

"We need to work on our technique, I'll grant you that," Teddie said, his voice warm, inviting.

"Speak for yourself."

He laughed that laugh that made me tingle all over—like we both had a wonderful secret to hide—which we did.

"You don't want more practice?" he asked, pretending to be wounded.

"Practice sounds perfect." I shifted the phone to my other ear as Miss Patterson peeked in the doorway. I motioned her inside. "But, right now I need to talk to you about a car. You wouldn't happen to be headed to the hotel, would you?"

"You read my mind. I'm meeting Reza at Babel for a run-through. Want to come watch?"

"That depends," I said. "On you and a certain Ferrari."

TEDDIE delivered the Ferrari and smoothed over my faux pas, so that was one less thing on my plate. I owed him.

Leaving Miss P to handle the office, I launched myself into the day. With Brandy dogging my heels, I headed off on my rounds. This was my young assistant's first major fight weekend. Layer that with a major club launch and this would truly be a test of her metal. By dawn tomorrow either the heat would have tempered her to steel or I'd be looking for a new assistant.

"First let's stop by the Kasbah," I said over my shoulder as I cleared a path through the crush of people already filling the lobby. "I'd like to check on our fighter-in-residence."

Carmen answered my knock. "Hey," she said, greeting us with a wan smile and motioning inside.

After yesterday the rooms resembled a mausoleum—not a child in sight. I introduced Brandy then asked, "Where are the kids?"

"Arrianna and Charles took them to the movies." Carmen looked tired and worried. "Those two are real treasures. Thank you for sending them our way."

"I thought you might get along."

"My husband offered them a deal," she explained. "Our foundation will pay for medical school for both of them if they will come work at the clinic for four years after they've completed their training. Of course, that's contingent on tonight."

The woman looked so distracted I couldn't resist giving her hand a squeeze. "It's going to be okay."

"Don't mind me—I'm a worrier." She shook her head. "After all these years you'd think I could handle this better. My husband knows what he's doing, but I still wonder whether experience is enough to make up for the fraction of a second his reflexes have lost to age."

I didn't think there were any words to offer her comfort. In the game of life, sometimes you just roll the dice and hope for your number.

"Is there anything my office can do to make your evening more enjoyable?"

"No, thank you. I usually watch from somewhere in the back—if I can stand it." Carmen gave me a weak smile. "The kids will be out until after the fight. They're going to Shark Reef, then to see the knights joust at Excalibur, then to ride the roller coaster at New York-New York. After that, I forget where they're going exactly, but it was quite an itinerary."

I handed her two passes to Babel, then thought for a moment and handed her two more. "Here, these will get you two, and Adrianna and Charles if they are so inclined and you have someone else to watch the kids, into the VIP section at the lounge opening tonight—we've planned quite a victory party. The champagne is already on ice."

"I'll be really glad when this is over," Carmen said, as she took the tickets.

"You and me both." I squeezed her tight.

Why didn't anyone ever tell me worry was contagious?

WITH Brandy in tow, my next stop was the Golden Fleece Room, the designated pressroom for this evening's festivities. A beehive of activity, the room was filled to overflowing with reporters, cameramen, and imposters special enough or clever enough to finagle a press pass, all charging around pretending to be important. And, as much as I hated to admit it, they were important—if the Babylon wasn't in the news, we were nowhere. And it fell to me to make sure the news was spun in the Babylon's best interests—about as easy as riding a wild mustang without a bridle.

Dane stepped in beside me as I paused in the doorway, looking for familiar faces. "Now I know how the Christians felt just before they were fed to the lions," he said, eyeing the rabid crowd.

I blew a lock of hair out of my eyes. "At least they had weapons."

"You have that rapier wit," he said, grinning down at me. "Does that count?"

"It'll have to do. Let's hope it at least evens the playing field," I said, as I tried to ignore the little flush of excitement at his presence.

"I'd put my money on you," Dane whispered in my ear. "Smarts, good looks, and experience—they don't stand a chance."

"And *you* are trying to make me nervous," I said as I gathered my wits, mustered my courage, and charged in to work the room. Brandy at my side, I was careful to introduce her to everyone I knew, and both of us to those I didn't.

Dane positioned himself along the back wall, presumably for the best view. Some help he was.

Finally Brandy and I made it to the far end of the room, where I caught sight of Flash Gordon holding court. She'd traded her tee shirt and jeans for a hot-pink dress that hugged her plentiful curves, and a white Chanel J-12 encrusted with diamonds hugged her wrist—who knew it took so much bling to tell time? The pink stilettos looked the same. Her red hair hung in a loose braid down her back, a few tendrils framing her face. Red and hot pink? Wasn't that some sort of a fashion faux pas? Faux pas or not, on Flash, somehow it worked.

Pushing Brandy ahead of me, we wormed our way through the gaggle of men Ms. Gordon always attracted.

"Hey, girlfriends," Flash said, cranking her personality to full wattage when she saw us. She gave Brandy a hug, and shot me a grin over the girl's shoulder. "You guys hanging with the riffraff, or what?"

"Just trying to keep you cannibals happy," I fired back.

"Man, that spread you sent down for lunch was amazing. My scale is going to yell at me in the morning." Flash ran her hands down her dress causing a collective intake of breath from the men who were watching. She pretended not to notice, but I knew every drool registered.

"Good thing most of your wardrobe is spandex, then, huh?" I said, unable to resist. Before she could dagger me back, I charged into the business of the day. "Did you guys get all the press releases and the updated list of our celebrity attendees?"

People gathered closer as I spoke; I raised my voice to be heard. "Everybody knows the routine for tonight? The special press section and all of that?"

Heads nodded. I fielded questions, then introduced Brandy again. "If you have any questions or if you aren't getting what you need, this is your go-to girl." I rattled off her cell number. "Each of you who have requested specific interviews should have gotten a response to your request. We are working hard to accommodate everyone within the time frame we have, so bear with us."

I paused and looked around. Everyone seemed to be on the same page. "Anything else?" I asked, in an attempt to wind things up.

"What about Jordan Marsh?" shouted the same brazen young thing who'd grilled me the other day.

"I told you to go bark up another tree," I said, my voice growing cold as I stared her down. "One warning is all you get."

She didn't heed the warning. "What's he like in bed?"

Several of the old-timers in the room groaned, then chuckled.

I motioned to Dane standing in the back of the room. Reading my mind, he stepped to the young woman's side. Grabbing her arm, he whispered in her ear.

"What?" she exploded. "I'm not leaving!" She tried to jerk her arm from Dane's grasp. Turning toward me, she shouted, "You can't throw me out!"

Smiling, I watched as he did just that—cowboys sure were real handy.

After a brief gloat, I turned my attention back to the rest of the gathering. "Now, where was I?"

"Teaching manners to a young dog," Flash said.

Some rewarded her with a chuckle—probably the ones who hoped sucking up would get them past the casual acquaintance stage. I could've told them they were wasting their time, but why spoil the fun? Flash only found attraction in the lure of the chase.

"Before that," I fired back. "Is everybody on board?" I paused for a response. Getting none, I continued, "I'm out of here, then. I'll leave Brandy to fill in any finer points I might have overlooked."

With a look of quiet confidence on her face, Brandy turned and began working through the throng one at a time.

Can I pick 'em, or what?

Chapter

S E V E N T E E N

♡

Walking slowly up the entryway to Babel, I marveled at the transformation since last night. Plush red carpet absorbed my footfalls and marked the path the celebs would traverse. Heavy velvet rope separated the carpeted area from the press corral, forming a chute. As the celebrities made their way through this gauntlet, they would be waylaid by local television personalities in a well-choreographed dance that my staff had timed down to the split second. Of course, since nothing goes as planned, some wiggle room had been factored in, but we didn't have much. Miss P's job tonight was to keep things on schedule. I would handle any temper flare-ups, and Brandy would ride shotgun on the DJ, keeping him well oiled, but not too.

Piece of cake.

The step-and-repeat hung at an angle at the end of the long

walk. Here the newshounds would have their photo ops. Each celebrity had been schooled as to what to do, how to stand, so each and every sponsor of the event would see their name in bold print in the photographs splashed across the morning papers all over the nation and the Internet. Such a star-studded event was a great marketing opportunity, and our sponsors paid handsomely for the privilege, so we had to make good on our promises.

The interior of Babel had been transformed into a fairyland of trees, sparkling with tiny white lights. Lit from below, the aquarium under the clear dance floor cast a shimmering glow. Fish, swimming lazily, cast uneven, ever-changing shadows. I still hadn't gotten used to the whole walking-on-water sensation. A fraud in the God department, I knew one day I'd step out on the thing and end up all wet.

With the retractable roof open, the rich desert air mingled with the heady aromas of the gardenia blossoms floating in crystal decanters that decorated the tables in the VIP area. The tables had been booked for a year even though each reservation required the purchase of a thousand-dollar bottle of champagne in addition to any other beverages of choice.

With the sun still high in the sky, the air was comfortable. However, heat lamps stood ready to chase away the chill after dark.

Taking a seat at the curved bar nestled under brightly colored tents, I watched Sean, our head bartender, as he checked the assortment of wine and spirits. Actually, since all I could see of him protruding from the cabinet behind the bar was his ass, I watched that.

Counting bottles, he would periodically call out a number, which would be noted on a pad by one of the barbacks. Tonight, the count was especially important—the various medicinal offerings would be high-end specialty stuff or call brands—no well drinks tonight. Most bars had gone to an automated measuring system to prevent theft and overpours, but the Big Boss thought that tacky. Not to mention it sorta peeved the bartenders to assume they were thieves. . . . The Big Boss was all about loyalty, a loyalty that worked both ways.

"How's your end stacking up?" I asked Sean.

Jumping at the sound of my voice, he banged his head then backed out of the cabinet.

A nice looking kid with spiked hair, a slightly receding hairline, and a ready smile, he held up a finger while he took the pen and jotted some numbers on the pad. When he finished, he stood, stretching his back. "This job is hell on the body—first the feet, then the rest."

"A small sacrifice for all the fun we have," I said. "You got everything under control?"

"More or less. We've got all the special requests filled, however I'm missing a bottle of 1995 Krug Clos d'Ambonnay, but I'll find it." He shot me a grin. "Or shoot whoever stole it. But if they drank it, I'm screwed."

"Sounds pricey." With my humble background, I was no oenophile, but, working for the Big Boss, I had traveled up the learning curve a bit. One thing I'd discovered—the more names a wine had, especially if they were words I'd never heard of and couldn't pronounce, the more expensive it was.

"I'm assuming you have Mr. Marsh's 1999 Bollinger on ice?"

Sean nodded. "And the Dom Pérignon for the Padilla victory party."

"Ah, the cheap swill," I said with a smile, then slapped the bar. "You're the best."

Instruments tuning up at the far end of the club screeched and wailed. Teddie and Reza, the band behind them, each had a mike in hand as they stood at the ready on the front of the stage.

Beating time on his thigh, Teddie counted down, "One, two, three, and . . ."

The band launched into a dance tune—one of Reza's I recognized but didn't know well. The two of them sang it as a duet. Used to seeing Teddie performing in a dress, this was new for me.

With a sinking heart I realized that whatever "it" was, Teddie had it. Magic happened when he had a mike in his hand and a song in his heart. And Reza sparkled when she sang with him— even without the makeup and the lighting.

Good for them, not so good for me.

Despite my inner protests, the song swept me up in its rhythm. Keeping time on the bar as I listened, I noticed almost everyone— the janitor mopping in tempo, the young woman cracking crisp white linens and settling them on the tables, the waitstaff going through their preparations, and Sean—were also entranced.

Toward the end of the song, Teddie noticed me hanging back by the bar. He waved, then blew me a kiss, as he wrapped it up. At my wolf whistle, he bowed deeply.

So how did I grow up to be the significant other to a shooting star in the music world? And where did I go to learn how to handle it? Mother always told me that one of the great cosmic jokes was the fact that so much of life was learned on the fly. So I was the butt of a joke—just another of life's little pleasures.

Happiness radiated from Teddie like warmth from a fire as he jumped from the stage and bounded over to me. As the band started in on another beat-driven tune, he swept me into his arms, whirling me around the dance floor.

His joy infectious, I laughed in spite of my heavy heart. Allowing the future to steal the fun from today would be a total waste, anyway.

When the dance tune came to an end, Reza segued into "At Last," one of her signature songs that really let her voice soar. I nestled in as Teddie pulled me close, my hand over his heart, his hand covering mine.

Lost in the pull of the music, in the thrill of being in Teddie's arms, I let myself wish it would never end.

Yet I knew, like wonderful songs, beautiful moments never last.

. . .

WHEN the song ended, I came crashing back to reality. After giving me a kiss that set me tingling, Teddie returned to his preparations. And I went looking for problems.

Amazingly enough, I didn't find any.

The Fates were toying with me, that I knew, but I was enjoying the calm before the tsunami. With the day rushing toward evening and all my ducks momentarily in a row, I paused as I walked through the casino on my problem-finding mission. Absorbing the energy shimmering off the crowd, I let it charge my batteries and light my inner smile.

No worries, not tonight, I told myself. At least no worries about my future.

A scrum of young men, laughing and slapping each other on the backs, burst through the entrance. Young women, all dressed to the nines, admired the men. Couples held hands. Anticipation lit faces. The whole world came to Vegas to shrug off worry and responsibility.

So where did I go to do that? I hadn't a clue.

My stomach, already roiling with worry over Torti Padilla and his family and Jimmy G, stabbed me with a sharp pain. On top of that, a headache threatened to join my ever-present heartache. With my stomach, my head, and my heart threatening mutiny, I ordered my mind to take control. For once it complied. Plastering a smile on my face, I fed off the excitement of the crowd.

Romeo's call caught me standing at the window that overlooks the ski slope and watching the skiers, unfettered by fear, fly down the hill. "Hey, Romeo. How's tricks?"

"I bet you get interesting responses to that question," he said, after a pause.

"You think?" I cringed, then resisted shouting for the paramedics as I watched one young lady do a face-plant into the icy man-made snow. "What would your answer be?" I asked him.

"Is this a test or something?"

"Just checking where you rank on the glibness meter." I watched the young woman right herself on her skis then push off downhill once again. She looked dazed, or half-looped. I made a mental note to ask about drinking and skiing—did they make them walk a white line or breathe into a tube? "Actually, that was a lie," I continued. "I'm trying to find my smile. Being silly sometimes helps."

"I'm pretty good at finding things," the young detective said. "Where was your smile the last time you saw it?"

"Cute." I felt a curl bend my lips—my smile had returned. "So, did you call just to cheer me up or what?"

"Actually, I wanted to tell you about my day," he said. "As you suggested, I did some research on the suppliers of bee venom— there aren't many. To my amazement, Glinda Lovato used her own name and credit card when she bought the stuff from an outfit on the Delmarva Peninsula."

"Stupid, but hardly convicting." Abandoning the skiers to their fate, I pushed through the front doors. Cars already stood six abreast at the valet desk as people in their glad rags streamed into the hotel.

"But, coupled with the other circumstantial evidence, it was enough to convince Judge Fury to sign a search warrant for the Lovatos'. I'm on my way there now."

"What do you hope to find?" I asked, as I breathed in the cool evening air.

"That smoking gun you mentioned."

"Numbers's perfume atomizer? Do you really expect it to be at the Lovatos'? I never took them for being quite that dumb." Although, I thought, Glinda wasn't exactly the brightest light in Vegas.

"Well, it's got to be somewhere."

Probably at the bottom of Lake Mead, or tossed under a bush on the Strip for someone to find and steal, I thought, but I wasn't going to burst the kid's bubble. Besides, searching the Lovatos' house might be the shove that pushed one of them over the edge.

Then maybe we'd have our killer.

· · ·

MISS Patterson, her head bent over a sheaf of papers, her brows crinkled in concentration, scarcely gave me a glance when I came through the office door. She'd already changed for the evening—her little black dress, gold heels, and large diamonds at her earlobes hit just the right note.

"Jeremy called," she announced. "He said they hadn't found somebody named Jimmy G yet, but he was chasing a hot lead."

"Track me down if you hear from him again, okay? Right now I need to change, then I'll be with the Big Boss in the VIP section for the fight." I kicked off my shoes and began unbuttoning my blouse as I headed into my office. "He's got some heavy hitters in town and I'm part of the dog-and-pony show."

Miss Patterson followed me, then leaned against the doorjamb, watching as I applied my war paint. "Brandy's tailing the DJ," she said. "As soon as you head out, I'm going to button things up here and head to Babel for the final preparations."

I slipped out of my slacks and top. The cleaners had delivered my outfit for this evening—a midnight blue sequined top and silver silk cocktail pants. My old standbys, the silver Jimmy Choos, and my own square-cut diamonds completed the ensemble. Like a chorus girl putting on her costume for the tenth show this week, I donned it all with indifference.

One last grimace in the mirror told me I looked the part I was to play. But something had changed, I thought, as I returned to my refection. This time I examined myself more closely, with more studied care. The same old, unexceptional me stared back.

The same . . . but different. Then it hit me—I felt sexy. When had that happened? And how? A side benefit to meaningful between-the-sheets time? If that was the case, with all the benefits of regular sex, it was amazing anyone bothered to get out of bed anymore.

"Have you seen Jordan?" I asked, willing my thoughts to divorce themselves from my libido—a valiant battle but one I was destined to lose if I spent any time around Teddie tonight. I vowed to steer clear until the night was well in hand, or I might embarrass us both.

"Jordan?" Miss Patterson's voice fluttered, then faltered.

"Yeah," I said as I stepped in front of her, waving my hand in front of her eyes, which seemed to have lost focus. "Jordan Marsh—you know the guy I mean—tall, graying temples, killer smile, great ass?"

"No."

I raised my eyebrows at her. "No? You don't know him?"

Stepping out of my way, she looked flustered. "I mean, no, I haven't seen him."

"I guess you wouldn't be this cool, calm, and collected if you had?" I asked, biting back a smile. "He was supposed to stop by for his VIP passes."

"Someday you're going to have to tell me all about him," she said, as she followed me to the outer door.

My hand on the knob, I paused. "Not a chance," I shot back. "I'm saving all my Hollywood scuttlebutt for that tell-all book I'm going to write." That, of course, was a lie, but it sounded good. I made a mental note to use it again at the first opportunity. "I'm headed to the Arena," I added. "I'll leave the passes here. If he comes before you go, fine. If not, lock up anyway—he knows how to find me."

MUSIC pulsed from the beehive of speakers hanging above the ring where Tortilla Padilla would rendezvous with his destiny in less than two hours. The technical crew made final adjustments, not only to the sound system, but to the lights and the projected screen images as well. Television cameras covering every angle were each manned by a cameraman shooting background shots. A few patrons dressed in evening finery with drinks in hand mingled in the ringside section—lesser VIPs who were most likely representatives of some of the sponsors. The real celebrities waited until they had an audience before making their entrance.

Jerry, a microphone hooked over one ear and extending to his lips, spoke rapidly as he gestured to his team of in-arena security people who had gathered at the side of the ring. He'd traded his informal attire for a dark suit, white shirt, and understated tie.

I made my way down to the floor, then waited until he finished his briefing and had dismissed his people before I stepped in beside him. "How's it shaping up?" I asked.

"A few surprises, but nothing major. We knew one senator was coming and had his security detail in place when another senator got wind of it and demanded to be front and center as well." Jerry ran a hand over his bare pate. "We've been scrambling half the afternoon negotiating with his muscle and PR people."

"The spin doctors are really my burden," I said, as I scanned the arena. "Why didn't you get my office involved?" On my second pass I saw Jordan and Rudy as they paused in one of the doorways. Waving, I caught their attention then motioned for them to join me.

"Fool that I am, I decided to take it myself," Jerry remarked with a chuckle. "I couldn't imagine the PR people could be that bad. After one particularly odious witch took a couple of bites out of my ass, I almost bailed and called you."

"Being barracudas is part of their job description," I said. "If it makes you feel any better, I've got the scars to prove it."

"Scars to prove what?" asked Jordan, as he and Rudy joined us. The two of them looked delicious, all spit-and-polished in their tailored suits and broad smiles.

"Scars on my heart to prove men can't be trusted," I replied as Jordan shook hands with Jerry, then introduced Rudy.

"You got to kiss a lot of frogs . . ." Jordan said, as he bussed my cheek, then grabbed my hand and hooked it through his elbow.

"To find your prince, I know," I said. "But nobody warned me about the toads."

Jordan gave me a knowing look. "Sweetheart, they come as a shock to all of us."

"How's our boy doing tonight?" Rudy asked.

I assumed he meant Tortilla Padilla. Rudy was his lawyer and had negotiated all the contracts for the fight. "Why don't we go see?" I said.

Rudy hooked my free hand through his arm. After saying good-bye to Jerry, like Dorothy, the Tin Man, and the Scarecrow, we charged off three abreast through the tunnel to find our main event. I hummed a few bars of "We're Off to See the Wizard," which earned grins from my two escorts.

Crash, his feet spread, his hands on his hips, blocked the entrance to the dressing rooms. "Hey Ms. O'Toole, Mr. Gillespi, Mr. Marsh."

"Crash." Jordan extended his hand, which was dwarfed in the big man's. "How's our boy doing?"

"He's doin' good. Real good." Crash glanced around then lowered his voice. "But between you and me, he's a bit jumpier than usual."

"There's a lot riding on tonight," I added. I saw the worry in Crash's eyes as he nodded at me, then stepped aside and opened the door.

"Go on in. He's expecting you guys." As I passed, Crash grabbed my arm momentarily and whispered in my ear. "Make him smile— it'll calm him down."

People invite me to parties as the comic relief, so I'm pretty confident of my talents in that department. However, when I got my first glimpse of Tortilla Padilla, his face drawn, his eyes worried, his posture stiff, I knew I needed to conjure championship-level flippancy.

The normally effervescent fighter sat on a training table, his feet dangling, his hands wrapped and bound into his gloves, his personality absent. Like a wooden puppet whose strings had been cut, he slouched, drawing in on himself. He looked up and managed a weak smile when we entered the small room, which smelled of Bengay, rubbing alcohol, sweat . . . and a whiff of fear.

If we didn't loosen up our man, I doubted he could stand up, much less throw a punch. Mother always said it takes two to make a good fight—although I don't think she was referring to prize-fights, the reference applied. And right now the fighter in Tortilla Padilla was MIA.

Jordan and Rudy, their smiles on the highest candlepower setting, rushed to greet Torti. With back slaps and high fives, they did their best to boost his mood. After a few minutes of the cocky-banter thing, I could see the stiffness in his posture ease a bit.

I shouldered in between Jordan and Rudy. "I don't follow the fight game too closely," I said to Tortilla Padilla, as three sets of eyes turned my direction. "But there's something I always wondered about."

"Do I worry about getting hurt?" the fighter asked, anticipating my question.

"No." I shook my head. "I've always wondered, with your hands laced into those gloves—you can't take them off by yourself, right?"

A serious expression on his face, he looked at me with troubled eyes and shook his head.

Keeping my face blank, I said, "Who holds your peter when you need to pee?"

A moment passed as the three men looked at me; nobody said anything. Then, almost in unison, they burst out laughing. In that instant, the tension fled, and the Tortilla Padilla I knew reappeared.

He leapt off the table, and grabbed me in a bear hug. Stepping back, his eyes dancing, he said, "That lady is called the peter-holder, and we check her credentials very carefully."

Since I couldn't grab his hand, I gave Torti's face a pat. "Knock 'em out, Champ."

PATRONS were streaming into the arena when Jordan, Rudy, and I left the locker room. Music thumped from the speakers at a decibel or two under my pain threshold. Spotlights played on the ring, amplifying the darkness in the rest of the cavernous space. Clad in the requisite tux, the MC for the evening prowled the ropes, waiting for his cue.

The energy of the crowd rose as Glinda Lovato, in her tiny orange bikini and heels, ducked through the ropes and sashayed around the ring. Several in the crowd signaled their approval with ear-splitting wolf whistles.

When she passed by me, our eyes locked and, for the briefest moment, her smile vanished. Then, she looked away, cranked her smile back to full wattage, and moved on.

That woman was angling for a fight, and she was going to get it. My Taser comment to Jeremy had been a joke, but now, as I watched Glinda's rippling physique, her feral grace as she moved around the ring, I wished I'd actually followed through. Of course, getting one of the stun guns past Security would have been a trick.

Glinda's sidekick, a younger, softer blonde in a hot-pink bikini and heels, stepped through the ropes and did her turn around the ring, eliciting more enthusiastic whistles. The two women apparently were going to tag team as the Round Card Girls for tonight's fight.

Jordan ducked out the side entrance so he could make his grand arrival when the timing was right. Rudy headed for the bar in the VIP section, and I made my way to the foot of the steps to greet the Big Boss and his party, who were descending from the entrance level.

After I said my hellos to all of his guests, my father pulled me aside. "Where's Teddie? Is everything good between you two?"

"Sure," I said, keeping my eyes on Glinda Lovato as she again paraded for the crowd. "He's running the show tonight at Babel, so he's staying up there, going through final preparations and all of that."

"I see." He gave me a piercing look as if trying to blast through my bullshit. He could try, but he was up against the master.

Finally it hit me that the Big Boss had no Mona on his arm. "Where's Mother?"

"Still pouting, I guess. I haven't talked to her." He put on a brave face. "You women."

"We are strange creatures, indeed," I said, as I took his arm. "Come on, we've got guests to entertain."

With Bakker Rutan, the stunning actress who insisted Las Vegas was too depressing to be seen in the daylight, on his arm, Jordan made his entrance to the roar of the crowd. As the spotlights captured them, they waved from the entrance, then made their way down to our little corner of the universe.

At the bottom of the steps, Jordan peeled away from Ms. Rutan, leaving her to fend for herself.

I gave him a dirty look as I went to rescue the actress from the embarrassment of not having a fawning fan near.

When I passed by Jordan, he whispered in my ear, "Be careful of that one. She's pretty, but she's poisonous. A real bloodsucker."

"With her aversion to daylight, I did wonder," I snapped, and was rewarded with a grin.

Ms. Rutan was tall and, in the current Hollywood mold, painfully thin. Her skin, pale to the point of translucence, pooled in her hollows, accentuating each bone. She wore a simple flowing sheath of the palest pink silk, which hung on her gaunt frame as if from a hanger—her body having no form underneath it. When she turned her eyes to me, they were cold, lifeless, and the palest blue—as if she'd been drained of blood and preserved in ice. Her face showed no welcome or hint of interest as I approached.

Introducing myself to our actress, I steered her toward the Big Boss's group. Pawning her off on him, I dove in and did the meet-and-mingle thing. Spying a couple of our corporate investors from New York that I actually liked, I joined them while the MC got the evening's undercard bouts under way.

Wetting my whistle with a glass of Bordeaux, I played my part, taking little interest in the fights until the bell sounded and the arena quieted as the announcer began his pitch for the title bout. My heart leapt into my throat. A giant hand squeezed my stomach.

A nervous hush fell over the crowd as the announcer turned the MC duties to renowned ring maestro, Winston Wiler. Dark hair giving way to silver, trim and handsome in his tuxedo, he bounced onto the stage. A spotlight followed him as he stoked the fires.

"Are you ready?" he shouted.

The crowd rewarded him with an anemic yell that barely elevated the underlying noise level.

"Are you ready?" he shouted again, much louder this time.

Now the crowd responded with a resounding, "Yes!"

"Tonight for the thousands of you watching, and the millions tuning in worldwide, the title of Undisputed Middleweight Champion of the World hangs in the balance." Mr. Wiler gestured toward a corner of the Arena. The spotlights immediately congregated there. "From the Ukraine, undefeated in his first forty-six professional bouts, holding the title of Middleweight Champion as well as a PhD in Romance Languages, Mr. Yvegny Kutz, also known as Doctor Demolition!"

Dressed in white, the current champion bounded down the aisle and stepped through the ropes. From the neck down, he looked every inch one of the best pound-for-pound fighters in the world. Above the neck, he had mousy brown hair that stuck out in uneven tufts—as if he'd put his head in a blender—a flat face, and a sullen expression. All rather pedestrian if you overlooked that angry, streetwise, chip-on-his-shoulder sneer. Doctor Demolition looked ready, willing, and able to fight—facts that knotted the worry in my stomach.

The crowd vigorously shouted, "Booooooo."

"And now . . ." Mr. Wiler shouted over the derision of the crowd, as fanfare trumpeted from the speakers.

The crowd stood, clapping and cheering. Feet stomped until I thought the roof would fall. The noise, the excitement, the release that came from yelling and booing, all combined into a heady rush, carrying me along.

"From the United States of America . . ."

The crowd let out a whoop. One particularly vocal guy in the stands above us shouted, "Knock the shit out of Kutz the Putz!"

While it was not resoundingly original, I seconded that emotion. Caught up in the frenzy, I felt like shouting something obscene, but I stifled myself. The Big Boss would be horrified. Come to think of it, I would be, too. What was it with me lately? Somewhere along the way I had started losing my grasp on me.

". . . the former undisputed, undefeated Middleweight Champion of the Universe, Tiny Tortilla Padilla!" Mr. Wiler had to shout into the microphone to be heard as the crowd went wild.

Pumping his fists and dressed in his signature red, white, and blue, Torti Padilla bounded down the aisle, through the ropes, and around the ring, his megawatt smile at full intensity. He pranced and preened. Throwing jabs and shadowboxing, he milked the crowd, working them into a frenzy.

While the boxers danced and flexed, the MC introduced the Nevada Athletic Commission, the sanctioning body for the fight. Each member made his way into the ring, slapped first one fighter, then the other on the shoulder, and basked in his one minute of fame.

On his way to the bar, Jordan stopped and said in my ear, "That European won't know what hit him—he's never faced a scrapper like Torti. The fastest hands and reflexes I've ever seen. And a wily fighter, to boot."

"Let's hope Dr. Demolition doesn't flatten our Tortilla," I said, in a feeble attempt at levity that fell flat. Both Jordan and I knew, if this fight was one fight too many, Torti could end up with scrambled eggs for brains.

"Mex retired with the titles," Jordan said, as he eyed the fighters in the ring. "After tonight, they'll be his again."

I clung to his confidence the way a swimmer caught in a riptide clung to a rope tethered to shore.

Jordan continued his search for a fresh drink and I turned my attention back to the ring, where the MC was now introducing any and all boxing luminaries in the crowd. One by one, they waved to the crowd as they made their way into the ring. There, they greeted each fighter.

The buzz of the crowd grew with each former fighter introduced, with each obscure official taking his place in the ring, with each senator who insisted on mingling with the important people.

Anticipation ignited the crowd like a torch to tinder. They clapped. They jeered.

The bottled-up energy and emotion shot my blood pressure through the roof.

"And now," Mr. Wiler shouted, his voice tinged with excitement. "One last man who needs no introduction. An olympic champion, as a professional this fighter defeated seventeen world champions, won ten world titles in six different weight classes . . ." The MC fell silent, and stepped aside.

Oscar de la Hoya stepped through the ropes.

The crowd exploded.

Oscar greeted the fighters, lingering with Torti Padilla. He waved to the crowd and flashed a smile, then stepped out of the spotlight.

With the introductions made and the ring clearing, Mr. Wiler added his trademark, "Are you ready to rrrrrumble?"

The crowd went berserk. If I'd been in the stands, I'd probably be wearing more beer right now than I could drink in a month.

Crash, his face a mask, eased through the ropes and settled into Torti's corner, his bucket at the ready.

With relatively little fanfare, the referee for the evening took over as the fighters stepped to their corners to shrug off their capes. When ready, their trainers stuffed in their mouthpieces, whispered last words in their ears, then sent their charges to the center of the ring. Bouncing on their toes, shaking their arms at their sides, the fighters glared at each other as the referee laid out the rules.

They hadn't thrown a punch and I was already a wreck as I watched Torti return to sit on the small stool in his corner. His hair glistened with styling gel, but his face was wet with sweat. His dark eyes were two holes of intensity, windows to the soul of a champion. His face, drawn tight with concentration, showed no fear.

Did he have one more valiant fight in him?

The Big Boss stepped in by my side. "I've got a hundred Gs on our man," he said.

"Last I heard, the line had Dr. Demolition eight to five," I said, as I sipped my wine, my eyes never leaving Torti. He might not be showing any fear, but I wasn't so lucky—my hand shook, my heart pounded.

The bell rang and the fighters shot off their stools, springing to the middle of the ring where they touched gloves and separated. Dancing around each other, they threw tentative jabs, testing, teasing. Torti saw an opening and pounced in a flurry of jabs. Several landed with meaty thunks against the champion's midsection.

So close, I could hear Dr. Demolition's grunts of pain as he absorbed Torti's blows.

Desperate for first blood, the crowd roared, urging the fighters on.

One of our VIPs, an unlit cigar in his mouth, shouted at the fighters from just below their feet. "You get that Ruskie SOB!" He grabbed the cigar from his teeth and punctuated the air in emphasis.

As a battle cry, it didn't quite have the rousing effects of "Remember the Alamo" but I gave him an A for enthusiasm.

Both fighters lowered their heads and fought in earnest now. Some punches landed, other glanced off. Sweat beaded and trickled in rivulets down the lean bodies. Torti landed a hook to the European's jaw. His head snapped around, flinging sweat over the crowd. Dr. Demolition faltered.

Torti dropped his left hand slightly and somehow, like a mountain lion after a fawn, the champion jumped through the opening. His wicked uppercut caught Torti in the jaw. Sweat flew. The crowd hushed. Torti staggered back.

The bell rang.

I almost fainted.

Torti wobbled to his corner and plopped on his stool. He tried to focus as Crash broke an ammonia tube under his nose. A couple of whiffs and the fighter's eyes opened wide.

"Damn it, Mex," Crash growled at his fighter in a voice loud enough for half the VIPs to hear. "You cocky son of a bitch. You been dropping that glove since you was fifteen. Don't you learn nuthin'?"

Torti flashed him a broad grin, which was brilliant, even with the mouthpiece.

I could see the red welt on his jaw where the punch had landed. My jaw hurt for him.

Glinda Lovato sashayed around the ring carrying a large sign over her head signaling Round Two. The crowd whistled and jeered as she preened for them, drinking in their adulation.

My father, still at my side, took a sip of his drink as he watched the spectacle with hooded eyes. "Our fella got lucky there," he said, displaying his flair for the obvious.

Too nervous to speak, I grunted in reply as Round Two got underway.

That uppercut apparently got Torti's attention. This round he was a different fighter. Gone was the tentativeness. From the bell, he attacked his opponent. Stepping in, a flurry of punches, then backing out. Waiting, testing, then another attack—keeping Dr. Demolition off guard and flat-footed.

The general consensus in our group was a decisive victory in Round Two for Torti—so each fighter had won a round.

Great, only ten more to go.

This time, when Torti returned to his corner, Crash gave him a nod, then squirted water into his mouth, but said nothing.

I watched as Glinda's counterpart took her turn around the ring announcing Round Three.

Curious as to where the evil Ms. Lovato had gone, I eased to the corner of the ring and poked my head around. Glinda had stepped off the stage and was rooting in her purse. She pulled her cell from the bag, stared at it, her brows creased in an unreadable expression. When she caught me looking, she glared at me and stuffed the phone back into her satchel.

The bell sounded, jangling my already frayed nerves. Round Three was under way. Torti again came out wailing away, but this time, the Champion was a bit more prepared. He blocked some of the punches, and landed a few of his own. By the end of the round, I was woozy from holding my breath. Torti had bloodied the European's nose and Dr. Demolition had repaid him with a shot to his right eye, which was beginning to swell.

The crowd chanted, "Torti, Torti, Torti."

Their fighter responded by raising his hands and doing a few air jabs as he pranced back to his corner. Crash slapped an ice pack over Torti's eye as he whispered in his ear.

From her elevated perch, Glinda glowered down at me as she waited her turn to do the number thing.

I was matching her stare-for-stare when my phone rang, scaring me into breaking eye contact. With a practiced motion, I glanced at the number then flipped the thing open with one hand, pressing my other hand over my ear. "Hey, Jeremy."

"I found our man," he said. At least that's what I thought he said.

"What?" I shouted over the noise. "You're going to have to speak up." With a nod to my father, I moved toward the stairs. "You found him?" I bounded up the stairs two at a time. The noise grew a little bit less the higher I went.

"We found him at a fleabag out on the Boulder Highway—the Nurse-A-Nickel, or something like that." Jeremy couldn't hide the excitement and relief in his voice. "They had him trussed up like a sheep during shearing season. But they only left one guy to guard him."

I didn't want to know what Jeremy had done to the hapless guard, so I didn't ask. "Who took him there," I asked with my last breath, as I hit the top of the stairs.

"His daughter, if you believe that shit."

Glinda Lovato!

In the entranceway to the Arena, I whirled to gaze down at the ring.

Glinda was gone.

Chapter

EIGHTEEN

I scanned the crowd—no sign of a tall muscular woman in a bikini nor the kind of attention she would garner if she were nearby. Damn!

"Jeremy, I've got to go," I shouted into the phone. "Bring Jimmy G here; I want to talk to him. This whole mess stinks like week-old fish." I didn't wait for Jeremy's reply. I pressed the push-to-talk button. "Jerry, we got a problem."

"I'm all ears." From the background noise it sounded like our Head of Security was still inside the Arena.

"Do you see the Round Card Girl in the orange bikini—the older one with all the muscles?"

After a moment he replied, "No, only the younger one."

I turned and began striding toward Security. If I could get to the monitors, maybe I could draw a bead on Ms. Lovato. "Find her," I barked. "Now! Don't let her off the property."

Repocketing the phone, I continued scanning the crowd as I dodged patrons and headed for the elevators. In front of me, I caught a head of black hair, slicked straight back, bobbing and weaving as someone made their way toward me—in a hurry. Peering side to side, I finally found an opening and got a good look.

Daniel Lovato.

And he looked pissed.

His head down as he charged forward, he hadn't seen me . . . yet. I ducked into a side corridor. Peeking around the corner, I watched as he strode in my direction.

Suddenly, his head snapped up. Fury colored his face. His eyes, dark and menacing, glared from under the shelf of his brows. His mouth pulled into a sinister line.

I turned to see who he was looking at.

Glinda Lovato.

Again I pushed to talk. "Jerry, Ms. Lovato is in the Arena corridor just outside the casino. Get your people on her. I don't want to lose her."

"Wilco," Jerry said.

I left the channel open so I could hear the staccato chatter between the security personnel. Holding my breath, I watched as Daniel closed in on his unsuspecting wife.

Glinda didn't see him—she was busy scanning the crowd as if she'd lost something . . . or somebody. A chill raced down my spine when I realized that somebody could be me. She'd been behind me . . . Had she been following me?

At the last minute Glinda saw her husband and tried to turn and run. But, quick as a snake, Daniel grabbed her arm, whipping her around to face him.

I saw his mouth move, but I couldn't hear what he said.

Glinda whirled on him, reared back, cocked her fist, then let it fly. Throwing her weight behind the punch, she caught her husband off guard. His arm in front of his face was too little, too late.

He staggered back, stunned, then fell to his knees clutching his nose. Blood oozed between his fingers.

Jumping from my hiding place, I propelled myself toward them. I roared, "Glinda! Stop!"

Her eyes narrowed when she saw me. With a kick to her husband's ribs, she bolted into the casino, disappearing into the crowd.

"Security, she's headed into the casino," I shouted into my phone as I rushed toward Daniel.

Still on his knees, blood dripping from his nose, he forced himself to his feet.

I skidded to a stop beside him. "Are you okay?"

The blood enhanced the murderous look on his face. Grabbing my arm, he jerked me toward the casino. Drawing shallow breaths, he tried to force air back into his lungs. "You're coming with me," he growled, one arm still clutching his side. He paid no attention to the trickle of blood.

"Daniel . . ." I resisted.

"We've got to get that bitch," he snarled, his voice stronger now, his grip like a vise on my arm. "When we do, you'll have your answers. Okay?"

He knew just what button to push.

"Okay." I nodded, ignoring my gut feeling that I had just crossed the line between bravery and terminal stupidity. "Security," I barked into my phone. "Where's the woman now?"

"She just cold-cocked one of our personnel and stole his elevator pass."

"Where's she going?"

"She jumped into the number five service elevator," replied an unidentified security guard. "We're watching, but it hasn't stopped yet. It looks like she's headed for the roof."

"This way." I steered Daniel through the casino, then through a set of spring-loaded double doors into the service area. The door to the other service elevator was just closing. "Hold that elevator!"

A hand shot out, keeping the doors from closing, then forced them open again. I pushed Daniel through the narrow opening, then darted in myself.

Right into the solid chest of Paxton Dane. I was never so glad to see anyone in my whole life. "What are you doing here?" I managed.

He grinned down at me as the doors closed and the elevator began its laborious ascent. "I was monitoring the action on the fight in the Sports Book when I heard all your chatter on the security channel. I saw the woman in the bikini and lit off after her."

"You know, in Texas, a guy could probably get arrested for that." I tried to smile, but only managed a grimace. "Apparently she's going all the way . . . to the roof, I mean."

"She had that loose look about her. Anyway, we're right behind her and there's not too many places she can run up there unless she can fly that helicopter."

We both looked at Daniel. He shook his head.

"So she can't get far, which is good news," Dane said, then his smile evaporated. "However, I do have a bit of bad news."

"Go ahead, ruin this *wonderful* evening," I muttered, as I swiped at a few dots of Daniel's blood soaking into my silk pants.

"She has a gun."

"A gun?" My blood ran cold. I had a cell phone, a tube of lipstick in the wrong color, and my keys—so I had jack and Glinda had a gun. Terrific. "She got past Security packing a piece?" Heads were going to roll . . .

"No, she took it off the guard at the same time she took his elevator pass."

Almost as bad—inept was only one step above incompetent—and tonight, both were probably lethal. Holding my phone to my lips, I interrupted the chatter over the Security channel. "The woman in service elevator five is armed. Repeat, she has a handgun. Three of us are in pursuit."

"We're right behind you," Jerry replied. "But we have to wait for an elevator. You got the last of the two."

"For the record, your mugged guard's ass is a grape," I added as I silenced the phone and stuffed it back into my pocket. "That gun sorta tilts the playing field in her favor, don't you think?" I asked the two men riding with me. "Stuck in this box and lit up like Macy's at Christmas, we'll be like fish in a barrel."

"Agreed," Dane said as he pulled a handkerchief out of his back pocket and extended it toward Daniel. "Here, you look like you could use this."

Without thanks, Daniel grabbed it and pressed it to his nose. "I'm going after my wife," he said, his anger barely contained. "You two stay here. If she shoots anybody, it should be me."

"And that would be *so* helpful," I snorted. "But if you're angling to get shot, no need to worry—I'll do the deed myself if you had anything to do with any of this mess."

Dane's eyes danced as he gave me a quick lopsided grin.

"However, first," I continued. "If we can find Glinda, maybe you, Daniel, can keep her occupied while Dane and I flank her?"

As I knew he would, Dane opened his mouth to object.

I held up my hand. "Don't start with me. I'm the highest ranking member of the cowboy club here tonight."

"Yes, Ma'am," he said, but he looked like he didn't like it. "Let's kill these lights."

"Better them than one of us," I said, pretending to be brave.

Dane opened the breaker box and doused the lights, plunging us into darkness. As the doors opened, we flattened ourselves against the sides of the elevator, protecting ourselves behind the small section of wall on either side of the opening. First Dane darted out. Crouching, he zigzagged, then threw himself behind one of the multitude of equipment enclosures dotting the rooftop. Daniel went next, with me following closely behind.

Following Dane and Daniel's lead, I crouched on my haunches. Dane turned to me. "Can you ditch that top? The sequins are catching the lights from the Strip—you glow in the dark."

I skinned the thing over my head and dropped it. The wind raised goose bumps on my exposed flesh.

"Ready?" Dane asked. At our murmurs of assent, he pushed off. Like a giant, amorphous monster, the night swallowed him whole.

Daniel followed.

I waited a few moments, taking in my surroundings. Glinda, hiding under the blanket of darkness, could be anywhere, watching, waiting, her gun at the ready. Why did she pick here for a confrontation? Sure, Security was closing in on her when she darted into the service area, but why not stop before the roof? She could've led us on a merry chase—if getting away was her goal, her odds would've been better below. What game was she playing? And was her husband part of it? And where would she pick for the final confrontation?

To my left, perching on the far wing of the hotel, I could just make out the hulking outline of the helicopter, its blades drooping like saplings under a heavy, wet snow. To my right, the darkness deepened toward the edge of the building. Large square shapes, patches of black against a starry sky, formed a maze of air-conditioning condensers, electrical junction boxes, and communications repeaters. A restricted area, guests were not allowed on this part of the roof—it was for service personnel, window washers, and the like. So far, I had precious little to rejoice about, so I reveled in the fact that if Glinda started shooting, she wouldn't accidently perforate an innocent bystander.

I didn't follow the men, choosing instead to angle behind their path. A few steps into the darkness I banged my shin on a protruding pipe. Stifling an expletive, I stepped over, then worked my way more carefully.

In front of me and to my right, Dane and Daniel were just moving shadows in the deepening darkness. A moment of panic seized me. I could hear my mother's voice: "Stay together. There's safety in numbers." Someday I was going to have to start listening to her.

Abandoning my solo mission, I moved to rejoin the men.

A sharp prod in my side and an arm around my neck brought me up short. I stiffened.

"I've been waiting for you," Glinda hissed in my ear. She poked me with the barrel of the gun. "I'll use this if I have to."

She tightened her hold around my neck, pressing, cutting off my air.

I bent backward, away from the pressure as the gun jabbed into my flesh. "You're just making this worse," I managed to whisper.

"Shut up," Glinda ordered. "You've really fucked up my day. All I need is one more little excuse to shoot you. I'd really like to shoot you."

I couldn't breathe. My focus telescoped down into pinpricks of twilight.

"You think you're so important—always sticking your nose where it doesn't belong," Glinda growled in my ear, her voice breathless.

She loosened her hold around my neck slightly, and I sucked in deep lungfuls of air. "Fucked up *your* day?" I spat, when my head stopped swimming. To hell with the gun—going out in a blaze of glory, fueled by fury, was more my style.

"You had to go looking for my father. You must've found him. My guy doesn't answer his phone." Glinda jabbed me angrily. "So, you're my father's replacement. Seems sorta fitting, doesn't it?"

"What part am I supposed to play?" I asked, trying to keep her talking. Eventually, I hoped, the two guys would figure out I wasn't behind them and come looking.

"Just shut up." Glinda jerked me backward. Step by step, my

body held tightly to hers, her arm around my neck and the gun in my side, we eased back into the darkness. She pulled me up the last step.

I angled my head and looked down and behind me.

Oh God! My heart leapt into my throat. We were balanced on the raised ledge that formed the edge of the building!

"Daniel," Glinda called into the darkness, her voice tinged with panic. "We're over here."

Both men, now just shapes that mingled with the others, whirled at her voice. They bolted toward us.

When Glinda had them where she wanted them, she shouted, "That's close enough."

Both men stopped, thank heavens. Dane had a damn-the-torpedoes, full-speed-ahead look on his face. If he did that, we'd all go over the edge.

With Glinda focused on the two men, I squirmed, testing her grasp.

"Don't." Glinda prodded me closer to the edge with the gun.

"Your beef isn't with Lucky. Let her go," Daniel said. "You hurt her, there'll be hell to pay."

Damn straight, I thought.

"Tell them, Daniel, tell them what you did." Glinda's imperious voice rang in my ear. "Tell them!" she shouted.

She jerked me. My foot slipped. I fell to one knee. The other leg dangled over the edge. Bile rushed into my throat. The world swam. I could see people walking below—they looked so small. An insane notion gripped me: If I let myself go I could fly.

A cold wind slapped me in the face.

Dane bolted forward.

"Don't," barked Glinda. "I'll let her go." She loosened her grip, and I slipped further over the edge.

I clutched at the ledge, but my fingers couldn't find any purchase. Slowly, they slipped. I couldn't hold on.

With one arm under my shoulder, Glinda pulled, helping me scramble back onto the roof.

For once I was glad she was even stronger than she looked.

She jerked me to my feet, the gun pressed to my side.

"What do you want him to tell us?" I asked, shaking now. Cold, scared, and really, really pissed, I tried to keep my voice calm, conversational—a Herculean feat—the bitch was getting really tiresome.

"He's responsible for it all—for Numbers," Glinda's voice cracked, and she swallowed hard. "For the money, the bets . . . everything."

"Then why'd you kidnap Jimmy G?" I kept prying, prodding, trying to distract her and keep her talking, as I waited for the right moment.

"As leverage."

"Leverage?" I tried to ease away from the edge, but Glinda yanked me back.

"To get Daniel to talk. Those two, they're thick as thieves." A high-pitched giggle escaped her. "Oh yeah, Daniel would do anything for my dear old dad."

"Even lie to get him back?" I asked, poking a hole in her thin logic.

She jerked at the slap of reality.

"I heard Numbers was doing you and doing your husband on the sly," I said, using the only weapon I had. Despite the cold wind, sweat trickled down my body. My breaths came in quick, shallow gasps.

Glinda's veneer cracked. She laughed, then—a laugh tinged with madness. "The bitch played me alright. And she thought she was playing Daniel." She stiffened as her focus shifted to her husband. "But she was fucking the Devil himself."

"And she was a great lay," Daniel said, his voice flat, emotionless.

Apparently Glinda didn't expect that. For the briefest instant, she dropped her guard.

I balled my fist and hit her in the face with the back of my hand as hard as I could.

She staggered, absorbing the blow. But she loosened her grasp.

I ducked out of her arms. I threw myself sideways toward Dane.

Out of the corner of my eye I saw Glinda raise the gun.

In that instant, Daniel launched himself at his wife.

A report shattered the stillness of the night.

Dane caught me and we both fell to the rooftop. Scrambling, we whirled around.

Thrown backward, Daniel lay on his back. He moaned and struggled to move.

Glinda, her mouth forming a silent scream, teetered on the edge of the building. Still clutching the gun, her arms whirled as she tried to regain her balance.

As one, Dane and I pushed ourselves to our feet and leapt for her, but we were too late.

With a panicked look at us, she fell backward and disappeared into the night.

Time froze, burning that instant into my memory.

Then, the world refocused, and I rushed to Daniel. Dropping to my knees beside him, I gently pressed him back on the ground.

Dane leaned over the edge of the building and peered down. I saw him reach for his phone, but I couldn't hear what he was saying as I turned my attention fully to Daniel.

He groaned, and then his eyes found mine as they struggled to focus. "Are you okay?" he asked, his voice a hoarse rasp.

"I'm fine. Be quiet. Let me have a look at you." Gently, I ran my hands over him, feeling for the warm dampness of blood. I found it on his right shoulder. Hooking my finger through the tear in his shirt, I ripped the fabric, pulling it away.

Daniel grunted.

A dark slash cut the outer muscle of his shoulder. Oozing blood, it looked grisly in the dim light, and probably hurt like hell. I probed the area, feeling for worse damage.

His breath hissed through his teeth as he sucked it in. He tensed against the pain, but said nothing.

He'd gotten lucky—the neat little gouge was the extent of his injury.

Dane dropped to his knees beside me. "How bad is it?" he asked.

"She just winged him." Raising my eyebrows, I looked at Dane.

He shook his head. Glinda hadn't been as lucky as her husband.

"I called the cops," Dane said. "Actually I called Romeo and told him what had happened, and he said he'd bring the cavalry."

"And the paramedics?" I asked, as I tore a piece of Daniel's shirt and pressed it to his wound. I had no idea whether that was the right thing to do, but it couldn't hurt.

"Them, too. And I alerted Security that we had things under control up here."

"Under control? That's rare," I said, but was unable to conjure a smile. My teeth chattered. Suddenly, I was cold . . . so cold.

"And I released the elevators. Apparently, after we arrived. Glinda turned them off from up here so they couldn't go back down," Dane added.

"I was wondering why the cavalry hadn't showed up." I could feel the wet warmth as Daniel's blood soaked the thin, cotton wad I pressed over his wound.

Dane put his arm around me, and pulled me tight against his chest. Then he kissed my temple. "Pretty stupid thing you did there. You could've been killed. I would not have been able to handle that."

His arms felt nice, strong and safe. I relaxed as the adrenaline eased its hold on me, and I started shaking. "I figured that could happen either way, so I picked my poison."

"Are you okay?" he whispered against my hair as he pulled me tighter.

I nodded, but couldn't stop trembling. Glinda had died. And she'd almost taken Daniel and me with her.

"Tell me one thing, was she right?" Daniel asked, his eyes clear and focused now. "Do you have Jimmy G?"

"Jeremy Whitlock found him," I replied. "He's okay."

Daniel lay back and shut his eyes, surrendering.

I thought I saw the glint of a tear leak out of his eye and I wondered if Daniel fully appreciated the fact that the man who had saved his father-in-law was the man Daniel himself had worked so hard to put in jail.

At that moment, the elevator doors burst open, shedding a cone of blinding light into our near-darkness.

"Lucky?" Teddie shouted, his voice tight. "Where are you?"

I pulled away and gave Dane a weak smile. "Over here," I called.

Dane let his arm fall from my shoulder as the sound of running footsteps came closer.

Teddie dropped to his knees beside me. "Are you alright? Security told me what was going on. I damn near died waiting for the friggin' elevator."

"I'm okay." I took Dane's hand and pressed it over the scrap of shirt covering Daniel's wound.

Looking into Teddie's face, all my emotions bubbled up. I shook my head. "No, I'm not okay." I buried my face in his shoulder.

Stroking my hair, he held me until the shaking stopped.

THE next thirty minutes passed in a flurry of activity. The police arrived with the paramedics. Teddie found my shirt and I covered myself. He didn't ask why I had taken it off; I guess it really didn't matter.

Waiting on the edge of the chaos, I was ready to give my statement to Romeo when I heard the call go out over the security channel.

There was an emergency. The paramedics were needed immediately.

Tortilla Padilla had collapsed.

MY heart in my throat, I turned and ran. Teddie and Dane jumped through the open doors of the waiting elevator after me. We rode in silence, the seconds stretching to interminable minutes.

We bolted through the service area and into the casino, now packed with the fight crowd, juking and dodging our way against the tide of people streaming out of the Arena.

My heart pounded. Oh please, let him be okay. The children's faces swam in front of me.

The fight was over, the Arena half-empty when I hit the entrance and threw myself down the stairs, Teddie and Dane on my heels. Torti wasn't in the ring. He had to be in the locker room. Security motioned us through.

The room was hushed and reeked of ammonia. A tight cluster of people circled the training table in the center of the room.

Elbowing my way, I pushed to the front.

The doctor from the Nevada Athletic Commission bent over the red, white, and blue clad body lying on the table. Holding the fighter's eyes open with his fingers, he shined a penlight into first one then the other.

Torti's hands, still bound into his gloves, hung toward the floor. They didn't move.

No one spoke. I couldn't breathe.

The Big Boss glanced up at me from the other side of the table, his eyes concerned, his mouth a grim line. Jordan gripped Rudy's elbow, their faces blank as they stared at the prone body.

Crash stood at the edge of the group. Tears streaked his face.

I didn't see Carmen.

Closing my eyes, I willed the fighter to move.

Teddie gripped one hand, Dane the other.

The big clock above the door ticked off the seconds.

I heard a faint cough. Then another. One of Torti's hands moved, I was sure of it.

The ice around my heart began to melt.

Then a weak torrent of Spanish, and I grinned.

"What'd he say?" Teddie asked, his voice a whisper in my ear.

"Nothing I'd repeat in polite company." If the guy could cuss, he had to be okay.

"Out of my face," Torti ordered, this time in English, his voice stronger.

The doctor backed off. One of the paramedics helped pull the fighter to a seated position as he swung his legs over the side. Steadying himself, he lifted his head.

For the first time, I got a good look at his face. One eye was swollen completely shut, the other a mere slit. The right side of his upper lip was swollen and an angry bruise covered his right cheekbone.

A smile lifted the good side of his mouth as he looked at me through the slit of his one good eye. "I won," he said, simply.

After a moment, the small crowd erupted—everyone backslapping and high-fiving anyone within reach.

I hugged Torti and whispered in his ear. "This is your last fight. I'm not going through this again."

"You sound just like my wife." He shot me that grin again even though it looked like it hurt.

"The voice of reason." I backed away as the crowd parted and I saw Carmen hurrying toward her husband.

She launched herself into his arms.

I tapped the doctor on the shoulder. "He's going to be okay, right?"

The guy folded his stethoscope as he eyed me. "He's healthy as a horse. Just dehydrated and probably a bit overexcited."

Overexcited? I could identify. At least my pulse was returning to normal—whatever that was—and my heart no longer threatened to burst through my chest.

"Do me a favor," the doctor continued as he stuffed his equipment back in his emergency kit. "Force-feed him Gatorade and water before he starts on the champagne."

WALKING through the casino, hand in hand with Teddie, I was trying to make sense of the evening—and failing miserably. Like the rope in a game of tug-of-war, my emotions pulled me one way then the other. Glinda had died. Somehow, I couldn't work up too much sympathy. Daniel had been shot—I'm probably just one of a good-sized crowd who thought he had it coming.

I'd hung over the edge and looked into the abyss—which would probably give me a serious case of post-traumatic stress disorder. Did workman's comp cover that? And if it did, would it pay for a suite at the Ritz while I recovered?

Love had reduced Jordan to irrationality, and he seemed totally unconcerned. Teddie was morphing into a rock star, Dane was campaigning to take his place in my life, Mother was acting stranger than usual and the Big Boss was one unhappy camper.

The lone bright spot was that Torti had survived a pummeling.

And I wasn't sure any of it mattered. My give-a-damn had finally bit the big one.

God help me. I needed a vacation. But who had the time?

"Damn." I braked to a stop in the middle of the party that was Saturday night in the casino. "What time is it?" I flipped my phone open and looked at the digital readout—accurate to one millionth of a second, or so they said. Eleven o'clock! "Teddie! You've got to go!"

The party had started without him.

"It's okay," he assured me, patting my hand and giving me a worried look. "This is more important."

"You act like I'm some kind of pansy-ass." I hated being patronized and worried over—he knew that. "I am not going back to the roof to fling myself off, if that's what you think." I pulled my hand from his and gave him an encouraging push toward the elevators.

"Go. I've gotten by just fine for thirty some-odd years without you, I'll get by fine when you leave." Ouch. I cringed, but the words had already escaped. Bad timing. Clearly I had lost my grip.

Teddie whirled on me. "Is that what you think? That I'm just going to walk right out of your life?"

"Of course not." I lied. My tenuous control on life had completely unraveled. I didn't understand anything anymore. Not even myself. "I promised Romeo I'd give him my statement. I'll be there for your set, okay?"

He brushed the hair out of my eyes, then gave me a very sweet kiss.

No doubt about it, he was one of the good guys.

But where would he be the next time I needed him?

Chapter

N I N E T E E N

♡

When I returned to the roof, I found Detective Romeo barking orders like a drill sergeant. While I waited, I took a seat on a mechanical box on the roof. It was probably some electrical thing and would zap me in the ass with fifty thousand volts. I couldn't work myself up to caring.

Right now, I had a debt to repay. I grabbed my phone, scrolled through the list of numbers, then hit send.

Flash answered immediately. "Whatcha got, girl?"

"I'm on the roof. You need to be here . . . now."

"Where exactly are you?" she asked, her voice dropping into a serious tone.

"Take the number five service elevator. I'll clear you through," I said, then rang off. After I'd talked to Security, I repocketed my phone and casually surveyed the rooftop. Cops crawled over the place like ants. Romeo talked with Dane, taking notes as he listened. The paramedics had Daniel on a gurney as they attended to him. His shoulder bandaged, he looked like he might live—at least for another day.

Boosting myself from my perch, I wandered over to him. "How're you doing?"

Before Daniel could answer my question, one of the paramedics piped up. "Him? He's one tough nut. We see him at least twice a month for something. Hell, he's broken those ribs so many times, I'm amazed they don't have to reattach them with wire and superglue."

He chortled as Daniel looked at me with those dark, inscrutable eyes.

"Rugby," the paramedic continued, as he shook his head. "Brutal sport. Ought to be outlawed, in my opinion."

As they wheeled him off, Daniel broke our gaze only when he disappeared into the elevator.

What was that about? Daniel didn't play rugby—he was more of a squash kind of guy.

No sooner had the doors shut than the set to the second elevator opened and a frantic Jimmy G burst through, followed closely by the Beautiful Jeremy Whitlock.

"Where's Daniel?" Jimmy G asked when he caught sight of me, rushing in my direction. "My son-in-law, he's okay, right? That shrew hasn't finally succeeded in killing him, has she?" Jimmy grabbed me by the arms and stared up at me.

"Daniel's fine, Mr. G." I peeled one of his hands from my arm and led him over to the box I'd been sitting on. How was I supposed to tell him about his daughter? "Sit here." I patted the spot next to mine.

"I ain't interested in sittin'," the little man growled. Nervous energy pulsed through him as he paced in front of me. "I want to see Daniel. Where is he?"

"They've taken him to UMC. A bullet carved a nice little groove through the muscle—it's not bad."

Jimmy G stopped his pacing and stared at me. "Glinda shot him?"

"Grazed him," I said. "Why'd you think it was her?"

"She was always after him." He shrugged as his eyes skittered away from mine and the openness in his face closed down. "Where is she?"

From the look on his face, I could tell he knew what was coming. "She didn't make it. I'm real sorry, Mr. G."

His face blanched. "Did Daniel kill her?"

"No. She fell."

His eyes met mine and held them. For some odd reason I thought he looked relieved.

"Do you think one of these guys could give me a ride to UMC?" Mr. G asked, the energy returning to his voice.

"Why don't you take the limo." I nodded at Jeremy, who had been standing to one side. "Jeremy can help you."

As Jeremy led Mr. G toward the elevators, Romeo materialized at my shoulder.

"This has been the weirdest evening," he announced. "That guy didn't look too busted up about his daughter."

"Just because somebody's family doesn't mean you have to like them."

Romeo nodded sagely. "Yeah, I've got this cousin who's a real wart on the world's ass."

"There's one in every family," I mused out loud, wondering who in my family would qualify. Right now, I didn't think I wanted to go there. "Is there any other reason your evening has been weird— beside the obvious?"

"I found that smoking gun," he said matter-of-factly, as if talking about tomorrow's weather.

My head snapped around, my eyes locked onto his. "The atomizer?"

"It looks like the one from the video, but it's hard to tell," he said, as he stared over my shoulder. "We're pulling fingerprints off it now and looking for matches. The lab is running a sample of the contents. I'd bet you a Ferrari there's bee venom in there—it didn't look like perfume to me."

"Where'd you find it?"

"In Mrs. Lovato's vanity—stuck in the back of the drawer."

Pretty convenient, I thought, but I didn't voice my opinion to Romeo. "Since you seem to have this mess tied up neat and tidy, do you still want my version of tonight's excitement?"

Romeo pulled out a pad of paper, his pencil at the ready. "Give it to me short and sweet."

I gave it to him clipped and dirty, but he let me go anyway. Perhaps he sensed my mood was plummeting like . . . well, like a body falling through space. Perhaps he planned to grill me later. Perhaps it no longer mattered—I didn't care.

Right now I was very late to a party.

Parties are great . . . when you're in the mood. Tonight my mood wasn't even pleasant, much less festive, but duty called.

When I stepped off the elevator into Babel, the sounds of riotous joy jolted me like an unwanted caress, forcing me further into my black hole. The crowds had left the red carpet area—apparently all the celebrity appearances had been made and duly recorded. I went in search of Miss Patterson.

I found her, a smile on her face, tiredness bracketing her eyes, and an elbow resting on the bar as she watched all the frivolity from relative safety.

The empty stool next to her called my name. Settling onto it, I kicked off my shoes and motioned to Sean. He mouthed the words "the regular"? I nodded and held up two fingers, signaling I wanted a double.

"Sorry I'm late. I didn't mean to leave you holding the bag," I said to my assistant as I ran a hand through my hair. My reflection in the mirrored glass behind the bar stared back at me. I grimaced. Next

Halloween I could dress up as myself and scare the hell out of everybody.

Miss P put a comforting hand on my arm. "I heard about Mrs. Lovato. Are you okay?"

"Functional is the best I can muster right now," I said as I took a long slug from the glass Sean slid down to me. "Everything looks like it's going well here. Were there any hitches?"

"Minor ones, nothing more." Miss P gestured toward the dance floor. "Your DJ has fallen right in line. He's kept the whole place on its feet."

"You're going to make a great Head of Customer Relations," I said as I contemplated giving her the keys to the kingdom on the spot and walking away.

"Don't you dare," Miss P replied, as if she could read my mind.

I took another pull on my drink. The warmth spread through me, but instead of the usual comfort, I felt half-sick.

As Miss P had said, the dance floor was indeed filled with gyrating bodies. Celebs and their friends packed the table-service area. Thankfully, many of them mingled with the hoi polloi. Jordan danced with a blousy blonde who couldn't keep her hands off him. Bakker Rutan watched all of it with cool aloofness from the sidelines.

Scanning the crowd, I caught sight of Brandy . . . dancing with Romeo—he must've taken a shortcut through the service area. Playing hooky from the crime scene?

I couldn't even muster a smile. With the long night in front of him, no one would rue him a quick dance or two—I certainly didn't.

The music set ended, and the dancers drifted to the tables and the bar. Jordan disengaged himself and came over to give me a hug. Holding me longer and tighter than usual, his hug felt good.

When he released me, I picked up my drink and held it up in toast. "To friends," I said, then waited for Jordan, Rudy, Miss P, and Jeremy, who bellied up to the bar just in time, to join me. "I'd be lost without you guys."

We all clinked glasses as the band took the stage and Teddie bounded out. At first the crowd didn't pay much attention. But within a minute or two, and with several impersonations under his belt, Teddie had them in the palm of his hand. When he introduced Reza, the crowd went wild—chanting and clapping in time to the music as she stepped into the spotlight.

Jordan leaned into me as he tapped his toe to the beat. "I knew Reza could sing, but Teddie is amazing," he shouted into my ear. "He's got a real future."

Watching the two of them make magic did nothing to improve my outlook on life, but I said I'd be here, so here I was. Teddie's future? Did it include me?

God, I sounded like a broken record. I slammed my mind shut to that topic and gave myself an internal tongue-lashing. Was I pathetic or what? Like a pig in slop, I had wallowed in self-pity until I'd shrouded myself in gloom. I *so* needed to get over myself. Grabbing Jordan's hand, I bolted off my stool. "Dance with me."

Apparently the man knew an order when he heard one. He let me pull him into the crush of people as the band segued into a slow song—the song Teddie had written for me.

Jordan folded me into his arms, and we swayed to the beautiful melody.

I rested my head on his shoulder and lost myself as Teddie sang about falling in love with a girl named Lucky.

THE music soothed the savage beast inside me. Actually, *Teddie's* music did the trick—and the memory of him next to me, his skin on mine, the look in his eyes when he caught a glimpse of me. He grounded me, gave me a port in a storm I'd never had. Self-sufficient to the last, I wasn't sure I was comfortable with being only one half of the whole. But I couldn't have it both ways—being in love was like being pregnant—an all-in proposition.

Surprising even myself, I stayed at the party through Teddie's first set . . . and his second. Somewhere around two, I found my second wind. Hours ago I had sent a grateful Miss P home with her Aussie. Brandy had left to take Bakker Rutan back to her plane so she could see the sunrise in Malibu. Jordan and Rudy partied on.

Torti and Carmen had made an appearance, drunk some champagne, and reveled in congratulatory back-slaps. Swollen and red, the fighter's face looked like raw hamburger, but he smiled anyway, savoring the sweet taste of victory. I had a feeling it would be his last—in the ring, anyway.

The crowd was still thick and the night very old when Teddie came to find me. Still juiced on the adrenaline rush of performing in front of a packed house, he pulled me into the throng for a couple of dances. A few people congratulated him, slapping him on the back. One young woman asked for his autograph . . . on her underwear . . . which she still wore. Teddie declined with a grin.

He and I decided to leave when the high rollers made it rain—throwing twenty-dollar bills over the crowd—and creating chaos. Darkness faded to light in the east when we pushed into the night and turned for home.

A new day.

And none too soon.

A comforting silence between us, we strolled hand in hand.

The energy of the evening still pulsed through me. "Are you up for a hot tub?" I asked, even though I knew he'd agree to just about anything that involved less clothing.

"For a start," he said as he leaned over and nibbled my ear, sending little sparks of anticipation arcing through me.

An instant of guilt flashed across my synapses—terrible images fought for my attention, but I wouldn't let them in. Glinda had died. I hadn't. Life, in all its wonder, went on.

And sex with Teddie would be the best reaffirmation of that I could think of. Not to mention, it sounded like fun.

Forrest had abandoned his post. The doors of the Presidio

were locked tighter than a virgin's knees. Teddie fished his key out of his pocket and let us in.

The bird greeted us with a long torrent of foul language. The bird! I'd forgotten all about him. Apparently the service had also as Newton danced about in his uncovered cage. Either they'd forgotten, or they'd come really early.

I stuffed a piece of very brown apple through the bars. The parrot eyed me, let loose a flurry of expletives, then grabbed the food.

"There is something so right about that bird landing on your doorstep," Teddie said as he watched the bird rip into his apple slice. "You two were meant for each other."

"I think you need to explain that remark." I skinned my top over my head. "That is, if you want any of this," I said, adding what I hoped was a seductive tone to my voice as I stepped out of my silk pants.

"You both are totally devoted, yet somehow manage to keep a sense of self intact—you refuse to let life defeat you." Desire lit Teddie's eyes as he stepped in front of me, watching me dispense with my clothes. "And you both aren't very subtle when it comes to what you want—I like that."

I reached to unhook my bra.

"Here, let me help you. God, you wore the black underwear tonight—my favorite," he sighed, as he dispensed with my bra in the blink of an eye. "Although, the red is nice, too . . ."

"You like it all." I laughed. I watched Teddie's face—which I found endlessly fascinating as his emotions marched across it. The prospect of sex intrigued him—that wasn't hard to see. But there was something else. As he looked at me, drawing me close to him, I knew what it was—it was the prospect of sex *with me* that excited him. And I'd been told by people who should know that from a man's perspective, that equated to the love a woman sought.

As I recall, I'd been more than a little disappointed at that revelation. I wanted more than that—I wanted his company, his nearness, always. My mother accused me of wanting more than life had to give. I didn't see any sin in that—disappointment, maybe, but no sin. Besides, I always did aim high.

Yes, I wanted more. But for now, I'd settle for what I had.

Already having tossed my bra aside, Teddie's hands worked their way into interesting places.

My breath caught. "You promised me a hot tub, remember?" I choked the words out as my throat constricted with desire.

"Give me a minute," Teddie murmured as his mouth sought my exposed flesh. "I'll make you forget that promise."

On the verge of surrender, I slapped his hands away and pushed him back. "It's more fun if you linger a bit, and don't rush headlong to the end."

He looked at me, his eyes wide in feigned bewilderment. "Who says?"

"Come with me," I said, as I led him into the darkness toward the hot tub. "Tonight it's your turn to beg."

EXHAUSTED, sated, satisfied, and wrapped in Teddie's arms, I couldn't find sleep. Images, snippets of conversation, worried at the edges of my consciousness until I finally gave up.

Careful not to disturb Teddie, I eased myself out from under one of his arms and out of bed. Pulling the duvet, I covered him, then gently touched his face—he was every good thing life had to offer. And he seemed to love me—one of life's little miracles. I pressed a kiss to his brow.

He didn't stir. God, to be able to sleep like that . . .

Two cups of coffee and Flash's front-page exclusive—with photographs—only added to my agitation. I'd made good on my promise to her—the story was probably good for another raise—and she owed me. Reading through it twice, looking for clarity and not finding any, I finally folded the paper and put it aside.

I was jerky and out of order, like a heavily spliced B-movie reel, and the trauma of the night before played over and over through my head.

Something wasn't right.

The thought nagged at me like a hangnail.

Pushing myself to my feet, I glanced at the clock—ten thirty. Daniel said he always took Gabi to the new playground in Summerlin after church. Today, of all days, I had no idea whether they would stick to their routine, but it was worth a shot.

If I hurried, I could make it.

AFTER parking the Porsche, I unfolded myself. Shielding my eyes, I scanned the playground. A few soccer games were under way on the fields—kids in their uniforms running madly, parents cheering them on—while traffic flowed on the Summerlin Parkway behind them. The playground, a huge conglomeration of wooden towers and bridges connected by the requisite monkey bars and several ladders with slides to make escape possible, sat in the middle of the patchwork of sports fields.

One lone little girl with long dark hair climbed a ladder, then launched herself down the slide. Peals of laughter wafted over the distance between us. Her father, his back to me, applauded.

Gabi and Daniel.

When I eased onto the bench next to him, Daniel glanced at me, but said nothing. If he was surprised to see me, he didn't let it show.

Lacing my fingers together, I held one knee as I leaned back. Closing my eyes, I held my face to the sun—luxuriating in its warmth. "Did you tell her?" I asked in a quiet voice, careful Gabi couldn't hear me.

"Daddy, watch this," Gabi called.

Daniel clapped then said, "Wonderful, Honey!" Then he lowered his voice and said to me, "Not yet. I don't know how."

I didn't either.

"Kids really grab you by the short hairs," he continued. "They crawl inside your heart and you find yourself doing the most unimaginable things to protect them."

"Is that what you've been doing? Protecting her?" I opened my eyes and raised my head so I could watch Daniel's face. "You let Glinda beat you so she wouldn't turn on her daughter, didn't you?"

"I don't play rugby; draw your own conclusions," Daniel said, his hackles rising. What man would want to admit his wife beat him?

"You could've walked."

"Gabi's not mine. Her mother would have taken her," he said, his face open, his pain easy to see. "Then who would be there for her?"

Gabi rushed over to her father. "Dad, you're not watching." Then she cast an eye my direction. "You're the lady from the hotel, right?"

"Pretty smart for a munchkin," I teased.

She rewarded me with a smile.

"Honey, let me talk with Ms. O'Toole for a minute." Daniel urged his daughter back to the playground. "We'll both watch."

Mollified, she bounded back to the jungle gym.

When Gabi was out of earshot, I said, "I know Numbers had you in her sights—we made the connection to JoJo."

"Pretty quick—that connection took me awhile." Surprise flickered across Daniel's face. "Look, I know you well enough to figure this isn't a social call. And it isn't to rehash what went down last night. So why don't you lay it out."

"You got rid of two birds with one stone, and that bothers me."

"Just because it turned out good for me doesn't mean I did anything wrong," Daniel said, his voice quiet, holding a hint of threat in it.

"True, but I've been wondering, why the shark tank?" I watched Gabi as she swung across the monkey bars, occasionally glancing at us to make sure she had our attention. "You knew about Numbers's severe allergy to bees. With all the bees chasing around that evening, you could've applied the venom and tossed her under a bush. Everybody would've thought she was accidently stung. No investigation. The killer walks."

Daniel absorbed all of this, but said nothing. A small tic fluttered in his right eye.

"But you wanted an investigation," I continued.

Daniel smirked, but his eyes wouldn't meet mine. "If I killed her, why would I want an investigation? That would be crazy."

"Not if you wanted to frame your wife for the murder."

"Hell of a risk. I'm a lot of things, but stupid isn't one of them," Daniel growled.

"I'll agree with that—not stupid but very clever. You pressured the police to investigate Jeremy knowing full well that would get everybody's knickers in a twist. And we all played our parts in your drama to perfection. I went on the warpath, and followed all your well-placed clues, each of which led back *not* to you, but to your wife."

"What clues were those?"

"The little charade on the twelfth floor, making darn sure all of it would be caught on tape; the convenient reappearance of Scully Winter, which was sure to attract attention; the perfume atomizer and the bee venom."

"Scully Winter vowed to kill me on sight. Why would he help me?"

"I don't know, but somebody with a lot of stroke had to help him get that job. When his trial was over, I thought the people in this town would hunt him down, draw and quarter him, and spread him over the desert. No way would somebody offer him a job—and a good one at that. Not without serious incentive."

"Pure conjecture," Daniel stated.

"And the atomizer conveniently turning up in Glinda's vanity."

"She wasn't known for her intellect."

"And her credit card was used to buy the bee venom. You even stacked the deck making sure Romeo, Metro's greenest detective, handled the investigation. I wondered why not even one of the brass stuck his nose into such a high-profile case. Very clever indeed— and all of it points to Glinda."

"And nothing points to me," Daniel added.

"True," I said, and for some reason I wasn't too concerned

about it. After all, justice had been served. Numbers and Glinda both got what they deserved—and so did Gabi. I gave a rueful chuckle.

"What's so funny?" Daniel asked, not looking the least bit amused.

"I guess I have more of my father in me than I thought." A realization that made me smile.

"So, that's it? You're not going to do anything?" Daniel understood how the old guard worked. His hand shook as he brushed back his hair.

"Like you said, I can't prove anything." I watched Gabi as she performed for her father. "And those who owed the debt paid it."

Daniel sighed and leaned back. His guard dropped, exposing the price he'd paid—and would continue to pay.

"I'm not going to point anyone in your direction," I added. "But if they come sniffing around, I won't lie."

"I wouldn't expect you to." He looked at me, raw emotion clouding his eyes. He grabbed my hand as I rose to go. He started to say something, then thought better of it.

"Don't tip your hand, Daniel. Don't give me anything concrete. I won't step across the line and become an accessory. Are we clear? Just because I won't keep turning over rocks doesn't mean I condone anything." I pulled my hand from his, waved good-bye to Gabi, then turned my back and left.

DRIVING slowly back to the hotel, I wondered what I would have done had I been in Daniel's position. Probably the same thing. Did that make it right? No. But nobody appointed me God, judge, and jury.

Daniel would have to live with himself; but I could move on.

My phone jangled. One of these days I am going to break down and just have the thing permanently implanted. I looked at the number and the black cloud hanging over the day evaporated. I flipped the thing open.

Before I could say anything, Teddie announced, "I woke up

and you were gone. Where are you?" His voice, husky with sleep, sounded sexy as hell.

"Just tidying up a few loose ends. I'm five minutes from home."

"If I stay in bed, will you join me?"

"Don't move," I said, ringing off. I tossed the phone on the seat, then accelerated toward home. We had plenty of time before Rudy and Jordan got formally committed late this afternoon. A long, lazy Sunday in bed with Teddie . . . Heaven wouldn't be any better.

My phone jangled again—they could call, but, unless the hotel was burning to the ground, I was not going to work. Out of habit, I glanced at the caller's number—it wasn't the office.

"Mother? How are you? Dad has been worried sick."

"Oh Lucky! The worst thing has happened!" My mother sounded rattled, off center—which, come to think of it, hadn't been all that unusual lately.

My heart sank. Not today. I really was in no mood to rescue Mona from another poorly reasoned adventure. "What? What is so horrible you have to hide in your room for how many days now? Two? Three?"

"You'll never believe it," Mona said, her voicing cracking. "I didn't believe it myself at first."

"Are you going to tell me, or do I have to guess?" I wheeled into a parking space at home.

"Oh, you'd never guess . . . not in a million years," she said, as if we were playing a game.

"Mother!" I raised my voice in exasperation as I unfolded myself from the car.

"Lucky, I'm pregnant."

I stood there with my mouth open. For once Mona was right: I never would've guessed.

THE BEAT GOES ON . . .